GOLFING
LADIES

GOLFING LADIES

FIVE CENTURIES OF GOLF IN GREAT BRITAIN AND IRELAND

ROSALYNDE COSSEY

FOREWORD BY VIVIEN SAUNDERS

ORBIS · LONDON

The author/compiler thanks the following people who have helped to ensure the accuracy of Chapter 9, by delving into early minutes, ascending to lofts in the middle of winter to ascertain names on cups, telephoning, writing, and speaking to octogenarians and nonagenarians, most of whose memories proved invaluable: Cynthia Andrews, M. Angus, Vera Atkinson, Betty Baird, Jean Bald, Betty Braithwaite, Catherine Campbell, Mae Charles, Janet Cleghorn, Peggy Coker, J.S.C. Collier, Betty Crips, P.V. Deacon, D.E. Deykes, H. Drake, M. Duncanson, Nancy Eastabrook, G. Lloyd Ellis, V.I. Foster, Stella Garrow, Betty Gibbs, Maureen Given, Joan Grey, Mary Greig, Ursula Hall-Thompson, Pamela Harker, Gillian Hickson, Margaret Hood, Muriel Horrocks, Bridget Jackson, Meg Jones, Brenda Jordan, Mary Kay, Ria Kenny, N. Luker, Margaret McLaren, Dorothy Matthewson, Elizabeth Meek, Marian Menzies, Mary G. Menzies, Wanda Morgan, Betty Morris, Teddy Morrison, L.D.C. Murray, Dorothy Payne, Barbara Nicklin, Muriel Price, M.P. Rennie, Sharon Roberts, Joan Rothschild, Gwen Scott, Marion Scott, M. Sheel, Wendy Shotter, Jen Smith, Margery Sykes, Ishbel Tinley, Anne Tunney, Evelyn Wand, Vivian Wilde, Vivienne Weaver, Nan Williams, Joan Wood and Joyce Valentine.

The author also thanks the LGU for their courtesy and hospitality while she was researching at St Andrews, and Michael Hobbs and Maureen Millar for their advice during the preparation of the book for publication.

Illustrations

Action Photos/H.W. Neale 71, 95, 102 left and right, 120, 175, 185 right; BBC Hulton Picture Library 66, 67, 81, 89, 91, 98, 116, 143, 149, 152, 167, 179, 181; Peter Dazeley Photography 40, 76 left and right, 100, 184 left, 185 left; Mary Evans Picture Library 108, 115; Golf Illustrated 36, 53, 106, 119, 159 right, 161; The Illustrated London News Picture Library 159 left; International Sports Co. Ltd. 126; The Mansell Collection 11, 20–1, 25, 28, 133, 134, 137; Maureen Millar 22, 33, 62, 84, 113, 130; The Bert Neale Collection 184 right, 186 left; S & G Press Agency Ltd. 75, 92, 121, 176, 180; Phil Sheldon 61, 77, 78, 186 right; Topham Picture Library 65, 72, 166; Women Golfers' Museum/photo Tony Gorzkowski 13, 26, 30, 31, 34, 63, 85 (on loan from the Ladies' Golf Union), 129, 156, 256; Women Golfers' Museum, Edinburgh 45, 69, 105, 110, 171.

FRONTISPIECE: 'A Lady Golfer Braves the Rain' (Mary Evans Picture Library)
PAGE 9: Vivien Saunders at Roehampton Golf Club (All-Sport/M. Powell)

Typeset by Inforum Ltd, Portsmouth
Printed in Great Britain
ISBN 0–85613–656–5

FOR LADIES WHO LIKE TO KNOW THE
BACKGROUND TO THE STATE OF PLAY

Women have been associated with the game of golf since the early sixteenth century and have been regular players of it for the past hundred years. During this time, they have usually been described as 'ladies'. Today, the governing body of the amateur game and its four national organizations in England, Ireland, Scotland and Wales use 'ladies' in their titles, as do most amateur championships and the one major open individual championship. The professional association uses 'women', thereby avoiding confusion with the American professional association. Magazines and newspapers identify their articles and reports with both terms. The club title is 'Lady Captain', with the exception of Wirral, the club managed entirely by women, whose captain is called 'Captain'. One of the first groups of women to play golf consisted of fishwives, but they were referred to as ladies, and were preceded in their connection with the game by royalty. Years later, members of the newly affluent middle echelons of society realized the possibilities and fascination of golf and they used the term 'ladies' when naming their clubs, championships and organizations. Much of their legacy is still cherished and most of this book is their history.

Contents

Foreword

As something of a student of the game of golf –
with a fair knowledge of the history of the game myself – I looked
forward with great interest to Rosalynde's new book. However, I
had no idea when setting out to read her manuscript for the first
time what a very enthralling and absorbing few days lay ahead of
me. The book is an absolute delight. The factual history of the game
is interspersed with just the right blend of anecdotes and, at times,
an appropriately just caustic comment. It gives a marvellous
viewpoint, not just of golf through its development, but it also
sheds a great deal of light on the changing role of women and on
society itself. I was quite amazed with the depth of research which
had clearly gone into compiling the book and give my heartiest
congratulations to Rosalynde on such an excellent work. It is not
just a book for the serious-minded championship golfer to enjoy. It
is one which woman golfers – and many, many men – will find an
absolute must for their golfing libraries.

Vivien Saunders

The
Female Connection

The first known woman to be connected with golf was Henry VIII's first wife, Catherine of Aragon. During Henry's second campaign in France, when he besieged and razed Thérouanne, she mentioned the game in a letter to Henry's 'cleric', the man who kept the English army fed, equipped and fit. This Master Almoner was the son of a butcher and cattle-dealer from Ipswich and his career progressed swiftly until he became the eminent Cardinal Wolsey. Catherine wrote on 13 August 1513: 'Master Almoner from hence I have nothing to write you but that you be not so busy in this way as we be encumbered with it, I mean as touching my own concerns for going further when I shall not so often hear from the King. And all his subjects be very glad I thank God to be busy with the Golfe for they take it for pastime; my heart is very good to it.'

The original of this letter no longer exists but there is no reason to doubt its authenticity for the state of golfing affairs in England at that time would undoubtedly have invited comment from such a lady.

Catherine came to England in 1501 to marry Henry's elder brother, Prince Arthur, but he died four months after the wedding. Relations with Spain were important, as was Catherine's dowry of 100,000 crowns' worth of plate and jewels. After arguments about the consummation of her first marriage, which eventually resulted in a papal dispensation, Henry married her in June 1509. It is possible that during her time in England she introduced certain customs from her native country. However, with regard to golf, it is more likely that the English were already playing the game, having learned it from the Scots.

The game had been declared illegal in Scotland in 1457, 1470 and 1491, because some Scots preferred playing golf to practising archery in readiness for war. An edict of 1424 banned football but did not mention golf, so the Scots may well have started to play between 1424 and 1457. James II's ban of 1457, dated 6 March, stated: 'It is decretyt and ordanyt yt wapinshawingis be halden be ye lordis and baronys spirituale and temporale four tymis in ye yeir. And at ye futball and ye golf be utterly cryt donne and nocht usyt . . . and as tuichande ye futball and ye golfe we ordane it to be punyst be ye barony un-lawe.'

The insistence on quarterly displays of arms and the necessity for instant readiness for war abated after the signing of the peace-making Treaty of

Westward Ho! Devon, 1873. The gentleman's chivalrous attentions seem a little excessive but do not appear to be deliberate distraction

10

Mary Queen of Scots was tall and tough and capable of enjoying golf in all weathers. Judging from the victorious roll from the drummer boy and the graceful but triumphant dance of the ladies above her, Mary may have just sunk a very long putt

Glasgow in 1502 and the Scots and the English were officially friendly until the Battle of Flodden on 9 September 1513. The English probably began to play golf during this time, enjoying the game their King's sister's husband enjoyed. Henry's sister Margaret had married James IV of Scotland, a golf addict, and although Henry enjoyed tennis, hunting and hawking the recreation of his cousin and his cousin's subjects undoubtedly would have interested him, his wife and their subjects.

Catherine wrote about golf to the Master Almoner, but to Henry she concentrated on affairs of state, including the Battle of Flodden, in her capacity as Governor of the Realm and Captain-General of the armed forces in the King's short but frequent absences. As his wife, she was experiencing a heart-breaking time, trying to produce a male heir. She had given birth to a still-born daughter in January 1510, a boy in January 1511, who died two months later, and another boy in 1513. He also did not survive. The next year she produced yet another who soon died, and another was delivered prematurely still born. Her only surviving offspring was her daughter Mary, born in 1516. It is unlikely that a woman who was enduring 'a ceaseless, desperate round of pregnancies and childbeds' would have actively taken up a new sport. However, the phrase 'my heart is very good to it' shows that she was thoroughly interested in the game, and was the first recorded woman in the history of golf to express her interest and enthusiasm.

Pictorial proof that women of all ages have enjoyed the game of golf is not uncommon. However, 'The Golfing Girl' by Aelbert Cuyp (1620–91) may have had a boy as the 'sitter': for centuries it was customary to dress very young boys as girls

On the playing fields outside Seton

The next woman known to have a golfing connection was Mary Queen of Scots, though she did not write about it herself. At her trial, she was castigated for having played golf two days after the murder of her husband Darnley, in 1567, 'on the playing fields outside Seton'. There were no specially designated golfing areas in the sixteenth century. Mary is also reputed to have stayed at St Andrews in 1563 and to have played golf there in what perhaps was a mild winter. At the time of his death, Darnley was recovering from 'some obnoxious disease, probably syphilis'. The place where he was staying was burned down; he himself was strangled. Mary was not a grieving widow, having been disenchanted with Darnley's behaviour for some time, and had no reason for depriving herself of healthy recreation. On the other hand, any behaviour, real or imagined, which could have cast aspersion on her would have been cited at her trial. Her accusers seem to have chosen golf as an example of her heartlessness and callousness, traits which had overtones of guilt. Mary had joined in games with some similarity to golf in France and probably succumbed to the influence of the Scottish version. And she was responsible for the eventually widespread use of the word 'caddie'.

The Scots pronunciation of 'caddie' sounds like the French 'cadet', and Mary included many cadets in the retinue which she brought over from France after the death of her first husband, the Dauphin. Cadets were younger sons of the French aristocracy and some came to Edinburgh as her pages. The word was at a later date used to refer to people of no particular

occupation who wandered the streets of Scottish cities looking for work – such as carrying, shovelling and conveying messages. 'Caddie' had connotations of 'porter', and evolved into the word for the person who 'ported' certain items – golf clubs.

Four-century embargo

After these royal connections, women do not appear to have actually played golf until the end of the eighteenth century. However, a few instances of women's involvement with the game, as auxiliaries, occur during the seventeenth and eighteenth centuries, times when most women led an extremely restricted existence, centring on domesticity and the social round. Their activities, unless they were the activities of royal witches, murderesses, actresses or novelists, attracted little attention. In Scotland, in 1608, people were imprisoned for playing golf on the Sabbath, especially 'the tyme of the sermonnes', and in 1612 a kirk session rebuked a woman for *instructing* her son in the mysteries of golf in the town's kirkyard on a Sunday. Such restrictions were modified by James VI in 1618: 'That after the end of divine service, our good people be not disturbed, letted or discouraged from any lawful recreation – such as dauncing, either for men or women, archerie for men, leaping, vaulting, or any other such harmless recreation.' However, he prohibited: 'the said recreations to any that are not present in the church at the service of God before their going to the said recreations'. This Sunday embargo is evident today. The Old Course at St Andrews is closed on Sundays in order to give the course a rest. Originally it was not available for golf on that day so that all the citizens of that locality could exercise their ancient and established rights of walking on their own municipal lands.

Golf's first widow was probably the former Mistress Magdalene of Carnegie, who married the Marquis of Montrose in 1629. Montrose played golf on the eve of his wedding and after considerable liquid refreshment, consisting of stirrup cup at the 19th, he paid his fiancée a brief visit. Only nine days after his marriage, he requested that clubs and balls should be fetched from St Andrews and he played in a dedicated fashion thereafter. Montrose was a teenager at the time, as was his wife, and the effect on his marriage of his addiction to the game is unlikely to have been healthy.

Later in the century, ladies were obviously expected to appreciate the game of golf for, among a set of songs written to appeal to the court and to high society (the *Westminster Drolleries*, published in 1671), is the following verse:

> Thus all our life long we are frolick and gay,
> And instead of Court-revels, we merrily play,
> At Trap, at Rules, and at Barly-break run;
> At Goff, and at Foot-ball, and when we have done
> These innocent sports, we'll laugh and lie down
>   And to each pretty Lass
>   We will give a green Gown.

Leaving aside the reasons for presenting the Lasses with Gowns, and the poet's appreciation of alliteration – the only example in the verse – why should the gown have been that colour if the ladies knew nothing of the green grass on which Goff and Foot-ball were played?

First recorded instructions

Sixteen years later, the first recorded instructions for playing golf were written in a two-year diary of Thomas Kincaid, the son of a surgeon apothecary of Edinburgh, who studied medicine, language, archery, religion and other subjects. The diary covers the period from 6 January 1687 to 12 December 1688. An entry for 9 February states: 'I rose at 7. I thought upon the method of pathologie and on playing at the golve. I found that in all motions of your armes ye most contract your fingers verie strait and grip fast any thing that is in them, for that doth command the notion exactly and keeps all the muscles of the arme verie bent.'

Kincaid possessed a talent for succinct thought and was obviously interested in economy of words because after he had written a long dissertation on the best methods of playing he condensed his findings, putting his views into verse:

> Grip fast, stand with your left leg first not farr;
> Incline your back and shoulders, but bewarre
> You raise them not when back the club you bring;
> Make all the motion with your bodies swinge
> And shoulders, holding still the muscles bent;
> Play slowly first till you the way have learnt.
> At such lenth hold the club as fitts your strenth
> The lighter head requires the longer lenth
> That circle wherein moves your club and hands
> At forty-five degree from the horizon stands.
> What at on stroak to effecuat you dispaire
> Seek only 'gainst the next it to prepare.

The first person to describe a golf match was also a Scot, the Reverend Thomas Matheson, Minister at Brechin. He had discovered that the fate of golfers lay in the hands of the divine, and he had decided that the divinity was female. Published in 1743, 'The Goff – an Heroi-Comical Poem' was in three cantos and cost four pence. In Canto I he wrote:

> O thou Golfinia, Goddess of these plains,
> Great patroness of GOFF, indulge my strains,
> Whether beneath the thorn-tree shade you lie,
> Or from Mercerian tow'rs the game survey,
> Or 'round the green the flying ball you chase,
> Or make your bed in some hot sandy place;
> Leave your much lov'd abode, inspire his lay
> Who sings of GOFF and sings thy fav'rite's praise.

Later he discussed women's curiosity about the game:

> With equal warmth Pygmalion fast pursu'd
> (With courage oft are little wights endow'd),
> 'Till to Golfinia's downs the heroes came,
> The scene of combat, and the field of fame.
> Upon a verdant by, by Flora grac'd,
> Two sister Faires found the Goddess plac'd;
> Propp'd by her snowy hand her head reclin'd,
> Her curling locks hung waving in the wind.
> She eyes intent the consecrated green,
> Crowded with waving clubs, and vot'ries keen,
> And hears the prayers of youths to her address'd,
> On either side the sprightly Dryads sat,
> And entertain'd the Goddess with their chat.
> First Verdurilla, thus: O rural Queen!
> What Chiefs are those that drive along the green?
> With brandish'd clubs the mighty heroes threat,
> Their eager looks fortell a keen debate.
> To whom Golfinia: Nymph your eyes behold
> Pygmalion stout, Castalio brave and bold.

Castalio won the match, the commencement of which the Reverend Matheson described with seemly excitement:

> Forth rushed Castalio and his daring foe,
> Both arm'd with clubs and eager for the blow.

Forty years later the first ladies' golfing society was in existence, although it was not documented until 1810. Women golfers were described in the first volume of the *Statistical Account of Scotland* (Edinburgh, 1791–9).

> The golf, so long a favourite and peculiar exercise of the Scots is much in use here [Musselburgh]. Children are trained to it in their early days . . . When speaking of a young woman, reported to be on the point of marriage: 'Hout', they will say: 'how can she keep a man who can hardly maintain herself?' As they do the work of men and their strength and activity is equal to their work, their amusements are also of a masculine kind. On holidays they frequently play at golf; and on Shrove Tuesday there is a standing match at football between the married and the unmarried women, at which the former are always the victors.

First ladies' competition
By 1810 the fishwives of Musselburgh, who claimed to have started their society in 1774, had obviously drawn attention to their prowess at golf because an entry dated 14 December in the minute books of Musselburgh

Golf Club states: 'The Club resolve to present by subscription a new Creel and Skull to the best female golfer who plays on the annual occasion on 1st Jan. old style (18 Jan. new) to be intimated to the Fish Ladies by the Office of the Club. Two of the best Barcelona handkerchiefs to be added to the above premium of the Creel. Alex. G. Hunter, C.' The phrases 'female golfer' and 'fish ladies' probably refer to the same group of women, for it is unlikely that the fish ladies were intended to tell the other women of the town about the competition. The prize – the basket which they carried on their heads with their part of the catch – would have been of interest only to fishwives. The names of the winners, and the duration of the competition, were not recorded. The club would have had no real reason for publishing the ladies' annual achievements, for undoubtedly the fish ladies were illiterate.

A few years later, in the eighteen-thirties, ladies at North Berwick were attending golf meetings on a very regular basis. We know that they watched and that they enjoyed the luncheon which followed the end of the round. The general involvement of women with golf at this time was portrayed by James Fullerton Carnegie, who also defined their role in the game, and consolidated the sex of the golfing divinity, in 'Golfiana', published in 1833:

> The game is ancient, manly and employs
> In its departments women, men and boys.
> Men play the game, the boys the clubs convey,
> And lovely woman gives the prize away.
> When August brings the great, the medal day,
> Nay more! though some may doubt, and sneer, and scorn,
> The female muse has sung the game of golf.
> And traced it down with choicest skill and grace
> Through all its bearing to the human race,
> The Tee, the start of youth – the game, our life,
> The ball, when fairly bunkered, man and wife.

In 1842, women were responsible for a change in Rule IV of the original thirteen rules laid down in 1744, although not through their playing of the game. A verse 'From Sanctandrews', from Blackwood's *Edinburgh Magazine* of 1819, sets the scene:

> It is in sooth a goodly sight to see
> Be east and west, the Swilcan lasses clean,
> Spreading their clothes upon the daisied lea,
> And skelping freely barefoot o'er the green.
> With petticoates high kilted up I ween,
> And note of jocund ribaldry most meet;
> Fram washin' tubs their glowing limbs are seen
> Veiled in a upward shower of dewey weet!
> Oh! 'tis enough to charge an anchorite with heat.

The washerwomen plied their trade by the burn and spread out their washing on the ground and whins by the side of the second hole. Provision was made in 1842 in Rule IV for washing tubs and their paraphernalia – in other words movable obstructions. The rule legislated for a ball lying on clothes or within a club's length of a washing tub: clothes could be drawn from under the ball and a tub might be removed. Sixteen years later, the drawing of clothes from under the ball was stopped, and lifting and dropping behind substituted; the tubs remained 'movable obstructions' until they were ruled off the course.

Vanguard of a restless age

Such are the known connections of women with golf until the mid-nineteenth century, when a measure of emancipation stemmed from the economic climate of boundless business opportunity during the early Victorian era. In 1855, Mrs Wolfe-Murray from, according to the geography of golf journalist Mabel Stringer, Cringlettie or Craiglettie, appeared regularly on St Andrews links with two clubs, and was apparently indifferent to the unflattering opinions expressed by the townspeople. She enjoyed her game, but attracted a great deal of adverse criticism, and was looked upon with horror by all the men and some of the women of St Andrews – a vanguard of a restless age indeed. Adventure and a measure of liberation from their previously narrow lives were being sought by many women. But complete emancipation from the bonds of masculine prejudice, particularly where property, wealth, education, employment and government were involved, was rarely possible. Women vented their frustration and excess energy on the sports fields, playing particularly tennis, cricket, hockey and golf.

For years, ladies were accustomed to accompanying their husbands, brothers and children on holiday, when the men would golf and the ladies would remain housebound, obedient to the social round, occasionally permitted to be present as spectators around the links. Through observation of the men's performances, they perceived the delights of playing a similar game themselves, and eventually rebelled against their former roles of mere onlookers and presenters of prizes.

First ladies' club

By 1867, ladies were playing golf regularly at St Andrews, and in the same year, more than 250 years after the first men's golfing society was established, they formed the St Andrews Ladies' Golf Club, the first universally recognized ladies' golf club in the world. Five years after its institution, the club's activities were featured in the second leader of the *St Andrews' Gazette and Fifeshire News*. The report described the club's struggle for existence and noted that its remarkable success had led to the establishment of ladies' golf in England and elsewhere. The leader also mentioned that the ladies' game was limited only to strokes of the putting variety. Nineteen years after the club was formed it had 500 members.

The St Andrews ladies were followed by the ladies of Westward Ho! in

North Devon, who formed a club in 1868. The Reverend H. Gosset, vicar, who had visited St Andrews, planned a course in a quiet corner near the Northam Burrows, where the inequalities of the ground were expected to offer lady players interesting and exciting hazards. They could thus play on an established course and also practise the game at home on their croquet lawns. At Westward Ho! only one club, a putter, was allowed. The rules stated that a ball could be taken out of a bush, off a road, or out of a bunker for a penalty of one stroke. If a ball was lodged in water, the player could extract it, change it if she wanted to, and then tee up before playing again – all for a one-stroke penalty. Loose impediments of any kind could be lifted on the putting green, which was considered to extend four putters' lengths around the hole. It was mandatory that everyone present should stand still, and not speak aloud while any player was aiming at or striking a ball. If a ball was split into pieces, a new one could be put down. This incurred no penalty in stroke play, but a one-stroke penalty in match play. Additionally, no member of the Ladies' Golf Club was allowed to bring a dog with her in case it should hunt and disturb the sheep on the Burrows. By 1878 five golf clubs had been formed.

Many women, particularly younger ones, knew a great deal about the game, apart from the use of a putter, to which most of them still confined themselves. One young woman changed the result of the men's Open, which was won by one stroke, through her knowledge and observation of the game. At the second last hole of the 1878 championship at Prestwick, Jamie Anderson was at address for his tee shot when a young girl pointed out to him that he was not on the teeboard and that he would be disqualified if he took his shot from where he was standing. Mr Anderson teed up again, this time within the designated area, and holed in one. Had he not done so there is very little doubt that he would almost certainly have lost the championship.

Six years later, by which time there were nineteen ladies' clubs, the first recorded analysis of the game by a woman was published. It was written by a young girl who attempted to describe the game to her non-golfing uncle at his request:

> The game of golf is a very good game. Most people like it very much; even babies play it when they are quite young. The balls you play with are very hard indeed, and they might kill anybody if they got hit very hard with them. When you play golf you first take a little sand and make a little heap, and then place the ball at the top of it; then you take a club called a driver, and hit the ball; that is called driving. Then if you get a good way from the hole, but too close to take a driver, you take an iron club and play up to the hole; when you are close to the hole you would take a club called a putter and when you get into the hole you count your strokes, and whoever gets into the hole in the least number of strokes it is their hole; and if the two people who are playing get into the hole in the same number of strokes, it is called a halved hole.

Boaters, wasp waists, long skirts and elaborate hair styles did not spoil ladies' enjoyment of the game. The style of this lady's body turn is admirable even today, although the bent arm could be criticized. This is Minchinhampton, Gloucestershire, in 1890

During the eighteen-eighties, fourteen ladies' clubs were instituted, and the practice of playing for a variety of prizes was well established. Here are some examples from Great Yarmouth: silver scent bottle, grouse-foot brooch, golf buckle, photograph frame, silver button hook, pencil case, golf brooch, sweepstakes, golf club bag, golf ring.

Putting games abandoned

By this time, some ladies had forsaken the gentility of the putter for strokes that demanded full swings. One English lady, Issette Pearson Miller, who started playing in 1887, did not at the time know of any other English ladies who played the full game well, but she was assured by a Scots gentleman,

Issette, née Pearson, Miller and some of her initial advisers: on the extreme left, her future husband, T.H. Miller, and on the extreme right (top), Mr Talbot Fair, one of the LGU's first vice-presidents

who was a competent player, that there were several ladies in Scotland who could halve a match with him by receiving only one stroke a hole. As soon as ladies experienced the excitement and fascination of the full game of golf, they abandoned their putting games. This coincided with their insistence on even more freedom in other fields. There was also a fashion for fresh air.

By 1893, the year of the formation of the Ladies' Golf Union (LGU), there were more than fifty ladies' golf clubs (see Appendix 1, page 244 for names and dates). After the institution of St Andrews and Westward Ho! (reconstituted in 1893), Musselburgh and Wimbledon were formed in 1872. Musselburgh ceased to function in 1887 because of general lack of interest and illness among its leading members, but was reconstituted in 1896. Wimbledon was instituted as the Ladies' Scottish but declined after it had existed for a few years and was reconstituted in 1890 as Wimbledon Ladies. Five years after the formation of the LGU, there were 220 ladies' clubs, in addition to those to which a few ladies were admitted.

Women have been meticulous in their organization of the game of golf ever since they adopted it in large numbers in the 1890s. They instituted championships, developed a unique handicap system, initiated international matches, coped with the vicissitudes of restrictive and changing fashions, fought antipathy, apathy, and a dearth of money in a dignified and resolute manner, and eventually instituted a professional circuit. Their first task, however, was to organize themselves into recognized establishments which, through strength of numbers, persistence and ubiquity, could not be ignored.

Ladies Are Born Organizers

Early in 1893, members of the Wimbledon Ladies' Golf Club had become interested in organizing a ladies' championship. They sought the advice of Laidlaw Purves, a leading Wimbledon golfer and an experienced organizer. Mr Purves suggested that all ladies' golf clubs should be invited to participate, and that their opinions should also be sought about establishing a ladies' golf union. Circulars were sent to all the known clubs, and a meeting was arranged for 19 April 1893, at 2.30 p.m. The meeting was held at the Grand Hotel, Trafalgar Square, London, and was attended by ladies from St Andrews, Barnes, Blackheath, Eastbourne, Great Harrowden Hill, Holywood, Lytham and St Anne's, Minchinhampton, Southdown and Brighton, and Wimbledon. Officers were elected, and a general meeting was planned for the following Friday to discuss and pass the rules which were to be drawn up by the new-born council.

This preliminary meeting instituted the Ladies' Golf Union, which grew quickly in numbers, strength, influence and power until it became one of the foremost governing bodies in ladies' sport. The founder members, encouraged by Mr Purves, did not wish their organization of the game to emulate the conditions under which male golfers played. The gentlemen suffered, in Mr Purves's words, 'an oligarchy of each Local Club ruling over its own individual members, and a great oligarchy of an ancient and venerable club ruling over the golfing world'. Instead, the Ladies' Golf Union was intended to represent all ladies' golf clubs, and the clubs were to have the opportunity of voting and legislating its rules.

Hounsom Byles entitled this illustration 'The Ruling Passion' in 1895 at a time when ladies had most forcefully established their right to play on territory which had formerly been the preserve of men. Whether the lady actually connected with the ball from this angle is debatable

For seven years Laidlaw Purves had attempted to form an English golf union, with the cooperation and approval of distinguished male golfers. Irishmen had formed a union in 1891, followed by Welshmen four years later, but Scotsmen waited until 1920 and Englishmen until 1924. When Mr Purves realized that his efforts were failing, and when the ladies, having heard of his attempts and reputation, solicited his help, he abandoned his aim of organizing male golf and devoted his attention to the ladies. If the ladies of the 1890s had not welcomed the prospect of a united democratic organization, their attempts to play golf on full courses rather than putting courses only would have failed. Small disparate groups would not have succeeded in establishing their rights to play on areas which had formerly been the preserve of men.

As despotic as the Czar of Russia

Laidlaw Purves and Mr Talbot Fair were the LGU's first vice-presidents. Purves looked after the interests of England south, Talbot Fair, England north, H.S.C. Everard, Scotland, and T. Gilroy, Ireland. Blanche Martin Hulton was the first honorary treasurer, and the first honorary secretary was Wimbledon member Issette Pearson Miller, a most dynamic young woman. With initial advice and encouragement from Mr Purves, she made the business of the union her life's work, lobbied for and retained support, instigated new schemes, and tolerated little interference with the growth of the game to which she was devoted. Assisted by a few of her lady golfing friends, and encouraged by knowledgeable male golfers, she was responsible for the initial organization of the union's work, the editing of its handbook, the institution of its handicap system, and the birth of many championships and tournaments. Her will was strong and she coped positively with opposition. One journalist, after losing an argument with her, stated: 'Miss Pearson is as despotic as the Czar of Russia.' And a few years after the creation of the LGU she answered the criticism: 'You ladies quarrel so much over golf – you are always having rows' with the reply: 'Well, you gentlemen made the rules by which we have to play, and they are so ungrammatical and illogical that not any two of you can expound them in the same way.'

Miss Pearson, who possessed an above average stature and consequently

Issette's devotion to her beloved golf did not always ensure her popularity either with the ladies she was encouraging or with the gentlemen. She is seen here in one of her more mellow moods, taking tea with T.H. Miller (left) and Laidlaw Purves

a dominating appearance, was, however, not always popular, and some people resented certain manners and customs upon which the union insisted. In particular, people resented being ordered about when following a match, and Miss Pearson was subjected to a great deal of criticism when she ordered some experienced golfers to stand back when they were already many yards behind the players. However, her hard work and single-mindedness of purpose were generally admired and soon her name and the phrase 'ladies' golf' were almost synonymous. At the time of the union's second annual general meeting, the organization had expanded from a group of enthusiastic pioneers into a membership of more than 2000.

The original Rules of the LGU were: 'The Rules of the game shall be those published in 1892 by the R & A GC [Royal and Ancient Golf Club] of St Andrews and shall be known by the Union as the Rules of the Game of the Ladies' Golf Union.' The purpose of the union in 1893 was:

1) To promote the interests of the game of golf
2) To obtain an uniformity of the rules of the game by establishing a representative legislative authority
3) To establish an uniform system of handicapping
4) To act as a tribunal and court of reference on points of uncertainty
5) To arrange the Annual Championship Competition and obtain funds necessary for that purpose.

The original draft of the constitution also made provision for the formation of a social club in London, the appointment of a paid secretary at a small annual salary, and the establishment of a Professionals' and Caddies' Benefit Fund. The objects of the LGU today are:

a) To uphold the rules of the game, to advance and safeguard the interests of women's golf and to decide all doubtful and disputed points in connection therewith
b) To maintain, regulate and enforce the LGU system of handicapping
c) To employ the funds of The Union in such a manner as shall be deemed best for the interests of women's golf, with power to borrow or raise money to use for the same purpose
d) To maintain and regulate International Events, Championships and Competitions held under the LGU regulations
e) To make, maintain and publish such regulations as may be considered necessary for the above purposes.

The first general meeting proposed that all associated clubs should submit their local rules and bye-laws to the council, and that the union should have power to advise on the removal of those local rules which were unnecessary or contrary to the laws of golf. Blanche Martin Hulton considered that it would be beneficial to club secretaries to have an impartial group to whom they could refer, particularly with regard to local rules, which caused considerable difficulties in open competitions and inter-club matches.

First LGU clubs

At a meeting in London on 5 May 1893, Wimbledon and Lytham and St Anne's were elected. In June, Ashdown Forest, Blackheath, Kenilworth, Minchinhampton, Royal Belfast, Royal Portrush, Southdown and Brighton, Tunbridge Wells and Warwickshire were elected. These were followed in November by Barnes, East Sheen, Folkestone and Littlestone, and shortly after by Barham Downs, Clapham Common, Cotswold, Eastbourne and West Lancashire. A design for membership badges had been approved, and these were soon worn proudly and – considering that few women at that time drew attention to themselves or even made speeches in public – bravely. The badge had become obsolete by 1922.

The financial structure of the union was based on entrance fees and subscriptions from affiliated clubs. Clubs with under 100 members paid an entrance fee of £2 2s (£2.10) and a yearly subscription of £1 1s (£1.05). Clubs with 100 to 200 members paid £3 3s (£3.15) entrance fee and an annual subscription of £2 2s (£2.10). Clubs with memberships of over 200 paid £5 5s (£5.25) in entrance fees and £3 3s (£3.15) in annual subscriptions. A club with under 100 members was entitled to one delegate to represent them; clubs with 100 to 199 members were represented by two delegates, and clubs with 200 and upwards, three. By 1947, after two world wars and the depression with the consequent economic upheavals, the entrance fees were the same, and the annual subscriptions had gone up by only a little more than 300 per cent. The highest entrance fee payable in 1982 was £5.25, and subscriptions were decided through the four national organizations on a per capita basis.

By 1896, the union had made its importance and necessity felt, and delegates from twenty-eight clubs attended a council meeting in the following year. For the year ending 20 April 1898, the twenty-six entrance fees and

The intense concentration of both players at Portrush, County Antrim, in 1895 hopefully aided the lady in making her putt

the annual subscriptions totalled £65 2s (£65.10), and entrance fees from the championship amounted to £57 10s (£57.50). Sales of the annual handbook, brooches and so on amounted to £20 7s (£20.35), bank interest was 10s 2d (51p), and stock in hand £7 7s 6d (£7.37½). After deducting costs for printing, stationery, badges, prizes, postage, bank commission and the expenses of the honorary secretary and honorary treasurer, there was a 'balance being profit' of £18 3s 8d (£18.18). Earlier that year, the railway companies had granted 1st and 3rd class return tickets to certified golfers for 'a fare and a quarter' and many compartments were taken over by groups of women golfers. Soon caddie masters were receiving complaints that ladies were arriving at clubs early in the morning and were engaging most of the caddies, leaving few for the men.

A few months after the official formation of the LGU, some Irish lady golfers met in Belfast, and instituted the Irish Ladies' Golf Union (ILGU). The first meeting, in December 1893, was presided over by Mrs George Shaw. It elected Miss Clara Mulligan honorary secretary, and the Countess of Annesley president. The ILGU was well established by the following spring, although at first there were only four member clubs – Royal Belfast, Royal Portrush, Lisburn and Dungannon. By 1904 there were eighteen clubs, and Miss Mulligan, who became Mrs Inglis, played a major role for many years in the ILGU's organization.

Scotland was the next country to form an association, through the initiative of Miss Agnes Grainger. Scotland played in international golf for the first time in 1902, but was overwhelmingly defeated. Miss Grainger realized that the Scottish ladies must gain more experience than was provided by club and inter-club events. She organized the ladies, visited every club in Fife and Midlothian, among others, and then requested that a Scottish Ladies' Championship should be played on the Old Course at St Andrews. Some gentlemen were critical, and doubted that the Old Course was suitable. They deemed it too severe a test for ladies. They also wondered if there would be a sufficient number of entries to justify a championship. Miss Grainger's reply was: 'There may be five or there may be fifty.' On 16 June 1903, the championship began with forty-six entrants. It was decided to hold the following year's championship at Prestwick St Nicholas. Miss Hamilton Campbell and Miss M.J. Allison, the captain and honorary secretary respectively of St Nicholas Ladies' Golf Club, suggested that an association be formed to finance and conduct future championships. By the time the competitors met, Miss Hamilton Campbell had the constitution already drafted and the Scottish Ladies' Golfing Association (SLGA) was instituted.

Wales also instituted its union in 1904, and for a while enlisted the aid of Mabel Stringer, an experienced LGU official, who served as assistant secretary for five years. Miss Stringer urged the institution of an English championship in 1906 and also the formation of an English Ladies' Golf Union, but this was considered unnecessary, because the LGU had its headquarters in England and no one saw the need for two unions similarly based geographically.

Vicissitudes of the handbook

Initially, the work of the LGU – the organization of meetings, championships and communications, the publication of the union's handbook, and the establishment of its handicap system – was carried out from Issette Pearson Miller's home in Northumberland Avenue, Putney. Miss Pearson placed great importance on the handbook, issued annually since 1894, as she knew the powerful role that communications and an official point of reference could play in the vital matter of consolidation and solidarity. In 1900, when the price of the handbook was 'Two Shillings Post Free 2s 4d', the cost of publishing became so great that the LGU, which had lost £35 on its publication the previous year, considered abandoning it. The women's magazine *Gentlewoman* thereupon provided financial support, but Miss Pearson warned that if the book was not a success the following year it would not be issued again. At this time it was sent free of charge to all associated clubs.

In 1902 the handbook was published after the advertised date because the new printers had difficulty in obtaining the type and other materials. Additionally, copy and proofs had been received late; the honorary secretary thereupon instituted a deadline for receipt of information, and communications from the clubs were looked after by ladies residing in the counties where the clubs were situated. The sum of £35 was contributed to the publishers by the LGU as costs were increasing – but sales were not.

Maud Titterton watches Dorothy Campbell drive off at the Ladies' British Open Amateur Championship at St Andrews, Fife, where it was played on the Old Course for the first time in 1908. Miss Titterton, later Mrs Gibb, beat Miss Campbell, later Mrs Hurd, at the 19th

Only 200 copies of the book were sold during the next year, and *Gentlewoman* withdrew. The handbook was taken over by the Golf Agency, who insisted that it contain at least thirty pages of advertisements. The 1904 edition also included names of courses, stations and distances from London, and details of 1st, 2nd and 3rd class ordinary and weekend return fares. The advertisements were intended to prevent the previous yearly losses; 300 copies of this edition were printed and, apart from those distributed free of charge, all were sold.

During the next year, putting, approach, bogey and foursomes competitions were omitted from the handbook, as the book had become too large to be viable. In the following year the honorary secretary therefore proposed to leave out the names and addresses of all players who did not have a handicap. The book was increasing in size but sales were not. Miss Pearson thought that 1000 copies could be sold to the union's 150 affiliated clubs. She and her colleagues considered not publishing the handbook until a large sale was ensured, and discussed making its purchase compulsory. In May 1906 they decided that if each club took six to eight copies, sales would be about 1000. Each club was accordingly obliged to take a certain number of copies according to the size of its membership. When the clubs realized that the book could be continued only under these conditions, they agreed. By 1912, each club with under 100 members took three copies, from 100 to 200 six copies, and 200 and over nine copies.

In the 1914 handbook, which had increased in price to 3s 6d (17½p), Issette, now Mrs Miller, asked members to support the advertisers, as it would be impossible to publish it in future without the advertisements. She wrote: 'Our members may have every confidence in accepting the statements they make in their announcements' and thus predated the Trade Descriptions Act by many years. The handbook survived, although it was not, of course, published during the world wars. It experienced several changes of name, and eventually lost its initial comprehensiveness. Before World War I it was thicker than *Golfer's Handbook* is today. After World War II it lost its hardback cover and was published with all records omitted in order to keep the price at pre-war level. Advertisements were obtained by the LGU staff, not an agent, thus saving a commission.

Today the handbook is a paperback, often so badly bound that the leaves fall out. It is distributed free to all eligible bodies and individuals may buy copies direct from the LGU. Meetings, decisions and policies are not reported as they were in Issette's day. The book is no longer *The Golfeuse vade mecum sans omission* as it was described in the 1897 edition. Now titled *The Lady Golfer's Handbook*, it is more useful to organizers than players.

Mabel Stringer, an intimate friend of Issette Pearson Miller, was a devoted and hardworking pioneer of the game, involved with different aspects of it for more than sixty years

Lady Golfers' Club

Another early endeavour of the LGU was the attempt to establish its own lady golfer's club. In 1900, negotiations were entered into with the Victoria Club for Ladies, 145 Victoria Street, London. Members of the LGU could join either as full members or at reduced rates for nine months – if the LGU could guarantee 200 members. Unfortunately there were not enough applications

so the agreement was not signed. By 1911, the growth in the number of affiliated clubs resulted in a need for more secretarial assistance and larger offices. As Issette wrote: 'Just as we were wondering what to do, we got the chance of forming a Lady Golfers' Club . . . at 3 Whitehall Court.' The premises contained a large room for meetings, sufficient bedrooms, and up-to-date luxuries, and the ladies soon achieved a reputation for the excellence of their club. Not long after they were in working residence, it was reported that: '

> The ladies really are a most enterprising folk. For instance, they have made a practice putting green in one of the courtyards. Rather good for the heart of London. The first putting competition was to have been held the other day, but the weather was unpropitious and Mr Hornby promptly devised a putting course in a large empty room. Nine holes there were of it and a most enjoyable competition was the result.

During the 1920s the dining room, with its shaded lights, was described as a rest cure for those who had eaten to jazz music. The Lady Golfers' Club enjoyed popularity for many years before merging with the Golfers' Club in the nineteen-sixties.

In 1904 the LGU invested £100 as a reserve fund, so that the annual income could be expended safely, and the honorary treasurer, Blanche Martin Hulton, was responsible for the appointment of two trustees. By 1908 the LGU had acquired a president – HRH Princess Victoria of Schleswig-Holstein – and agreed that the accounts should be audited by chartered accountants. Two years later, colonial members visiting Britain were provided with letters of introduction and could become temporary honorary members of clubs for a period not exceeding seven days. The ladies had tried to institute this in 1898, and all but four of the clubs present at that particular meeting had voted in favour of the rule. Three of these four could not conform 'owing to being in the hands of the gentlemen's clubs' so the ladies decided not to introduce the facility.

By 1912, the LGU had over 500 affiliated clubs and bankers, solicitors, auditors, trustees and two secretaries for county golf. A committee of handicap managers had been formed in the previous year, and this was soon divided into two, one for the north and one for the south. And Issette attempted to resign. Her reasons were that she no longer had sufficient time because she had married, changed residences and had more household duties to attend to. However, all her colleagues felt that it would be a national calamity for golf if she did not continue as honorary secretary. During the previous year, a presentation of an aquamarine and diamond pendant had been made to her in recognition of her eighteen years' hard work in the interests of women golfers. She made a conventional, self-effacing reply which included the statement that 'the work was her play'. She was made a life member just before World War I and was elected vice-president in 1919. She retired in 1921.

Applause from the suffragettes

The LGU grew in strength and achieved popularity and favourable publicity at a time when other groups of women were upsetting the whole nation through their dedication to the suffragette movement. Golf and golfers attracted a share of the women's need to spread their gospel. The words 'Votes for Women' were found inscribed on greens, etched with acid, initially at Birmingham and then in other areas. Miss Cecil Leitch's victory over former Open Champion Harold Hilton in 1910 was much applauded by the suffragettes. The margin of the victory was not important – the gentleman gave her a half (a stroke on alternate holes) and she won by only one hole – but the fact that such a challenge had been made, accepted and won boosted their fighting spirit. On one occasion, 'suffragists' removed the red and white flags on Balmoral and replaced them by purple ones bearing legends 'appropriate to the good cause'. They were also reputed to have burned down a clubhouse. On another occasion, a group of suffragists interrupted a game between Mr Asquith and Mr McKenna. A plain-clothes

The suffragettes made much of Cecil Leitch's victory over Harold Hilton in 1910, and the match attracted a great deal of attention to the ever-growing popularity of ladies' golf

Mabel Stringer presented this stirringly patriotic trophy for the scratch aggregate competed for by the members of the United Services Ladies' Golfing Association, which was founded in 1914

detective in attendance had difficulty in controlling the women and he invited the caddies to help. However, the suffragists had secured the support of the Caddies' Union, so they refused to assist. The caddies were not enamoured of the government at the time, as the matter of whether insurance stamps should be paid by clubs or by caddies was rousing a considerable amount of antagonism.

In 1912, a journalist stated in the magazine *Ladies' Golf* that he had been asked to deny that 'the Women's Suffrage Golfing Society is about to put on the market a ball called the Asquith'. And in 1913 the same magazine published the following under the title 'Post and riposte':

> Suffragists who have been told off for pillar-box work are respectfully requested to declare an armistice for those days on which county matches are being played through the post [results were posted]. And presumably the regulations will be so framed that it will be no benefit to a side to win the match if they lose the post. In previous years these encounters have been decided by match play, but the new suggestion is that in future they should be of a totally different stamp. Under this scheme the expression 'beaten at the post' will assume a new and terrible significance.

As the influence of the LGU spread, many affiliated associations were formed. In 1911 Lady Ellis Griffith approached Mabel Stringer for assistance in founding a Ladies' Parliamentary Golfing Association (LPGA) for the relatives of members of both Houses of Parliament. Mrs Asquith, wife of the Prime Minister, was the LPGA's first president. Their first championship was won by Mrs James, later Lady Craig, wife of the Prime Minister of Ulster. At the 1912 meeting, handicapping was difficult because many ladies were unfamiliar with the rules and regulations: they were accustomed to playing only an occasional round, during which they rested when they were tired. Sir John Barker offered a trophy for an annual match between teams representing both Houses, and the first one was won by the Lords. The LPGA's second president, Mariota, Countess of Wilton, presented an Inter-Association Scratch Challenge Shield in 1921 for annual competition among four associations – the Medical, founded a few months before the LPGA, the LPGA, the Legal, founded in 1912, and the United Services' Ladies' Golfing Association (USLGA). The Legal has remained open to blood relatives of members of the relevant professions and today refuses to admit some practitioners. The USLGA membership was originally open to blood relatives of 'Gentlemen holding or who have held His Majesty's commission in the Navy or Army'. It was founded in 1914. After the Armistice, qualifications were extended to 'members on their own services rendered as a militant section of the Navy, Army and Air Force'.

In 1921, the Veterans' Association, open to members over fifty years of age, was formed through the foresight of Mabel Stringer. In 1923 the Girls' Golfing Society (GGS) followed. Its qualification for membership was that each girl should have been accepted as a competitor in the Girls' Open

Championship. The GGS's first president was Joyce Wethered and Mabel Stringer endowed the society with a Founder's Scratch Challenge Cup. Among other associations were the London Irish Medical Golfing Society, The Stage, and the Women's Automobile Sports Association. In 1936–7 the Vesta Society was founded for members of recognized golf clubs resident in the British Empire overseas, in order to establish a freemasonry of women golfers throughout the Empire. A trophy was presented by Mabel Stringer in the form of a Grecian urn in bronze with a silver plinth, the urn crowned by flames of an ever-burning fire. Through the opening of a matchbox was seen the word 'Vesta' [as in today's 'Swan' matches] so that women golfers of the Empire could see that 'the fire was kept alight'.

Ladies' subsidiary role

During the 1920s, all LGU subscriptions from clubs were doubled, temporarily, and the entrance fees for championships and LGU handicaps were raised. Additionally, the ladies were becoming discontented with their subsidiary role in the government of the game. One contemporary complaint was: 'Women play all their games under entirely man-made rules . . . will a representative of the LGU ever be invited to sit on a yet higher authority?' Today's editions of the Rules of Golf, as approved by the R and A and followed by the LGU, use masculine terms. There have been some illustrated books for women simplifying the better known rules, but a full edition of the Rules using feminine terms – 'she shall be deemed', 'her ball', etc. – has yet to appear. Also, in the Rules of Amateur Status published in the current LGU handbooks, the words 'his' and 'he' appear twelve times, the word 'her' only four times.

In 1925 an innovation occurred at a meeting of the LGU. A woman, Mrs Lewis Smith, took the chair at a Council meeting, the position having always previously been occupied by gentlemen. In 1926 the LGU re-instituted its pre-war competition book, which had to be signed before starting a round or scores would not be accepted, and issued a 6d (2½p) book of LGU rules containing information from the handbook. The Executive Council debated whether, for LGU purposes, Monmouthshire was in England or Wales. They decided for Wales. During the same year it was agreed that the LGU should be represented on the Council of the National Playing Fields Association.

The LGU had more than a thousand affiliated clubs by the beginning of 1927, as well as 400 colonial clubs, which affiliated through their own unions. By 1931 the description of the colonial clubs had changed – they were called 'Unions in British Possessions'. Today they are 'British Commonwealth of Nations (Overseas)'. Coulsdon, Surrey, was the 1000th club to be affiliated to the LGU. The honour of being the 1000th was almost achieved by the Woodsetts Artisans' Club, founded in 1898, which at that time had sixty men and twenty women members. Qualifications for membership were residential, either in Woodsetts village or Shireoaks. However, one club resigned, so Woodsetts became the 999th.

Well organized, the LGU was enjoying financial prosperity, and was

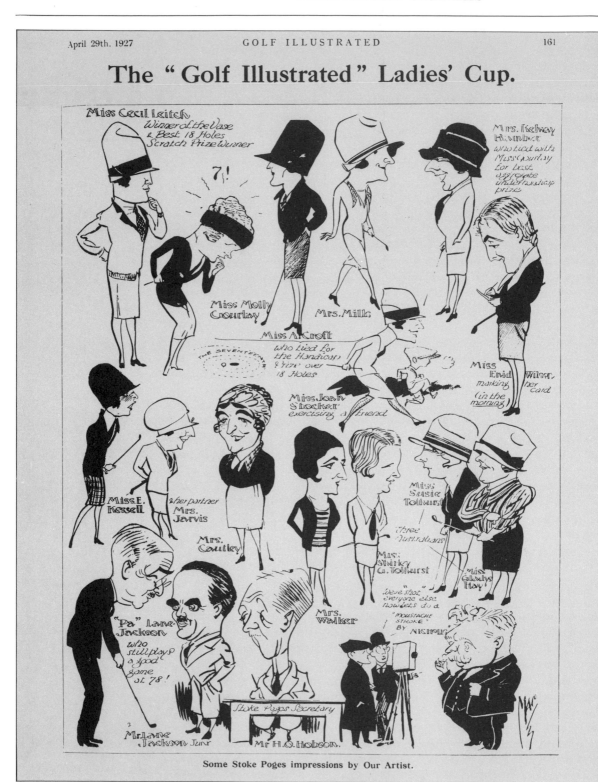

Some Stoke Poges impressions by Our Artist.

balancing a sheet of £3285 in 1927. This was not a large sum of money, but the ladies were not trying to make money. After the subscriptions were raised in 1922, the LGU showed a profit, so they lowered the subscriptions in 1923. In return, the LGU provided: silver and bronze medals each year for competition among members; handicapping by managers; the working out of Standard Scratch; and the welcoming of delegates to meetings. The union also offered help and advice, allowed eligible players to enter for the Ladies' Championship at reduced fees, and provided clubs with copies of the handbook. But a strong undercurrent of discontent had been growing among club members for some time.

Discontent and dissension

The dissension was about the management of union affairs, performed by a small and unrepresentative group of members who lived in or near London. There were demands that the people who made the decisions should be drawn from clubs in all areas. In 1927, the union had ten representatives for the northern division of England and Wales, ten for the southern division, one for Scotland and one for Ireland. These representatives formed the Executive Council which managed the union. They also paid their own expenses, which were not excessive because the majority lived near London, where most meetings were held.

The largest meeting in the union's history was held on 8 February 1928, to debate and vote on the reconstitution of the LGU. Five hundred and fifty-eight delegates from all parts of the kingdom travelled to London for the meeting, which commenced at 10.30 a.m. in the Aeolian Hall, moved to the Hotel Cecil at 3.15 p.m. with a further 400 people attending the annual 'At Home' in an adjoining room, and continued at the Hotel Metropole for a further hour and three-quarters from 6 p.m. onwards. Sir Harold Reckitt took the chair. Never had any item on any of the union's agenda raised so much interest. Powerful and emotional speeches were made by the ladies, some of whom were in tears. Many feared that any interference with the traditional structure of the LGU would weaken it and ultimately cause its demise. Others were adamant that it was not representative and that the power of making decisions lay with too few people.

The three constitutional principles debated but defeated at that meeting were: that the union was to head a neutral governing body following the establishment of an English association – this would give the four countries equal rights and each country was to deal with its own local affairs; that the annual general meeting would in future be held with restricted representation, with full representation at the annual meetings of the national associations – this was considered necessary because the present size made clear discussion and legislation impossible; and that there should be an executive council of fifteen, two each from Scotland, Wales and Ireland, three from the northern division of England, with two each from the Midland, south-western and south-eastern divisions. The possibility of a national English association was defeated because of the expense. It was also considered unnecessary because the majority of players resided there. The meeting

In the 1920s ladies' golf was well established and even regarded as something of a social accomplishment. Matches between gentlemen and ladies no longer generated raised eyebrows but rather lighthearted comments, as in this artist's impressions

favoured representation at the annual general meeting by a delegate from every club. The fifteen-person council principle was defeated because the majority considered that county representation was preferable to divisional representation.

Issette Pearson Miller, although she had retired from her official position seven years previously, signed a letter explaining a further proposed constitution which was sent to many clubs. The ladies debated and voted against at an extraordinary general meeting on 10 July 1928, at which proxy votes were allowed. The new constitution provided national or county representation on the Executive Council for every club, with travelling expenses granted to council members if they lived more than thirty miles outside London. Six standing committees were also suggested, composed of members of the Executive Council. This EGM heard arguments about whether proportional or divisional representation was the more suitable and whether or not fares should be reimbursed out of funds. The latter caused a great deal of indecision and strong feeling: some ladies were indignant that their subscriptions should subsidize other ladies' fares.

The best committee

Cecil Leitch made the brilliant but impractical comment that the best committee was a committee of one, provided that the right one was chosen. Miss Leitch was against the proposed reconstitution as she considered that the business of the union would still be carried out by those who could travel to meetings easily. She expected either regular attendance at meetings and therefore heavy expenses because of reimbursement of travelling expenses, or else management by a few ladies who lived in or near London, the latter item being the initial cause of the ladies' dissension. Miss Leitch was in favour of England having her own association, but was twenty-four years ahead of her time. She was quite convinced that paying all the representatives would bankrupt the LGU. As most clubs were affiliated and fewer fees were anticipated, she wondered how the union could obtain the money. Miss Leitch was then a member of the Executive Council but after the July meeting she wrote to the LGU tendering her resignation. She received a letter expressing deep gratitude for her work and connection with the union.

All clubs now had votes in the election of councillors to represent them. The union was considered to be truly an association of clubs. Representatives for Scotland, Ireland and Wales were elected by clubs affiliated to the three national unions and associations and to the LGU. There was one representative for every thirty clubs in those three countries, and England's representatives were elected through the county organizations, with the additional provision that a county club with 100 affiliated clubs within its own boundary was entitled to elect a second representative, but that representative's travel expenses would not be reimbursed.

In 1931 the union had forty-two councillors – thirty-four for England, one for Ireland, five for Scotland and two for Wales. During this decade the union's affairs were consolidated and remained stable, due substantially to

the efforts of Miss M. MacFarlane, who was connected with the union for thirty-five years, for most of that time in the office of secretary. The ladies obtained larger administrative offices at 38–40 Eccleston Square at an annual rent of £176, excluding rates and other incidentals.

Preserving history

Conscious of the need to preserve their history and prestige for the young and future generations, the ladies initiated the idea of forming a museum to exhibit objects relating to the origin and growth of women's golf. The suggestion was made at the annual dinner of the Veteran Ladies' Golf Association in April 1938. Women golfers rallied to the appeal, treasured items were donated and loaned and the Women Golfers' Museum was officially opened in the April of the following year. Issette Pearson Miller was president, Mabel Stringer chairman, and the committee consisted of M.H. Benton, E.T. Bolton, Doris Chambers, D.I. Clark, R.F. Garnham, Blanche Martin Hulton, Cecil Leitch and H.B. Rabbidge. The museum was originally housed at Whitehall Court, stored safely during World War II, and was thereafter exhibited in different clubs, including the Devonshire and the Nineteenth. This limited the people able to view the collection to members of those clubs, or their guests, until the mid-1970s when Colgate, who were at the height of their golf-sponsoring phase, rehoused it at Colgate House, Oxford Street, London, although written requests for appointments to view were necessary. Cecil Leitch performed the opening ceremony at the age of 86.

When Colgate withdrew from golf sponsorship, the museum was homeless for some time. The exhibits were nearly transported to the USA, but this intention was discovered during a conversation between the museum's solicitors and the current chairman of the trustees, Miss Maureen Millar – daughter of Cecil's sister, May Leitch Millar. Today the museum, which still acquires important items, is on loan to the National Museum of Antiquities, Queen Street, Edinburgh, suitably displayed and on view free of charge to the public. It receives a small subsidy from the LGU and was officially opened on those premises in February 1982 by the current lady champion, Isabella McCorkindale Robertson, aged 46.

Immediately after World War II, the LGU was in a parlous state. Income had dwindled through lower membership in affiliated clubs and fewer affiliating and affiliated clubs, but staff, rental and other expenses still had to be paid. This did not prevent the entries for the 1946 Ladies' Championship at Hunstanton being high and when Miss MacFarlane retired as secretary in November 1947 the testimonial fund for her had reached £5023, and amounts were still coming in from overseas. In 1948 the LGU had its first Scottish chairman of the Executive Council, Mrs Wallace Williamson. Two years later there were 1249 affiliated clubs and an excess of income over expenditure for the first time since the war – £35 10s 11d.

Once again there were discussions about a reconstitution of the LGU and one of the major points of dissension was the unwieldy size of the Executive Council which, because of expenses, was eroding the funds. The statement

After a chequered history before, during and after World War II, the Women Golfers' Museum found a permanent home in Edinburgh in 1982. It was officially opened there by the then current lady champion, Belle, née McCorkindale, Robertson, pictured here at the end of a shot

was made: 'The LGU is the predominating and governing body of women's golf which at present is untouched and unassailable.' In 1951 a sub-committee was set up to investigate the formation of an English association, and a proposal was made to reduce the number of councillors. Lady Katherine Cairns was chairman of this sub-committee and it was largely the result of her persistence and vision that the English Ladies' Golf Association (ELGA) was created. At one meeting, delegates were asked to vote on whether or not the investigation should continue, where the legal expenses to form such an association should come from and if the LGU was autho-rized to spend funds for such a purpose. Lady Katherine Cairns solved these problems with perspicacity and speed.

There were three plans: to form ELGA and consequently reduce the LGU council; to reduce the Executive Council with consequent alteration in the system of representation; to organize ELGA on lines acceptable to the LGU when ELGA applied for affiliation. The English ladies were anxious to form their own association quickly and when at one meeting a member of the platform said she thought that the new organization could not be effected by the end of the year, there were shouts of 'Why not?' from the hall. The scheme to reduce the number of councillors suggested that the England northern division, with 351 clubs, should have 5 councillors, the England Midland, 212 clubs, 2 councillors, England south-east, 283 clubs, 3 council-lors, England south-west, 85 clubs, 1 councillor, Ireland, 13 clubs, 1 council-lor, Scotland, 206 clubs, 2 councillors, and Wales, 90 clubs, 1 councillor. The Executive Council was eventually reduced from 44 to 10 – England had 6, Scotland 2, Ireland 1 and Wales 1.

Birth of the ELGA

The ELGA was formed at a meeting on 21 November 1951, with the majority of 654 for and 31 against. LGU meetings had always been kept in order by the ringing of a bell from the platform, but when the Irish, Scottish and Welsh delegates departed together with the LGU's bell, the meeting was called to order by the clinking together of two glasses. Lady Heathcoat Amory, formerly Joyce Wethered, was the ELGA's first president, Mary Holdsworth secretary, and Mrs Barnes treasurer. The English were gratified that the ELGA had two ex-LGU chairmen in office.

At the February 1952 meeting of the LGU, a new LGU flag was presented in memory of Miss MacFarlane, who had died in 1951, by Doris Chambers and unfurled on the platform. It flew first at Muirfield for the Curtis Cup and obviously brought golfing luck on that occasion. The original LGU flag had been presented to the LGU by Mr T.H. Miller and Mr Smith Turberville in 1895. When it flew at St Andrews for the first time, in 1908, it withstood the gales and the R and A's flag did not.

The ELGA now managed her own domestic affairs – championships, county golf, and the appointment of representatives, but not the handicap-ping system nor the standard scratch scheme. All four countries were autonomous, and appointed their representatives to the LGU's committees. Thus the structure envisaged by Mabel Stringer became reality.

In the spring of 1954, the LGU transferred its headquarters to Sandwich Bay, paying 1 shilling per annum in rent to West London Leaseholds, through the generosity of Sir Aynsley Bridgland. In the same year, Lady Katherine Cairns gave a flag to the ELGA. Its design incorporated the cross of St George with a Tudor rose at the centre and the letters 'E, L, G, A' at the four corners. The SLGA held its fiftieth anniversary dinner in this year, the speakers including Charlotte Stevenson Watson Beddows, Mrs Wallace Williamson, Noël Dunlop-Hill and Cecil Leitch. The LGU had an unhappy series of anniversaries. Its fiftieth occurred during World War II, and at its sixtieth it was nearly bankrupt. However, for its seventieth it was provided with an iced cake decorated with golf balls, and had made a profit of £1200 over the previous twelve months.

The closest of closed shops
During the 1960s, the LGU was likened to 'the closest of closed shops, which worked because of the very small number of players likely to be affected by the policy of the Council'. Its 1952 reconstitution had ensured that every councillor could work in harness with a deputy and so ensure continuity of policy and full representation at all meetings, so it was still the case that very few delegates performed the necessary tasks and made the decisions. Hierarchically the structure of the government of the game could be likened to a pyramid: at the base were the club committees; above these were the officials who organized the various counties and associations. On the next step in the pyramid were the area councils, above them the national associations and unions, and at the top the members of the Executive Council of the LGU. This is its structure today.

Also during the 1960s, the LGU was recognized as the feminine counterpart of the R and A throughout the world and tried to institute an Open Championship. It was premature in its efforts to obtain suitable sponsorship and failed (success not coming until 1976 with the 1983 event cancelled because of lack of TV coverage; in 1984, however, with lavish sponsorship and TV coverage, the event seemed likely to assume higher status, assured if the United States' LPGA stars continue to participate). The LGU inaugurated a stroke-play championship, instigated training schemes, and concentrated on its Standard Scratch Scheme, the handicap system and the organization of tournaments. A working committee, drawn from the four associations and unions, was announced to investigate the streamlining of administration and financial responsibilities between the LGU and the national governing bodies, the services of a professional adviser being enlisted for finance and administration.

In 1970, after many years of defeats in international matches, one former British champion was asked: 'What's wrong with British women's golf?' Her reply was that the fault could be with the LGU, because the Council belonged to a different generation from the players. She considered that the Council should have some younger representatives who knew at first hand the difficulties and the life-styles of the younger players. The LGU were aware that younger players were entering administration at club and county

level and stated that they hoped the trend would continue. The most recent
event inaugurated by the LGU was for seniors (over fifty years of age) in
1981. Two of the most promising players in the UK today had both won
major national championships well before their eighteenth birthdays. The
lady champion of 1981 was in her mid-forties, while the 1983 winner was
also over forty. The current president is in her sixties and has been involved
with golf at all levels for most of her life. Hopefully, any generation gap will
not affect the future.

During the 1970s, the LGU managed to inaugurate an Open, and raised
its per capita subscription by more than 250 per cent. A move of headquarters to 12, The Links, St Andrews was also made, the lease at Sandwich
Bay having expired. The current premises are suitable surroundings for the
working administrators of such a long-established body, suitably designed, properly heated and carpeted, spacious, and with one of the best
views in the world from the boardroom – the 1st and the 18th of the Old
Course. The LGU Executive Council currently consists of president – the
thirteenth since the first in 1908 – honorary treasurer, chairman, and two
councillors and two deputies each from England, Ireland, Scotland and
Wales. It has three sub-committees – International Selection Committee,
Regulations Committee, and Scratch Score Committee, and representatives on other golfing bodies. It holds one AGM and five Executive Council
meetings a year. Subscriptions are paid by each home country, according
to the number of members entitled to play on each club affiliated to their
national organization. The two secretaries administer the council's policy
with regard to running tournaments, handling finances, and liaising with
overseas affiliations.

In 1982, the ELGA had 280 officials, advisers and representatives, 1128
clubs, and 93,550 members; the ILGU had 229 affiliated clubs with 117
official representatives, organizers and managers, and 21,048 members; the
SLGA had 335 clubs, 126 elected officers, representatives and official advisers, and 30,660 members; and the WLGU (Welsh Ladies' Gold Union) had
108 clubs, 98 organizing officials and representatives and 8203 members.
The officials and representatives of the overall governing body, the LGU,
numbered 47 in 1982. This gives a total of one official for every 229.7 playing
members in England, Ireland, Scotland and Wales. Leaving aside club
committees, whose members average about seven for each club, but including, conservatively, a captain, honorary secretary and handicap secretary,
the figure becomes one official for every 25.4 players. Apart from the 1800
affiliated clubs in England, Ireland, Scotland and Wales, the LGU in 1982
also had 17 affiliated overseas unions and associations, comprising 3809
clubs, as well as 61 other affiliated clubs in many parts of the world.

The LGU's first telegraphic address was 'Issette, Churton'. Later on it
became 'Issette, Sandwich', and today it is 'Issette, St Andrews'. A portrait
of Issette Pearson Miller hangs on the wall of the LGU boardroom. Her
pioneering organizational work endowed women golfers with a substantial
legacy, and she will also always be remembered for her prodigious success
in instituting the LGU's handicap system. ◖

Catching
the Colonel

The uselessness of the club handicapping systems which were in vogue in the early eighteen-nineties was forcefully implanted in Issette Pearson Miller's mind by one particular incident early in her golfing career. After missing a train, she filled in the hours before the next one by visiting an unfamiliar course. There was a ladies' club and she found a partner for a match. After only a few holes, Issette realized that she should be giving strokes not receiving them. Each lady was playing from her respective club handicap, and the unevenness of the match impressed upon her the necessity of investigating existent handicapping systems. She discovered so much inconsistency that when she and her colleagues eventually formed the LGU in 1893, they insisted that one of the principal aims must be to establish a uniform system of handicapping. They instituted their system in 1896 and it quickly spread to many ladies' clubs in the four home countries and around the world. Their system was similar to a scheme adopted by Wimbledon in 1874 and favoured by Laidlaw Purves.

Handicapping was in a chaotic state, because each club calculated the par of the green and players' handicaps by its own method. This inconsistency did not affect club competitions, but inter-club and open meetings presented secretaries and handicapping committees with time-consuming decision-making. Many committees were ignorant of the difficulties and variations of courses other than their own, and so could not take these into consideration, or determine the relative merit of players. Mabel Stringer, one of the LGU's first handicap managers, described the confusion:

Irish champion May Hezlet had strong views on, and wrote prolifically about, the game. One method of handicapping which she favoured was to give up the appropriate number of holes at the beginning of the round and then play level throughout

Mrs Jones goes steadily round in 80 and is put at scratch; Mrs Brown hands in a wobbly card of 85 with a 7 on it and gets 5. At Wimbledon in 1893 Miss Pearson was back marker at scratch, and the limit was 24. At West Lancashire some of the members were plus 1 and the limit was 30. Lady Margaret Scott and Mrs Wilson-Hoare were scratch at Minchinhampton, where the limit was 25. But at St Anne's, where the limit was also 25, there were several plus players, Mrs Ernest Catteral being plus 5. At Littlestone we went up to 36 and our lowest player was 10.

One club in the south of England had a player with a handicap of 96!

Home handicaps a mockery

The majority of clubs handicapped from a scratch score made by the best player in the club, ignoring the fact that if that player were matched against a champion she would need more than a few strokes to make the match a fair one. Some clubs who possessed a well-known scratch player gave her a 'plus' handicap and the resultant table of handicaps in that club made a scratch player out of one whose standard of play in comparison with a champion should have been rated at 10. The only method of handicapping in existence was handicapping players in relation to other players of the same club, not by a standardized method of assessing players against a ground score which had also been established in accordance with a standardized method. The lack of a universal system made a mockery of handicaps obtained on home courses. A scratch player in a small club would probably be beaten by a player with a 16 handicap at a large club where the status of scratch could be obtained only through intense competition and against enormous odds.

Laidlaw Purves and the ladies of the LGU considered that the adoption of a system which was approved by all the clubs belonging to the union would be the best method of handicapping and would be fairer in competitions which ladies from different clubs entered. Then the secretary of the LGU could obtain a list of the handicaps of all members from all clubs and circulate that list to all clubs. The handicapping committee of each club could then allot visiting players a suitable place on their competition list and each player would find herself competing against a lady of her own standard or against a common standard. The sending of lists to all clubs was feasible in the days when only about twenty or so clubs belonged to the union. Later on, and for many years, changes in handicap were published regularly in the handbook and in other periodicals.

The problems presented by the variations in the courses could only be overcome if each club calculated the par of its own green by a method agreed upon by all clubs. In that way, the scratch scores of each green would give a standardized guide to the amount of handicap allowed in both match and stroke play on the different greens. Pars of the green varied enormously in the eighteen-nineties. Leaving aside the fact that courses, standards of play and equipment have changed, as well as methods of assessing Standard Scratch Score (SS), a comparison of pars of the green of twenty-eight courses shows that they varied by as much as forty-four whereas today the variation of those same courses is eight (see Appendix 3).

Margin for unavoidable accidents

Issette and her colleagues instituted a system of striking a scratch or bogey score for each hole of each course, and thus obtained a universally recognized LGU method of establishing the par of the green. The ladies decided that if it took a first-class player two strokes to reach the green, two more should be added for putting out, and the regulation figure for that hole should be 4. They applied the same principle to each green, added two or

three strokes 'for unavoidable accidents' to each total of nine holes, and decided that all handicaps should be related to the score so obtained for the eighteen holes. Three scores were to be the average for each player's handicap, and those scores had to be made on a prize or medal day. Handicaps were limited to 25, as the ladies considered that anyone who required more than that number was 'a very crude performer'.

The par of the green was therefore fixed at a score that a champion lady golfer would find great difficulty in lowering. Some long-established clubs already had champions among their members, but the newer ones had to be visited by competent players. However, the honour of 'taking par' for the LGU was considered a very high one and leading players willingly took on the work. In the early days of the system, a hole under 120 yards was usually a 3, one under 280 yards a 4, and one under 320 yards a 5. Once the par of the green of a club had been carefully ascertained, the two best scores returned in a stroke play by each player were noted, the best score was doubled, and the difference of the average of these three from the par of the green was the player's handicap.

Best score	75	Average	77
Doubled	75	Par of the green	72
Next best score	81	Player's handicap	5
	231 ÷ 3		

As the ladies had fixed the handicap limit at 25, no player could receive a handicap unless she had returned two scores within that number added to the par of the green. Laidlaw Purves disliked the idea of doubling the best score; he considered that a handicap should be based on the difference from par of three best scores. He maintained that the method of handicapping on a suppositional score – i.e. best doubled – was a fundamental error. The ladies eventually agreed that his was a more accurate method, but not until 1913, and handicap managers then underwent many weeks of hard work in order to adjust the system.

Two other features of the LGU's system were that each player should have the same handicap at every club she played at, and that no player could be 'plus'. If plus was possible, then the par was considered too liberal. No one could be 'scratch' either, unless she had proved her right to the title, preferably by winning the Ladies' Championship, which automatically earned her that honour. By 1900 the LGU ladies considered that their system ensured that an LGU handicap was a fair assessment of a player's form. But not all clubs used the LGU system, and those who did not were faced with internal difficulties and arguments.

One method of handicapping which May Hezlet, the Irish lady champion, favoured was to give up the appropriate number of holes at the beginning of the round and then play level throughout. This worked well for medium handicappers, but a scratch lady playing against, say for

example, a 24-handicapper could arrive on the first tee 19 holes down, and it would therefore be unnecessary to start. Another plan adopted in some clubs was to reduce a player after a win in proportion to the amount of handicap which she had had at the time of playing – from 20 to 18, from 15 to 13, from 10 to 9 and so on.

Such inconsistency shouts for reform

Handicap committees of clubs which did not use the LGU system expended much time, work and thought in arranging relative handicaps fairly, but some of their players were always discontented and convinced that the committee's sole intention was to prevent them from winning prizes. These committees tried to reduce everyone to a general level, with the object that all matches might work out evenly, preferably being decided on the last green or after a tie. The committees were happy if all matches were closely fought, and if no player proved herself a long way ahead of the field.

Club members were usually annoyed when youngsters, beginners or players who had not attended meetings for some time returned astonishingly low scores. The committee's competency was queried in such cases, but the members often considered it was unfair to cut a beginner's handicap before she had a chance of establishing her true form. Sympathetic committees agreed that beginners seldom did themselves true justice in their first few competitions, and that, through nervousness and anxiety to play well, they usually played either way above their eventual form or way below it. Committees also had difficulties with regard to the handicaps of those who had been absent from competition for a long time, as they had no way of knowing if such players had been practising regularly or if they had not wielded a club for months. When committee members recognized the name of such a player on the competition entry sheet, they usually allotted the player her former handicap, but received an unpleasant shock when her score was noted and found to bear little relation to that handicap.

Some committees turned handicapping into a guessing game, and others based their decisions on favouritism. If a popular member of a club won a few prizes, the committee often let her handicap stand, but if a less-popular member won, she would be brought down quickly. Other club committees took little account of actual scores, and reduced players automatically after a win. On match days, handicapping committees could raise or lower handicaps as they thought fit, and non-committee members had no rights to query their decisions. Many members did not agree that a reduced handicap was a token of the committee's approval and appreciation of a lady's standard of play, and thought that it was too severe.

Further difficulties facing players and committees included the fact that players in open competitions had to declare the lowest handicap obtained at any club they belonged to, and some clubs had bye-laws stating that competitors had to play off the handicap allotted to them on the course at which the event took place. Handicap committees at open meetings were rarely successful at placing players with handicaps obtained through a

different system on level terms. Competing for prizes at such meetings was often on a level with tossing a coin. Some clubs who considered that their members were under-handicapped – because they were rarely among the winners at open meetings – put up all their handicaps a few days before a meeting, thereby enabling their members to take all the prizes.

As Issette said: 'Such inconsistency shouts for reform.' The LGU did not insist that all clubs affiliated to it should use their system, but many clubs which adopted it found it advantageous and usually did not revert to their previous club system. Some clubs worked two systems – their own and the LGU – but concentrated most of their efforts on establishing sound club handicaps. When an LGU competition occurred, however, all members wanted to enter, and so their neglected LGU handicaps had to be validated quickly, thus making a convenience of it. This was considered unfair on other competitors, whose LGU handicaps were properly certified over an approved length of time.

Ladies who adhered to the LGU system experienced a friendly rivalry concerning the size and alteration of their handicaps. If a player's handicap was too high or too low, other ladies usually recognized the fact, even if the player was a member of another club. The ladies generally found out if all the handicaps in a particular club were, on the whole, too high or too low. These points were frequently discussed – with the result that all players did their best to obtain a correct LGU handicap.

To encourage their system of handicapping, the LGU in 1897 decided to give a silver medal annually to each associated club. The medal was won by the member who returned the lowest aggregate of four scores under union handicap during a medal competition. The LGU also gave a gold medal to be played for over a neutral links by the winners of the silver medals in each year.

The ladies realized that one difficulty of the system was the impossibility of handicapping without sufficient scores, and some players objected to returning the required number. Many considered that score play was extremely dull, but the LGU insisted that it was the only sound basis on which to establish handicaps. In several clubs the home handicapping system went up to 40 or 50. When this was the case LGU players considered that the handicapping was a farce. A player who needed 40 or 50 strokes to help her round an 18-hole course was either so inexpert that she ought not to be playing at all, or else she returned scores which, after the deduction of her handicap allowance, brought her nett scores down to the sixties. The general opinion was that 18 or 20 was suitable for ladies who had played for about a year. Although the ladies recognized the discontent that would be caused if all clubs adopted this limit, they considered that it would improve the standard of golf. They therefore left the limit at 25, to include beginners. They realized that all players tried to play to their handicaps and therefore the higher their handicaps were the less need and incentive they had for practice and improvement. The handicapping principle was thus laid down in accordance with best form, not average play.

By 1897, four handicap managers had been appointed – for Cheshire,

Customary prizes for ladies in the late nineteenth century ranged from scent bottles through brooches to button hooks; medals were always popular. The LGU in 1897 decided to give a silver medal annually to each associated club. These are scratch medals from North Berwick, East Lothian

Bolton, Kent and Folkestone; these ladies worked out the handicaps and returned them to the club secretaries on special forms ready for medal returns. After each medal competition, the forms went back to the handicap manager, who altered the handicaps where necessary and forwarded a new list to the club secretary. The scores were then sent to the LGU's honorary secretary for publication. The LGU pioneers were initially pleased with the basis of the system, having proved that: 'As every player handicaps herself by the scores she returns there can be no complaint about the handicap committee not recognizing her merit.'

Extra days

By 1900 several clubs were designating extra days every month on which scores could be returned for handicap purposes, under strict medal-play rules. They considered this advisable because if the monthly medal day was wet or windy, there was little chance of returning a characteristic score. Players who belonged to more than one club advised the assistant honorary secretary for handicap managers of these clubs of any differences in handicap.

Improvements and alterations were continually taking place on many courses and course records were often broken. This entailed alteration of the par of the green, and subsequently more work for the champion takers of par. If a par was raised because of alteration to the course, handicaps remained the same, with the par difference added; similarly the same principle applied if the par was lowered, until players had made better gross scores after the alteration. But if a par raised because a club member came to scratch who had not formerly been a scratch player, the gross scores remained the same and the handicaps were raised by the same number as the par.

No one could become 'scratch' without a certificate from three players who were already scratch and production of proof of scores by her handicap manager. Players who had not returned a sufficient number of scores to allow the handicap committee to certify valid handicaps were allowed to compete on half handicap. Around 1901 the LGU ladies found that, in inter-club competitions, their practice of adding one-third (six strokes) to the handicap of a player from a short course playing on a long course, and deducting the same from a player accustomed to a long course and playing on a short course, was unsatisfactory. So they added one-half to the handicaps of players from short links who were playing on long links, and subtracted one-third from the handicaps of players from long links when they were playing on short links (see Appendix 2). The ladies had divided all affiliated clubs into two classes: first class was for ladies' clubs playing over gentlemen's links and for ladies' links of a par of 76 and over; second class consisted of clubs playing over ladies' links of a par of under 76 and of those playing only 9-hole courses.

The LGU system grew in popularity. By 1905 there were fifteen handicap managers and a complete revision of club pars was necessitated by the fashionable, and more general use, of the rubber-cored ball. This was a

heavy task, and a thankless one, as no one wanted their handicaps raised. But most players admitted that their revised handicaps were correct in comparison with the current champion scratch players, to whom the handicaps were related. And all over the country lady golfers were answering the question: 'How is the handicapping to be done – by a committee or by scores?' The majority opted for the latter solution because they found that 'when six or eight people get together, no two of them could agree to another's form'.

Issette maintained in 1906 that the system was gradually winning its way:

> Players are beginning to realize that the system of giving the lowest handicap that a player has in any club, at an open meeting, is very unfair and hard on some players as the best player in a club is often put at scratch, and even plus, quite regardless of her form compared to a champion player. Some of the LGU handicaps are much too high; this is because the players will not take the trouble to return scores and get a correct handicap; but now that the handicap managers have agreed not to certify any handicap for an open meeting unless scores are returned and a correct handicap obtained, I think we shall see an improvement.

Handicap managers could refuse to certify a handicap for an open meeting, unless at least ten scores had been returned during the previous twelve months, and two of these scores had to be returned during the two months prior to the meeting; exceptions to this were handicaps of 4 or under, illness, or lack of reliable information from handicap managers.

By 1907 one strong objection to the LGU system was raised through the concerted voices of members – and that was its limit of 25. Many clubs found that their players could not return scores low enough to come down to that figure. The ladies eventually decided that there really was no reason for clubs to limit their handicaps to 25, if that would prevent them from using the LGU system. They could go up to whatever figure the club committee decided was advisable.

Clubs were realizing that a universal system was useful and necessary. Yorkshire made an important step when the Ladies' County Club decided to adopt the system throughout the county and found the results satisfactory. Many clubs in other areas now worked the LGU system only. But the LGU ladies were still finding it difficult to make players realize that perpetual scoring was not necessary, and that if scoring for Extra Day was allowed on any day at all, much better scores would be returned than would ever be returned on medal days, and therefore the handicaps would be too low. The suggestion that a member could return scores on any day she wished also caused objections because if a member wished to compete for a prize she might record her scores ten days in succession, and would be able to obtain a handicap in ten days, although she might be completely off her game at the time.

The system migrates

By 1908 Blanche Martin Hulton had 'toured the world' and had spoken to representatives in both islands of New Zealand about the handicapping system and the management of competitions. Medals were sent out for competition, one for the North Island and one for the South Island. Her stepson was the secretary of the Tasmanian Union and his members had approved his report of the handicap system and instructed him to write 'home' for full particulars of rules and regulations.

Many lady golfers now agreed that 'To say you were scratch in the LGU meant a very great deal.' By 1909 a bronze medal was competed for annually by those holding handicaps from 26 to 40, and in 1910 players with handicaps over 25 were allowed to take out cards on any and every day they wished. In 1911 all players were permitted to make one score a week for handicap and could choose their own days for doing so, if they had previously announced their intentions. And by this time, the handicap managers had recommended that there should be two classes of player (where clubs had sufficient members): silver and bronze. Thirty-seven players had now been officially listed as being 'scratch', but there was still no 'plus'. By 1912, the LGU ladies had decided that the handicap limit was not to exceed 40.

In 1913, Laidlaw Purves's initial suggestion that players should be handicapped on their three best scores, instead of best score doubled plus one other score, was adopted. Every player was re-handicapped on her three best scores of the years 1911, 1912 and 1913. It was considered that this would lead to greater accuracy and that the long handicappers would be able to hold their own with the scratch players a little more easily. Issette warned that everyone should make sure that they had a third score representative of their form, or there could be difficulties with regard to certifying handicaps in the following year. The ladies were given a full year's notice of this change, but Issette reported that: 'Alas! the wailing is loud.'

On the advice of the handicap managers, whose work was voluminous and voluntary, and as a result of many requests, on 1 January 1915 the LGU handicap was limited to 20 for the silver class and 36 for the bronze class. The limit of 20 for the silver division remained in force until 1931 when it was changed to 18, as it is today. By 1920 two extra scores per week were allowed for handicap purposes for both divisions.

The system stymied

And then along came 'plus' – in the person of Cecil Leitch, the first lady to occupy that position. Actually Miss Leitch did not receive any strokes within the system during her official competitive years, and on one occasion she had to give 25. Her sister May had to give 50 in the same competition – and she won it. However, Joyce Wethered stymied the system. She did not play in many open meetings nor return sufficient scores under LGU rules and regulations. She was put at plus 1, when other ladies who had registered the necessary number of scores were put at plus 2 or plus 3. This was considered a definite flaw in the system.

Joyce Wethered, who stymied the LGU handicap system by not returning sufficient scores under LGU rules and regulations. Miss Wethered, later Lady Heathcoat Amory, is seen here receiving the trophy after beating Cecil Leitch in the Ladies' British Open Amateur Championship at Troon, Ayrshire, in 1925

Thus the system in use today evolved. Men had been officially permitted to mark cards for ladies since 1913 and soon after it was resolved that 'If the local rules of the Club prohibited a man member from marking a card for a lady, a prominent notice to this effect must be posted in the Club House and the LGU must be notified.' Information concerning the marking of cards by men is published in the LGU's handbooks today. The general opinion of male golfers, including that of amateur champion Harold Hilton, was that the system of handicapping adopted by the LGU embodied an excellent principle. However, the men did not institute a general system of handicapping until the 1920s.

After World War I, handicaps were revised at the end of 1920 on scores returned in 1919 and 1920, and players on 4 and under were revised solely on scores returned in competition. Since the 1920s, sliding scales for permitted increases on lapsed handicaps have undergone various revisions, as have the number of strokes added or subtracted for playing on longer or shorter courses. The durations of the validity of handicaps have varied from six months to three years, and the permitted number of extra-day scores has developed from none for some players to any day for everyone. The bronze and silver divisions have been further divided. Today the LGU recommends that everyone should return at least six cards a year, and handicaps lapse if four cards are not returned within each handicap year, which runs from 1 February to 31 January.

A bronze division player, 36 to 30, is handicapped on her best score; bronze from 29 to 19 are handicapped on their two best scores; 18s must return four scores averaging less than 18 to get the star off; 18s to 4s are handicapped on the average of their four best scores; 3s stay starred until they have returned four cards which average 3¼ or less above SS and these are recorded by handicap advisers; 3 and under handicappers must return scores on at least two courses in addition to the home course, and the average of the four worst of the six best is the handicap.

It is easier today to gain and retain a handicap than it was in the days when a handicap manager could ask for ten cards if she considered it necessary. The handicap managers carried out a difficult and time-consuming chore and their work was completely voluntary. In 1922 players were requested, owing to the expense of postage, to enclose postage with every application for certification. Around 1930, the suggestion was made that the LGU should institute a central handicapping bureau, and take the work away from the handicap managers. It was felt this would lead to greater uniformity, as the work was in the hands of 200 ladies and it was doubtful that they were all interpreting the regulations in the same way. Another reason was that a player would not have to decide which course to play on for handicapping purposes. The suggestion was not taken up, and the ladies missed the opportunity of being far in advance of their time and instituting a unique centralized system.

During the 1930s, some clubs still held to their own systems of handicapping, but this was generally considered a lower form of reckoning. The handicap regulations for the 1932 Ladies' Championship stated that

players must have an LGU handicap of 6 or a club handicap of 3. Ladies were considered easier to handicap than men as they played truer to form and if men were handicapped on the LGU system the results would be farcical. Men approaching championship level – 3 to 4 – held national handicaps, the rest were handicapped by their local clubs. The men agreed that their handicaps should be different on different courses, and worked out among themselves who should go down after winning and vice versa. The ladies claimed that they obtained much fairer results with their system than the men with theirs.

SS assessment

The ladies also decided to make use of the men's scheme for SS assessment. This scheme had been put into operation, evolved by the British Golf Union's Joint Advisory Council, found satisfactory, and revised in 1933. The ladies decided to deduct 10 per cent from the men's figures. Tests had shown that the pitch of a woman's drive was 12½ per cent less than a man's, but the run on the ball was nearly as long. The LGU SS was taken under normal summer conditions and it was of no concern that handicaps could be played to only in summer because there was little competition golf in winter. There had at one time been different pars of the green for summer and winter conditions, but these ceased, with the exception of affiliated clubs in Singapore, India and other countries which have wet and dry seasons.

The chief benefits of adopting a version of the men's scheme were that the SS committee would no longer be required and the SS could be worked out by the LGU in conjunction with visits of scratch players to the courses and by collaboration with county officials in the matter of granting additional course value. This was judged a more efficient system and would save the LGU money. At the 1937 championship at Turnberry, white posts were placed at intervals of ten yards – the length of the pitch of a tee shot being considered to be 175 yards. The officials stood in the rough, noted where the ball landed, and then strode step by step to measure the run.

After World War II, in 1947, the LGU scrutinized the SS on all affiliated courses but, as it was impossible to cover all the courses immediately, handicaps were being obtained on revised and unrevised courses. At the Sunningdale Open Foursomes, handicapping the women therefore presented problems, and it was eventually decided that they should play off 4. This worked well, and it was observed that a good woman golfer plus one first-class man golfer could hold two first-class men on level terms. In the men's versus women's matches at Stoke Poges, if the ground was hard and worn, the women could reach the green with two woods, making a half an almost impossible handicap for the men.

In the early 1950s the difficult task of the handicap managers was discussed. The LGU supplied the stationery and the players the postage, but they were seldom able to leave their records for a single day. By 1955 there were 250 handicap managers, all appointed by the Executive Council of the LGU. They took their records with them wherever they went, and, as the handicap year then ended on 31 December, the work they had to complete

during the Christmas period undoubtedly led to some domestic disruption. Jeanne Bisgood suggested that extra-day scores should be dispensed with altogether, and a one-year validity for all handicaps was introduced. Hitherto they had been valid for two years after the year in which the necessary number of scores had been returned. The change was made because the handicaps were obviously unrealistic, as some scores could be three years old, and the work of the handicap managers would be lessened.

Junior handicaps were inaugurated in 1959. These could be obtained with three cards returned over 9 holes, as it was thought that it was easier for the under-fifteens to concentrate over 9 holes than over 18. Their handicaps started at 50 – 45 today and an age limit of twelve – with the standard scratch of the selected 9 holes doubled, as were the scores returned, and the usual deductions made. Players in this category today, as with senior veterans and disabled ladies, must return two scores annually to retain a handicap.

SS revised again

In the nineteen-sixties all scratch scores were revised in order to bring the British SS in line with the USA and the Continent. The LGU's chairman, Mary Holdsworth, stated that the SS in Britain were higher than anywhere else in the world, but during the previous fifteen years courses had become easier because of improvements in greenkeeping and equipment. Clubs had eliminated large patches of rough, and filled in some hazards, in order to get more people round in less time. Miss Holdsworth hoped that 'eventually men and women would play the game on level terms, with handicaps as the only concession'.

Also in the nineteen-sixties, the suggestion was made that anyone who could not play to a 36 handicap would not be given a handicap at all. It was not implemented, although it might have improved standards, because most ladies thought that the smaller clubs would suffer. One handicap manager was faced with the task of writing out handicap certificates for two ladies who had never played below a 50 handicap and who wished to enter an open meeting. The advice she received from an LGU official was:

> Small wonder you were embarrassed having to write those certificates – and there is certainly nothing in the rules which allows you to withhold the certificates. I believe this is cropping up in most clubs at the present time – and it is a sign of the times – we are getting new members into clubs, not even young people, but older people, who are taking up the game and, as I see it, with little prospect of ever playing to 36. From my own experience on the Council, this question has been coming up from time to time, but we adhered to the fact that we posed a limit of 36 and anyone who put in three cards would be allowed that limit. I myself do not see how we can depart from that policy, once they are accepted to Club Membership.
>
> I find the whole trend of rising handicaps difficult to understand. Leaving out the fact that all SS were reduced on February 1st this year [1963], the sheets that were returned to my own club on 1.2.63 were

quite amazing. 2½ sheets of Silver Division players and 8 sheets of Bronze Division players. Slowly and by degrees in the last 3 or 4 years this position has been building up – and I am sure that it really means that we must accept the fact that a new type of member is coming into the Clubs – the only good thing is that the Clubs will survive, which in effect, means that the Clubs being full, their subscription to the LGU will be maintained. So, in turn, the LGU will survive.

I still think it is impossible not to give a 36 handicap to those who have not put in one card to 36 – because I think it would preclude quite a number of players from ever achieving a recognized handicap.

Another regulation of the 1960s stated that a player who did not belong to a golf club could not gain a handicap, but that was unpopular, and today individual members of the LGU and the national associations may obtain handicaps. There was also an unsuccessful plea for a return to two-year validity for handicaps. The roles of the handicap managers were abolished in 1966 and the keeping of the handicap records was placed in the hands of club secretaries or club handicap secretaries. Handicap advisers were appointed for each county. This spread the work into the hands of many more people, with representatives from the national associations and the LGU available to advise on any problems which the secretaries or handicap advisers could not handle. This system is used today, the main reference being the regulations published in the LGU's handbook.

Personal responsibility

Pleas for handicaps to be valid for two years were again heard in the nineteen-seventies, but the LGU hoped that an 'honest handicap' would always be acquired by taking out a reasonable number of cards, not only taking them out in dry weather when the ball was running well, or just putting in the minimum number of cards and withholding best scores so as not to reduce handicaps. Organizers were asked to look very carefully at handicap certificates at open meetings, but, in comparison, it was stated that 'one probably has to accept a man's handicap as genuine as they do not yet have certificates.' In 1974 the LGU advised that people should return four cards each year, the idea being that scores of 135 and 145 giving a 36 handicap would stop. Today the LGU recommends that six cards a year should be returned, and handicaps are valid for one year only. A player's handicap is her own personal responsibility – despite the figure on the notice board – and this has spread the work even further. Actually the system almost runs itself. Handicap advisers receive very few queries about handicap regulations, but they do receive enquiries about the rules of golf.

With regard to current and constant surveillance and adjustment to the SS, champion players today do not visit all LGU affiliated courses taking pars as did the early pioneers, although some do advise the LGU under certain circumstances. The backbone of the game – the club golfers – would receive a welcome fillip if the champions did visit. The opportunity to see a champion player in action at one's home club even once a year would give an

enormous boost to morale and standards. In 1982 343 members of the 1800 clubs affiliated to the LGU in England, Ireland, Scotland and Wales were registered as having handicaps of 3 or under. So each of these players would have to visit 5.24 clubs each year.

SS today is measured, the score being the responsibility of each club. Measurement must be performed by a qualified person who is 'competent and experienced in the handling of surveying instruments or a qualified surveyor, taking into consideration course ratings, course groups and course values'. The course rating is based on the average length of run on each of the eighteen holes. The run is measured in yards/metres and the decimalized rating table starts at 2.7 for up to 100 yards (91 metres), and goes up to 5.5 for 561 yards (513 metres) and over. The course group is based on the average amount of run during normal spring and autumn conditions. For example, if there is an average run of from 6 to 10 yards (5 to 9 metres), 1 is added to the course rating. The scale ranges from adding 2 to subtracting 3. The course value takes into consideration all the hazards, flat or hilly terrain, open or guarded greens, narrow or wide fairways and exposure to the elements. It ranges from subtracting 1 to adding 2.

The ratings of each hole are added up and the groups and values are either added or subtracted. The LGU SS of a course is the score expected from a scratch player in normal spring and autumn conditions of wind and weather. The LGU definition of a scratch player for SS purposes is a theoretical golfer who consistently averages a carry of at least 180 yards (165 metres) from the tee and whose second shot on a par 5 hole carries at least 170 yards (155 metres). All SS are fixed by the national SS committees through their executive councils in accordance with the LGU's SS scheme.

Courses measured under the LGU scheme are shorter than others, and handicaps, no matter what the system, can be misleading, because of the card-and-pencil fever which attacks so many golfers, often reducing them to bundles of nerves with their games completely shattered. Also, there never has been, nor is there now, any method of stopping a golfer four-putting deliberately on the homeward half if she desires to keep her handicap up and has been doing too well. Pot-hunters are adept at keeping their handicaps higher than they should be, and status seekers keep them lower. This would still apply if handicaps were worked out on average play, instead of best form.

The Colonel's contribution
Handicaps are related to the SS of each course, but the pars of each hole often add up to a higher figure, because committees may allot figures for each hole if the LGU SS is used as the par of the course. *Chamber's Dictionary* states that 'bogey' is 'in golf the score for a given hole or for the whole course of an imaginary Colonel Bogey, fixed as a standard; the bogey score for a course is higher than par'. For instance, the SS of one particular course is 67, but the ground scores of each hole are 4, 4, 3, 4, 3, 4, 5, 4, 4,; 5, 3, 5, 4, 3, 3, 4, 3, 4 = 69. The terms bogey and par today are in Britain interchangeable, although Americans and, increasingly, British

players refer to a bogey as one over par for the hole, a double bogey two over, and so on.

Colonel Bogey was born in 1891. Hugh Rotherham and other male members of Coventry had instituted a prize for competition against the ground score, which proved popular. They visited Great Yarmouth and explained the idea which received a great deal of interest. A popular song of the time – autumn 1891 – was:

Hush! Hush! Hush!
Here comes the Bogey man!
So hide your head beneath the clothes
He'll catch you if he can!

At Great Yarmouth two players were playing unsuccessfully against the ground score which was catching them when one remarked: 'This player of yours is a regular bogey man.' The name was adopted by Great Yarmouth, whose secretary visited the now defunct United Service Club in Hampshire. He introduced his imaginary friend as a steady but not brilliant golfer and explained the bogey man game. A ground score was quickly worked out for the new member and, as every member of that club possessed a forces rank, a title had to be found for him. A commanding officer's rank was the only suitable one for a person who never made mistakes but who could penalize erring culprits, so they gave him the title 'Colonel'.

The Colonel is a slightly kinder adversary than that theoretical scratch player who plays exactly to the SS each round and, as the ladies who watched his growing popularity in the eighteen-nineties decided, a player can catch him, aided by her handicap, on whatever course he plays, provided she is playing at best form.

For Women
of Many Lands

Ladies have played in international matches since 1895, when England played Ireland at Portrush. Issette Pearson Miller captained the English team, and experienced some difficulty in assembling her players on the first tee on time, because they had attended a dance the previous night which lasted well into daylight. England won, by 34 points to 0. Six played on each side, and scoring was by holes. The ladies played this match on the Saturday after the Ladies Championship, and found it a 'profitable and amusing' way of filling in the time before the English caught the night boat home from Belfast. The next match was played for the same reasons, also in Ireland, at Newcastle, County Down in 1899, and again England won, by 37 points to 18. In 1901 another match was played before the championship at Aberdovey and this time Ireland won. This time scoring was by matches, the result being 5 to 2.

Soon after this, Mr T.H. Miller, then a vice-president of the LGU, presented a trophy consisting of an oblong piece of silver with the names of the four countries in copper at the top. It was made by Messrs Carrington & Co. of Regent Street, London, and is played for today. In addition, the captain of the winning team holds the Hugh C. Kelly Cup. The matches between England, Ireland, Scotland and Wales were originally called 'the internationals', but this was changed to 'home internationals' during the nineteen-thirties to distinguish them from matches played against countries outside these islands.

In 1898 Issette was excited about 'the essentially dramatic enterprise of an International Competition between the women golfers of England and America'. Seven years later, the Ladies' Championship at Cromer attracted sufficient American entrants to make such a match possible. The match was referred to as 'America versus England', even though the English side contained Scottish and Irish players. England won by 6 to 1. The members of their team were Dorothy Campbell, Lottie Dod, Alexa Glover, Mary Graham, May Hezlet, Florence Hezlet and Elinor Nevile. The American team members consisted of M.B. Adams, Georgie Bishop, Harriot and Margaret Curtis (of whom more hereafter), Frances Griscom, Miss Lockwood and Mrs G.M. Martin.

The Curtis sisters immediately offered to present a cup for further matches, but agreed that the difficulties and slowness of travel might

Jill Thornhill, member of the Curtis Cup team for the 1984 match at Muirfield, intently measures a putt during the match. She has been prominent in ladies' amateur golf for many years, and was lady champion in 1983

The English home international team in 1914. Left to right: (standing) Edith Leitch Winifred Martin Smith, Mrs Sumpter, Gladys Ravenscroft, Cecil Leitch; (second row) Muriel Dodd, May Leitch, Lettie Barry; (front row) Stella Temple, Mrs Cautley

prevent regular events. In 1909 the American association also offered a cup, but this was not accepted because the LGU thought they would have difficulty in selecting an official team. The Ladies' Championship at Royal Portrush in 1911 attracted many overseas entrants, and a match called 'American and Colonial versus Great Britain' was played, Great Britain winning by 7 to 2. At Burnham in 1923 the Ladies' Championship provided sufficient international players for another match, 'Overseas versus the Rest of England', which the latter won by 6½ to 2½. The American entries for the 1930 Ladies' Championship were so numerous that a match was arranged once again. Joyce Wethered asked Molly Gourlay to choose the British team and Great Britain won by a two-match margin at Sunningdale.

Pioneering sisters

By this time, regular matches in both countries were feasible and the Curtis sisters' offer of a cup was soon officially accepted. Harriot and Margaret were pioneering and generous golfers and eminent American champions. Harriot won the US Ladies' Championship in 1906 and Margaret beat her in the final in 1907. Margaret also won in 1911 and 1912, was runner-up in 1900 and 1905, and competed in the championship until 1949. Both sisters, incidentally, had definite views on match play 'honours' – they considered that whoever won the hole should decide who teed off first at the next. They presented their cup 'for biennial competition between teams from Britain and the USA, with the proviso and hope that other countries would join in later', and their aim was 'to stimulate friendly rivalry amongst the women golfers of many lands'. However, by tradition, the Curtis Cup has been contested only by the women of Great Britain and Ireland and the USA, and run by the governing bodies of those countries.

As it was an official match, the first Curtis Cup necessitated meticulous organization, fund-raising and constant communications between the ladies on both sides of the Atlantic. In March 1929, Margaret Curtis sent a copy of her personal guaranty (*sic*) to Cecil Leitch:

> 28 July, 1928
> I will give a guaranty of $5000 per match for the first ten matches played, to be used in defraying the expenses of the members of such team or teams as cross the Atlantic Ocean to compete.
> This will help out Canadian, British, French teams, etc, as well as America, and I think at the end of ten years . . . the various golf associations ought to be able to look after their own finances.
> There is only one condition attached . . . complete anonymity.

In February 1930 the LGU decided to send teams to the Dominions, France and the USA, provided that the LGU were able to raise the necessary funds. In the same year, the USA offered to make the first journey, to the UK, in order to give the British time to collect enough money, and stated that Margaret Curtis would present a cup for international competition between Great Britain, France, Canada and the USA.

Some of the international medals worn by Cecil Leitch, who represented her country from 1910 to 1928

Raising money presented problems to the British. In 1930 the LGU requested clubs to subscribe a minimum sum equal to the donation of 2s 6d (12½p) per member to the International Match Fund (IMF), but by July it stood at only £1088 19s 6d (£1088.97½). The LGU also decided to charge gate money at championships in order to boost the fund. They attempted to charge for the first time at the English Championship in 1930 at Aldeburgh, but were prevented from doing so because that course was on common land. The magazine *Fairway & Hazard* published a list of donors, and, between announcing their intention to publish and doing so, the fund increased by nearly £700. In a letter published in that magazine, a reader calculated that if every lady who played in the monthly medal paid 3d (little more than 1p) towards the IMF, this would raise £4712 a year.

The LGU's current chairman, I. Huleatt, wrote to Margaret Curtis on 10 July 1930:

> In my letter of 11 March, I told you that the LGU had started an IMF for the purpose of sending teams abroad and that we would give you a definite answer about the proposal this month. Unfortunately, the response has not come up to our expectations and, therefore, we are unable to fix definite dates with you, but this we hope to be in a position to do next year. The LGU is doing its utmost to raise the sum required.

The reply stated that financial support for the proposed matches was assured in America. This probably came from the $5000 ten-year guaranty from Miss Curtis. During research for this book, a letter of enquiry was written to the USA but brought forth no clarification, nor was any mention found in the accessible records of the LGU. Undoubtedly Cecil Leitch would not have betrayed a confidence and perhaps the condition of 'complete anonymity' was too complete.

Like whales scattering minnows

The LGU was not raising money only for the Curtis Cup. In 1931 Monsieur André Vagliano presented a silver challenge trophy to be competed for annually by teams from Britain and France, the matches to consist of three foursomes and six singles. The first match took place at Oxhey, with Joyce Wethered the leader and Noël Dunlop-Hill non-playing captain of the British team, which won. This was the first international event in which British players were sponsored by the LGU. On 4 February 1931, the LGU accepted invitations from abroad to sends teams to the Dominions and also to play regularly against America and France. When this was announced, former amateur champion Sir Ernest Holderness warned the LGU that financing the Walker Cup (the equivalent of the Curtis) had always been difficult and that the problem could be worse for the women than for the men. He hoped that the LGU would 'take heed of the dangers if there should be brought before it any ambitious programme of international matches. When international matches attain the scale of Davis Cup matches,' he maintained, 'they tend to create professional amateurs; they set high standards of skill but destroy the fun of amateur events in which they scatter the genuine amateurs like whales scattering minnows.' He also stated that: 'No one could expect a married woman with young children to win championships. That is a shocking thought. It would be enough ground for a divorce.' The LGU persevered. The first Curtis Cup was played at Wentworth in 1932 and was referred to in the press as the 'Ladies International Match' and also as the 'Ladies Walker Cup', but these descriptions soon disappeared, and the cup swiftly became known under its proper name.

In 1933 the South African Ladies' Golf Union asked 'their parent body', the LGU, to send a team of girl golfers to tour, in order to stimulate interest

and to show what standards were like in the 'Mother Country'. Doris Chambers captained this team and the players included Pamela Barton, Diana Fishwick, Molly Gourlay and Wanda Morgan. In 1936 Mrs Philip Hodson, as non-playing captain, took a team to Australia and New Zealand in response to pressing invitations. During this tour, Mrs J.B. Walker won the Australian Championship and Jessie Anderson Valentine the New Zealand title; and Mrs Walter Greenlees and Phyllis Wade won the New Zealand Ladies' Foursomes. In 1938 a South African team visited Britain, but poor weather prevented them from playing at best form.

Four Curtis Cup matches were played before the outbreak of World War II. The USA won three times and Great Britain and Ireland managed to tie once. Before playing the Curtis Cup on American soil, Canada was always played and defeated. Of the eight matches held annually against France,

Left to right: Mme P.P. Munier, Mlle Tollon, Helen Holm and Mrs J.B. Walker stride out between shots during the Britain versus France match at Worplesdon, Surrey, in 1935

Great Britain had by 1938 won seven and halved one. Then it was time for the women and men of many lands to down clubs and up arms. During the steely years of inhumanity, there were special war rules for those who could snatch a few hours away from the horror. Players were asked to collect bits of bombs and splinters from the course in order to avoid damage to mowers, and were allowed to take cover – without penalty for ceasing play in competition – if guns were blasting or bombs falling. Red and white flags marked delayed action bombs, and balls moved by enemy action could be replaced without penalty. Balls lying in craters could be lifted and dropped without penalty, shell or bomb splinters on the greens could be removed without penalty. If a stroke was affected by the explosion of a bomb or shell or by machine-gun fire, another ball could be played from the same place, for a penalty of one stroke.

Pam Barton Days

After World War II, a golf magazine complained, in 1947, that 'For once the ladies are not setting the pace, and it is unfortunate that the Curtis Cup match will not be held, although a team is being sent to France.' Money was scarce as were the social conditions necessary to acquire a decent standard of play. The Americans had fewer problems and helped. On the initiative of Margaret Curtis as chairman, American lady golfers held one-day meetings to raise funds for the impoverished Britons. These were call 'Pam Barton Days' in memory of the lady champion who was killed during the war. The 'Days' were still continuing in 1950.

Diana Fishwick drives from the 18th tee during the 1930 match between Great Britain and the United States. Molly Gourlay chose the British team, Glenna Collett the American

The Americans visited Great Britain in 1948 for the Ladies' Championship and the Curtis Cup but their stay was a short one. Some, having heard tales of British austerity, brought their own supplies of food. They came, won both cups, and departed. American golfers organized themselves swiftly after the war and practised daily. British players worked, looked after their families, coped with unpredictable public transport and played an occasional match at their local club at weekends – conditions hardly conducive to the acquisition of international playing standards.

American lady golfers were not the only ones to recognize the British plight. In 1949 the Australian opera singer Joan Hammond gave the proceeds from two concerts to the Australian Ladies' Golf Union so that a team could visit Britain. An enthusiastic golfer and a good player (three times New South Wales champion), Miss Hammond had previously received support from Australian golfers which enabled her to come to Europe and establish a successful career. By 1950 the Australians had contributed £1000 to the IMF and continued to send food parcels until the end of 1953. British flood disasters that winter also brought gifts from Australian golfers.

In 1949 the LGU appealed for help in rebuilding the International Match Fund so enabling promising young players to bring British golf back to the high standard attained in the past. *Fairway & Hazard* suggested a donation of a shilling a year from every lady member of a golf club. Response was fairly favourable and a year later the fund stood at more

The 1934 Curtis Cup team at Euston Station, London, prior to their departure for the USA. Left to right: Molly Gourlay, Diana Fishwick, Doris Chambers, Diana Plumpton, Pamela Barton and Wanda Morgan

than £3000. However the pound was devalued and this reduced the money available for international matches by about 33 per cent. The women's section of the USGA (United States Golf Association) were officially informed of the state of the LGU's International Match Fund, and the Americans continued their fund-raising activities.

A new fixture joined the team events against France and the USA in 1949. This was a biennial match against Belgium, which Great Britain won every time it was played. The Australians toured the UK in 1950 and the matches resulted in England halving 3-all, Scotland winning by 3 to 2, Australia beating Ireland by 5 to 1, and Australia beating Wales by 6 to 0. Doris Chambers donated a cup in appreciation of the many gifts received from Australians and this was first competed for in 1951 in Victoria, Australia. In 1951 a touring team was sent to South Africa, captained by Mrs John Beck, and included Mrs S.M. Bolton, Jean Donald Anderson, Moira Paterson and Frances Stephens Smith.

Provision for juniors

In 1952, Great Britain and Ireland achieved her first victory in the Curtis Cup and it was 'Caps over the Mill' (a press headline) at Muirfield, a club with no lady members and no facilities for women. No provision had been made for a junior team to gain experience against American players, and this situation spurred the redoubtable Enid Wilson into action. She organized a match at Sandy Lodge which attracted huge interest and a large crowd of spectators, as well as much nervousness amongst the youngsters. During the next year, the LGU invited six affiliated unions – Australia, Canada, East Africa, New Zealand, Rhodesia and South Africa – to visit the UK to compete in a tournament to commemorate the coronation of Queen Elizabeth II. The LGU also announced that the Bank of England had agreed a special foreign currency allowance to permit ladies to compete in overseas international championships. The allowance was considered entirely adequate and also made provision for entrance fees and caddies; applications were processed through the four national associations and unions. By 1955, the International Match Fund showed a debit of over £500.

On 2 April 1956, the LGU announced that they had discussed with the USGA and the Misses Curtis a system by which other countries could participate in the Curtis Cup. The plan was that the match should be played every three years, with qualifying matches played in each of four zones. These zones were: America (the USA and Canada), Europe (UK, France, Belgium, etc), Australasia (Australia and New Zealand) and Africa (South Africa, East Africa, Rhodesia, etc). The winning country in each zone would send a team to contest the Cup every three years. The span of three years was chosen to ensure the continuance of existing international fixtures. Entry was to be optional, and a zone could send a country through to the final if unopposed. Venues selected were: 1959 America, 1962 Europe, 1965 Africa, 1968 America, 1971 Europe, and 1973 Australia. The finals of the Cup were to consist of a tournament in which all teams played each other, teams of eight to play three 18-hole foursomes and six 18-hole singles each day.

*During the 1930s ladies'
golf was enthusiastically
enjoyed and taken very
seriously on both sides of
the Atlantic, in many
parts of Europe and in
Australia and New
Zealand. Pamela Barton,
one of the most popular
lady golfers ever, played
victoriously at
championship level all
over the world. She
became the second lady to
hold the British and the
American titles in one year*

The LGU urged that each country should be responsible for paying its way.

Such a contest would have fulfilled the idea of being one 'for women of many lands' and might have sustained year-round interest in ladies international competitive golf all over the world. A permanent tournament would have raised the standards of amateur golf for ladies in countries where there was little international competition.

But the consensus of opinion was against the scheme. The Americans were sad that any changes were being considered, and British golfers realized that because of rotation Britain might have to wait forty-five years to host the event. It was also considered that the whole affair would be too costly, too vast, and too unmanageable. As golf was more popular in some countries than others, it would be unfair if the tournament stayed in a country where golf was relatively unpopular. Some people thought that the usual countries, Britain and the USA, would probably contest the finals. Others thought that the time span of three years was too long to sustain interest, and many realized that those who entered in the first year might not only have jobs to concern them in three years' time but also a home to run and families to look after and therefore would be unavailable for the finals. Additionally, the adequacy of the IMF was questioned, because its contributions came from the average club golfer and it was arguable whether their interest and support would continue if the Cup were played in the UK only once in nine years – or in France every twenty-seven years.

The scheme was not put into operation, but its outline may have laid the foundations for the Women's World Amateur Team Championship for the Espirito Santo Trophy, which was instituted by the French Golf Federation at the suggestion of the USGA. It was inaugurated at St-Germain, Paris, in 1964, and has been played biennially ever since. France won the inaugural event and has been second on three other occasions. Australia won once, Great Britain and Ireland managed to come second once, and the USA have won the rest. Three players comprise each team; the two best scores of each day go forward, and the winner is the team with the lowest of four daily totals. It is indeed an exciting tournament but has not the breadth of the 1956 scheme as it is only a four-day event. However, the political changes which have taken place in some countries of the four zones since the 1950s might have made that scheme even more impractical than when it was first considered.

Some individual achievements

In 1956, Great Britain and Ireland won the Curtis Cup for the second time and the cup was presented to the captain, Mrs Zara Bolton, 'to remain in the safe keeping of the Governor General of Northern Ireland'. In the same year the British junior team was awarded the Golf Writers' Association Trophy for its achievements during the 1955 tour of Australia and New Zealand. During this tour Veronica Anstey (later Beharrell), then aged eighteen, won the Australian Championship, the New Zealand Open Match Play Championship and the Victoria State Open. The trophy, awarded annually to the man or woman who, in the opinion of golf writers, has done most for golf

Enid Wilson was determined that juniors should get some good experience when the Americans arrived for Curtis Cup matches, and organized special tournaments for the youngsters in 1952. Through her knowledge of the game, her playing, her encouragement and her writing, Miss Wilson made an outstanding contribution to ladies' golf in Great Britain

The 1960 Curtis Cup was played at Lindrick, Nottinghamshire, and the USA was victorious, by 6½ to 2½. Our home team was: (back row, left to right) Angela Bonallack, Belle McCorkindale, Frances Smith, Marley Spearman; (front row, left to right) Philomena Garvey, Ruth Porter, Maureen Garrett, Janette Robertson and Elizabeth Price

during the year, was first presented in 1951. It was awarded to Elizabeth Price in 1952 and to Frances Stephens Smith in 1954. Since then only two other women – Marley Spearman in 1962 and Michelle Walker in 1972 – have received the award.

During the juniors' tour, the team's blazers were embroidered with Union Jacks. Formerly, when the LGU crest was worn, players were sometimes asked what school they were attending. In 1958 the decision that the Curtis Cup team blazers should also bear the Union Jack produced problems as players from Eire were eligible to play. The statement 'Ireland plays as one country' was made and the president of the ILGU, Daisy Ferguson, maintained that the decision made it difficult for any golfers from Eire to play in the team. The previous badge had embodied emblems of all four countries.

In 1958 the Curtis Cup was halved in the USA. This was the first time that any UK golf team, male or female, professional or amateur, had

avoided defeat in the USA. The Curtis sisters offered to replace the cup with a new one, but this was refused on sentimental grounds. Great Britain had by now won all of sixteen successive matches against France, and all her five matches against Belgium. In 1959, at the request of the LGU, these two matches were combined, and since then the Continent of Europe have competed against Great Britain and Ireland biennially for the Vagliano Trophy. Britain has won eight of the twelve confrontations and retained the trophy with a halved match once. The competition consists of four foursomes and eight singles of 18 holes on each of two days, with the foursomes being played in the mornings. Nine players and a non-playing captain may be nominated, with a win counting as one point, and a half point for a halved match.

A new international was inaugurated in 1959 – the Commonwealth Tournament – and teams from Australia, Canada, New Zealand, South Africa and Great Britain and Ireland competed on the Old Course at St Andrews. Nancy, Viscountess Astor, who was then president of the LGU, presented a trophy – a silver globe with the participating countries shown in gold. She also wrote a foreword for the commemorative brochure in which she stated: 'Though not a very good golfer, I am still an ardent one! I took it up years ago for my old age, and I have never been disappointed.' The Commonwealth Tournament has been played by teams from countries belonging to the Commonwealth every four years since 1959 in the UK, Australia, Canada, New Zealand, the UK, Australia and Canada. Great Britain and Ireland has won five out of the six tournaments. During the first tournament tour, prior to the first match at St Andrews, a junior team took on a combined Commonwealth team at North Hants and won their matches. This experience for juniors was instigated, once again, by Enid Wilson, who worked with the Golf Foundation to make it possible.

Five internationals
At the beginning of the 1960s the ladies were playing in three internationals – Curtis and Vagliano biennially, and Commonwealth, four-yearly. Then the biennial Espirito Santo was inaugurated – Curtis and Espirito being held in even-numbered years, Vagliano and Commonwealth in odd numbered years. Another permanent fixture was added in 1965 when teams from the four home countries began to participate in the biennial European Ladies' Amateur Team Championship. England has won it five times, and Ireland twice. On the occasions when juniors have played in the annual European Lady Juniors' Team Championship, Scotland and England have been the UK's only winners, Scotland once, England twice, since 1968. The format for these two championships is the same: each team nominates six players, and the competition consists of two qualifying rounds of 18 holes stroke play, with the best five scores counting. The final consists of two foursomes and five singles of match play on each of three days. Another biennial is the Femenino de Golf, held at the Club Compestre, Cali, Colombia, South America. The top thirteen in the previous tournament and the top six countries in the previous Espirito Santo Trophy are invited to participate, all

expenses paid. The UK finished 6th, 4th, 7th, 4th and joint 6th respectively in 1975, 1977, 1979, 1981 and 1983.

These tournaments are the main international team events which amateur women golfers may aim to participate in. The national associations and unions and the LGU frequently send teams and individuals to play in other national championships not mentioned here. And, of course, individual British players have done well in amateur national championships in many countries. Overseas players have won major British amateur championships too, and here the ladies' record is better than the men's. Out of eighty-eight contests for the men's amateur championship, twenty-three have been won by players from other countries; out of the eighty-one women's amateur championships, seventeen have been won by overseas players. This gives the ladies an 8 per cent better record.

In 1969 the LGU decided to discontinue the Vagliano for financial reasons, apart from presuming that the European Team Championship achieved a similar competitive standard. Louis Newmark ensured its survival by donating the entry fee from the Avia Ladies' International Tournament. This was the first time than an LGU amateur international match had financial support from a major international event. In 1970, £700 from the Avia was donated to the LGU for the Vagliano, and £1250 in different donations for the Curtis Cup. Louis Newmark continued its contribution until 1974 when the LGU received a grant of £2600 from the Sports Council to help with running competitions.

During the 1960s a trophy was given to the golf club which contributed the most money per lady golfing member per year to the International Match Fund. Donations from commercially sponsored tournaments, charity matches, and gate money and the sale of programmes helped the fund. In 1970 the LGU publicly thanked the trade for Curtis Cup equipment – Slazengers for bags, covers, hats, socks, gloves and cases; Perry Bros Ltd and Pringle of Scotland for clothes, and Dunlop Sports Ltd for balls. By the mid-1970s the International Match Fund had been made into a central fund with a proportion of annual subscriptions – in 1978 15p for annual subscription and 10p for the Fund – automatically allotted to it. Official sponsors are now solicited regularly.

Coaching the aspirants

Lady golfers from Britain and Ireland have generally been able to hold their own against Europeans but not against the Americans. After the defeat by 6½ points to 2½ at the 1960 Curtis Cup at Lindrick, the LGU asked for assistance from the Golf Foundation in the coaching of present Curtis Cup players and others near the standard. This was the first attempt by the LGU to institute a national coaching scheme. The Golf Foundation agreed to assist players aged from fourteen to eighteen, provided that the LGU formed a sub-committee to take charge. This group included Maureen Garrett, Wanda Morgan and Enid Wilson, and the first ten participants were coached at Sandy Lodge in October. This subsidized session, in the hands of top lady golfers, contributed to some improvement in standards. In the

Philomena Garvey played in the Curtis Cup six times and was an Irish international from 1947 to 1969

74

OPPOSITE: *Vicki Thomas during the 1984 Curtis Cup match at Muirfield. Miss Thomas is one of the best players ever produced by Wales*

BELOW RIGHT: *Jenny Lee Smith, now a successful professional and member of the WPGA, played in the Curtis Cup in 1974 and 1976. This is almost a textbook shot*

BELOW: *A successful shot for Tegwen Perkins, now Mrs Thomas, the first Welsh lady to play in the Curtis Cup*

following October, the Golf Foundation granted another £500 for this purpose, but the grant was discontinued the next year because of the difficulties caused by the overlap of this coaching with schemes already instituted by the national associations and unions. The Golf Foundation also preferred to devote its full attention to introducing and promoting golf in schools, which is its purpose under its constitution.

Regional training centres were in existence all over the country and arrangements were made for promising youngsters to play matches against former Curtis Cup players. The national associations and unions increased their already lively efforts. In 1967 the LGU instituted a winter training scheme, run on an area basis, but discontinued it the following year and encouraged players to concentrate on physical fitness instead. Scotland's 1969 winter training scheme was popular and England introduced a new scheme for finding promising juniors and a new competition for girls. During the 1970s efforts to increase playing standards were intensified and more individuals and teams were sent to gain experience by competing in different European championships.

But the efforts have been insufficient. British lady golfers have not been superior to American ladies since the early years of this century. Great Britain and Ireland were victorious against the USA when the players

themselves chose the teams, but the rate of success has been 96.43 per cent worse since the selectors from the relevant governing bodies have been officially involved. However Curtis Cup representation remains the highest ambition and the pinnacle of the career of amateur golfing ladies in team events.

Those who have played most often in this Cup are Mary McKenna and Jessie Anderson Valentine, seven times. Next are Elizabeth Price, Frances Stephens Smith and Angela Ward Bonallack with six consecutive appearances; Belle Robertson and Philomena Garvey also played six times. Jessie Anderson Valentine became a national heroine in 1936 when she holed a twenty-foot putt on the last green, thus winning and tieing the whole match. Frances Stephens Smith, Jeanne Bisgood and Elizabeth Price all won their singles in 1952, the year of the first victory, and in 1956 Jessie Anderson Valentine, Angela Ward Bonallack and Elizabeth Price also won their singles, after the UK had lost the foursomes 2 and 1. This again left a deciding match to Frances Stephens Smith, which she won at the 36th hole. Again in 1958, the result depended on the last singles, and again Frances Stephens Smith won it, this time by 2 holes.

Although in 1950 the format of the match was changed to 36-hole matches, at the request of the LGU, this reverted to 18-hole matches in 1964. The Cup is now contested over two days, on each of which there are three foursomes in the morning and six singles in the afternoon, with each country nominating eight players. A win counts as one point and a half as half a point. The event is played under the rules of golf in force in the country in which it takes place. During the twenty-two Cup contests, Great Britain and Ireland's fortunes have been in the hands of fewer than eighty players, with Frances Stephens Smith holding the record for the most outstanding individual performance – bearing in mind that this is a team event – as she won four and halved one of her five singles matches. The youngest lady to play was Jane Connachan, just sixteen years and three months, in 1980.

The British Curtis Cup record is slightly better than the Walker Cup's. Whereas the ladies have won twice and tied twice, the men have won twice and tied once, the ladies having played twenty-three matches and the men twenty-nine. The ladies' worst defeats, three in the USA and one at home, were in 1966, 1974 and 1980, on which occasions they were trounced by 13 to 5, and in 1982, by 14½ to 3½. Optimism, hunger for victory and hard work may contribute to a potential victory, but even if Canadian, French and other teams were to join the competition for this Cup it is doubtful if the Americans' immense superiority would be diminished for long, if at all. However, if the description of the 1911 match, 'Overseas versus the Rest of England' were turned into 'USA versus the Rest of the World', then at least the Curtis Cup would be 'for women of many lands' and the Curtis sisters' original intention would be fulfilled. ◐

Oh, no! Not again! Penny Grice expresses dismay during the 1984 Curtis Cup match at Muirfield, a match which resulted in a very narrow defeat for Great Britain and Ireland

The Great Divide

The trophy for the inaugural Ladies' Championship of 1893 cost £50, with players unsuccessful in the first round competing under handicap for a £5 prize. The ladies were not conscious that they might be injecting into the game any idea of playing for material gain rather than glory alone. Competing for a costly cup and a money prize did not taint the championship. The division between amateurs and professionals was little realized and generated little or no concern. However, when Amy Pascoe won the 1896 Ladies' Championship, the division was strengthened. Miss Pascoe had hired the professional golfer Peter Rainford to caddie for her; he coached and advised her before and during play and in between rounds. She was a highly intelligent and discerning woman who used his knowledge and constant supervision to obvious advantage. Miss Pascoe was not the only lady who employed a caddie devoted to her success, and most caddies became thoroughly involved with their hirers' fortunes. One competitor's caddie, after a missed putt, showed his disgust by rolling over and over on the ground with hundreds looking on.

The championship committee of the LGU immediately announced that professional golfers would not be allowed to caddie at the following year's event at Gullane. At an LGU meeting on 22 January 1897, the ladies proposed that the local greens' committee would allot the required number of properly qualified caddies to the players by a draw one week before the event, and no lady was to employ any caddie in a championship match other than the one allotted to her. The system was completely disregarded by the ladies at Gullane; the Orr sisters and others had professional golfers, including Ben Sayers, to caddie for them, and the championship was won by Edith Orr. The LGU reinforced its recommendation by soon making it a rule and, eighty-six years later, today's regulations governing play still include the following proviso: 'Amateur competitors may not engage as a caddie any professional or assistant professional, who is, or has been at any time, attached to a club or a member of a professional golfers' association.'

After banning professional advisers from their amateur championship, the ladies discussed the position of lady club professionals. Early in 1894, a contributor to *Golf* magazine had observed that the job of a club professional could be a new employment for ladies, but such people would obviously be

Wanda Morgan watches while her ball is retrieved from the Burn at St Andrews during the 1931 Ladies' British Open Amateur Championship. She was runner-up to Enid Wilson that year, and had to wait until 1935 for the title of lady champion

ineligible to enter amateur competitions. As there were no professional tournaments for women, nor any likelihood of such events in the foreseeable future, many potential lady club professionals were deterred from embarking on such a profession. The anticipated role, earnings and difficulties of lady club professionals had been thoroughly considered and analyzed as early as 1898.

Ladies were not expected to undertake arduous club duties merely from a love of the game and a desire to improve the play of their fellow golfers. They needed to increase their income, as they had proved capable of doing in other professions. Payment for instructing beginners varied throughout the year, and might earn a lady club professional £40, but combining the duties of green-keeper with that of professional meant a continuous income. A lady green-keeper employed by a club needed a boy as her assistant, to cut the grass and perform rough tasks, and she could probably earn £52 a year. Acting as housekeeper and caretaker in the clubhouse would qualify her for free lodgings. However, few ladies were able or content to survive on £92 a year, and a method of augmenting this amount would have been to master the art of clubmaking. Clubmakers served an apprenticeship as journeymen, working eight hours a day for five years, and their wage was 5 shillings (25p) a week at the beginning of their apprenticeship, rising by increments to £1. The hardship and drudgery of such an apprenticeship was a deterrent to ladies, but some gained sufficient knowledge with a few months' tuition from a qualified clubmaker to be able to prepare and repair clubs.

One contemporary forecast was that lady professionals would initially encounter difficulties and opposition but, as in other professions, the novelty would diminish until it was quite normal for each ladies' golf club to have its own woman clubmaker and professional, duly certificated by the Ladies' Golf Union. That forecast was for ladies. With regard to 'women taking up golf as a trade', it was considered that 'doubtless they would have to begin as the ordinary biped man does, as caddies, and rise by degrees to notoriety and championships'.

A game for all classes

Money was indeed important to lady golfers in the early years of the century. They agreed that golf was essentially a game for all classes, giving enjoyment to rich and poor alike, and recognized that it attracted as much interest from millionaires as from artisans. The rich could invest as much of their superfluous cash as they wished in the game while the poorer golfers could, by careful management of their resources, obtain as much benefit and pleasure without having to spend more than they could comfortably afford. The ladies observed that one of the most obvious aspects of the game was its levelling influence, which created a kind of universal brotherhood on the course, with all class distinctions being totally ignored for the duration of the game.

If golf were played solely for amusement, not on a serious competitive level, it was far less expensive than hunting, shooting and fishing. The

current price for irons was 5 shillings, with woods half as much again. This meant that clubs were easily within reach of everyone. But the advent of the rubber-core ball in 1902 added to the cost of playing, because the gutties, which they replaced, could be refurbished with lighted matches and remake machines, whereas the rubber-core, if it suffered a cut, could not be satisfactorily repaired. Most ladies realized that a first-class player could easily spend £100 a year attending all the available meetings, with their accompanying social demands. An average golfer might need to spend only £30 per year for equipment and entrance fees for the ladies' championships and a few meetings but the game could easily be played, for pleasure only, for less than £5 a year.

To offset some expenses of the amateur game, a few ladies wrote about golf and golfing matters in periodicals. In 1890, Marrion Verron discoursed on how 'the female mind is struck with the loneliness of the game. Meeting here and there a solitary golfer with his caddie on the bluff shoulders of the light-house hills at Cromer, his opponent nearly 100 yards ahead and striding along as if for dear life.' She was followed by other ladies, including Blanche Martin Hulton, Amy Pascoe and May Hezlet. The latter found her golfing career expensive but she was able to write for a newspaper for £100 a year and was grateful for such a sum.

Miss Pascoe and Miss Hezlet published books about golf which included helpful hints on the playing of the game. The fact that they were writing about golf for money drew no adverse criticism. The excesses of some lady golf-writers caused Amy Pascoe to comment: 'Reports of open meetings leave much to the imagination, the writer usually being some hours' railway journey from the scene of competition. Newspaper interviews and sketches of lady players are even more emotional and less moral.' She cited one article in a 'sixpenny' under the heading 'Potent Putters, Golf Giants, Drastic Drivers':

> The lady of this week, whose reproduced photograph we sincerely hope is a libel on her character, is unknown to us and fame . . . (but she may have a sweet swing). We open and read – but of her bicycle! her favourite jam! and bootmaker! The element of golf is eliminated altogether. That Potent Putter, Golf Giant, Drastic Driver is an imaginative creation of an interviewer. Where is our sixpence? Far better it had been spent on a 'remade'.

Expenses for county matches

As the ladies increased their golfing activities, the financial aspect was more widely discussed and by 1910 they were arguing publicly about whether or not players competing in county matches should receive expenses. Paying expenses so that the better players could compete enabled the richer countries to produce the best teams. The arguments produced strong feelings, articles considered to be anti-LGU were published, and a split occurred in the LGU which led to the formation of the National Alliance. Distinct tension was apparent when members of the two factions

met at open meetings. Adherents of one would not sit at tables with members of another, nor would they even speak in the changing rooms. The ladies eventually reached agreement. The American system had at first been used for county golf but soon proved too unwieldy to organize and a divisional system was instituted. One of Issette Pearson Miller's final opinions on the matter was that as every club could at least afford one away and one home match, all the better players would in time have the chance to play for their county, and there would be no question as to their amateur status. The Alliance ran the first few English Championships, but by 1914 the rift was healed and the re-united LGU managed that championship until the birth of ELGA.

Issette and Miss M.E. Phillips, honorary secretary of county golf, strongly disagreed about financial organization, and there was a year-long debate about a possible discrepancy in the accounts. The minutes of a December 1909 meeting were reviewed and the statement made that when Miss

Issette Pearson Miller and Cecil Leitch (second from left) anxiously watch during the 1923 Ladies' British Open Amateur Championship, which was won by Doris Chambers

Pearson first heard of the practice of paying players' expenses she thought it made them professionals. However, after enquiries, she stated 'on the very best authority' that it did not affect amateur status. Issette did not state who the 'very best authority' was and at a meeting in May the following year she read out this opinion from *Field* magazine:

> Whatever the ladies decide, the men will always adhere to the same view that golf had never been a subsidized game, and that to play in a representative capacity its players should reject financial aid, either of unions or individuals. Far better would it be, therefore, to abandon the competitions which apparently exact a financial sacrifice of those who enter them than persist in violating one of the sacred golfing traditions.

County golf, which had been organized by a sub-committee of the LGU since 1901, presented problems because some clubs were not affliliated to the union. Tips, printing, postage and other expenses connected with county golf had always been paid by the LGU and Miss Pearson proposed, at a meeting in December 1910, that the expenses of the honorary secretary of county golf (Miss Phillips), rent for greens and hire of rooms for meetings should be paid by the LGU. The ladies of Prince's, Mitcham, and certain other clubs objected, maintaining that those who did not contribute (non union clubs) could not expect to be treated equally with those who did. The ladies eventually reached agreement, but the ethics of money being paid to golfers for playing were permanently founded and the matter of expenses was accordingly treated with almost reverential care. Today, a 'player may receive expenses, not exceeding the actual expenses incurred . . . provided that in the case of a County event such event has been approved for this purpose by the County's National Union.'

Prizes and vouchers

The LGU became very strict about prizes and recommended that prize vouchers should not be exchanged for wearing apparel or consumable goods. Nor would they condone the giving of equipment. Players ineligible to compete in amateur competitions included those who accepted as presents – or were given facilities to buy at prices below those usually charged – golf balls, golf clubs or other merchandise, when those presents

The LGU Barnehurst Challenge Trophy – presented by Mrs C.H. Gray, who with her husband owned the Barnchurst club. The trophy is no longer played for, nor is the club in existence, and the trophy reposes behind glass in the Women Golfers' Museum

were made or the facilities granted for advertising purposes. The latter condition was an escape clause, for it is doubtful that anyone did, or does, relacquer woods, fudge names on irons, paint out names on balls, and so on; that would defeat the purpose of the donation. When a first-class player was known to be playing with a particular make of clubs, other players bought them.

By 1912 lady club professionals, although rarities, were well known. Mrs Gordon Robertson had been professional for some years to the Prince's Ladies' Club at Mitcham. Miss Lily Freemantle was professional to Sunningdale Ladies, and Miss D.M. Smyth to Le Touquet. Just before World War I, one golf magazine expressed surprise that there were not many more ladies enjoying the employment of professional golfer, and that few clubs were trying to secure them. The advantages of having an instructor of the same sex seemed obvious, and lady professionals were expected to become increasingly important in future years. Ladies were willing to accept other ladies as club professionals and instructors, but the concept of lady professional players was irrelevant. In 1914, Mrs R.P. Graham was appointed secretary to the Edgware Golf Club, the first woman to occupy such a position.

During World War I, Ida Kyle taught golf in a girls' school, thereby releasing a man for the front. In 1920 she was forced to apply for reinstatement as an amateur and this was granted as she was considered to have acted on patriotic grounds. This same year, the LGU modified some of the definitions of amateur status, for not all the men's criteria, which they tried to adhere to, were suitable for them. The ladies added two reservations. One was that a schoolmistress could receive a salary for teaching golf if she was a bona fide teacher of other subjects, without forfeiting her amateur status. The other stated that 'a player in a County match, or taking a Scratch Score on behalf of the LGU may receive her expenses without forfeiting her amateur status.' Later on, the LGU resolved that members of the Executive Council on union business were entitled to be reimbursed out of union funds – 3rd class return fare or an allowance of a penny per mile for motor expenses in Great Britain and Ireland – for travel between the lady's place of residence and London.

Entering open tournaments

After World War I, ladies frequently competed in open tournaments, whether amateur or professional, although they were not always popular. In July 1919, Muriel Dodd MacBeth, lady champion in 1913, was invited to play in the Cruden Bay Tournament. Play was over two rounds, the lowest sixteen to qualify. She competed in the first round and returned a score of 96. Many male players returned higher scores, one scratch player returning a 98. In 1920, Dr Elsie Kyle, who had reached the final, match play, stage of the Cruden Bay in 1909, tied for the sixth handicap prize in the Men's Open Tournament at St Andrews. In the following year Ida Kyle and Molly Griffiths competed in the Eden Tournament at St Andrews but did not qualify for the final. In 1927, Miss M.C. White won the North Foreland

Club's Victory Shield Open Tournament by 2 holes. She belonged to North Foreland and beat Mr Cardell Martyn of Sunningdale; she was the first woman ever to win an open tournament. A team of ladies competed on level terms in the Braid Hills (Edinburgh) Tournament in 1927. They were Charlotte Stevenson Watson Beddows, Mary Wood, Doris Park Porter and Edith Nimmo and were beaten in the first round. Women competitors were barred from that competition in the following year, as they were from other open events.

Poppy Wingate, then assistant at Templenewsam, Leeds, competed in the Leeds Professional Tournament in May 1933, the first woman to participate in a British professional tournament. Meg Farquhar Main, who had been an assistant professional at Moray Golf Club, and was an assistant in a golf club-maker's shop in Elgin, competed in the Scottish professional championship at Lossiemouth in June 1933. Then aged 22, her first round left her only seven strokes behind the winner at that stage, and her aggregate of 331 for the four rounds was 30 strokes better than some of her male rivals. She was the first Scottish woman to compete in a professional championship in Scotland. Nearly a score of women, with male partners, have been victorious in the Sunningdale Open Foursomes since 1934, and in 1982 the all-woman final was won by two British professionals, Michelle Walker and Christine Langford.

During the 1920s, ladies wrote both instruction and criticism about the game, in articles and books, and reported matches whether they played in them or not. In 1922, the new R and A definition of an amateur golfer, effective after 31 December 1922, caused the LGU to ask for advice about the status of a freelance journalist who wrote theoretical articles on golf for a firm which had engaged her obviously because of her skill as a golfer and not as a writer. The LGU wondered if the amateur status of Joyce Wethered and Cecil Leitch would be affected if they received royalties for their books in 1923, and also payment for future articles. Henry Gullen, secretary of the R and A, reassured them that journalists who wrote theoretical articles were excluded from the new clause in the definition which stated that amateur golfers could not receive 'a salary or remuneration, either directly or indirectly, from any firm dealing in goods relating to the playing of the game'. Books and magazines were not 'goods'.

A pathetic idea

Eleanor Helme, who was a paid worker of the LGU and whose duties included reading proofs, secretarial work and providing press reports, caused controversy when she entered an LGU tournament and reported on the matches she played in. She described one match she played against Joyce Wethered in 1924 as a feet-wiping exhibition, saying that she enjoyed being a doormat, and that crowds were kind to under-dogs. She considered that the shots up to the hole made her feel distinctly uncomfortable: 'If the shot went through [what about] that dear old lady with her hat on.' And she also observed that 'this Special Correspondent had roving eyes searching for the sensational in other matches. Rove it never so wildly, no eye can

penetrate a wall of spectators.' In 1931, Miss Helme declaimed that the idea that a lady could play first-class golf and also earn a living was 'pathetic'. Miss Helme said that lady club professional jobs were almost impossible to come by; that there was no livelihood to be made out of golf; and that there were not half-a-dozen posts in the whole of the UK in which golf knowledge was of the slightest use. She thought it was possible, in time, that there could be opportunities for women golfing journalists, but that a journalist must put competitive golf aside and give the paper her best. The majority of golfers, she maintained, were not prepared to do so. She estimated that competitive golf required an annual three-figure expenditure and that the dilettante writer who put the game first was unlikely, indeed extraordinarily lucky, to earn that amount in the course of a year. She also maintained that 'golf was a lucky incident, not the reason I became a journalist capable of earning a living'. Miss Helme was a golf editor for magazines and golf correspondent for newspapers.

Protecting amateur status was an important aspect of ladies' golf in the nineteen-thirties. The LGU, faced with the adventure of sending teams abroad, agreed that expenses must be paid, and, despite the precedent of county golf, were worried that the true spirit of amateurism would thereby be impaired. However, as international competition would promote friendship amongst countries and raise standards, and as not participating might damage British golfing prestige abroad, they overcame their scruples. When *Golf Illustrated* organized a fund with a target of £3000 to send male professionals to the USA to play in the US Open and the Ryder Cup, the LGU donated £10, thereby acknowledging the contribution that professionals could make to the game. In the press, ladies received the generous comment: 'If it were not for women golfers, professionals would make very poor incomes.' Expenses for prestige events abroad, councillors and county players were condoned, but positive material incentives to women golfers were not. Joyce Wethered stated that: 'Ladies are not paid for playing, but they are playing when they are being paid for.'

Attempt to define professionalism

In 1930, Sir Herbert Austin offered a 'baby' saloon car to the Women's Automobile and Sports Association for their tournament at Wentworth. The offer had to be refused because valuable prizes were not looked upon with favour by the authorities. The car was withdrawn and a silver trophy presented in its place. In the same year, Molly Gourlay aired the impracticability of the current rules of amateur status. By then, if a lady had the opportunity to pay just a shilling for a set of golf clubs she could do so as the relevant rule did not stipulate full payment. She suggested that the rules for amateur status should exclude only those who carried for hire, who taught or played for money. She pointed out that the LGU had recently asked the R and A whether a group of girls who were going to Florida with their expenses paid would forfeit their amateur status or not. The answer was that they would forfeit. So some went and paid their own expenses and others – some of them better players, who might have gone –

Molly Gourlay selects a club under the watchful eye of her boy-scout caddie at a sporting gymkhana at Leeds Castle, Kent. The competition in which she played raised money for the Kent Playing Fields' Association

did not for they could not afford it. It was not an official match. 'Personally,' Molly Gourlay wrote, 'I cannot think how any existing regulation covers such a contingency, although I was quite sure that the R and A would reply as they did.' She suggested that the rules for amateur status should be abolished and professionalism defined instead: 'A professional is one who caddies, teaches, or plays for money.' Had the suggestion been implemented it would have helped some contemporary and future first-class players to continue gaining competitive experience and would have boosted standards.

In 1934 the LGU added the word 'amateur' three times to its regulations – for home internationals, international matches and county matches. At a council meeting on 24 April 1934, a condition laid down by the championship committee prohibiting players in the championship from reporting on it and on the home internationals was reconsidered because the stricture had not been publicized until after the entries had been received. It was decided to withdraw the condition with regard to that year's championship, but it was enforced subsequently. In the same year, the R and A advised that: 'Firstly amateurs must not exploit their skill and secondly they must not allow their skill to be exploited by others. For these reasons journalists who are good players should be careful to see that all references to their prowess at the game are omitted from the articles they write.' Seven players had notified the LGU that journalism was their usual and recognized vocation, and were told that the restriction in Clause 3(c) of the Amateur Definition did not apply in their cases. 'Clause 3(c): for remuneration – under own names or description from which they can be recognized report a golf competition or match in which they are taking part, if journalism is not their usual recognized vocation.'

Miss Wilson's status

Enid Wilson, who had been publishing articles since she was eighteen years of age, and who had won the Ladies' Championship three times running, was refused entry to the next championship at Royal Porthcawl. In 1933 Miss Wilson had written captions of an instructional nature for a series of photographs. The LGU asked her if she had been paid, for if she had been paid she was no longer an amateur. Miss Wilson said that she was no longer interested in international matches and then, to test the situation, she sent in her entry for Royal Porthcawl. The R and A advised the LGU that, on the evidence submitted, the Council was of the opinion that Miss Wilson was exploiting her skill at the game. Accordingly she was no longer eligible to play in amateur competitions. Her entry could not be accepted, although it was agreed that should she wish to apply for reinstatement they would do what lay in their power to further her application.

So Miss Wilson, who like the ladies earlier on in the century had to boost her income, retired from competitive amateur golf at the age of twenty-four. She took a job at Lillywhites, designed a complete range of golf equipment, became a regular correspondent for *Golf illustrated* and other magazines, and retired as golf correspondent for the *Daily Telegraph* in the

the 1970s. Her contribution to the game through her skill, knowledge, criticism, comment, encouragement and reporting during more than four decades was enormous and she was invited to play in amateur events – society and club matches and so on.

The debate concerning the division between professionals and amateurs continued and some ladies considered that the amateur status problem was by far the biggest one the LGU had yet to face. The call came again: 'An amateur under modern conditions cannot be defined, so define professional instead.' Then, in 1935, Joyce Wethered made a highly successful tour of the USA. One contemporary comment was: 'It is to be regretted that Miss Wethered cannot get enough competitive golf in England.' It was not a matter of getting enough competitive golf; it was a matter of money. She was already golf adviser at Fortnum and Mason, wanted to travel, but did not have the resources. So when offers were made, she accepted, playing fifty-two matches in four-and-a-half months. She is reputed to have received £40 per match and there were other sidelines.

The Golf Ball, held annually in London, attracts many leading golf stars. Here Enid Wilson tries a shot at one of the side shows at Grosvenor House, Park Lane, in 1931

So there were at least two first-class players, as well as the lady club professionals, who could play in amateur events only by invitation. As women were welcome in only a few open events and there were no professional events for women, at least a decade of promising golfers was denied the chance of seeing them in action regularly.

In April 1935, the LGU chairman, Miss D.I. Clark, and Mrs A.C. Johnston interviewed representatives from twelve London newspapers and seven news agencies. Their intention was to secure greater publicity for LGU international matches and touring teams and better cooperation between the LGU and the Press. The ladies' pursuit of publicity was admirable, for they undoubtedly understood that publicity generates sponsorship, which in turn leads to higher standards and therefore more money. If the ladies had kept up their efforts they might have anticipated the achievements of their American colleagues, who did not set up their ladies' professional circuit until after World War II. The LGU ladies had the opportunity, and support from their contemporaries, and the chance, through consensus, of making LGU events 'open'.

An Open should be open

At an annual general meeting of the LGU in 1935, Noël Dunlop-Hill proposed that the Ladies' Championship should be open to all women golfers, amateur or professional. The championship players present wanted the women professionals back again to compete with them, as they feared that the leading players could be lost to the game and standards therefore be lowered. Agreement by women golfers to recognize the professional and give her the right to play in an open championship would help to set the highest standards. A few ladies considered that the championship was no longer the 'Blue Riband' of the game; others thought that the fair and open spirit of the game could only be kept, under modern conditions, by drawing a clearly defined line between amateur and professional. Some insisted that as the rules laid down by the R and A had been adopted and accepted they must be adhered to – with the exception of the championship. Diehards were worried that the membership of the union would be damaged by a split in its ranks; that to declare the championship open would encourage professionalism among younger players and therefore commercialize the game; and that if they were to hold an open, other events would admit professionals also.

The resolutions at the meeting were that the Ladies' Amateur Golf Championship should be replaced by a championship on similar lines, but open to all lady golfers, whether amateur or professional, and that all members of clubs affiliated to the LGU, whether amateur or professional, should be eligible to obtain LGU handicaps. Surrey proposed a resolution that the word 'amateur' should be deleted from all LGU events. Noël Dunlop-Hill suggested, seconded by Durham, that the Open should be truly open, with all other events remaining as they were. Her amendment was carried, but the resolutions were not passed.

Brilliant lady golfers continued to face the difficulties presented by the

Pamela Barton at the age of nineteen after winning major titles on both sides of the Atlantic

division between professionals and amateurs. Faced with a large and unexpected bill, lady champion Pamela Barton published 'A Stroke a Hole' in 1937 but was told she was not entitled to accept any payment without infringing her amateur status. The advice from the R and A was that it was quite in order for Miss Barton to write a book – provided she did not gain from it. Then another lady champion, Wanda Morgan, joined Dunlop as a liaison officer and was thereafter designated a non-amateur. One contemporary comment was: 'As long as the powers that be continue to insist that conditions today are the same as in 1893 these things are bound to happen, and the standard of ladies' golf will suffer.' Rulings about expenses were frequently inconsistent. When plans were being made for the 1938 visit by the South African ladies, the R and A decided that the LGU could defray expenses if the visitors played as a team, but not if they played as individuals in championships. If a British lady who was providing hospitality and looking after a visiting player did not have enough accommodation in her home, another ruling stated that she was not entitled to put her guest up at a hotel and pay for her.

Post-war shambles

After World War II, amateur tournaments were slow to recommence and male professionals were experiencing hard times. They had little equipment to offer in their shops, no money coming in from reshafting, and 2000 male golfers were competing for £200,000 on the playing circuit. Although more women were taking up employment than before the war, golf presented few opportunities as the profession was already overcrowded. Other sporting authorities were sponsoring coaching, matches and competitions in order to provide a growing pool of high-class players, but the LGU did little, owing to self-consciousness about amateur status and its own parlous financial state. There were few first-class lady players, and the LGU had no funds to support schemes to encourage young players. They considered that the responsibility for reaching a decent standard lay with local female golf officials and clubs, not only for the sake of their own ladies' sections but for the good of the game as a whole. The enthusiasm of a few devotees ensured that ladies' golf did not collapse completely, and the debate about professional/amateur status continued.

In the late 1940s Philomena Garvey's amateur status was queried by the LGU because she was working in a Dublin store and helping in the firm's sports department. They requested the R and A to give a ruling and were informed that her status was not affected. Later on, Meg Farquhar Main regained her amateur status, as did Wanda Morgan and Joyce Wethered.

For women on average incomes, championship and international golf were too expensive and, of course, if the game were played only by those in higher income groups, or if only those well-off were available for international matches, the game could have become a farce. The better a player became, the more she played, until she was spending nearly all her time on golf. The expense of full-time golf often caused retirement from competitive golf or entry to the non-amateur ranks; few risked the stigma

Jean Donald Anderson played in the Curtis Cup three times and in the home internationals seven times before turning professional

of shamateurism. By 1953 the golf trade had supposedly opened its doors to first-class women golfers who could perform advisory work for club golfers. Jean Donald Anderson turned 'professional' and enjoyed the life, although she complained that there was one drawback: the lack of tournaments in which she could play. She would willingly have foregone any prize just to be allowed to compete.

A constitutional problem

Meanwhile the LGU had a constitutional problem. The rule that no professional golfer could be eligible to hold any office within the framework of the union mystified delegates at an annual general meeting. No one could clearly define 'framework' and 'office'. The elected officials considered that if a club had a professional she could not be its secretary, but did not know if she could be captain. The constitution plainly stated: 'Every annual amateur member of an affiliated club shall be a member of the Union' but the position with regard to the president of a club was unclear. During its six decades of government, the LGU had carefully avoided unwelcome laws or interference with the domestic arrangements of clubs and approached this problem with their usual seriousness. They took legal advice, and ascertained that no woman professional was eligible to be a member of a committee or council of the union, but clubs could select anyone they wanted as secretary or captain. The governing body continued without official provision for a professional to participate in its functions, to give advice and thus undoubtedly improve standards. Noël Dunlop-Hill once again raised her opinion about declaring the Ladies' Championship open but hardly anyone agreed.

In 1958 the LGU was criticized for not sponsoring promising young players nor assisting with finances. The comparison was made with the Lawn Tennis Association, who helped players but were not accused of shamateurism. Officially the LGU did not act, apart from paying justified expenses. Then, in January 1962, women were allowed to join the Professional Golfers' Association (PGA), founded in 1902, 'on the same basis as men'. The PGA said that women could become full members after serving for a certain time as professionals or assistants at clubs, and could also register as playing professionals and compete for the PGA tournament prize money six months after being accepted.

Plans were submitted in February to the PGA for the first women's professional tournament, on the grounds that it would boost British golf; act as a first-class incentive to young players; and in the hope that the scheme would encourage commercial firms to add a little prize money to the usual trophy awards for women. The scheme called for twelve women professionals, and did not come to fruition. Few women were willing to risk playing for a little prize money in one tournament and, having turned professional, then be unable to play in other events. Comparisons were made with the US ladies' circuit where, in 1962, players were competing for prize money in the region of $200,000. UK women professionals were only helping to sell golf equipment, and although they could be members of the PGA this did not ensure their futures: they had to be accepted by the

golf clubs where professionals would hire them as assistants. There were no tournaments where women could compete amongst themselves for money prizes. The prospect of specially sponsored tournaments for women seemed remote until there were enough women to make such events worthwhile – and there was no prospect of there being sufficient women available until there were enough specially sponsored tournaments.

In March 1962, Colonel Harry Reed, secretary of the PGA, discussed the possibility of a women's Open with Mary Holdsworth, secretary of the LGU, but definite proposals were not made, although the Colonel said that he would like an Open to take place. In May, PGA member Mrs Eileen Beck of Wentworth entered for the Open, in order to gain experience. But the R and A championship secretary Brigadier Eric Brickman stated: 'The question of the inclusion of women has never been contemplated. The championship committee do not intend at present to alter the system.' Also in May, the LGU announced that they would hold a women's Open at Hoylake in June 1963. The LGU were confident that sponsors would be sufficiently interested to provide finance and make it possible for US lady professionals to participate. The sponsors did not appear. By November 1962 the LGU had abandoned the idea.

Few opportunities for girls

During the nineteen-sixties, many firms continued to recognize the prestige that accrued from employing first-class sportsmen and giving them paid leave to play, but the usefulness of sportswomen on their staffs had less appeal. Although it was the custom, apart from economic necessity, for both girls and boys to find jobs when they had finished their education, with regard to sports, and particularly to golf, there were opportunities for boys but not for girls. Boys who attained Walker Cup standard could earn a living at activities related to golf, but girls who reached Curtis Cup standard had very few opportunities. The PGA had admitted women, who could now wear its tie! The organization was simply not interested in any of the difficulties which women were experiencing. There were few club jobs for women and very little money to play for. The LGU guarded the amateur status regulations with the strictness of a kind of maiden-auntly Beefeater.

Nevertheless, professionalism still attracted certain women, including Philomena Garvey, Elizabeth Price and Gwen Brandom. All three were reinstated as amateurs some years later, the latter saying: 'I am an outcast as a pro and I want to enjoy again the fun of being an ordinary golf club member.' This 1967 Irish champion ran Dublin's only fully equipped indoor golf clinic for some years. Elizabeth Price established herself as a journalist, took over from Wanda Morgan at Dunlop and from Enid Wilson on the *Daily Telegraph*. A few girls found jobs as representatives for golf equipment and other sports firms, and others found temporary work – in the off season – as secretaries, petrol pump attendants, hairdressers, baker's assistants, and so on. A lucky few found permanent jobs where kind employers allowed them plenty of time off for both practice and playing.

One girl, already a proven international, reviewed the prospects for

earning her living while at university, but could not find anything that would fit in with golf, except an offer from one man who said: 'Yeah. Let's play everywhere and gamble. We'll win lots.' Wondering what it would be like to turn professional, she phoned a large sports equipment firm to see what the prospects were. The firm phoned the LGU. The LGU phoned her a few days before Christmas and said: 'If you don't turn pro by January 1, we'll turn you pro.' An enquiry about prospects is hardly 'taking any action for the purpose of turning professional', which is the relevant phrase in the amateur status regulations.

Miss Saunders gets going

In 1969, Vivien Saunders, whose work for women professionals equates with Issette Pearson Miller's work for the LGU, turned professional, entered and performed creditably in the few available tournaments in Britain and in the same year obtained her player's ticket for the American circuit – the first European to do so. By 1974 she and Michelle Walker were the only British women tournament-playing golf professionals. Michelle Walker attacked the US circuit and obtained a contract at the Pacific Harbour Club in Fiji, reaching a play-off in 1976 on the US Tour. Vivien Saunders taught, played, wrote illuminating books and many articles, and spent a rewarding time on the staff of the Fairmile Hotel, Surrey, in addition to other golfing activities. But she could not *play* for all her necessary income in Britain and she had disliked the life in America.

When the Colgate LPGA championship was played at Sunningdale for the first time in 1975, the popularity of the event showed players and spectators that a professional circuit would enhance women's golf in the UK. Nearly 100 golfers presented a petition to the LGU pleading that women's golf should be declared open. One leading lady player complained that players could not be officially sponsored but were expected to play full-time if they were to have any chance of being chosen for the international teams. The chairman of the LGU replied that there were various ways and means for counties and countries to cover the expenses of certain individuals in major events but so far as she knew they had never been really used. The LGU attempted to persuade the R and A to relax the amateur status rules but the R and A were unsympathetic. The rules were strict and sponsors had to receive full R and A backing. At the Ladies' British Open Amateur Championship at Royal Porthcawl, some players shared nine to a flat; others went without meals as they could not afford them; and one player was charged £65 for five days in a guest house, an expense which prevented her from paying for the services of a caddie.

In 1975 the LGU were forced to cancel their planned inauguration of the Ladies' British Open Championship as the potential sponsors, Steiner, did not agree to support it for the three years requested. Also in 1975 the Colgate at Sunningdale lacked BBC television coverage. Vivien Saunders published a letter suggesting that complaints to the Head of Sport, BBC, might prevent this happening again. Colgate circularized the clubs. The ladies wrote, and phoned. One overwhelmed duty officer muttered dejectedly: 'Oh no, not

One of twelve nominated for the Curtis Cup in 1932, Wanda Morgan poses for the record

Vivien Saunders at the height of her powers. Miss Saunders has played the game at all levels and in most countries. The existence of the WPGA is mostly due to her tenacity and she is probably the most highly qualified ladies' coach the game has produced

one of you bloody women golfers again.' Television coverage improved.

The status of UK women professional golfers had yet to be established. Women could be admitted to section F of the PGA, but could not play in their tournaments, attend meetings or vote. They had no rights, although they were eligible to wear PGA ties. The Sex Discrimination Act at the end of 1975 enabled Miss Saunders to request the PGA for changes; she also suggested to the LGU that they should institute a professional division within their own constitution. The LGU did not. The PGA said that a constitutional change needed twenty members to propose it and there were not twenty members. Sharp letters were exchanged.

Pleas from some players that surely some tournaments could be open to professionals were largely ignored, with the eventual exception of Joan Rothschild, Avia organizer, who declared that, as from 1978, the tournament would be open to professionals as long as they played with amateurs. She maintained that the Avia was an open tournament and she did not care if the players were members of anything or of nothing at all. In response to the information that the PGA had a rule that non-PGA members could not play alongside members she said: 'I don't see how the PGA can dictate terms when they do so little for the women in their associations.' Sadly, she changed her mind for the 1982 championship, as some of the professionals, practising for an event nearby, joined the Avia participants only for tea and socializing. Understandably furious, she said: 'If you want to play, play. If not, go away.'

Birth of the WPGA

In 1976 the LGU inaugurated the Ladies' British Open, initially through the generosity of an anonymous donor and eventually sponsored by Pretty Polly. Even so, by the beginning of 1978, of thirty-two major fixtures, none catered for lady professionals. Miss Saunders rallied the ladies into forming their own Women's Professional Golf Association (WPGA). She met marketing magnate Barry Edwards, through an inventor's attempt to sell a lining-up aid for women golfers, and Carlsberg brewed up some money. Officially launched in May 1978, the WPGA had £15,000 from Carlsberg, Vivien Saunders as chairman, and founder members who included Jenny Lee Smith, Beverly Lewis, Lynne Harrold and Michelle Walker. By the end of the year, as result of the efforts of Barry Edwards, the sponsorship for the 1979 season was close to £100,000, and nearly twenty girls turned professional. By 1982 professionals were able to play for about £150,000, a figure that seemed likely to rise to nearly £500,000 for 1984.

The ladies' professional circuit succeeded because it was formed at the right psychological moment and because one of its pioneers was a determined woman who would not be defeated, just as in 1893 the LGU succeeded because one of its pioneers was a determined woman who would not be defeated.

By the late 1970s, men were accustomed to the fact that women had access to, and proven ability for, many hitherto male-orientated occupations. The Colgate sponsorship set the example in the UK; the galleries found the girls

BELOW RIGHT: *Chipping to the 16th green at Northumberland, during the 1981 Ladies' British Open, is Jenny Lee Smith, who won it in 1976 as an amateur and was runner-up as a professional in 1982*

BELOW: *Cathy Panton receives the Ladies' British Open Amateur Championship trophy from Cecil Leitch at Silloth, Cumbria, in 1976. Miss Leitch, who was born in Silloth, won the trophy in 1914, 1920, 1921 and 1926*

charming to watch; television showed how attractive women's golf was; and sponsors, through the expertise of Barry Edwards, realized they could obtain wide coverage for comparatively little money.

When women professionals were first allowed to enter regional PGA events, some of them finished ahead of young male assistants. This was considered 'demoralizing for the lads'. Women playing alongside men at this level knew that they could enhance their prospects on their own tour. Heading the money winners on the women's professional circuit in 1979 was Cathy Panton, followed by Muriel Thomson the next year. And in 1981 and 1982 Jenny Lee Smith topped the lists and won around £14,000 each year, a sum which can provide an adequate standard of living. In 1983, Muriel Thomson topped the Order of Merit while Beverley Huke was leading money winner. In contrast, an amateur, without forfeiting amateur status, may accept a 'prize, prize voucher or testimonial in Great Britain and Ireland of retail value not exceeding £150', and receive all expenses under certain, rather broad conditions, a way of life which is adequate for some.

Initially the WPGA had one paid worker, its executive director, Barry Edwards, who found the sponsors and managed organization and administration, a press officer, a chairman and a committee of six who attended to

the playing details. The association carried responsibility for running women's professional golf throughout Europe. Members of the WPGA automatically belonged to Class F of the PGA and, to become eligible for Class A (club professional) or Class B (full assistant), had to serve five years on the tournament circuit and pass tests in teaching club repairing and the rules of golf at Lilleshall. Towards the end of 1982, the WPGA and Barry Edwards severed connections, argued in the High Court, and resolved their differences with financial compensation for him and a firmer base in the PGA for them.

The UK now has flourishing amateur and professional circuits. The results of the Ladies' British Open Championship show that during its seven years' existence nine amateurs and seven professionals have been winners and runners-up. Sir Ernest Holderness misprophesied. Top players have failed, on at least three occasions in the past fifty years, in their call for women's golf to be declared 'open', but many players at all levels now believe that the division caused by these two circuits is a luxury which the playing standards of the golfing population of the country cannot afford.

Women golfers at all levels – club, county, area and national – have for ninety years been vociferous and democratic in deciding how their game should be organized. Their next decision, through overall consensus, may be to open the game. If Surrey's far-sighted proposal of 1935 were to be implemented, the division would disappear and the lack of consciousness about money that was present at the 1893 championship would reappear, although changed in character, and all women golfers would enjoy, now as then, the same status.

Geared up for Action

Practicality, comfort and a fashionable appearance have been contra-
dictory factors in golf clothes for many years. In the early eighteen-
nineties, any fashionable lady who tried to raise a club higher than
her shoulder was impeded by a large hat, full-length dress with long
ballooning sleeves, two full-length petticoats, combinations and a tight-
laced corset. This was the usual attire for ladies during the years in which
they made the transition from the putting green to the full course. Full-
length broderie anglaise looked pretty and elegant on the putting green in
summer, and alternated with white, pale blue or cream serge suits, while
floral hats were fixed rigidly to masses of hair meticulously coiffed in the
Pompadour style.

Although the ladies had, since the eighteen-forties, the opportunity of
wearing bifurcated skirts or bloomers, owing to the pioneering work of Mrs
Amelia Bloomer, who advocated emancipated dress for women, few
adopted them for golf. Even the advent and popularity of the safety bicycle
in the eighteen-nineties, which had been preceded by the velocipede fifty
years earlier, did not tempt many golfers into the wearing of cycling
breeches. Costumes with belted jackets and short skirts were available for
alpine climbing devotees but few golfers took to these either. Some ladies,
however, adopted long belted jackets and barely flared skirts, which gave a
more masculine outline and expressed their lack of willingness to accept
their former restricted existences.

The bustles of the eighteen-seventies, the tiered creations of the eighteen-
eighties and the flowing styles of the eighteen-nineties would not have
hindered a full swing, although a lady had to be wary of revealing an ankle
and thus displaying a lack of modesty, unless she wanted to, but corsets
were a decided restriction. A standard pattern for corsets restricted and
altered the shape of the body above and below the waist. The garment was
cut very short at the sides, to encourage the hips to protrude, and had a deep
point in front; twenty-eight whalebones curved in at the waist and out
immediately below and above it. Wearers resembled inverted forks – bent
round above the hips, then straight to the ground. Combinations had
low-cut necks and reached inches below the knees, as did voluminous
chemises which were tucked into drawers.

In the course of research for this book, a lady successfully hit full shots

Lady Margaret Scott in the fashionable golfing gear of the 1890s. Leg o'mutton sleeves and tiny wasp waist were compulsory

with air balls in the privacy of a secluded sheltered garden while wearing simulated bustles, tiered dresses and long skirts. She also purchased a 'basque', wore it sixteen hours a day for a week, and then donned the garment, under trousers and a sweater, for an early morning practice round on a charming course in Kent. The wearer, who is fairly supple, found that her suppleness was impeded as she tried flat swings, hockey-style swings, upright swings, right elbow high in the air in the style of Lady Margaret Scott, and her normal swing. All the swings were possible but after three holes exhaustion set in. There followed scores of eight on a par four, five on a par three – where a quick curtsey was found to be the most effective method of retrieving the ball from the tin – a seven on the next par four and complete defeat on the par five 7th when the rough had not been cleared in three. The experimenter thereupon putted – very long putts – across the fairway to a shed, removed the basque and stuffed it in her golf bag, and concluded that the ladies of the eighteen-nineties either possessed the stamina of titans, or else they cheated and either loosened or threw away their corsets.

Long skirts which blew in the wind and acquired wet hems from damp grass presented problems for years. The ladies used initiative. In 1893 a 'New Forest' skirt was popular. Its length could be adjusted, from twelve

Even tighter waists for the winners of the Ladies' British Open Amateur Championship. It is doubtful that Lady Margaret Scott played in her de rigueur *coat, or Mrs Ryder Richardson in her jacket*

inches off the ground for wearing while playing on the links, to three inches off the ground for wearing while walking home. This skirt had a tuck, hidden under which were buttons so that a piece of cloth nine inches deep could be attached when the extra length was required. It also had a leather 'bottom piece' which, when consciousness about ankles or the effect of wet grass necessitated, could be changed for a cloth piece, dry and respectable, for entering the club house. Another early device for coping with long skirts was a 'harem' pin. This secured the middle of the front of the hem of the skirt to the same part at the back.

Later on, a wide dark length of elastic was worn around the waist and slipped down to the area of the knees when skirts became wayward in the wind. This device was widely referred to as a 'Miss Higgins' after the lady who invented it. In summer, skirt hems were threaded with wire to keep them down. Skirts had stiff petersham belts which emphasized wasp-waists. For wet conditions, skirts were bound with leather or braid, from which mud could be sponged. This was a difficult chore – one women's magazine stated that the only satisfactory method of removing mud stains from a golfing skirt was to dye the skirt the same colour as the mud.

Ostrich feathers for a medal round

One woman who had been sitting in a London park in the morning, as was the custom at the height of 'the season', did not change her clothes before playing a medal round at her nearby club. She played in a long skirt with a little train, and a large hat trimmed with ostrich feathers. When Harriot Curtis visited England for the first time, she 'stepped off the boat in a most beautiful get-up and with such a lovely hat adorned with a high ostrich feather, on her way to a golf championship'. The feather did not survive the gales and drenching rain which occurred at that event.

Leg o' mutton sleeves made even a glimpse of the ball on the backswing impossible, so either the left sleeve was pinned flat, or an elastic strap was worn around the left arm. When sailor hats with very broad brims were in vogue they were pinned, insecurely, to huge piles of hair. Straw hats were fastened under chins with elastic or ribbons. By the 1900s, stand-up collars and wide striped ties, which gave a more masculine line, were fashionable. Hats were adorned with club colours and ties were similarly patterned. Starched stiff linen collars had to be endured, and the higher the collar the more chic the wearer was considered. Plain stand-up collars produced little discomfort but highly glazed double collars, worn as deep as possible, meant that players almost had to peer over the sides of these collars, and the left side of the neck frequently acquired a painful red sore. When fashion permitted soft silk collars, comfort improved, but collarless blouses often caused wearers unaccustomed to the sun to suffer the severe discomfort of blistered red necks.

Rubber-soled footwear was not available, and thick-soled shoes were studded with nails. Heavy boots, with heel guards resembling horseshoes, were also worn; these weighed over thirty ounces – each. Thick heavy coats, lined with materials of the same weights and colours as blankets, were worn

By 1900 skirts were a wee bit off the ground, and precious lengths of chiffon were permitted to tie down hats which could wander in stiff breezes

in winter and wet weather. Apart from the discomfort of wearing a heavy coat, these interfered with free arm action.

The early golfing outfits were in general heavy, cumbrous, uncomfortable, unhygienic and impractical. Men laughed at the unsuitability of ladies' golfing attire and referred to them as 'mirth-inspiring damsels'. One gentleman did not comment on their dress but referred to 'billiard table legs, leathery faces and clumsy great paws'. He had either a lively imagination or privileged knowledge – legs?

Problems and advice

In the early 1900s the ladies tied the newly fashionable pancake-shaped motorcaps down with voluminous veils, often of chiffon. They were claustrophobic, but kept the hats firm, and the hair under control, not blowing around, or off, or into the eyes. Corsets and other items for the nether regions improved. A 1902 advertisement in a lady golfer's publication cited ladies' knickerbockers – from 1 guinea (£1.05) or, lined, from 1½ guineas (1.52½p) – and also detachable gaiters to the knees, at 2 shillings (10p); the knickerbockers enforced the still mandatory wasp waist. The Patent Shapely

Skirt Association offered accordion-pleated divided skirts, at 3 guineas (£3.15); these were a similar hoved-in shape to the knickerbockers but longer, and were available from Mme Goldschmidt, Court Dressmaker, Cromwell Road, South Kensington, London SW. C.T. Taylor advertised corsets which were 'pre-eminently suitable for every athletic pursuit' and the lightest and the most supple in existence. 'There are no heavy side steels, and the flexible side supports are unbreakable. They are made in fifty different shapes to suit every figure. There are no *vertical* [emphasized] joins, and splitting or tearing of the material . . . impossible.' They sold for from 10s 6d (52½p) to 3 guineas (£3.15).

By 1904 practical advice about clothes for lady golfers stressed the necessity of a short skirt. Experts considered that nothing looked more untidy or was more unsuitable for games than a long skirt, because the hem dragged in the mud or else the wearer suffered exhaustion from the effort of keeping it off the ground. In wet weather long skirts hampered movement and were soaked with the moisture from the grass. Short skirts – 'really short, not simply a couple of inches off the ground' – were judged more workmanlike and comfortable. Ladies were advised that skirts should be well cut from thick material such as tweed or serge as these would not blow about in the wind, and should have side fastenings, plain strappings or stitching around the hem, but no elaborate trimmings which would not withstand rain. Some serges cockled up in the rain so only those guaranteed to withstand hard wear were suitable. The best hemlines were those which were a trifle shorter at the back, because short skirts dropped at the back, particularly after several drenchings.

Nice boots with short skirts

With short skirts, ladies were advised to wear nice boots, and to ensure that the whole ensemble was plain and neat, well-made and smart, but not trimmed excessively, or gaudy. Cheap boots were a false economy as good boots kept their shape but cheap boots needed frequent repairing. Brown or black boots were the only choice; brown were usually made of softer leather and looked smarter, but black wore better and withstood the onslaughts of mud and wet. Pigskin or porpoise hide was recommended for rough wear, and the best pattern for winter boots consisted of one which laced halfway up the leg and then buttoned over with flaps. The soles projected, and such shoes were heavy; however, they gave great protection. Playing in tennis shoes in summer was not advised because some players found them tiring.

Gaiters made of cloth or leather were worn because shoes quickly filled up with sand, and the edge of the skirt rubbed against the ankles and made them wet. Ladies were also advised to have studs or nails in the soles of the boots, so that a firm grip could be gained in wet or slippery conditions. But the drawback to nailed shoes was that they were uncomfortable for walking on pavements and tiring for long distances, and the additional weight made them heavy. Also, unless the soles were extremely thick, there was always the danger of the nails coming through into the feet. One make of shoe –

1911 and skirts had crept up to ankle length; jackets and skirts were a little looser too. The feather in Elsie Grant-Suttie's hat was a gesture to fashion not superstition

Scaife's Patent – possessed indiarubber studs, and aluminium nails were also available. Nails put in singly, rather than arranged in clusters, formed the most efficient grip.

Many ladies were of the opinion that a great disadvantage of golf was that it increased the size of the hands and feet. It was impossible to play well if restraint was felt in any article of dress, particularly tight boots. Muscles which were constantly being exercised needed sufficient room for expansion, with the result that 'the more one played the larger the hands and feet became'. Another disadvantage of golf was the damage that being outdoors in all types of weather caused to the complexion. But the ladies thought that the 'new life' was very much healthier and hoped that sunburn and freckles had a charm of their own.

Shady hats and gloves

It was difficult to find any headwear that would stay on firmly and not wobble in the wind. Tam-o'-shanters were useful if they had velvet crowns as the bands would stay on and resist the elements. American ladies rarely wore hats but the British climate was less suitable for such a custom. Most ladies thought headwear was essential because it looked tidier and gave a more finished appearance. Shady hats in summer, if not extravagantly fashionable, and therefore extravagantly large, were useful for protection from the sun. Turn-down collars made of the same material as the skirt, worn with lace or silk ties, were considered suitable. Some ladies found that heavy coats in cold weather controlled the swing, and counteracted any tendency to overswing. Golf jerseys were favoured and these were 'easy to make, taking about a pound and a quarter of wool. Instructions from D. Head & Son, Sloane St, London, twopence.' Gloves were usually worn, for the protection of soft pale hands, and were often made of soft washing chamois leather. Men's old white kid gloves turned inside out were also used and pronounced most efficient. The ladies frequently tried to adopt one particular colour for their golfing outfits and then matched all their accessories to it.

Conscious of the fact that, ten years after the formation of the LGU, lady golfers were still curiosities, May Hezlet insisted that:

> anything that makes the wearer conspicuous is out of place on the links. Outrageous or indifferent dressing raises remarks about 'athletic woman'. We must prevent disparaging remarks which are too apt to be made after a large ladies golf meeting. Non-golfers were delighted to find something to criticize. The aim of all lady golfers of the present day must be to abolish the absurd but popular belief, which must have started somewhere, that 'a golfing girl' is a weird and terrible creature clad in the most extraordinary garments, striding along with self-possessed walk, and oblivious to everything but her beloved game.

In 1905 Burberry's maintained that the real solution to a lady golfer's

problems lay in their (patent) coat – free-stroke with pivot sleeve. 'Test your present coat thus', they exhorted.

> Buckle a belt tightly round the waist, tie the sleeves at the wrists, then put both arms straight up. If you can't do this without lifting the collar and body of the coat YOU WANT A PIVOT SLEEVE IN WHICH YOU CAN. The coat permits the ARM to be swung around like a mill sail without dragging. The body of the coat won't lift when both arms are held straight up. No other sleeve is fit to golf in or will ever be used again after this.

Cecil Leitch played in her first golfing competition in 1908 with her hair in a plait which reached half way down her back, and wearing a long-sleeved blouse, mid-calf-length skirt and spats. She was only seventeen and her appearance was uncriticized. Two years later, during her match against Harold Hilton, she wore a longer cream serge skirt striped with blue, a long-sleeved white blouse with the collar turned down, and a green and red tie fastened with a sparkling pin. Blue stockings and tan shoes completed the outfit, and her hair was fastened with combs. Not all the ladies copied her practicality, although Mrs Asquith always played without a hat, whatever the weather. In 1909, Gladys Ravenscroft played in a championship with her sleeves rolled up, thereby shocking the gallery.

In 1912, lady golfers and their requirements attracted the inventiveness of manufacturers and one useful aid was a hat-pin with a detachable head which was slipped on to the point after the pin had been passed through the hat. This obviated the annoyance of a protruding point or a lost pin. The head of a driver was deemed a suitable finish for the hat pin of a lady golfer. The registered name of this device was 'The Duke' and it became very popular. However, just before World War I there was a widespread bare-headed fashion owing to a long spell of good weather, but by 1920 hats were essential for golf and cloches, berets and bandeaux were worn.

Comfort and ease of movement

Ladies were realizing that, although the whole ensemble had to be carefully considered, the most important aspects of clothes for golf were comfort and ease of movement. Tight sleeves and ill-fitting blouses were impediments which could cause the loss of a match. Distinctions were made between shirts and blouses; shirts were worn for sport. These had to be well-tailored, with sleeves close-fitting at the armholes and set in properly to the shoulders. Kimono or magyar sleeves were restrictive and therefore not tolerated, and shirts were cut with plenty of room at the front and back so that they would not pull in any way.

Cecil Leitch advised ladies to avoid full skirts, but not to make them excessively narrow. She was often asked if her skirts were the exact width of her stance for full shots. She replied that they probably appeared to be so but that this was by accident rather than by design. Miss Leitch had her skirts made from a plain pattern which allowed a hem width of 56 inches around

An almost calf-length skirt and a bow in the hair were permitted attire for the 17-year old Cecil Leitch before World War I

the hem; 8-inch pleats gathered this width into both the back and front of the waistband. She liked men's tweed materials and, as these were usually sold in 60-inch widths, a yard and a quarter was enough to make one skirt, with two patch pockets. She also advocated shirts, especially styles with which ties could be worn. Some players were inclined to overlook the fact that the width at the bottom of the skirt was not the only item of importance; the width around the knees was equally so.

Miss Leitch and her colleagues played in all weathers; and the difficulty of keeping hands warm in winter prompted her invention of a pattern for golfing mittens, which did not interfere with the grip. The golfing mittens were made of soft wool and had a long cuff which fitted over the cuff of a jersey. They were easy to knit and when finished resembled an ordinary glove which had the palm cut out and the fingers and thumbs cut off. Her instructions were:

> An ordinary cuff is knitted and about half the stitches are then knitted for about an inch and a half, when sufficient must be cast off to allow for the thumb; again the remainder are knitted until of a sufficient length to cover the whole of the back of the hand; these are then cast off and loops crocheted for three fingers and thumb. A loop around the forefinger will be found to interfere with the grip. This is the only form of covering for the hands which does not interfere with the grip of those players who do not play in gloves.

A golfer is a cardigan

Knitted coats and jerseys became inseparably linked with golf – a 'golfer' is another word for a cardigan – and stockings were chosen to match them, or to tone in with ties or shirts. Stockings were available 'in checks or stripes and (if you are sure of your ankles) will add in no small measure to the charm of your appearance'. Silk stockings were not considered suitable for golf, and cotton ones were a poor economy as they made the feet sore. Thick woollen stockings were found serviceable and comfortable in winter, and thin cashmere stockings in summer. Two-piece knitted outfits prevailed in the 1920s, but were impractical in the rain. At the English Championship at Cooden Beach in 1924, one player became waterlogged after a sudden storm. Her knitted skirt was badly drenched; it lengthened and became so heavy that she could hardly walk, and by the time she reached the 18th playing was impossible. There were no rules for such an occurrence. Could she retire to the clubhouse to change her skirt, or could some one carry her from shot to shot? She was allowed to change into a spare skirt and won admiration for obtaining permission to cover an unprecedented disaster. Other ladies who played in bulky knits suffered from temporary loss of equipment, particularly when playing out of bunkers, as balls rebounded and became lodged in pockets or in folds of jumpers.

Breeches were occasionally seen in the 1920s too. At a 1921 match between the Legals and the United Services at Stanmore, two players who had travelled to the course on motorbikes wore their riding gear of

breeches for the round. Long waists, lowered down to the hip, were fashionable and some players, including Joyce Wethered, thought that a little restriction in that area helped to counteract a lady's general tendency to overswing.

The 1920s brought knits, cloche hats, dropped waists and far more freedom, comfort and ease of movement

Berets and bandeaux

Molly Griffiths popularized the beret for golf in 1920, while Cecil Leitch frequently favoured an extremely practical bandeau. The problem of studs on shoes improved, for nails which could be screwed into soles were on the market. Leather coats were found to be useful in winter, but clothes specially advertised for golf often had too many pleats in the skirt and so blew out annoyingly in the wind, or else they were so tight that they made walking around the course painful. Bobbed hair was popular and skirts developed into a sensible, much shorter, length. At the Ladies' Championship at St Andrews in 1929, Eleanor Helme compared the fashions with those at the same championship on the same course twenty-one years previously. She remarked on the shorter skirts and the lengthening of the shots, and prophesied that in another twenty-one years, if the lengths of the shots and skirts proceeded in the same direction and at the same pace, spectators would need 'a telescope to follow one and a microscope to discover the other'. But, twenty-five years later, one gentleman declaimed authoritatively: 'Shorts for men and scanty dress for women will naturally never appear on a golf course. The dignity and deportment of the game just could not abide it.'

In 1933, Gloria Minoprio's contribution to the 'dignity and deportment of the game' did not endear her to the LGU. Their official statement was that they 'deplored any departure from the traditional costume of the game'.

The object of their outrage was the extremely well-cut, close-fitting navy trousers the lady wore in the English Championship. Her outfit included a turtle neck sweater and woollen cap of the same, navy, colour; her make-up was a mask-like white; and she played with only one club. She received front page publicity in the newspapers but the LGU's official 'organ', *Fairway & Hazard*, did not mention her. Miss Minoprio never clarified her reasons for using only one club, nor her reasons for the extraordinary make-up. Her practical outfit – the trousers had straps beneath the insteps in the fashion of ski pants – can be seen today in the Women Golfer's Museum, Edinburgh.

Sic Transit Gloria Monday

Apart from a polite nod on the first tee to her opponents, Miss Minoprio communicated with no one, playing as if in a trance, or under the influence of auto-hypnosis. Her club, which was similar to a modern two-iron, enabled her to putt, drive, approach and get out of bunkers well, but she could not loft the ball, nor pitch over a hazard, nor obtain any backspin nor any distance other than from a first-class lie. She played in the championship six times, thus giving golf journalist Henry Longhurst the opportunity of titling his piece 'Sic Transit Gloria Monday' five times in succession as she lost the first day of each of the first five times she played; on the sixth occasion the title ran: 'Sic Transit Gloria Tuesday' as the lady had survived into the second day's play. In the 1935 championship her outfit, which was exactly the same, attracted little attention because other competitors wore waterproof trousers, baggy and unrevealing, because of the appalling weather.

Miss Minoprio was a trained conjuror; if she intended her outfit and her preference for one club as a publicity stunt to boost her profession she made no attempt to endorse it. The rules of golf did not include specifications for clothes for women; the lady was years ahead of her time by being the first woman to play in a major British championship in practical, comfortable and exquisitely designed trousers. Conventions are not often broken until the moment is socially and psychologically right. At that time one player who drove off in a competition with the sleeves of her blouse rolled up to the elbows elicited the comment from a spectator: 'She looks as though she has just done a day's washing.' The lady overheard the remark and quipped back: 'And it would not be for the first time.'

Pam Barton's straight arm aid

Soon a 'caddyless golf belt' was available to lady golfers. It had compartments for money, powder and handkerchiefs and, most importantly, contained a stiffened pocket for cigarettes and matches. Another advertised 'aid' was a straight left golf sleeve made of leather or canvas which men were encouraged to practise in to assist the efficiency of the all-important left arm. Pamela Barton, when practising between the 1935 and 1936 Ladies' Championships, had great difficulty with her pitch and run. Her short mashie approaches into the wind caused her so much trouble

By 1932 the emphasis on fluid lines and comfort was paramount as this shot of Diana Fishwick shows

that she virtually put her left arm in a straight jacket. This was made of strong canvas and was further strengthened with bone – long, tough slivers of bone that stretched from the top to the bottom of the sleeve, which was long enough to cover her elbow. Thus imprisoned, her arm, she wrote, 'was as incapable of bending as I could ever hope to make it. I kept it bound up like this for three-quarters of an hour three or four times a week until I felt, in the unconscious way mastery does steal over a set problem of golf if you have persevered, that my left arm could do its work unaided. It could and did.'

By the end of the decade, divided skirts, often called trouser skirts, were worn for golf and trousers were available with a small pleat fastened with a zip on each leg; gores kept the back of the waist neat. The trousers were available in five fittings in five different leg lengths. The transition from wasp waists and full-length skirts to loose blouses and trousers had been accomplished in a little over thirty years. Whereas three decades before players adapted their ordinary clothes as well as they could for sports, just before World War II there was a tendency to adapt specially made comfortable sports clothes for ordinary wear. Insistence on practicality and comfort was becoming a priority, and maintaining a smart appearance on the golf course soon became a minor consideration.

Trousers versus skirts

After World War II, restrictions generated by clothing coupons resulted in motley colour schemes and styles, but golfing gear gradually settled down – to a general shapeless untidiness and remained so for many years. Jean Donald Anderson was referred to in the press as a 'sartorial sensation' when she wore waterproof trousers in the final of the 1948 Ladies' Championship, and in the early 1950s skiing clothing was popular among women golfers. Teddy Tinling, who designed the uniform for the 1954 Curtis Cup players, maintained that a woman looked untidy if her ensemble included more than two colours. He saw one lady who looked so untidy that he had to look at her several times and count up the colours twice before he realized that the reason for her unkempt appearance was that she was wearing seven colours. Mr Tinling was also of the opinion that women should never wear slacks. 'No woman,' he said, 'however beautiful, looks as good in slacks as she does in skirts.'

Pamela Barton holds the Ladies' British Open Amateur Championship Trophy in 1936. Each year a heart-shaped plaque engraved with the winner's name and date is added to the trophy

A few years later, Henry Cotton wondered 'why lady golfers have given up so readily the golf skirt for the doubtful elegance but possible convenience of ski pants or the shorts . . . but the shorts are here to stay and on certain individuals have gallery appeal extending beyond their nattiness and mere convenience to wear.' He also pleaded: 'Please let the world be spared the sight of all women in slacks.' And one magazine demanded: 'If girl golfers must wear slacks on the course and not neat skirts then for Heaven's sake get slacks that look nice and not like tights.' In the late 1950s, appeals were made to the LGU to ban competitors from wearing Bermuda shorts. The Americans wore them at the 1956 Ladies' Championship at Sunningdale and many British golfers followed their example.

British manufacturers were requested to supply skirts with pleats at the back so that the wearer would not see them fluttering while putting. If it were possible to find neat skirts, with at least one pocket, some ladies thought that trousers would lose their popularity. But, at the time, off-the-peg golf skirts were either pleated all round or else pencil tight, and golf shirts pulled out from the waist at the first practice swing. Properly tailored waterproof clothing was not available, and requests were made for water-proof skirts which fastened with buttons or zips, and hats with brims. The requests were ignored. Shirts with rubber discs around the waist area, intended to prevent the shirt from riding up, were available but these were ineffective for full shots. A 'Fairway' golfers' hat was advertised. It was showerproof, had a strap and buckle at the back to adjust to fit any size of head, and tapes to tie under the chin, although these could be concealed. Another advantage of this hat was that it could be folded flat in a golf bag, and was obtainable in scores of tartans and plains, or made up in a customer's own material; it was supplied with press studs which were not sewn on in case they spoiled the line.

RIGHT: *Sensible precautions against the weather were permitted and in general use by 1957, as Philomena Garvey demonstrates*

In 1962 Enid Wilson published an article about the difficulty of purchasing waterproof shoes that were flexible and not too heavy. Most women golfers bought rubber shoes because no other type was available. Manufacturers responded to her criticism within a week and one firm said that they had been working on the problem for some time, thought that they had overcome all obstacles, and would soon be presenting a suitable range of shoes. The range was for men. In early 1965, plus twos – abbreviated plus fours – were seen at the Girls' Golfing Society meeting, as were pork-pie hats. Plus fours, incidentally, were so called because the trouser lengths were cut and hemmed four inches longer than the wearer's full length in order to give the required overhang when tucked up.

Minis and hot pants

Marley Spearman, lady champion of the early nineteen-sixties, attempted to dignify the amateur circuit with well-cut, but not extravagant, outfits. Her flair for fashion and attention to detail initially set her sartorially apart from many contemporaries, but some eventually and successfully imitated her style. She also caused a greater sensation, in Australia, than Miss Minoprio had caused in England thirty years earlier, by wearing well-cut tight scarlet trousers. The mini-skirt fashions of the mid-nineteen-sixties liberated lady golfers from skirts that flapped as they putted – few seemed to have appreciated the merits of the kilt – and then tights became commonly available and removed the necessity for wearing garments that needed suspenders attached. Officialdom disliked minis. The 1972 Curtis Cup team was issued with trousers, but the LGU was wary of minis; one comment was that the lady golfer would be made more conscious of her own contours than those of the green.

But hot pants had already appeared on the golf course. In June 1971 one lady champion arrived in hot pants to play in a large open meeting. This caused the lady captain of the host club to call a ladies' committee meeting which lasted two hours. It was decided that hot pants could not be worn without a skirt. This was a disappointment to the male members of the club and they took exception to the ban. In July 1974 one player who turned up in a see-through blouse to play in an exhibition match was asked to cover up, and did so when informed of a 'Jackets will be worn' rule. This action was not popular with all of the male exhibitors.

Mainland Europeans and Americans seem to have had little trouble in finding well-cut trousers and toning tops, but it is only in the last few years that British manufacturers have understood the special needs of lady golfers. Shapelessness and untidiness are still common on the golf course but the availability of colourful, attractive, fashionable and practical clothes from several specialist manufacturers, including the 'Golf Girl' range launched by a lady golfer in 1978, may end this image. Since Mrs Joan Rothschild instituted a prize for the best-dressed competitor in the Avia, the improvement in smartness in that event has been noticeable. After nearly a hundred years, women golfers may swing freely while knowing that they look their best.

Everyone will play so perfectly

As with clothes, the evolution of certain items of golfing equipment has made the game easier for ladies. One forecast at the beginning of the century was that 'at the rate at which golf is progressing now, there will probably be no need of handicaps as everyone will play so perfectly by the aid of all the new inventions; that happy day, however, will be some time in coming.' That 'happy day' may never arrive, but the fact that ladies achieved drives of over 200 yards with hickory-shafted weapons and gutties, while wearing ramrod corsets and impractical unhygienic clothes, is hardly believable to today's club golfers, who have access to unrestrictive clothes, non-cut balls and matched sets of clubs of an infinite variety of weight and length specifications.

The fish ladies who competed in 1811 for the fishing creels and handkerchiefs used feather-, wool-, flock-, or hair-stuffed balls made of leather. The earliest British mention of making a ball with feathers occurred in *The Goff*, written by Thomas Matheson in 1743:

ABOVE: Featheries
BELOW: Gutties

> Lo, tatter'd Irus, who with armour bears,
> Upon the green two little pyr'mids rears;
> On these they place two balls with careful eye,
> That with Clarinda's breasts for colour vye,
> The work of Bobson; who with matchless art
> Shapes the firm hide, connecting ev'ry part,
> Then in a socket sets the well-stitch'd void,
> And thro' the eyelet drives the downy tide;
> Crowds urging Crowds the forceful brogue impels,
> The feathers harden and the Leather swells;
> He crams and sweats, yet crams and urges more,
> Till scarce the turgid globe contains its store.
> The dreaded falcon's pride here blended lies
> With pigeons glossy down of various dyes;
> The lark's small pinions join the common stock,
> And yellow glory of the martial cock.
>   Soon as Hyperion gilds old Andrea's spire
> From bed the artist to his cell retires;
> With bended back, there plies his steely awls
> And shapes, and stuffs, and finishes the balls.

A piece of tanned leather was cut into curved strips, soaked, sewn up and turned seam-side in, leaving a quarter-inch slit through which feathers were inserted. The amount of feathers stuffed into each ball was the same as the amount needed to lightly pack a gentleman's top hat. Goose feathers, which had been boiled to make them pliable, were stuffed in with an iron rod about 18 inches long, and a smaller instrument pushed in the last few feathers. Then the slit was stitched. The leather shrank on drying out and the feathers expanded – thus producing a hard ball. The size of the ball was measured with calipers. In order to aid visibility, the finished ball,

ABOVE: *Hand-hammered gutties*
BELOW: *Machine-made gutties*

OPPOSITE: *Hammered, moulded or machined, the dints and bumps on balls have always been considered of the utmost importance due to their effect on the ball's flight. The 'Bramble's' raised pimples made it popular with devotees in the early 1900s*

already pale, was enhanced with white paint, the first person to do this being Thomas Kincaid who, on 25 January 1687, 'collured a golve ball with white lead'. The whole procedure took a long time and only a few balls could be made in one day. Towards the end of the 'feathery' era, they cost up to 4 shillings (20p) each.

Rubber balls were being made in the UK by 1830, but no one seems to have tried to play golf with them, although this may have been done and voted a disaster. Then in the 1840s a cheaper ball became fashionable. Gutta percha, the dried milk from the rubber tree, was moulded from sheets into balls of different sizes and these were available from 1848. Dark in colour, they must have been difficult to find, and painting them white was impossible. When a new ball was first used, soaring flight was not possible. The smoothness caused it to dip. After it had been hacked about by a few shots it flew more efficiently; as a result nicking and hand hammering quickly became common practices. The gutta sold for about a shilling (5p). Shortly, surface patterns of various kinds became the norm.

Demise of the gutta

In 1871, Captain Duncan Steward of St Andrews made a ball of wound rubber thread wrapped in gutta percha, and this principle was used for the Haskell rubber-cored ball thirty years later. Captain Steward also made a ball which combined pieces of cork, metal filings and solvent in 1876, and he patented this composite ball, which was harder and longer in flight than a non-composite. Another composite was made of rubber, cork and leather, moulded and vulcanized, the mould being lined with canvas to indent the surface. Called the 'Eclipse', it was described in 1892 as 'a soft india rubber ball which goes off the club with the silence of a thief in the night. Good ball in wind, easier to keep straight, but will not rise quickly from the club.' Many composite gutties were invented, each supposedly superior to the others, and these were superseding the non-composite gutta when the Haskell rubber-core was introduced from America in 1902. The gutta took over from the feathery because it was cheap and could be melted and re-made, but the new wound one was so rewarding to hit that players would pay 2s 6d (12½p) for one, at a time when clubs cost only 5 shillings each. Guttas and gutties were solid and had to be hit exactly in the middle of the club, but a mis-hit with the new ball brought fewer difficulties. At first, the rubber-cored balls were so scarce that as much as £1 10s (£1.50) were paid for them. They were made mechanically, not by hand, and consisted of elastic rubber threat wound round a core.

British manufacturers soon took out patents for the new ball, and this prompted the Haskell company to sue a Glasgow manufacturer, but they lost the case because of the former use of the idea by Captain Steward. During the court proceedings, one of the witnesses was Mrs Hickinbottom from Derbyshire who had for some time made children's balls by winding bits of elastic around a core and coating them in rubber solution. She demonstrated this process, with its accompanying smells, in court to the judge. Between 1902 and 1905 about a hundred patents for golf balls were

registered in Britain but legislation about standardization of sizes or weights did not occur until after World War I. Featheries had been numbered in sizes from 25 to 33 dram weight; guttas and gutties were similarly numbered but were smaller in size. When troy weights were used, in the late eighteen-eighties, dwt – pennyweights – described them, a 32½ being about the weight of today's ball.

Joyce Wethered analyzed the improvement in ladies' golfing standards in the early years of the century and deduced that the reason was the introduction of the rubber-cored ball. It was easier to hit further with the rubber-core, and the new ball behaved better when a shot was topped or only half-hit. It continued to run, whereas a mis-hit gutty staggered on for a few yards and then stopped dead.

Ladies soon found the new balls easier to play with, and a round with a rubber-cored ball needed only half the exertion of one played with a gutty. Hard hitters, including Miss M.A. Whigham, frequently drove up to 214 yards with the gutty, but hitting the new ball hard was often a drawback, as rubber-cored balls would not fly properly when hit hard and sometimes split in half. A lady's lack of strength no longer prevented her achieving the distance essential for competent play on long courses. The LGU kept pace with the higher standards made possible by the new ball and in 1905 completely revised the pars of the green.

Weights and sizes

In 1920 the R and A ruled that the weight of the ball should be no greater than 1.62 ounces and the size no smaller than 1.62 inches. In 1931 the USGA decided that 1.68 inches should be the maximum diameter and 1.55 ounces the maximum weight; they changed the weight to 1.62 ounces in 1933 but kept to 1.68 inches in size. English champion Elsie Corlett considered that the lighter (1.55 ounce) large ball would help women golfers. Although the ball required more control and therefore had to be hit more accurately, she found that she did not hit so many haphazard shots and did not find the game so tiring. The harder a ball is hit, the more it expands and the more distance it covers; women, she thought, would find the lighter ball easier to compress or flatten out. She also discovered that the lighter ball soared much higher, stayed in the air longer and sat up higher on the turf, thus making fairway shots easier. The R and A discouraged the general use of the lighter ball in 1935. In 1951 a joint committee of the R and A and the USGA recommended that both sizes should be legal in all countries, but the decisive meeting of the USGA over-ruled the recommendation. Another attempt at a world-wide uniform ball was made in 1974 but agreement was not reached. In early 1982, the LGU decided, following the lead the men had given, that as from 31 January 1983, the big ball – 1.68 inches – should be used for all open tournaments but not for international events.

Apart from size and weight, there are three main types of ball – one-, two- or three-piece. The three-piece, which is the most widely used, has a cover, rubber thread and rubber core. About 25 yards of rubber thread are

The one-piece Dunlop DDH, constructed on a 12-pentagon principle, has 360 dimples, compared with the more usual 336

stretched in winding to over 200 yards. Each ball has over 300 dimples and each dimple is ten times as wide as it is deep. A two-piece has a moulded inside and a cover, and a one-piece is only hardened and moulded. That intricately constructed little object that must be cajoled into a hole measuring 4¼ inches in diameter and at least 4 inches deep with the use of as few strokes as possible in accordance with the rules of golf has been white in colour for nearly three centuries; the current vogue for 'optics' may or may not be fleeting.

Evolution of the tee

Another major piece of golfing equipment, which underwent eventual improvement, was the tee. For centuries, players or their caddies made their own tees from sand. Caddies used to carry little bags of sand with them before the introduction of sand boxes; some of the boxes remain, and are often used to designate the teeing areas for visitors. Cecil Leitch in 1924 complained that 'Very few lady players make their own tees. This, when we think over the matter, is a great mistake. The task may be an unpleasant one, especially when the sand provided for the purpose is wet, but it is not wise to try to play from a tee one does not fancy, nor is it fair to the caddies to complain about the ball having been badly teed after the shot has been a failure. If a player make her own tee, she has only herself to blame in the event of a missed shot caused by the work having been badly done.'

One aid advertised for ladies in 1920 was described as an adjustable sand tee. It was a triangular piece of apparatus which released sand to the height of individual requirements. At the same time, an india rubber tee was introduced and advertised as being very useful for ladies who did not want to get their hands wet from sand. It had a strip of leather moulded to hold the ball at one end and a weight at the other to keep it from swaying. This was not, however, the first rubber tee.

In 1889 a rubber tee of similar shape to today's long un-notched plastic tees was patented but its popularity did not last; apart from the fact that it deprived caddies of an important part of their work, it wobbled. There was an attempt to introduce steel tees in 1896, and aluminium tees were still being manufactured in the early 1930s but were discontinued as clubs objected to the damage they caused to mowing machinery. In 1905 disposable cardboard tees were patented, but were undoubtedly useless in wet conditions. Wooden tee pegs were common in the late 1920s and plastic tees were used after World War II, although these were not easily obtainable in Britain for some time, owing to the government's drive for exports.

Improvements in clubs

Apart from the usefulness of various improvements in balls and tees, improvements in clubs have been of special value to ladies. In 1898, Amy Pascoe wrote: 'Our physical and mental capacity to use a driver being no longer an hypothesis but an historical fact, it became no longer possible to break a record using a putter only, or to carry off the monthly medal with a game resembling croquet.' Before that 'historical fact', driving putters were

often used for low shots into the wind and players could tee up and obtain some distance with these; there were also approaching putters, as well as putting putters.

Brassies, which had been available for decades, were made on similar lines to drivers, but had a brass plate on the sole which protected the wood from contact with earth and stones. It also made the club heavier and more able to cut through long or thick grass. The shaft was usually a little stiffer than the driver's and the face was more laid back, so that it was easier to pick the ball up off the ground. The appropriate modern equivalent to a brassie is a 2-wood.

The 'metal woods' which in early 1982 were being sold in professionals' shops almost as quickly as they could be stocked, seem particularly useful to the less supple, and to those lady golfers who have previously played hockey, an important rule of that game being never to lift the stick above the shoulder. The ladies of the nineteenth century had, for corsetry reasons as well as the impropriety of showing an ankle, similar problems. How much earlier could they have started playing properly on the 'long course' if there had been available, instead of a wood with a brass inset, an iron with a wooden inset? These first appeared in 1896. The Mills club had an aluminium framework filled in with wood. By 1900 clubheads which had previously been made of wood were being made from aluminium and were available in matched sets with only the loft varying.

The ladies of the early years of this century found such clubs very useful. Aluminium clubs of all sizes, shapes and weights were easier to play with than cleeks, and a mid-spoon (the equivalent of a 4-wood) sent a ball about the same distance as a cleek. It was intended to take the place of all ordinary approaching irons, but did not require so much practice and needed very little cleaning. However, the ladies observed that the balls went off the irons with a cleaner truer sound than off the aluminium surface. The company which made them did not re-establish its business after World War I.

Tobies, baffies, cleeks and jiggers

Clubs in use at the beginning of the century were not numbered as today's are. They had names which described what they did, or were originally for, and all clubs had their special merits. A short wooden spoon called a 'toby' was an excellent substitute for a cleek, and was similar to the brassie except that the shaft was short and stiff; it was especially serviceable in long grass. Spoons had stiffer shafts and more loft than the grassed (slightly lofted) drivers, and such clubs were referred to as being 'well-spooned', i.e. well-lofted. Spoons were long, middle, short or baffing – terms which referred to the length of the club and the degree of loft. The baffy – which took its name from baffing, meaning to loft it high, or baff it, into the air – had a well-laid-back face; it approximates to today's 5-wood.

Cleeks varied in club-head shape from long thin heads to short broad faces with the weight concentrated at the back of the centre of the head, as it was found that more power could be gained when they were made in that way.

Cleek shafts were longer and thinner than irons and sometimes showed a little whippiness. They were particularly useful in windy weather, as balls flew more truly off the surface, and were less affected by wind than those hit with a wooden club. The word 'cleek' is related to a word which means catch or snatch away with a hook.

Irons were made in many different patterns, ordinary driving and approaching; some had twisted necks, some had shafts commencing in the centre of the club instead of the heel. There were cleeks, driving irons and driving mashies, bulgers, baps, approaching irons, jiggers and mashies. A wooden niblick, and later on an iron niblick, had a very small head and was 'well spooned'; it was useful for getting out of ruts or holes which the longer heads of the spoons could not effect. The word 'mashie' derives from the word 'to mash' – to pound or stamp one's way; niblick comes from 'neb', the nose or beak of a fowl, which was appropriate for a club with a type of beak to it. A jigger was a thin-faced iron club, longer than a putter, used for run-up shots. It had about the same loft as a 6-iron.

Some of the weapons of war the ladies used eighty years ago can be equated, roughly, with those in standard sets today:

People are still working on the production of the perfect club. These date from the nineteenth and early twentieth centuries: (left to right) rutting iron, said to be shank proof; putter; torpedo 'lofter'; Tom Morris putter; niblick; cleek; torpedo driver; and ladies' driver with a brass sole plate

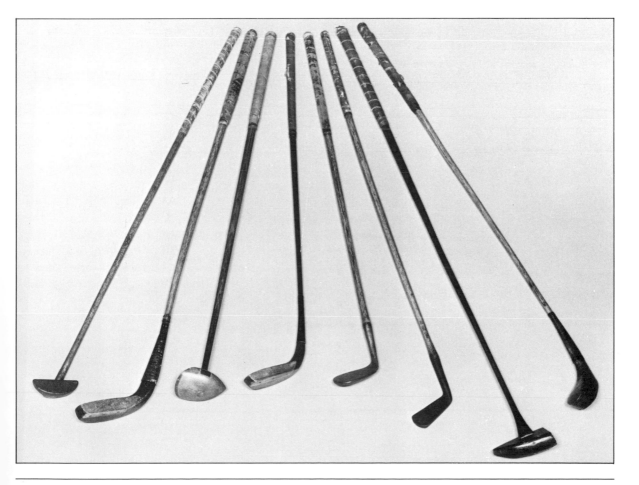

Cecil Leitch possessed extraordinary stamina, as the weight of her clubs confirms. From left to right: her palm-under grip; the ducking right knee betrayed by the fold of her skirt; and the virtual walk-forward which reveals the power she has just expended

Driver	1-wood	**Short spoon**	5-wood	**Mashie niblick**	7-iron
Brassie	2-wood	**Baffy**	5-wood	**Niblick**	9-iron
Long spoon	3-wood	**Mashie**	5-iron		
Mid-spoon	4-wood	**Jigger**	6-iron		

At the turn of the century there were hundreds of variations in the heads, weights, loft and patterns of clubs. But they all had one thing in common – hickory shafts. Hazel, thorncuts, apple, pear and beech were superseded by hickory around the eighteen-fifties, the hickory being imported from Tennessee, USA. A well-seasoned hickory shaft was long lasting, provided that it was kept in an equable temperature and not left for long periods in excessive damp or heat. The shafts were termed 'whippy' because, like horse whips, they were flexible. Light clubs and slender shafts were advised for ladies, and beginners were told not to use clubs which were excessively springy. Ladies were also advised to take good care of their clubs, particularly through protecting wooden clubs in wet weather. Leather faces were considered difficult to handle in wet weather as the ball slipped off the surface, and players who had all their clubs faced with leather were told to rub a little chalk on the face before each stroke as this would stop the ball slipping.

Iron clubs, which were then not made of rustless metal, could be worn away with constant cleaning or disuse. Shafts often broke. Lady champion Gladys Ravenscroft had trouble with them in a match just after World War I. She said: 'Oh, I expect those are the ones I lent the wounded Tommies to play with,' and then picked up another and continued until the same thing

happened again. At that time there were no restrictions on the number of clubs a player could use in competition, although most ladies settled for about seven. One lady champion used twenty; she also had the services of a sturdy caddie.

When steel shafts became available, aided by the world-wide shortage of hickory, the game was again made easier for ladies. Steel shafts permitted harder hitting because they did not suffer from torsion (twisting of the shaft), whereas hickory shafts were considered more exacting as they needed more precision in timing and accuracy. The first patent for a steel shaft was taken out in 1894 by T. Horsburgh, a blacksmith who played off plus four at Baberton, but he could not persuade the professionals to use steel instead of hickory because the longer-lasting steel presented the threat of loss of income. He sold his patent to an American, which is ironic because all the hickory came from the USA and the depletion of the Tennessee hickory forests was one of the reasons for the eventual legalization of steel shafts. The USA legalized steel shafts in 1924, the UK in 1929.

At the height of her prowess, in the nineteen-twenties, the weights and names of Cecil Leitch's clubs were: driver, 20 ounces (exceptionally heavy); brassie, 12 ounces; spoon, 13 ounces; heavy iron, 15 ounces; mashie iron, 14 ounces; heavy mashie, 16 ounces; light mashie, 14 ounces; niblick, 16 ounces; putter, 14 ounces. In the nineteen-thirties, Joyce Wethered's woods had steel shafts, her irons hickory, and her set consisted of driver, brassie, spoon, and irons 1 to 10. Duplicate sets of her clubs could be bought from Fortnum & Mason and were made by Gibson of Fife. Similar sets bearing her name were made in varying lengths and weights – woods from A to D and irons A to E, D and E being suitable for men.

Enid Wilson, who continued her childhood hobby of carpentry through-out most of her life, personally designed a set of clubs in the nineteen-thirties. The set included a wooden cleek for close lies, and irons with the weight concentrated at the back of the blade. Both woods and irons were available in four different weights graded to the height and strength of the user. In 1963 Miss Wilson saw a girl playing with a set she had designed for Gradidges in the nineteen-thirties. 'They were my grandmother's', said the girl. Miss Wilson was quite pleased. The girl had done a nett 59.

Thereafter, many leading lady golfers gave their names to sets of clubs, some of which they designed themselves, including Jessie Anderson Valentine, Jean Donald Anderson, Vivien Saunders and Cathy Panton. There are today just as many designs, weights and length specifications for ladies' clubs as there are for men's, although the discovery of a 1982 advertisement for a huge stock of clubs 'including some for left handers and women' shows that the ladies have no reason to be complacent about the matter. ◯

The
Male Connection

When Juno discovered that Jupiter was in love with Io, Juno's priestess, Jupiter transformed Io into a heifer. She then wandered all over the world, before finally settling in Egypt, where she was restored to human form. This Trojan-Roman myth has a variation. When Io came to St Andrews in the shape of a cow, she was grazing in a field when one of the 'Clubmen' sliced and struck the cow, causing her instant transformation into a woman again. The golfer instantly laid a curse upon any woman who entered 'the sacred place, averring that he had been put off his play by this circumstance. This then became the law, even to this day.'

Andrew Lang published this parody in 1892, by which time ladies had decided to play on full-length courses, not only on putting grounds. Prior to this adventurous decision by the ladies, men had little objection to the ladies amusing themselves with putting games, provided that they did not have to join them. Mr Lang had not always been averse to women golfers, for around 1873 he and a friend played the first mixed foursome, with ladies from the St Andrews Ladies' Golf Club. But he wrote:

> Next morning early I fled, into the wilds of Athole, with a price on my head, while my male opponent (English) put Tweed between himself and mischief. We only retreated just in time; our partners were left to the female tongues of St Andrews. I was much the oldest of the nefarious foursome, and ought to have known better; anyway, my side lost, and I had to pay the stakes. But what an awful example of iniquity did I thoughtlessly set.

By sheer persistence on the part of the female sex, ladies' golf became an accepted sport, and an entertainment worth watching. This report dates from 1912

Both the concept of wickedness and, more particularly, the unpopularity of women's presence on territory which had formerly been the preserve of men, were evident for many years, and some vestiges remain. However, the ladies of the eighteen-nineties ignored, as far as possible, published and spoken antipathy, and steadily persisted with their chosen sport. Many ladies had support from male relatives, but those who did not showed admirable qualities of tenacity, purposefulness, dedication and even temerity. Since then, the gentlemen have shown animosity tempered with occasional admiration, confusion, and high regard. And the men have also

WHEN LOVELY WOMAN STOOPS TO—GOLFING

COMPETITORS IN THE LADIES' CHAMPIONSHIP AT TURNBERRY

MISS GLADYS BASLIN   MRS. HENNING JOHNSON   Rita Martin   MISS GLADYS RAVENSCROFT, AND THE WAY IN WHICH SHE WON THE TOURNAMENT

THE FINAL ROUND OF THE LADIES' CHAMPIONSHIP AT TURNBERRY: MISS RAVENSCROFT PLAYING OUT OF A BUNKER

THE FIVE SISTERS LEITCH—CECIL, CHRIS, EDITH, PEGGY AND MAY, WHO PLAYED IN THE TURNBERRY TOURNAMENT

Miss Neil Fraser and Mr Hilton

Mr B. Darwin. (Driving).

Miss L. Moore Who beat Mr Hilton

Captain C.K. Hutchison

Miss Ravenscroft Who won both her matches

Miss Chambers. A bunker shot.

Miss V. Hezlet.

H.D Gillies who lost to Miss Ravenscroft

disagreed about how ladies should play, if they should play, and with whom and where they should play. This selection from the gentlemen's writings tells the story.

Impossible to putt and languish

In 1887, Sir Walter Simpson, Bart., stated his objections to the presence of ladies on the golf course:

> You can ride at a stone wall for love and the lady, but what part can she take in driving at a bunker? It is natural that Lady Diana should fall in love with Nimrod when she finds him in the plough, stunned, broken-legged, the brush, which he had wrested from the fox as he fell, firm in his lifeless grasp. But if beauty found us prone on the putting green, a 27½ embedded in our gor lock, she might send us home to be trepanned. No! at golf ladies are simply in the road. Riding to hounds and opening five-barred gates, soft nothings may be whispered, but it is impossible at the same moment to putt and cast languishing glances. If the dear one be near you at the tee, she may get her teeth knocked out, and even between the shots, arms dare not steal round waists, lest the party behind should call 'fore'.

With such thoughts uppermost, it is surprising that Sir Walter managed to play golf at all. He continued:

> I have seen a golfing novel indeed; but it was in manuscript, the publishers having rejected it. The scene was St Andrews. He was a soldier, a statesman, and orator, but only a seventh-class golfer. She, being St Andrews born, naturally preferred a rising player. Whichever of two made the best medal score was to have her hand. The soldier employed a lad to kick his adversary's ball into bunkers, to tramp it into mud, to lose it, and he won; but the lady would not give her hand to a score of 130. Six months passed, during which the soldier studied the game morning, noon and night, but to little purpose. Next medal day arrived and he was face to face with the fact that his golf would avail him nothing. He hired and disguised a professional in his own clothes. The ruse was successful; but alas! the professional broke down. The soldier, disguised as a marker, however, cheated, and brought him in with 84. A 3 for the long hole aroused suspicion and led to inquiry. He was found out, dismissed from the club, rejected by the lady (who afterwards made an unhappy marriage with a left-handed player) and sent back in disgrace to his statesmanship and oratory. It was as good a romance as could be made on the subject but very improbable.

Sir Walter was an expert on the theory of the game but not a brilliant player; one contemporary champion stated that a first-class amateur would have to give him about a third. He was also a frustrated fiction writer, for it was he himself who wrote the 'improbable romance'. Jealousy may have

Unfortunately gentlemen versus ladies matches do not figure frequently on many clubs' calendars, and players miss out on a lot of fun. At the Stoke Poges, Buckinghamshire, contest in 1911 the fun was very obviously not missing. The men gave the ladies a half and won by 16 matches to 7

influenced his opinion for it is likely that he knew of Mrs Stirling's *Sedgley Court*, a successful novel with a golfing theme published 30 years earlier.

In 1890, Lord Wellwood analyzed the problems which women golfers presented to men golfers:

> Women's rights: we do not know that a claim for absolute equality has as yet been made; but the ladies are advancing in all pursuits with such strides, or leaps and bounds, whichever expression may be thought the more respectful, that it will, no doubt, not be long before such a claim is formulated. How is it to be met? Now it will not do for the men to take too high ground in this matter. Want of strength is not a sufficient objection, because everyone knows that for clean hitting more than strength is required. And besides, in the mere question of strength and endurance there are some men with whom it would go hard if they were pitted for a summer's day single against some ladies we wot of. Again, it will not do to urge that the game is unfeminine. It is not more unfeminine than tennis and other sports in which ladies nowadays engage freely. No; if any objection is to be entertained, it must be based on most subtle grounds.

Lord Wellwood then discoursed upon the abstract right of women to play golf at all, their right to play 'the long round' with or without male companions, and their right to accompany matches as spectators:

> On the first question our conscience is clear. We have always advocated a liberal extension of the right of golfing to women. Not many years ago their position was most degraded. Bound to accompany their lords and masters to golfing resorts, for the summer months, they had to submit to their fathers, husbands, and brothers playing golf all day and talking shop the whole of the evening, while they themselves were hooted off the links with cries of 'Fore!' if they ventured to appear there. We therefore gladly welcome the establishment of Ladies' Links – a kind of Jews' quarters – which have now been generously provided for them on most of the larger greens. Ladies' links should be laid out on the model, though on a smaller scale, of the 'long round', containing some short putting holes, some longer holes, admitting of a drive or two of seventy or eighty yards, and a few suitable hazards. We venture to suggest seventy or eighty yards as the average limit of a drive advisedly; not because we doubt a lady's power to make a longer drive but because that cannot be done without raising the club above the shoulder. Now we do not presume to distaste, but we must observe that the posture and gestures requisited for a full swing are not particularly graceful when the player is clad in female dress. Most ladies putt well, and all the better because they play boldly for the hole without refining too much about the lie of the ground; and there is no reason why they should not practise and excel in wrist shots with a lofting iron or cleek.

Hints to ladies on where, how and when they should play were occasionally tempered with useful suggestions

The presence of ladies on courses other than putting grounds exercised the gentleman's chivalry:

> The expediency of their playing the long round is more doubtful. If they choose to play at times when the male golfers are feeding or resting, no one can object. But at other times – must we say it – they are in the way; just because gallantry forbids to treat them exactly as men. The tender mercies of the golfer are cruel. He cannot afford to be merciful; because he forbears to drive into the party in front he is promptly driven into from behind. It is a hard lot to follow a party of ladies with a powerful driver behind you if you are troubled with a spark of chivalry or shyness.

But the matter which most worried Lord Wellwood was being watched by ladies:

> It is to their presence as spectators that the most serious objection must be taken. If they could abstain from talking while you are playing and if the shadow of their dresses would not flicker on the putting green while you are holing out, other objections might, perhaps, be waived. But, apart from these positive offences against the unwritten laws of golf, they unintentionally exercise an unsettling and therefore pernicious influence, deny it who can. You wish to play your best before them, and yet you know they will not like you any the better if you best their husband or brother. Again it seems churlish not to speak to them; if you do, the other players will justly abuse you. It may be stated parenthetically that one of the party is sure to speak to them; because (to their praise or blame be it said) few foursomes do not contain one ladies' man.

Hopeless infatuation or brutal indifference

Also in 1890, one Member of Parliament, described as a fairly good golfer, wrote: 'No self-respecting golfer, unless hopelessly infatuated, ever plays with women when male opponents are available. On the contrary he usually regards them as interlopers, frames rules with the express object of keeping them at a distance, and at most tolerates their presence with an absolutely brutal indifference.'

One eminent amateur champion who was also an accomplished golf writer changed his initially strong opinions against women playing golf into equally strong reasons for their participation. On 9 April 1893, when the ladies were discussing their plans to institute a ladies' golf union, he wrote to the future honorary treasurer, Blanche Martin Hulton:

> I have read your letter about the proposed Ladies' Golf Union with much interest. Let me give you the famous advice of 'Mr Punch' . . . *don't*. My reasons? Well, women never have and never can unite to push any scheme to success. They are bound to fall out and quarrel

on the smallest or no provocation; they are built that way. They will
never go through *one* Ladies' Championship with credit. Tears will
bedew, if wigs do not bestrew, the green. Constitutionally and
physically women are unfitted for golf. They will never last through
two rounds of a long course in a day. Nor can they ever hope to defy
the wind and weather encountered on our best links even in spring
and summer. Temperamentally the strain will be too great for them.
The first Ladies' Championship will be the last, unless I and others
are greatly mistaken. The Ladies Golf Union seems scarcely
worthwhile.

The writer was, according to Cecil Leitch, Horace Hutchinson, and he had
just published '*Miseries of Golf*', one of which included being asked by his
opponent, just as he was starting, if he had any objection to his wife and
sister-in-law walking round with him, as he wished to introduce them to the
game. However, six years later, Mr Hutchinson criticized:

. . . those golfers of the Tory school who object on principle to women
on the links. Their objection, according to their lights, is a perfectly
sound one. It is their lights that lead them astray. These lights seem to
show the woman on the links as a talkative, irresponsible person,
without real knowledge of the game or real interest in it, treating the
solemn matter as if it were a mere affair of a game of croquet at a garden
party. This may have been the light in which women on the links really
appeared in the generation of the Tory golfers; but that generation is
passing away, and being succeeded by another in which woman yields
nothing in golfing interest and knowledge to the most crusted golfer of
the other sex. Her enthusiasm even passes his; she is as keen and alert
in regard to every point of the game as any male golfer ever can be, and
in point of execution she is often quite the equal of some of those who
would have her removed from the green. As for talking or moving 'on
the stroke', such an enormity is quite unthinkable for her. In fine, she is
capable of being as good a golfer in the most complete sense of the
phrase, as any man; she has no need for suffrance, she has only to
claim her right to play on the links with the best. It is only to open the
Tory eye to the dawn of the new light that [I] gave this justification . . .
certainly not that the golfing ladies' cause, through any weakness of its
own, requires it.

In the same year, 1899, Mr Hutchinson was also happy to maintain that
golf contained no conditions that made it essentially unsuited for ladies'
playing, and that it could be played as gracefully and as ungracefully by men
as by women. He considered that ladies should play over the long course at
St Andrews because the one specially designed for them there was too short
for the needs of the 'modern' feminine golfer. This course, the Jubilee or
Third Course, was then patronized by those lady golfers who wanted
something more strenuous in the way of a game than that supplied by the

Ladies' Putting Courses. It was formally opened by Mrs McGregor, wife of the St Andrews Provost, on the day on which Queen Victoria's Diamond Jubilee was celebrated in that burgh, and originally consisted of 12 holes. In 1912 it was extended to 18 holes and in 1939 Willie Auchterlonie began its reconstruction, which was finished seven years later.

Congestion on the courses

Despite his advocacy of this course, Mr Hutchinson suggested that elsewhere there were excellent ladies' links, suited to their modest length of driving, and that they should restrict their activities to them and not attempt to play on the longer links of men, where carrying bunkers was beyond them. He had another reason for this qualification. Writing about the incursion of ladies on men's links, he said that it intensified problems of congestion.

> No doubt [men] felt that it was a hard and discourteous thing to deny the ladies equal rights even over private courses. Obviously, on the public courses they had the equal right and they were not shy of claiming it. On the private courses we used to hear at first: 'It's absurd, these ladies not sticking to their own course; they can't drive far enough to be able to appreciate the long course.' But then it very soon became evident that they could drive further and play better than a large number of the male members of the Club, which rather knocked the bottom out of the argument. As a rule, some compromise was effected, the ladies being restricted to certain hours – after all, the men were generally workers, so that they had the more claim to have the course at their disposal in their hours of leisure.

As an example, Mr Hutchinson mentioned one club where one afternoon a week was reserved for ladies, and those whose handicap was four or under could play at any time and on equal terms with the men. This was judged a satisfactory system for it kept off the links

> the inefficient lady players who would be apt to block the green and whose right place is their own short course, while it freely admits those who are capable of appreciating the blessing of the long course and are quite as good golfers as the average of the men who they will meet thereon. As time goes on it appears as if we should be fortunate if the ladies do not take exclusive possession of the links, and only allow us men upon them at the hours which are the least convenient.

J.H. Taylor, who won the Open five times, advised longer courses for ladies. In 1902 he suggested that, despite the difference in strength and stamina, the courses set apart for the use of ladies should be longer and that the hazards should be made more difficult. As the Ladies' Championship was decided over a course that had been laid out for men, Mr Taylor thought that it was unfair to any competitor accustomed to a short course to be faced

with the task of playing in the principal event of the year upon a long one. He thought that the best women golfers were those who had learnt to play the game on men's courses: they were freer in style, 'more at their ease with the absence of anything cramped in their play'.

Mr Taylor also considered that the real reason

'The Proper Position for a Drive': jokes and cartoons concerning the sexes playing golf together abound

> of the ladies taking up the game with so much keenness must be attributed to the fact that their husbands and brothers were playing day by day and naturally they did not wish to be left completely out in the cold. In this decided favouritism for golf, the ladies have displayed excellent judgement. It is not exercise of a too violent description, it is far superior to cycling and it is not an expensive recreation. While in the act of playing every muscle of the body is brought into use and should be under control.

He was full of praise for ladies' putting abilities, and admired their natural delicacy of touch, which enabled them to score over the majority of their male competitors. But he did not think much of their driving. 'Here it is that wrist play comes into operation and the absence of this power in ladies mediates against full and complete success.' Another fault was

> the very decided tendency for a woman to overswing. They are far too apt to think that a long swing is an absolute to secure a long drive. But here again they are wrong, for in so playing a stroke they simply, by excess of effort, defeat their object. As a matter of fact, a short, concentrated swing is all that is required in order to apply the fullest possible power to the greatest advantage.

Concerning the weight of clubs, he considered that women were most prone to make mistakes.

> She should never attempt to play with too heavy a driver or other club, for it is not true that a heavy club equals distance advantage. When swinging a club, a considerable expenditure of physical force is rendered necessary, the result being that instead of being able to play freely and at her ease, she evolves an ugly and a laboured style and the damage done irreparably it is impossible to surmise. The task of controlling her club is too great, and once perfect control is lost, the prospect of success is gone.

But Harry Vardon, who won the Open six times, considered, in 1907, that ladies used weapons that were far too light for them. He wrote:

> A man only uses a club of a certain weight because experience has proved that it is the best one and most effectual for its purpose, and usually he has a very great reserve of strength which could be employed with heavier clubs if necessary. There is no reason why

ladies should not employ clubs of good average weight instead of featherweights. By doing so they would spare themselves a great amount of exertion, and they would certainly get better results, for it is always much more difficult to get good results with a light club than with one of medium weight. With the featherweight the swing is very liable to get out of gear. It is cut short and is apt to wander out of its proper direction. There is, in fact, no such control over the club as there is when one can feel the weight of the head at the end of the shaft. A lady may require clubs a trifle shorter in the shafts, but this is the only difference which need exist, and it is not of itself sufficient to make any perceptible difference in weight.

Mr Vardon was of the opinion that the standard of ladies' golf in the UK was improving every season and that the best of gentlemen golfers would need to give at least a third [six strokes] to achieve an equal game. He also thought that they were excellent pupils, taking more notice than men of hints given them and retaining parts of the lessons longer. 'They are painstaking,' he said, 'and if she begins to play early enough in her life, adopts sensible methods, and is possessed of an average amount of athleticism, I can see no reason why any lady should not become a very fair golfer.' He advised ladies to 'learn properly, and practise much; and – well, yes, do the rest like a man, and not as if there was a special woman's way.'

Golf is the same for ladies as for men

James Braid, the first player to win the Open five times and the first man to write an instructional book on golf for women, nearly agreed about the 'special woman's way'. 'Golf may be, and is, the same game for ladies as for men,' he said in 1908. 'But the physical difference between them necessitates some variation in system, at the same time that they induce others which have to be guarded against.' But he did not quite agree with Mr Vardon about the weight of ladies' clubs, and considered that they needed lighter clubs than men, 'but not so much lighter as they may think', and recommended the weights of a lady's driver and brassie as 11½ and 12½ ounces. He thought that ladies were excellent pupils, but qualified this by saying that there was a shorter limit to the skill that they may attain than there is in the case of the average man golfer; but he requalified this with the statement: 'There is no reason why any healthy lady should not play a sound game of golf.'

Mr Braid was also a golf course architect and had views on ladies' tees.

In placing them, they should always be put so far forward that the bunkers that are intended to catch the men's second shots are also in good place for the second shots of the ladies. This is of more importance than getting the hazard right for both tee shots and seconds when they have been laid out for the men's game; therefore, having to make a choice, devote chief attention to the test of the second shot, and put the tee so far forward that this will be done.

Edward Ray, winner of the US Open Championship in 1920 and the Open in 1912, firmly believed 'that the idea that heavy clubs result in long drives being obtained is the reason why so many ladies make little progress. The weight of their clubs,' he declared in 1912, 'should be determined by their power to swing them; it follows therefore that if the clubs are on the heavy side, the user is at their mercy, for they have no control whatever.' He advised lady golfers to rely on accuracy, to a large extent, to make up for physical shortcomings, and if they obtained this they would be surprised what a decent length of stroke would follow. He also advocated that ladies should not use stiff-shafted clubs, as these needed strong wrists to be wielded successfully, and he thought that a little suppleness in the shaft undoubtedly assisted the player.

Mr Ray had some advice about making tees, and was sensibly cost-conscious: 'When making a tee bear in mind that, if on an inland course, sand costs money. To go on your way leaving a pyramid behind you is to draw attention to your lack of skill; there is no necessity to build up a high tee, for you should learn to play the stroke from as small a tee as possible. By doing so, playing through the green will not appear such a hopeless task.' But Mr Hutchinson did not quite agree. Ladies, he said: 'seem to have a lofty minded idea that there is something not quite right about putting the ball on a high tee – that it is rather on a par with potting the

This boy-versus-girl contest at Birmingham in 1932 produced tough combat. Here Wanda Morgan is bunkered in her match with Francis McGloin, runner-up in the 1931 boys' championship

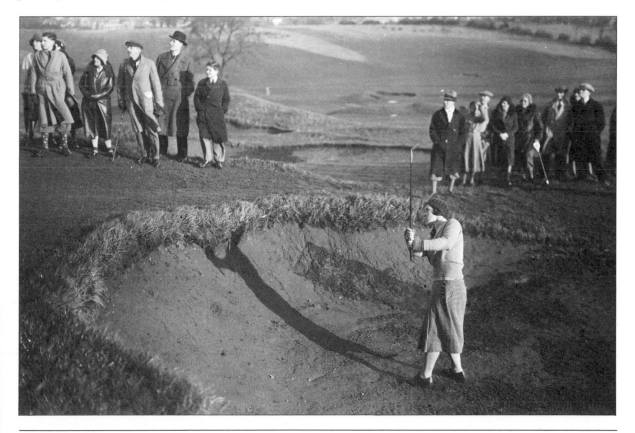

white at billiards.' Writing in 1919, he said 'It is splendid of them to have such fine and noble ideals but it would be to their practical advantage to forget them now and then.' He also advised ladies to tee the ball much higher going down wind for that way they would find it easier to 'give it that hoist into the air which is essential for its getting advantage of the favour of the breeze'.

These two gentlemen did not even agree about ladies' attitudes to the game. Mr Hutchinson gave an optimistic picture:

> She brings to bear upon it an even more than masculine solemnity. Her earnestness is grim and terrible; there is no modern player of the male sex who would fulfil more perfectly all the requirements of the old time golf. Woman, in fact, has justified her claim to equality with men on the links, and the sooner he can be brought to understand it the better for the comfort of the sexes.

But Edward Ray was

> convinced that in ladies' golf despondency is rife. That the game is a difficult one goes without saying. Enthusiasm is half the battle and although the road is a weary one, a little of this will generally assist you in your task. The person who lacks ambition is not one likely to distinguish herself at any sport, for, without it, she plays in a lackadaisical manner. If the tee-shots are topped she reflects that it is all in the game. She uses the expressions: 'It might have been worse' or 'I thought so'. This may be a philosophical ways of taking things, but not one calculated to eradicate the fault.

The healthy game that knits the frame

By the beginning of World War I, golfing ladies had attracted some admiration for their enthusiasm for the game, their ability to compete among themselves, and their attempts to play against the gentlemen. In 1906, Ronald Ross had ended a long poem entitled 'Golf' with this verse:

> When lovely woman deigns to grace
> The green, our game to share,
> With welcome meet we love to greet
> Her gentle presence there.
> Long may she play, the while she shirks
> No wife or maiden's duty,
> The healthy game that knits her frame
> And tints her cheek with beauty.

And when Dorothy Campbell beat Florence Hezlet in the final of the Ladies' Championship at Royal Birkdale in 1909, the extraordinary excitement of the event prompted these lively verses from George Harold in a poem which he entitled 'The Final':

Shrieking stewards, rushing madly
Over all the course,
In excitement tripping gladly
Into sand or gorse,
Mighty crowds, the bunkers swarming,
Rushing on ahead,
While the green-men, loudly storming,
Scorching language spread.

Engulf'd and swallowed in the turmoil
'Cause of this array,
While the rushing crowd their clothes soil
Coolly do they play –
Two fair ladies bravely striving,
Each with mighty heart:
Now they're putting! Now they're driving!
With consummate art.

Two fair ladies, dainty, graceful –
Nervous? – not at all;
Of the thronging crowd unmindful,
Philosophical;
Though a fate, unkind and cruel,
Hang o'er all they do,
Yet how well they take their 'gruel'
'Sportsmen' through and through.

And the difficulties of competing with men were considered by George Batchelor, after a team of men had defeated a team of women, even though the ladies received a half:

Try no more, ladies, try no more;
Despite your best endeavour,
You must confess that, by the score,
Men are (by half) too clever.
But sigh not so, my fairest foe,
In future let us rather go
In *partnership* together.

As well as orientating themselves within, or ignoring, the various attitudes of the men and their conflicting advice, generations of women golfers have had to endure primitive club facilities and prohibitions on the times they were permitted to play, and those facilities and prohibitions were ones considered suitable by male club members. In the eighteen-nineties, old drafty sheds were frequently the only places provided for changing and socializing. In 1900, at a golf club in Hertfordshire, the original clubhouse was extended at a cost of £500, but when a small ladies' clubhouse was

erected in the following year the expenditure was £60. The membership consisted of 200 gentlemen and fifty ladies. Now £60 is not even one-quarter of £500, which would at least have been fair, and the ladies were not consulted. At the same club, in 1905, the rotation of the holes was changed and a rule was introduced which said that ladies must invite men to play through at all times and not drive from the first tee until all the men had started. Writing about this rule in the nineteen-seventies, the male author added: 'I cannot help thinking that even in these days such a rule might gain a good deal of support in some clubs.'

From 1902 onwards, a golf club in Kent displayed a notice which read: 'Women are admitted to play on the course only on suffrance and must at all times give way to members.' Players from far away and not so far away places with strange sounding and not so strange sounding names visited the club just to see that notice, which in 1927 was amended to: 'The Committee wish to draw the attention of members again to a request that ladies be not introduced to play when the green is crowded. It should be remembered that ladies play only by courtesy. And it ought to be understood that when they do play they must at all times give way to members.' There may be some small difference between the meaning of the two notices but it takes an acute brain to find it. The same club had for years a prominent notice which stated: 'Women playing golf in trousers must take them off before entering the clubhouse.' In the early nineteen-fifties the club stated that there was 'no bar to women playing', and a 1982 phone call elicited the information that 'there are no restrictions on women playing if accompanied by a member.' This in itself, of course, is an almost insuperable restriction, and there are a great many private clubs which today have similar restrictions.

Dogs and women are not allowed in

In 1926 at a Surrey club, a father took his daughter around as he played, just for the walk as it was a fine day. Members reacted with horror. Around the same time, at another club, an attendant refused admission to ladies on the club premises on the grounds that 'dogs and women are not allowed in'. Actually, dogs today sometimes warrant better treatment than women. Some clubs permit male members to take their dogs into the clubhouse with them but not their wives, nor playing nor non-playing female companions. Golfinia will one day ensure that all members of committees who enforce such rules lose all their matches by a 'dog licence' – 7 and 6 (the cost of a licence in pre-decimal coinage).

In a 1938 guide to golf courses of the 250 listed, 104 had restrictions varying from 'Women are not permitted to play at the weekends', 'Women are not permitted to play on Saturdays, Sundays or Holidays' to 'Women are not permitted to play'. Fifteen public courses were listed, and even at one of these there was the restriction 'On Saturdays and Holidays women are not permitted to start before 3 p.m. and they must invite men players through at all times.' Today's Equal Opportunities Commission, set up in the nineteen-seventies, could have monitored the latter, as it was a public course, but it

cannot do anything about private courses. In a 1982 letter to a popular golfing magazine, which allotted four pages out of its total 108 pages to ladies'/women's golf, the male writer inserted the statement: 'We don't have ladies' tees at Muirfield as we don't hold with sex discrimination.' Muirfield has no lady members.

After World War II, club restrictions on women members and women golfers worried leading players and writers. One golf magazine warned: 'We know there is a great prejudice against women in some club houses, but we do not agree with it . . . golf clubs who want to keep women at the door are just burying their heads in the sand, and if they don't have a good stocktaking before long their whole body will be buried and a cross marked RIP above it to mark the resting place of a once-famous club.' Restrictions also annoyed the industrialist Lord Brabazon of Tara, to such an extent that he wrote in 1952:

> I believe the trouble is that so many golf clubs will not cater for the girls – for the women, and after all if you are a young married man and you want to play golf it is not a very pleasant thing to go down to some golf club where women are looked upon as almost a weed or an excrescence which is not required anywhere near the place. Many clubs have this outlook on life, and if women are not going to be welcome at golf clubs they are not going to allow their men to go there. And you've got to remember this, that the arbiter in the home as to how a man spends his leisure is, very largely, the woman and if she is not going to be made welcome at a golf club and if she is not going to be allowed to play at a golf club or if there is not going to be accommodation for them to eat and be merry and social she is not going to allow her young man there. It is high time that many of the old people in charge of some of the old golf clubs realized that the club has got to be a social thing with women there, so that everybody can find amusement. If you take that attitude, then you will find that many people will come. Even if the women cannot play, so long as they are welcome to be there to lunch and to sit about or to take part in some form of occupation – even a very tiny women's course, or putting green or tennis courts or something to amuse them – they will go there, and once you can get a lot of people then you are on the way to prosperity for your club. But if you look upon the whole thing as something which is only for men as it was twenty years ago, then your club is as good as dead.

They make the club a happy club

Gary Player stated in the nineteen-sixties: 'I feel women golfers deserve to play on a course just as much as any man does. I, for one, wouldn't want to belong to a club that didn't allow women. They make the club a happy club. If it wasn't for the women, we wouldn't have many parties at most of our clubs. They also support the pro shop.' Many club secretaries agree that if it were not for the women's support their clubs would not be in profit. Some

men argue that the backbone of men's golf is the weekend golfer, and that women's golf has no such similar body, because the weekend is a busier time for the housewife than mid-week. But, leaving aside the fact that the restrictions are not only in force at weekends, which came first, the restrictions for women or the busier time? Most clubs today have lower subscription rates for ladies than for men – but the ladies are not offered a choice about the matter.

When the Ladies' British Open Amateur Golf Championship was played on the Old Course at St Andrews in 1975, and competitors and officials were given the courtesy of the clubhouse, members resigned in protest. However, early the next year a mixed buffet evening held in the clubhouse was so popular that it was decided to hold more. It seems that the R and A were regressing. In 1954 on the occasion of the 200th birthday of the club, ladies had drunk champagne in the clubhouse and it was considered that a long-standing male bastion had been breached. This was not progress. An entry in the club's minute book for 9 September 1810, well over a hundred years before, states:

> It has been presented to the Meeting that the Rooms in the Golfer's Hall, hitherto used as a Supper room at the Ball, is now occupied as the Store for the local Militia. The Meeting request their Society respectfully to apply to Colonel Anstruther stating the Inconvenience to which the Ladies Honouring the Golfers with their Company must be subjected from the want of it – that Mr Patulla will give accommodation for the Stores in his loft in the immediate neighbourhood. And therefore to express hope that the Colonel will accommodate the Golfers on that evening.

Apart from their reverence for the 'sacred place', men have been bewildered about their female counterparts playing golf for a living. When women were allowed to join the Professional Golfers' Association on the same basis as men, in 1962 – apart from the secretary of the R and A confirming that women members of the association would not be allowed in the clubhouse – some rather supercilious statements were made. One magazine was typically grudging in its analysis: 'Possibly there could be some kind of future for good women golfers becoming assistants at golf clubs. Obviously they would be very good in the shop and we see no reason why they should not be able to teach. They might be particularly good at teaching golfers of their own sex.'

And the following statements were published in the same journal under the same editor within a few weeks of each other:

> The idea of women professionals has never been popular. She should be strongly discouraged, not because they are not capable but because many men are having quite a job making a living out of the game. Women have demonstrated their ability of competing with men, but we feel that professional golf is not one of these professions.

In all professions, careers and callings, on all legal, legislative and government bodies (with of course the exception of the Upper House) the gentle sex are now on equal footing with the gentlemen. Especially is this so in the case of sport. Golf is a fine example. With well run councils and well organized tournaments, the ladies have brought lustre and renown to the game. They have brought colour to golf. Ladies, we salute you.

However, some first-class players and top writers have not suffered crises of identity with regard to lady golfers. Henry Cotton has followed women's golf all his life. 'Many top ladies,' he said, 'have been my pupils and I have enjoyed playing with them and watching the best of them in action in competitions.' Mr Cotton even went to the length of stuffing balloons up his

Mixed foursomes at Worplesdon is one of the major highlights of the British golfing calendar. Here the 1948 winners, Wanda Morgan and Eustace Storey (left), are seen with Lady Heathcoat Amory (Joyce Wethered) and her husband, whom they beat in the 36-hole final

sweater to simulate women's bosoms to see how they got in the way. When playing in a tournament in 1946, he discovered that ladies, including his wife, were not allowed to use the clubhouse. So he refused to use it himself and, as he won, arrangements had to be made for the trophy presentation ceremony to take place outdoors.

Archie Compston thought that women had plenty of courage but not enough power, and criticized their artistic sense. He wrote in the 1930s:

> Golf is considered the most artistic game in the world. You would imagine that women would have an artistic sense, especially on the putting green. But on the golf course they seem to be absolutely devoid of it . . . The great failing with women golfers is lack of length from the tee and with the long irons. Lack of length is the principal reason why women golfers will never be able to play on level terms with men. And lack of length is due to lack of power in the wrists and fingers. Ladies start with a big disadvantage – they have not the physical strength. For them it has to be a game of rhythm combined with activity. And the trouble lies in blending this activity into the swing.

He advised swinging the club for five minutes a day without a ball, and advocated a dumb-bell routine to cultivate strength in the fingers and wrists. He considered that ladies were 'scared stiff' of developing muscles. 'Still, they have got to if they want to play golf well.'

As well as asserting, in 1947, that 'Pretty women behind your eye are better than bombs,' golf historian and writer Bernard Darwin wrote:

> Not only have ladies become relatively long drivers; they are also good all round wooden club players, accurate and trustworthy. They have to play many more brassey shots than men do, and that is, I am inclined to think, the strongest part of their game. Save in a few cases it is certainly better than their iron play, for which as a rule they lack something of the required 'punch'. They are essentially swingers rather than hitters and this is a virtue, but a virtue subject to some inherent weakness. It would be natural to assume that on the green, where strength is of no importance, and delicacy of touch a valuable gift, the ladies are man's equals if not superiors, but experience shows this assumption to be fallacious.

Mr Darwin was steadfast in his allegiance to women golfers:

> Indeed if some magician would summon up for me from the past just one of all the golf matches I have watched and allow it to be played over for me again like a gramophone record, I *think* I would choose the 37th at Troon [final of the Ladies' Championship (1925) between Cecil Leitch and Joyce Wethered]. It might perhaps be too agonizing, I might fall down dead towards the end, but I would risk it.

He also admired the LGU's work in developing their handicapping system:

> The ladies did exhibit a noble endurance. They, and Miss Pearson in particular, likewise exhibited a noble enthusiasm for a uniform system of handicapping. They worked it out in minute detail and now after many years the men's unions have begun, faint and perspiring, to imitate them. Granted that such a system is wanted, then the LGU is a wonderful achievement and if the ladies like it, that is all that matters and all is for the best in the best possible of worlds.

A smaller edition of the men's game

Tommy Armour, US and British Open winner, who reckoned that 90 per cent of all golfers score in the 90s, preferred teaching ladies. In 1954 he said:

> Some of the most satisfactory, most quickly developing pupils I've taught are those of the gentler sex. What often enables them to advance possibly a little faster than men is that seldom do they want to do the teaching. There are a number of men who are so full of golf theories, tips and hunches, they seem to have a burning desire to teach me instead of learning . . . Women are usually more inclined to accept and respond to instruction than men are.

He considered that basically there is no difference between men's and women's golf, women's golf being 'simply a smaller edition of the men's game'. But he stated that 'golf is comparative and on that basis the women can boast that the average of their scoring has improved at a more rapid rate than men's scoring'. He also suspected that the crowded golf courses of the day 'somewhat delay progress in women's scoring by not encouraging practice opportunities'.

In 1964 Gary Player wrote: 'Few things delight men more than to see a woman who is serious about her game stand on the tee and bang away at a drive with everything she's got.' He considered that women have a special advantage over men when it came to the short game, having a much more sensitive touch around the green. He agreed that lack of distance was a woman's big problem in golf and did not advocate the use of men's clubs, as they only minimized the yardage a woman would achieve off the tee; he advised whippy-shafted ones. He wrote: 'It is true that women lack distance on golf shots largely because they are not as strong as men. However, they do have distance-producing advantage over men golfers that should be incorporated into their swings. These advantages are suppleness, especially in the torso, and rhythm. They allow the woman golfer to take a smooth and full backswing with maximum turning of the hips.'

Mr Player also reckoned that women golfers were often the victims of too much advice, especially from male players. 'Unless your husband is a low-handicap player, I would take his advice with a grain of salt. Your pro is the person to see if you want first-hand golf instruction.'

Henry Longhurst said:

Ladies' golf has always suffered from lack of funds but the ladies have frequently proved themselves to be good fund raisers – both for their own sport and for charity. Here in the grounds of the Royal Hospital, Chelsea, in 1930, Diana Fishwick intrigues two Chelsea pensioners at a garden party in aid of the Actors' Orphanage

Men's amateur golf, for some reason which perhaps only sociologists could answer, seems to be losing its public appeal. Anyway, most of the 'news' in golf now [1968] concerns not amateurs – and this applies all over the world – but professionals and, in particular, how much money they win. This to the true lover of golf soon becomes monotonous, and it was against this background that I found myself recapturing all the old time excitement when watching the Curtis Cup match at Porthcawl. The answer is that 'given a reasonable course' the best of the women play just as well as the men, and are a good deal more decorative.

What scratch man, for instance, would have backed himself to beat Mrs Spearman or Miss Gunderson, who halved their match in 71, or to have stayed level last week with Miss Sorenson, the new Champion, and Miss White, who each went out at Prince's in 31. These girls play at a lively speed and in the best possible spirit, and if you want to watch golf at its best, go and see the Curtis Cup match.

And Pat Ward-Thomas, after watching a match between Marley Spearman and Angela Ward Bonallack, said the match had every element of greatness. 'As a championship match it was also incomparable . . . The prospect of watching a professional event this week [1964] is akin to that of being offered flat beer after a precious vintage wine.'

Another Ray, Ted, the comedian who took his stage name from the champion and at his best played off 7, advised people not to be patronizing to the ladies. In 1972 he said he had played with some wonderful women 'so lovely to watch, with perfect swings'. Once when playing at North Foreland he saw an attractive young girl on the practice ground and remarked to her: 'That's a very nice little swing, my dear. Carry on like that and you will become a good player.' 'Thank you, sir,' said Angela Ward Bonallack.

Alas, not all contemporary writers are up-to-date and sensible about women golfers. Michael Williams's report of the all-women finals of the Sunningdale Open Foursomes in 1982 had the word 'comedy' in the title, referred to a 'descent to Curtis Cup level', and was scornful of the fact that the women winners took three out of a bunker; the third went in. Mr Williams's sneer, published in 1982, is as anachronistic as Mr Lang's parody, published in 1892.

However, the man who really understood what golf means to women was G.K. Chesterton:

> Miss Meekins' drive tore eastward, like a bolt from an arbalest, trailing with it a memory of impact and the hallucination of a hack. The ball had been struck just where its invisible energy pulsated far down in its suppressed subconscious, and now it carried the triumph of crisis across the course. Drives there had been before, drives that had ended in a million lies, good, bad, indifferent, and circumstantial. Drives that had dropped on a million hummocks where the bright short grass lay all one way like brushed hair; on the edge of holes to refresh her like a bun and milk, or in them to depress her like an attack of indigestion. But this drive – ah!
>
> There was in it something more inspired and authoritative even than the best of the drives that were but its primitive precursors. It struck the earth not in the innermost declivity of the turf-embowered bunker, there to ricochet in the sand like a sterile shrapnel in the cold intoxication of the sea, but where it was hidden in an impenetrable forest of gorse and wrapped in the roaring dark.
>
> The destiny of a drive may depend on how destiny itself is driven, or words to that effect. Yet this is certain. People talk of the pathos and failure of plain women. But it is a more terrible thing that a beautiful woman may succeed in everything but golf.　◯

Commanders of the Course

L ady Margaret Scott, later Lady Hamilton Russell, was the first lady champion. She won the inaugural Open Amateur in 1893 and the following two. Only two other players have managed this in the championship's history – Cecil Leitch and Enid Wilson. After Lady Margaret's first win, her father, Lord Eldon, made the winner's speech for her, and after her third win he tried to present the LGU with a replica of the cup and to retain the original for his daughter. The LGU retained the cup and Lord Eldon had a replica made for his daughter.

Her style of play was described as 'dashing, fearless, fascinating', and her great advantage was the power of her second shot, particularly when faced

---

The following abbreviations have been used in this chapter:

Commonwealth Tournament	Commonwealth
European Ladies' Amateur Team Championship	European
Femenino de Golf	Femenino
Vagliano Trophy	Vagliano since 1959, against France before then
Women's World Amateur Team Championship for the Espirito Santo Trophy	Espirito
Ladies' British Open Amateur Championship	Open Amateur
Ladies' British Open Amateur Stroke Play Championship	Open Amateur Stroke Play
Ladies' British Open Championship	Open
Girls' British Open Amateur Championship	Girls'
English Ladies' Close Amateur Championship	English
English Girls' Close Championship	English Girls'
Irish Ladies' Close Amateur Championship	Irish
Irish Girls' Close Championship	Irish Girls'
Scottish Ladies' Close Amateur Championship	Scottish
Scottish Girls' Close Amateur Championship	Scottish Girls' Close
Welsh Ladies' Close Championship	Welsh
Welsh Open Amateur 54-hole Stroke Play	Welsh Stroke Play
Welsh Girls' Close Amateur Championship	Welsh Girls

Four semi-finalists at the Ladies' British Open Amateur Championship at Troon in 1904: Charlotte Dod, Dorothy Campbell, May Hezlet and Miss M.A. Graham

---

with unsympathetic brassie lies. She won with ease and seemed to be in a different league from her contemporaries, having played since childhood with her brothers, who also made their marks as first-class players.

In 1892 she won a championship at the Cheltenham club in which all the other players were men, and the next year, after her first championship win, she did a record 80 for the 18 holes; she also made the best scratch score of 70 – at that time the record – at Bath. When competing, she always wore a carnation for luck, and this was at the time considered somewhat frivolous. During the three championships in 1893, 1894 and 1895, Miss M.E. Phillips and Mrs Ryder Richardson were the only two of her opponents who obliged her to play the last 2 holes in order to win a match. As Lady Hamilton Russell, she won the Swiss Ladies' on three consecutive occasions (b.1875, d.1938).

Runner-up in the inaugural Open Amateur was Issette Pearson, later Miller, who was also runner-up the following year. She was one of the leaders of the government and organization of the game for thirty years, and without her determination and hard work it is doubtful that ladies' golf would have been organized so well and so early, bearing in mind that, in the eighteen-nineties, women rarely had the opportunity or the wish to unite for concerted effort. Miss Pearson was, in her day, the only lady who had always played from scratch. She also achieved five holes in one. She suffered from nervousness when playing and would be put off her game completely if faced with an opponent who could not take a beating cheerfully. One of her closest friends, Mabel Stringer, wrote that she had 'great autocracy' (d.1941).

First woman to write on golf as a profession

Miss Stringer herself was, in her own words, 'the first woman to write on golf *as a profession*', a calling to which she applied herself with the greatest dedication for many years after her first excursion into it in 1906. She also beat the future lady champion Maud Titterton Gibb when that lady was the only Scot to enter the Open Amateur in 1898, a feat which vexed Agnes Grainger, instigator of the SLGA. Miss Stringer 'took pars', was on the LGU council for twenty years, was instrumental in coping with the LGU's coyness about accepting trophies, helped to set up the Girls' Championship and pioneered various associations. Greatly devoted to her friend, Issette, she admired and strongly supported her efforts with regard to the organization of the LGU and the development of the handicap system, and she attempted to write a history of the LGU, intending to devote a chapter to each year of its history, but did not complete it. She published *Golfing Reminiscences* in 1924. When she 'officially retired' in 1924, her friends presented her with a collection amounting to £166 6s 6d (£166.32½p) and she used the money to install much-welcomed electric light in her simple little cottage home in Kent (b.1868, d.1959).

Semi-finalist in the first Open Amateur was A.M. Starkie Bence, who in 1898 held course records at Littlestone, 73, Brighton and Hove, 73 (twice), Eastbourne Old Course, 70 (twice), and Folkestone, 67 (old 13-hole course).

She won eighty-eight prizes between 1892 and 1898. She was also one of the first LGU handicap managers and maintained that her favourite part of the game was niblick play in sand bunkers.

The next lady champion was Amy Bennet Pascoe who won in 1896 and was prominent in county golf thereafter, being the first captain of Surrey. Two years after winning the championship she held records at Woking, 96, and Wimbledon, 73, and set records at Ranelagh, 78, Great Yarmouth, 86, Bushey, 88, and Surbiton, 88.

Miss Pascoe was a well-known, and plain-writing, chronicler of the contemporary ladies' golfing scene, and she described herself as 'not a bad golfer, though on account of her usual unsteadiness she is considered weaker than she is. Very good off the tee, and when once on the green; but the poorness of her iron play places her ball in a bunker and her game within easy range of the arrows of criticism.' She practised constantly, and her concentration on the game left her indifferent to everything including her appearance. Indeed for the final match of the Open Amateur, colleagues assisted her toilette, so that she would not disgrace them with an unsuitable appearance. She was a good putter, and a brave and determined fighter, but essentially a 'made' player, without the 'dash and power of the "fine insolent carelessness" of those who had played from early girlhood'.

In 1897, two members of the same family battled out the final of the Open Amateur, the first time this had occurred. Edith Orr won, beating her sister. During the championship, the sisters' father was horrified at the bets that were being made and the girls did not appear on the major championship scene again. There were three Orr sisters, all golfers, and they came from North Berwick. As women were allowed on the course there only before 9 a.m. or after 5.30 p.m., they upped early and were always ahead, never holding anyone up. Of Edith Orr a contemporary wrote: 'Her game has no weak point, but is critic proof. The Scotch-bred game of the latest lady champion is *sans peur* and *sans reproche*. She has complete command over all her clubs, but her approach play is extraordinarily accurate, the ball invariably being well up, and once on the putting green, she appears able to hole out in one from almost all parts of it.'

No one need despair of playing golf

Soon after the Orr sisters' triumph and departure, a seventeen-year-old became lady champion. Mary Linzee Hezlet, later Ross, won the Open Amateur in 1899, 1902, and 1907. She also won the Irish in 1899, 1904, 1905, 1906 and 1908, thus being only one below Joyce Wethered's all-time British championship record. The third time she won the Open Amateur, she and her sister Florence contested the final, the second set of sisters to do so. By winning the championship for the first time one week after her seventeenth birthday, she set a record as the youngest winner of a major British championship, a record which stood until 1981 when Janet Soulsby won the Open Amateur Stroke Play at the age of 16.

Born in Gibraltar, 'May' Hazlet started playing at the age of nine, and won her first competition at the age of eleven, playing with a driver, a cleek, a

mashie and a putter. Later on, her clubs were specially made for her by Gibson of Westward Ho! and Auchterlonie of St Andrews. At her best she played off plus 7. She gave up competitive golf upon her marriage in 1909. As well as writing many articles on golf and other matters for newspapers and magazines, she published *Ladies Golf* in 1904 and contributed to Horace Hutchinson's *The New Book of Golf* in 1912. She was encouraging to other lady golfers and was of the opinion that: 'No one need despair of playing golf. Anyone gifted with ordinary strength can train themselves by perseverance and trouble to play not only sufficiently well to amuse themselves, but really well' (b.1882, d.1969).

Her sister Florence, née Hezlet, Cramsie was also runner-up in the Open Amateur in 1909, runner-up in the Irish in 1905, 1906 and 1908, and an Irish international. Another sister, Violet, née Hezlet, Hulton, was runner-up in the Open Amateur in 1911, runner-up in the Irish in 1900, 1903 and 1909, and also an Irish international. Mrs Hulton retired as secretary of the ILGU in 1976 and died in 1982.

Early in the century, Rhona Adair, later Mrs Cuthell, won the Open Amateur twice, in 1900 and 1903, and the Irish four times, in 1900, 1901, 1902 and 1903. Around 1902 she changed her swing, and played with a much shorter one than previously. A contemporary wrote of her: 'Unlike most lady players, Miss Adair stands up to the ball in a manner quite worthy of any of the sterner sex. There is a determination and firmness in her address to the ball which is most fascinating to watch. Lady players, as a rule, appear to persuade the ball on its way; Miss Adair, on the contrary, avoids any such constriction in her methods by hitting very hard indeed.'

In 1899, Miss Adair played 36 holes with 'Old' Tom Morris at St Andrews on, as far as can be deduced, level terms. She won the 1st hole, and by the 36th hole she had still only won by this as Old Tom was determined 'not to be licket by a lassie'. Unerring straightness was a feature of her game. During a visit to the USA, she was faced with a drive of about 170 yards across a river from the tee. Two balls hit the bank and rolled back, whereupon she asked people in the gallery if there was an easier place. When told there was a point five yards to one side of where she had been aiming, she aimed at it, hit it and crossed the river. Later in life she featured prominently in the government of the game, including being elected President of the ILGU in 1930 (b.1878, d.1961).

Charlotte (Lottie) Dod won the Open Amateur in 1904, having made the transition from champion tennis player to golfer. She had won the Ladies Lawn Tennis Championship at Wimbledon at the age of fifteen in 1887 and won it four more times before 1893. Five years later, her golfing ability enabled her to hole the full course at the Hoylake men's links in 90, the best score then made by a lady (b.1872). Among her contemporaries were Lena, née Thomson, Towne and Mary Graham. Lena Thomson Towne won the Open Amateur in 1898 and carried off many scratch prizes at open meetings at Great Yarmouth, West Lancashire, Minchinhampton, Prince's and Ranelagh. Miss Thomson learned her golf in Scotland and entered competitions for England. She was captain of Wimbledon in 1892. Mary Graham, who

took the Open Amateur title in 1901, was also a bronze medallist in 1904, won the Scottish in 1904, and was a silver medallist in 1903 and runner-up in 1905 (b.1880).

The lady champion in 1905 was Bertha, née Thompson, Walker, the Yorkshire champion in 1902 and an English international for years.

More than 750 prizes

Another contemporary was Dorothy, née Campbell, Hurd, who was the first lady to win both the British and the American titles in the same year, 1909. Two years later, entering from Hamilton Club, Ontario, where she had been based since her marriage, she won the British again and carried the trophy to her adopted country, the first time it crossed the Atlantic. She gained more international honours than Cecil Leitch, although Miss Leitch had a greater championship record.

Dorothy Campbell Hurd won the Open Amateur in 1909 and 1911, the American in 1909, 1910 and 1924, the Canadian in 1910, 1911 and 1912, and the Scottish in 1905, 1906 and 1908. She was Western Pennsylvania champion in 1914; North and South champion in 1918, 1920 and 1921; Boston champion in 1922; Florida West Coast champion in 1923; Philadelphia champion in 1925, 1926, 1927, 1929 and 1934; Bermuda champion in 1931 and 1934; and Pennsylvania champion in 1934. She won more than 750 prizes in golf, played for the British against the USA in 1905 and 1909, and was a Scottish international in 1909, 1911 and 1928 (b.1883, d.1946).

BELOW LEFT: Rhona Adair, another lady golfer who had the distinction of beating a famous male golfer – in her case 'Old' Tom Morris

BELOW: Gladys Ravenscroft (right) became lady champion in 1912; Muriel Dodd won the following year

Maud, née Titterton, Gibb also won her golfing honours at this time. She won the Open Tournament at Edinburgh in 1907, the Open Amateur in 1908, and was South African champion in 1912 and 1913, Johannesburg champion in 1913 and Transvaal champion in 1913. She instituted the Transvaal Ladies' Golf Union in 1913 and ensured that it was affiliated to the LGU. The only UK club she belonged to was Musselburgh. She was thus 'claimed' by Scotland although she played for England.

Lady champion in 1910 was Elsie Grant-Suttie. She also won the Scottish in 1911 and was a Scottish international in 1908, 1910, 1911, 1914, 1922 and 1923. She was an ambulance driver in World Wars I and II, and instrumental in raising funds for an ambulance to serve the local community from North Berwick; this was put into service in 1939. At first there was a team of drivers, but after the war she carried on almost single-handed, always answering calls. She often drove the 48 miles to Edinburgh and back, and sometimes back again, in the one, long day. She was awarded the BEM in 1949 for this. On watching a match between top amateur ladies shortly before she died, she exclaimed: 'If only some of these girls would use their heads' (d.1954).

A good fighting temperament

Gladys, née Ravenscroft, Dobell was lady champion in 1912. She won the American in 1913, the French in 1912 and was Cheshire champion in 1912, 1913, 1914, 1920, 1921, 1926 and 1928. She was an English international in 1911, 1912, 1913, 1914, 1920, 1921, 1925 and 1930. Her grip was 'pulled with one hand and a slicer's with the other', and she had 'great physical advantages, plenty of power, a good free swing and a cheerfulness of disposition which, save when occasionally it overcame all attempts at seriousness, concealed a good fighting temperament'. In her later days, she refused to take a place in the Cheshire team in order to give the youngsters a chance (b.1888, d.1960).

Prominent among her golfing colleagues in her early days were Stella Temple and Madge Neill Fraser. Stella Temple was runner-up in the 1912 Open Amateur, was an English international and also played hockey for England. During World War I, exhausting work in France weakened her and she died in the 'flu epidemic in 1918 (b.1890). Madge Neill Fraser was a semi-finalist in the Open Amateur in 1910, runner-up in the Scottish in 1912 and a semi-finalist in 1906, as well as a Scottish international. She died on 10 March 1915, on active service at Kragujeratz, Serbia, where she was acting as volunteer nurse and chauffeuse. A hospital fund in her memory was subscribed to by golfers in many parts of the world.

Another player who gained international honours before and after World War I was Muriel, née Dodd, MacBeth. She won the Open Amateur in 1913, the Canadian in 1913 and the Indian in 1927. She was Cheshire champion in 1922, 1923, 1927, 1932, 1935 and 1937, and an English international in 1913, 1914, 1920, 1921, 1922, 1923, 1924, 1925 and 1926 (b.1891).

The next lady champion was Charlotte Cecilia Pitcairn Leitch, who won the Open Amateur in 1914, 1920 and 1921 (consecutive times played) and

again in 1926. Nicknamed 'Cecil', she won the Canadian in 1921, the English in 1914 and 1919, and the French in 1912, 1914, 1920, 1921 and 1924. She won the Roehampton Gold in 1928, the *Golf Illustrated* in 1912, 1913 and 1914, and was Middlesex champion in 1924. Miss Leitch was an English international in 1910, 1911, 1912, 1913, 1914, 1920, 1921, 1922, 1924, 1925, 1927 and 1928, and toured America and Canada in 1922. At the height of her playing powers she held more than twenty course records.

In 1910, in a match which attracted unprecedented attention and publicity and was made much of by the suffragettes, she beat Harold Hilton – receiving ten mascots from admirers and a half from him – over 36 holes. She halved with him in a match after World War I, he from the men's markers, she from the ladies', and beat Tom Ball (twice second in the Open) on the same terms. She was elected to the US Hall of Fame and, apart from her major championships, she won every important medal and prize during her fifteen years of competitive golf.

Miss Leitch returned from her American tour with the muscles in her forearm ruptured so badly that 'below the elbow they were torn from the bone'. She played no golf for two years, but came back winning. She wrote books and articles about golf, was prominent in the affairs of the LGU, was a

Left-hander May Leitch and right-hander Cecil Leitch (right) demonstrate their grips

committee member of the Women Golfer's Museum, lectured on the importance of the National Playing Fields Association, and inaugurated a five-club
competition which bears her name and was played for the twenty-fifth time
in 1982.

Palm-under grip, ducking right knee

The first modern-style 'star' of ladies' golf, Miss Leitch attracted a large
number of acolytes who followed her to all her matches and cheered her on.
One of five golfing sisters from Silloth in Cumbria, she startled the ladies'
golfing world on her first appearance in the Open Amateur at the age of
seventeen, and continued to startle it for many years, particularly in her
matches with her arch-rival, Joyce Wethered. A protegée of Issette Pearson
Miller and her many intimate friends, who made sure that she received the
right experience in the days when major tournaments were few, Miss Leitch
learned her golf by watching the male players on her home course. A feature
of her game was a palm-under grip and a ducking right knee.

'Cecil' brought to ladies' golf a most dominating personality and a more
masculine game than had ever been shown by one of her sex. She punched
her iron shots with more strength and vigour than any lady before her, and
used a wide stance with the ball well away from her. She was tall, strong and
tough and her personality was such that she distinguished herself in
whatever company she found herself in, or sought out. She was a born
leader and captivated the world of athletics through the determined and
forceful manner in which she hit the ball. She was the first woman to exhibit
power and artistry in iron shots.

Her rival, and eventual conqueror, Joyce Wethered, analyzed her particular qualities in 1922:

> For some years her name has been a household word as standing for
> a unique record in ladies' golf, and for that reason has attracted an
> amount of interest which is justified not only by her intimate know-
> ledge of the game but by her proficiency in putting it into practice.
> She also possesses a great asset in a quality which might very well be
> called generalship – a type of character which, from the psychological
> point of view, contributes very largely to the promotion of a player to
> the front rank. It is only necessary to recall for an illustration of this
> gift the number of occasions on which Miss Leitch has pulled desper-
> ate matches out of the fire, in order to realize the intensity with which
> she plays the game, and the additional fraction of concentrated ener-
> gy which she can summon to her aid in a close finish. I have had the
> good fortune to meet her in three consecutive championship finals
> over thirty-six holes, and can truthfully say I never wish to indulge in
> more exacting ordeals. She has the enviable facility of being able to
> commence right away with par figures or under, which gives a slower
> or less confident opponent a lot of leeway to make up, and an infinite
> amount of trouble to extricate her from a desperate situation.

Miss Leitch played no golf from 1939 to 1955, but friends coaxed her out of retirement by giving her a 4-wood, and with inimitable style at the age of 67 she reduced her handicap from 8 to 6. She is credited with three holes in one (b.1891, d.1977).

Her sisters May and Edith were also first class players. Edith, née Leitch, Guedalla won the English in 1927, was Middlesex champion in 1914, 1923 and 1930, and an English international in 1908, 1910, 1920, 1921, 1922, 1927, 1928, 1929, 1930 and 1933.

The two ladies, Miss Leitch and Miss Wethered, were dissimilar both in their attitudes to the game and in their personalities. Miss Leitch was dynamic and extrovert, Miss Wethered shy, shrewd and persistent. On the other hand, in their person-to-person tussles it was Miss Wethered who produced the fireworks, and Miss Leitch who had to deal with their effects. Their differences were also apparent in their attitudes towards practice. Miss Leitch was of the opinion that 'the right time to practice a shot is when a player is playing it well, and not when she is playing it badly. It is far easier to discover what one is doing correctly than what one is doing wrong.' Miss Wethered found: 'It is worse than useless to repeat shots in practice when once the correct result has been obtained; you are only wasting good strokes.' On their retirements from competitive golf, Miss Leitch vented her energies on the commercial world of antiques, and Miss Wethered bent her perfectionist's mind to gardening on a grand scale. Battles between the two always resulted in front page newspaper coverage and their endeavours ensured that women's golf had a prominent place in the sports scene.

Oh, Joyce, you will never play golf!

Joyce Wethered, later Lady Heathcoat Amory, won the Open Amateur in 1922, 1924, 1925 and 1929, and the English in 1920, 1921, 1922, 1923 and 1924 – an unparalleled record. She was also Surrey champion in 1921, 1922, 1924, 1929 and 1932. She was playing captain for the inaugural Curtis Cup match in 1932, played against France in 1931, and was an English international in 1921, 1922, 1923, 1924, 1925 and 1929. She made a highly successful professional tour of the USA in 1935, regained her amateur status in 1954, and was the first president of the ELGA. After her marriage she played little golf, apart from successful appearances at Worplesdon.

A sickly child who was not allowed to attend school, Miss Wethered began playing at the age of eight with her brother Roger, and played with boys and men all her formative years. When she was eleven, Roger viewed her attempts to play mashie shots in the style of J.H. Taylor with the comment: 'Oh, Joyce, you will never play golf. You won't study the game.' After World War I, Surrey were looking for a team and invited her to play – at the bottom. She exploded onto the golfing scene at Sheringham in 1920 when she defeated the then all-conquering Cecil Leitch in the English. Her appearance at Sheringham was entirely due to Molly Griffiths, who invited her along as companion. Miss Griffiths was runner-up in the Open in 1920; before that, during World War I, being too young to get into uniform, she

replaced a greenkeeper on the men's course at Sunningdale, and was soon after invested with the honourable order of life membership of that club. With Miss Griffiths as companion, Miss Wethered proceded to confound players and spectators alike with her phenomenal concentration which instituted a legend during the Sheringham match. As she was about to putt, a noisy train belched along, mightily disturbing the spectators. She took no notice and sank the putt. When asked afterwards: 'Didn't the train put you off?' she replied: 'What train?'

After winning the Open Amateur three times, she took a few years off from competitive golf and reappeared with a changed swing – 'no longer high, but a beautiful low trajectory' – and won the Open Amateur again. In two years of competitive golf in the UK she was defeated only twice, winning 71 out of 73 matches. During her USA tour she broke eighteen course records, outplayed many male champions, and showed that she was indeed capable of being the world's first top-flight woman playing professional. However, the world was not ready for her. She returned to Fortnum & Mason as golf adviser after her tour and worked in a parachute-making factory during World War II.

She was the first lady to popularize the Vardon grip and was the forerunner of the modern American swing – this latter observation being based on a film made on her American tour. 'Her swing,' wrote Bernard Cook in 1973, 'had much more in common with the Hogan swing of the 1950s than with the Vardon swing. The film reveals that she was beautifully wide both on the backswing and also on the forward swing. She made no early hit, she had no wrist flick, and she kept a perfect centre.'

She had an unhurried and rhythmic pace, was consistent, and could get psyched up for an important occasion to exactly the right degree. Her effect on the gallery was riveting, and sometimes calamitous to other ladies' golf. Some ladies who watched her decided 'in awe-stricken conclave that Miss Wethered did not pivot, and they remodelled their swings with catastrophic effect.'

Enid Wilson wrote that

> Miss Wethered was fragile in appearance, and there was nothing of the Amazon about her. Strength and stamina she must have had to withstand the physical and mental effort of a week's championship golf; but perhaps, knowing that her resources were not over-abundant, she evolved the most economical method to suit her physique, and by shutting out everything of an extraneous nature avoided the strain which others found so sapping and destructive, although this strain was not uncommon to her. Miss Leitch brought power into women's golf; Miss Wethered brought power combined with perfection of style and a hitherto unknown degree of accuracy.

The aspect of her rival's game which most impressed Miss Leitch was her putting. 'If I were asked to name the lady golfer whom I consider to be the best and soundest putter,' she wrote, 'I should say Miss Joyce Wethered

without a doubt . . . She has a sound method of hitting the ball which appears to be the result of study and practice. The firm stance, the still head, the short straight backward movement of the club head, the decided hit and the short follow-through are clearly demonstrated in her method of putting, and the results prove the soundness of it' (b.1901).

Contemporary with Miss Leitch and Miss Wethered was Doris Elaine Chambers, who won the Open Amateur in 1923, at the age of thirty-nine, having played in the championship for the first time in 1905. She was Cheshire champion in 1924, champion of India in 1914, and won the Veterans in 1937. Miss Chambers captained the 1933 LGU team to South Africa, and to Canada and America in 1934. She was non-playing captain of the Curtis Cup team in 1936 and 1948, and an English international in 1906, 1907, 1909, 1910, 1911, 1912, 1920, 1924 and 1925. She was president of the LGU from 1961 to 1963 and of the ELGA from 1958 to 1962. She was also overseas relations officer for the LGU, and was awarded the OBE. She took up golf at the age of fourteen, having only one club – a cleek – and bought the others one at a time. She retired in 1963 and in 1968 was reported to be attending practically every golf tournament in the country (b.1883, d.1983).

Another prominent golfer, and golf writer, who was active in many ways in the first three decades of the century was Eleanor Helme. She was women's golf correspondent to the *Daily Telegraph, Bystander, Morning Post, Tatler* and *Sporting and Dramatic,* and held, among other journalistic posts, the editorship of *Britannia*, and the golf editorship of *Eve.* She covered all the major championships from 1910 to 1939 and in 1935 broadcast the commentary on the Open Amateur from Newcastle, County Down, the first woman to broadcast such a commentary.

As well as playing 'top golf' – she represented England in 1911, 1912, 1913 and 1920, and was a bronze medallist in the Open Amateur in 1925 – she was a paid worker of the LGU, assisting with proofs, reports and press work. She organized and ran various championships and tournaments including the Girls' and the *Eve* and *Bystander* foursomes.

Among her publications were *After the Ball – Merry Memories of a Golfer,* 1931, *The Lady Golfer's Tip Book,* 1923, and *Family Golf,* 1938. When she retired from writing about golf, she devoted her time to children's books about pets, ponies, dogs and birds (b.1887, d.1967).

An almost reverential awe

Diana, née Fishwick, Critchley was the next British lady champion. She won the Open Amateur in 1930, the English in 1932 and 1949, the French in 1932, the German in 1936 and 1938, the Belgian in 1938 and the Dutch in 1946. She won the Florida West Coast in 1933, was Kent champion in 1934, Surrey champion in 1936 and 1946 and won the Girls' in 1927 and 1928.

She played in the Curtis Cup in 1932 and 1934 and was non-playing captain in 1950. She toured South Africa with the LGU team in 1933, played against France in 1931, 1932, 1933 and 1934 and was non-playing captain in 1948. She played for England in the home internationals in 1930, 1931, 1932,

1933, 1935, 1936 and 1947. She was chairman of the ELGA's selection committee in 1967, 1968, 1969 and 1970 and an international selector in 1970, 1971, 1972 and 1973.

When she won the Open Amateur, the British had been worried because Joyce Wethered was not playing and the top-notch American Glenna Collett was competing. The British feared the trophy would cross the Atlantic. As Bernard Darwin wrote: 'I imagine that when this youthful heroine first took the lead, the onlookers thought it a gallant but unavailing effort, and that as she went on and on and they realized she was going to win they were overcome by an almost reverential awe' (b.1911).

OPPOSITE: Doris Chambers (left) and Molly Gourlay at the London Ladies' Foursomes at Stoke Poges in 1934

Work it out for yourself

Among other prominent lady golfers who reached their peak in the 1920s and 1930s were Molly Gourlay, Mrs W.T. Gavin Hooman and Charlotte, née Stevenson, Watson Beddows. Molly Gourlay won the English in 1926 and 1929, the French in 1923, 192? and 1929, the Swedish in 1932, 1936 and 1939 and the Belgian in 1925 and 1926. She was Surrey champion in 1923, 1926, 1927, 1931, 1933, 1934 and 1938 and won the Veterans' in 1962. She won the Roehampton Gold in 1927 and the *Golf Illustrated* in 1929.

BELOW: Enid Wilson, accompanied by prop, drives off at Romford, Essex, in 1938

Molly Gourlay played in the Curtis Cup in 1932 and 1934, against France in 1931, 1932, 1933 and 1939, and was an English international in 1923, 1924, 1927, 1928, 1929, 1930, 1931, 1932, 1933 and 1934. She was a member of the LGU team to tour South Africa in 1933, and non-playing captain of England in 1957. At the age of 71 she was playing off a handicap of 5 at Camberley Heath, where she had been a member for half a century. She improved on this and when she retired from playing golf at the age of 73 she was playing off 4. During the early nineteen-thirties she suggested that the internationals should be called the home internationals to distinguish them from the other 'internationals'. She became a director of Messrs Simpson & Company, golf architects, in 1936, helped to establish the Commonwealth tournament, was chairman of the LGU from 1957 to 1959, and president of the ELGA from 1963 to 1965. She refereed the Avia for the first time in 1968 and accepted the invitation to maintain the post for the next ten years; among other posts, she commanded the referees at the fourteenth European Lady Juniors at Wentworth in 1981.

A bout of scarlet fever started her playing golf in earnest. At the end of World War I she was with the Voluntary Aid Detachment in Queen Mary's, Roehampton, but succumbed to the status of patient. She was not allowed to take violent exercise after that, so 'settled for golf'. She had some coaching but was mostly self-taught; she was not in favour of too much coaching, considering that 'you should work it out for yourself'. She joined the First Aid Nursing Yeomanry some years before World War II, on one occasion going on duty at Aldershot the night she came back from winning the Swedish Open. She was a staff officer in charge of the Auxiliary Territorial Service at Montgomery's HQ, went to Normandy with the first detachment of the British Liberation Army and was invalided home, mentioned in despatches and awarded the OBE (b.1898).

Mrs W.A. Gavin Hooman was very much an international golfer. She won the Canadian in 1922, the Swiss in 1924, and the Belgian in 1924. She was Middlesex champion in 1925, and an English international in 1910, 1911 and 1925. In 1923 in New York, receiving a half, she beat Jerome K. Travers, four times USA Amateur champion and 1915 Open champion by 8 and 7 over 36 holes. She represented the USA Red Cross against a team of professionals, playing twenty-six matches, and receiving a half, won 16, halved 4 and lost 6 (b.1886).

Charlotte, née Stevenson, Watson Beddows won the Scottish in 1920, 1921, 1922 and 1929, was East of Scotland champion in 1931 and 1932, and won the Veterans' in 1947, 1949, 1950 and 1951. She played in the Curtis Cup in 1932 and against France in 1931 and 1932. She was a Scottish international in 1913, 1914, 1921, 1922, 1923, 1927, 1928, 1929, 1930, 1931, 1932, 1933, 1934, 1935, 1936, 1937, 1939, 1947, 1948, 1949, 1950 and 1951. She was non-playing captain against France in 1939 and captained Scotland in 1921, 1922, 1923, 1930 and 1931. She was awarded the Frank Moran Trophy – for Scots who have done the most for golf – in 1964 and is credited with six holes in one.

Mrs Beddows reached the finals of the Scottish at the age of 62, and played

county golf for six decades, last playing for East Lothian in 1966. During World War II, the course at Gullane 'got into rotten shape', but 'the rot was stopped by Beddows who organized working parties of elderly club members and lady members to go out on to the course for weeding and bunker exercises' (b.1887, d.1976).

I am a slave to golf

The next lady champion was Enid Wilson, who won the Open Amateur in 1931, 1932 and 1933. She won the English in 1928 and 1930, the Roehampton Gold in 1930, was Midland champion in 1926, 1928, 1929 and 1930, Derbyshire champion in 1925 and 1926 and Cheshire champion in 1933. She won the Girls' in 1925, played in the Curtis Cup in 1932, and was an English international in 1928, 1929, 1930 and 1931. She was a semi-finalist in the American in 1931 and 1933.

Miss Wilson was deemed a 'non-amateur' in 1934 and had to retire from competitive golf at the age of twenty-four, although she did play when permitted and invited to do so. She pursued a vigorous career in golf journalism, writing regularly for most of the journals, and retired as golf correspondent of the *Daily Telegraph* in the mid-1970s. When she was first approached to write for the *Daily Telegraph*, her editor told her that there were no such people as lady golfers – they were women. A journalist since 1927, her crisp prose and no-nonsense approach did a great deal to air the difficulties experienced by lady golfers. Her criticism of the various governing authorities and her frank comments on selectors and various players did not always earn her popularity and favour. She was prominent in the encouragement of juniors whenever possible and was elected a vice-president of the LGU in 1978. Her first book, *'So that's what I do'*, written in collaboration with Robert Allen Lewis, was published in 1935, her second, *A Gallery of Women Golfers*, in 1961, and her third, *Golf for Women*, in 1964.

At the age of thirteen, Miss Wilson managed to get herself expelled from boarding school, because school interfered with her golf. She performed this feat by being extremely rude to her housemistress, with the use of some four-lettered words which she had overheard from some of her doctor father's patients. A few years later, she was playing in a tournament near her old school and noticed that the headmistress was one of her most ardent gallery followers. After the tournament she went to the school to thank her for her interest. She was given a 'royal tour' of part of the school and was introduced as being an 'ex-product' of the school, not an expelled product.

Initially her main difficulty as a golfer was with putting. Being a competent carpenter, she sorted that out by altering the lie of her putter to suit her upright stance; she trued the blade herself and this gave her the confidence to know that it *was* true. The putter, which she fixed in 1927, remained her faithful friend for many years. Through her prowess at the game, her ability to communicate, and the longevity of her involvement ('I am a slave to golf') her solo contribution to British women's golf remains outstanding. She served in the WAAF during World War II (b.1910).

Helen, née Gray, Holm was lady champion twice during the 1930s. She won the Open Amateur in 1934 and 1938 and the Scottish in 1930, 1932, 1937, 1948 and 1950. She was Lanarkshire champion in 1928, 1929 and 1932, West of Scotland champion in 1933, 1934, 1935, 1936, 1937, 1948, 1949 and 1950, and Ayrshire champion in 1935, 1936, 1947, 1948, 1950 and 1951. She played in the Curtis Cup in 1936, 1938 and 1948, against France in 1933, 1934, 1935, 1936, 1937, 1938, 1947, 1948 and 1949, and against Belgium in 1949; she was non-playing captain against both in 1951. She played in the home internationals in 1932, 1933, 1934, 1935, 1936, 1937, 1938, 1947, 1948, 1949, 1950, 1951, 1955 and 1957.

She was described as 'the most striking player since Miss Wethered'. She was 'not the most consistent and was capable of unexpected and perhaps light-hearted mistakes, but when in full tide of play she had a majestic power about her game and a capacity for playing the counting shot rarely seen. She "stood up and gave it one" ' (b.1907, d.1971).

13 under par

Runner-up to Enid Wilson in 1931 and lady champion in 1935 was Wanda Morgan. She also won the English in 1931, 1936 and 1937, and was Kent champion in 1930, 1931, 1933, 1935, 1936, 1937 and 1953. She played in the Curtis Cup in 1932, 1934 and 1936, and against France in 1932, 1933, 1934, 1935, 1936 and 1937. She played in the home internationals in 1931, 1932, 1933, 1934, 1935, 1936, 1937 and 1953. In 1929 she set an amateur record of 60 on the then par-73 course at Westgate and Birchington at an Open meeting.

Miss Morgan had to endure 'non-amateur' status for some years after she joined Dunlop as liaison officer but regained her amateur status after World War II and promptly won the Kent for the seventh time. She distinguished herself in all the tournaments she played in, even on one occasion winning her own Challenge Scratch Trophy, which of course she could not accept. As well as organizing and inaugurating tournaments, many for charity, she also gave clinics and was one of the most popular pre- and post-war golf figures. When asked, in November 1981, if she would have joined the professional circuit had it been going in her full-time golfing days, the answer was a long, drawn-out, heartfelt 'Oooh, ye-es!'

Miss Morgan initially wanted to be a cricketer but took the advice of her father who considered that a cricketer's day was over by the age of thirty-five but a golfer's day went on for ever. Her father played off scratch and her mother off 4. She started playing with only a 2-iron. Described as 'small in stature, great in power', she did not spend a tremendous time practising but would do so if 'off'. She always knew exactly where she was with her favourite caddie, Arthur Herrington: he smoked a pipe constantly and would point it downwards if she were down and up if she were up. She retired from Dunlop after thirty-one years' service in 1968 (b.1910).

The second lady to hold both the British and the American titles in the same year was Pamela Barton. She won the Open Amateur in 1936 and 1939 and the American in 1936, and was one of the few British lady golfers to be

Helen Holm intently watches the result of her attempt to crash one down the middle during the final of the 1934 Ladies' British Open Amateur Championship at Royal Porthcawl, Glamorganshire. Mrs Holm beat the 17-year old Pamela Barton by 6 and 5

elected to the US Hall of Fame. Miss Barton won the French in 1934, and was Surrey champion in 1935. She won the Roehampton Gold in 1935, 1937, 1938 and 1939. She played in the Curtis Cup in 1934 and 1936, against France in 1934, 1936, 1937, 1938 and 1939, toured Australia and New Zealand with the LGU team in 1935 and played in the home internationals in 1935, 1936, 1937, 1938 and 1939.

In her book, published in 1937, she wrote: 'Bogies I know are very fine things, but birdies are better. The flag is put there to be aimed at.' This book, *A Stroke a Hole*, devoted one chapter to each of eighteen holes taken from courses throughout the world where her golfing journeys took her. These were: the 12th at Brookwood, Surrey, the 1st at Canoe Brook, New Jersey, the 7th at Stoke Poges, the 3rd at Royal Mid-Surrey (men's), the 9th at Heretaunga, Wellington, New Zealand, the 9th at Newcastle, County Down, the 5th at Worplesdon, the 5th at Prince's, Sandwich, the 6th at Royal Wimbledon, the 18th at Southport and Ainsdale, the 15th at Royal Calcutta, the 4th at Gleneagles, the 1st at Hayling Island, the 14th at Turnberry, the 1st at Royal Melbourne, the 8th at Canoe Brook, New Jersey, the 2nd at Berkshire, Ascot Red Course, and the 6th at Sunningdale. Among the advice she gave was: 'Gentility never pays in bunkers.'

> Half measures never get anybody, especially golfers, anywhere. That is for your encouragement. In America in 1936 I practised five or six hours a day before the championship. First I played seven holes with two balls and that took two hours. Then I had an hour each of putting, driving and iron play. I believe that if I had kept a tally of the number of hours I have spent on golf courses, I should find that at least half . . . had been in practice. That also is for your encouragement.

At one time, she was unhappy with her putting, as she was not taking the club back straight. 'Thereupon she went to a vacant green, laid down two clubs so that the shafts made a groove for the head of her putter, and practised away relentlessly up and down the straight line. This improvised piece of machinery was effective, for she putted well thereafter and virtue was rewarded.' Archie Compston, one of her teachers, said of her: 'This girl's greatest asset is her attitude of mind. She has a wonderful power of concentration and wonderful fighting qualities coming up the home stretch where it matters most. Pamela Barton went out there to win.'

A WAAF officer during the early years of World War II, Miss Barton was killed in a plane crash while off duty. After leaving a dance, her escort pilot took off down wind and failed to clear an obstacle, having forgotten to turn the petrol taps on. He survived the crash but was killed shortly after (b.1917, d.1943).

Runner-up to Miss Barton in the 1936 Open Amateur was Bridget Newell, who was Derbyshire champion in 1935, Midland champion in 1936, won the *Golf Illustrated* in 1935, the Roehampton Gold in 1936, led the Derbyshire county team, played against France and was a reserve for the Curtis Cup. She died suddenly on the eve of the 1937 home internationals, which were

therefore abandoned. However, the Open Amateur which always followed the home internationals did take place, the best possible tribute to her. Miss Newell was called to the Bar at the age of twenty-one and two years later she became the youngest magistrate in England, sitting on the Matlock Derbyshire bench (b.1911, d.1937).

Winner of the first Open Amateur after World War II was Jean, née McClure, Hetherington Holmes. She was at that time the only lady with, of course, the exception of Lady Margaret Scott, to win it at her first attempt. She was honeymooning and her husband acted as caddie and adviser. She was Nottinghamshire champion in 1949, 1950 and 1951 and Essex champion in 1956 and 1957. She played in the home internationals in 1955, 1956, 1957, 1958, 1959, 1960, 1961, 1962, 1963, 1964, 1965 and 1966, and was non-playing captain of England in 1967 (b.1923).

All ladies' courses are too short

Frances (usually 'Bunty'), née Stephens, Smith was twice lady champion, in 1949 and 1954. She won the English in 1948, 1954 and 1955, and the French in 1949. She won the Roehampton Gold in 1969 and was Lancashire champion in 1948, 1949, 1950, 1951, 1952, 1953, 1954, 1955, 1959 and 1960. She played in the Curtis Cup in 1950, 1952, 1954, 1956, 1958 and 1960, and was non-playing captain in 1962 and 1972. She played against France and Belgium in 1955, in the Vagliano in 1959, toured South Africa in 1951, played in the Commonwealth in 1959, and was non-playing captain of England in the European in 1973. She played in the home internationals in 1947, 1948, 1949, 1950, 1951, 1953, 1954, 1955, 1956 and 1959. She is credited with eight holes in one. When she won the English at Woodhall Spa in 1954, she did the first 9 holes, which measured 3280 yards, in 30 – 3,3,4,3,1,4,3,4,5.

In the whole of her international career she lost not a single match. She started playing at the age of fourteen at Bootle where her father was professional, but World War II intervened and she was twenty before she 'started to take it seriously'. On the advice of Henry Cotton she played as often as possible from the men's tees. He told her: 'You are not really off scratch until you can play to scratch regularly from the men's tees.' She practised regularly all her playing days, particularly from bunkers and difficult lies. A pronounced halt at the top of the backswing was a feature of her game, but she was unaware of developing this deliberately. 'It just happens to me,' she said.

It was always a puzzle to her that women's tournaments were played off LGU tees: 'We can't beat the Americans if we allow that sort of thing,' she maintained, and she was of the opinion that 'under normal conditions all ladies courses are too short'. She was awarded the OBE for services to golf, and the Golf Writers' Association Trophy in 1954, and had her portrait painted by John A.A. Berrie. She was president of ELGA at the time of her death (b.1924, d.1978).

Another top golfer of the 1950s was Catherine, née Smye, McCann, who won the Open Amateur in 1951, the Irish in 1949 and 1961, was Munster

champion in 1958, Irish Midland champion in 1952, 1957 and 1958, and Leinster champion in 1948 and 1958. She played in the Curtis Cup in 1952, against New Zealand and Canada in 1953, and in the home internationals in 1947, 1948, 1949, 1950, 1951, 1952, 1953, 1954, 1956, 1957, 1958, 1960, 1961 and 1962 (b.1922).

Moira, née Paterson, Milton won the Open Amateur in 1952, and was Dunbartonshire champion in 1949 and Midlothian champion in 1962. She played in the Curtis Cup in 1952, against France in 1949 and 1951, and against Belgium in 1951. She played against Australia and South Africa in 1951, was non-playing captain of Scotland in the European in 1973, and played in the home internationals in 1949, 1950 and 1952 (b.1923).

Jeanne Bisgood, one of her contemporaries, won the English in 1951, 1953 and 1957, the Swedish in 1952, the German in 1953, the Italian in 1953, the Portuguese in 1954 and the Norwegian in 1955. She was Surrey champion in 1951, 1953 and 1969. She won the Astor Salver in 1951, 1952 and 1953, the Roehampton Gold in 1951, 1952 and 1953, and was South-Eastern champion in 1950 and 1952. She played in the Curtis Cup in 1950, 1952 and 1953, and was non-playing captain in 1970. She played in the home internationals in 1949, 1950, 1951, 1952, 1953, 1954, 1956 and 1958.

Miss Bisgood started playing golf at the age of nine, her enormous enthusiasm for the game being sparked off by Pamela Barton, who was always very encouraging to beginners. Her first handicap was 21 and she played off 12 just before World War II. She went up to Oxford to read history in 1941 'but found it a bit irrelevant', so joined the Women's Royal Naval Service. Being stationed at Stanmore she managed to play at Royal Mid-Surrey and Parkstone and by the time the war was over she was off 8. A barrister, her strong, very articulate views contributed to various aspects of the government of the game (b.1923).

A severe blow to Scotland

Two Scots ladies who also reached their golfing peaks at this time were Jean, née Donald, Anderson and Jessie, née Anderson, Valentine. Jean Donald Anderson was runner-up in the Open Amateur in 1948, won the Scottish in 1947, 1949 and 1952, the French in 1947, was East of Scotland champion in 1947, 1948, 1949 and 1953, and East Lothian champion in 1948, 1949, 1951, 1952 and 1953. She played in the Curtis Cup in 1948, 1950 and 1952, against France in 1947, 1948, 1949, 1951 and 1953, against Belgium in 1949, 1951 and 1953, and against New Zealand in 1953. She played in the home internationals in 1947, 1948, 1949, 1950, 1951, 1952 and 1953, and toured South Africa with the LGU team in 1951. She is credited with three holes in one.

In 1948 she achieved a 100 per cent victory record and was described as one of the successes of post-war golf. She took up an appointment with Golf Ball Development as a representative in 1949 but this did not affect her amateur status. When she did turn professional, in 1953, this was described as 'a severe blow to Scotland'. Playing in the first Curtis Cup after World War II, she was the only player to win her singles and foursomes. During the

Jessie Anderson Valentine at the end of a gloriously full swing in 1970

Triumphant winners of the Women's Spalding Tournament in 1957 – Marley Spearman (left) and Elizabeth Price

1951 South African tour she was noted as being an excellent ambassadress. She has been an inspiration to lady golfers for many years, particularly to the younger generation (b.1921, d.1984).

Jessie Anderson Valentine won the Open Amateur in 1937, 1955 and 1958, the Scottish in 1938, 1939, 1951, 1953, 1955 and 1956, the New Zealand in 1935, the French in 1936, the Girls' in 1933 and was East of Scotland champion in 1936, 1938, 1939 and 1950. She played in the Curtis Cup in 1936, 1938, 1950, 1952, 1954, 1956 and 1958, against France in 1935, 1936, 1938, 1939, 1947, 1949, 1951 and 1955, against Belgium in 1949, 1951, 1954 and 1955, toured Australia and New Zealand with the LGU team in 1935 and played in the home internationals in 1934, 1935, 1936, 1937, 1938, 1939, 1947, 1949, 1950, 1951, 1952, 1953, 1954, 1955, 1956, 1957 and 1958. She turned professional in 1960, was the first woman to receive the MBE (in 1959) for golf, and was awarded the Frank Moran Trophy in 1967.

'Wee' Jessie was given her first club at the age of five; at the age of eight she had three more, four more when twelve and a full set at the age of seventeen, by which time she had a handicap of 12. She retired from competitive golf in order to be a full-time partner in her father's sports shop, founded in 1899. Later on, Dunlop asked her to help them design a set of clubs. She did not regret her decision to turn professional, taught occasionally, and played in tournaments when permitted or invited. Dunlop presented her with a necklace of antique pearls to mark her twenty-five year involvement with them in 1981 (b.1915).

Among those flying the flag for Britain during the 1950s was Veronica, née Anstey, Beharrell, who won the Australian, the New Zealand and the Victoria (Australia) in 1955. She was Warwickshire champion in 1955, 1956, 1957, 1958, 1960, 1971, 1972 and 1975. She played in the Curtis Cup in 1956 and in the home internationals in 1955, 1956 and 1958, being non-playing captain in 1961.

On her return from her victorious Antipodean tour with the LGU team, Raymond Oppenheimer, who was then chairman of the R and A Selection Committee, paid her a special tribute: 'There was a young golfer who was given the chance and took it in both hands . . . I do assure you that when it comes to deciding the various international teams, and especialy the Walker Cup side, we will keep the name of Veronica Anstey very much in the forefront of our minds' (b.1935).

Playing like a pocket professional

The next lady champion was Philomena Garvey, who won the Open Amateur in 1957, and the Irish in 1946, 1947, 1948, 1950, 1951, 1953, 1954, 1955, 1957, 1958, 1959, 1960, 1962, 1963 and 1970 – an all-time record of fifteen times. She was Munster champion in 1951 and Irish Midland champion in 1951. She played in the Curtis Cup in 1948, 1950, 1952, 1954, 1956 and 1960, against Australia in 1950, against France in 1949, 1951, 1953, 1955 and 1957, against Belgium in 1951, 1953 and 1957, and in the Vagliano in 1957, 1959 and 1963. She played in the home internationals in 1947, 1948, 1949, 1950, 1951, 1952, 1953, 1954, 1955, 1956, 1959, 1960, 1961, 1962, 1963 and 1969. She turned professional in 1964 but was reinstated as an amateur later on. In 1947 she was described as 'The only discovery to emerge from the past season' and a year or two later on she was said to be 'playing like a pocket professional' (b.1927).

Elizabeth, née Price, Fisher was lady champion in 1959. She also won the Astor Salver in 1955, 1956 and 1958, the Roehampton Gold in 1960, was South-Eastern champion in 1955, 1959, 1960 and 1969, and Surrey champion in 1954, 1955, 1956, 1957, 1958, 1959 and 1960. She won the *Golf Illustrated* in 1951, the Danish in 1952, the Alberta in 1961 and the Portuguese in 1964. She played in the Curtis Cup in 1950, 1952, 1954, 1956, 1958 and 1960, the Vagliano in 1959, against France and Belgium in 1953, 1955 and 1957, and in the Commonwealth in 1955 and 1959. She played in the home internationals in 1948, 1951, 1952, 1953, 1954, 1955, 1956, 1957, 1958, 1959 and 1960. She was awarded the Golf Writers' Trophy in 1952. An assistant editor on *Fairway & Hazard* magazine for many years, she took over from Wanda Morgan at Dunlop and from Enid Wilson on the *Daily Telegraph* when those ladies retired. She turned professional in 1969 and regained her amateur status in 1971 (b.1923).

Twice-running winner of the Open Amateur, in 1961–2, was Marley, née Baker, Spearman (later Harris). She won the English in 1964, the Roehampton Gold in 1965 and the Astor Salver in 1964 and 1965. She was Middlesex champion in 1955, 1956, 1957, 1958, 1959, 1961, 1964 and 1965, and South-Eastern champion in 1956, 1958 and 1961. She won the New Zealand in 1964.

She played in the Curtis Cup in 1960, 1962 and 1964, the Vagliano in 1959 and 1961, the Commonwealth in 1959 and 1963, and was non-playing captain of England in the European in 1971. She played in the home internationals eleven times – in 1955, 1956, 1957, 1958, 1959, 1960, 1961, 1962, 1963, 1964 and 1965.

In 1965, she retained her Middlesex title without losing a hole; she played only 45 holes, won 33 and halved 12. As was said at the time: 'To go through a championship without losing a hole must be a rare distinction, if not unique.' Formerly a dancer, Mrs Harris (then Mrs Spearman) had her first golf lesson at Harrods and then took a course from Edward Holdright who told her that she could be an international within three years if she wished. She was. Mrs Harris had a strong flair for fashion and wore whatever was most suitable of 'the latest' whenever she played, in contrast to most of her contemporaries, who were still way back in the baggy-tweed-skirt era (b.1929).

Elizabeth, née Chadwick, Pook also won the Open Amateur twice running, in 1966 and 1967. She was North of England champion in 1965, 1966 and 1967, and Cheshire champion in 1963, 1964, 1965, 1966 and 1967. A girl international in 1961, she played in the Curtis Cup in 1966, the Commonwealth in 1967, the Vagliano in 1963, the European in 1967 and the home internationals in 1963, 1965, 1966 and 1967. At the time of her retirement from competitive golf in 1968, she held ten course records (b.1943).

During the 1960s the Open Amateur title went overseas six times, and the next British lady champion was Dinah, née Oxley, Henson, who won in 1970. She also won the English in 1970 and 1971 and was Surrey champion in 1967, 1970, 1971 and 1976. She was Daks Woman Golfer of the Year in 1970 and leading amateur in the Colgate European Ladies' Open in 1974. She won the Girls' in 1963, the English Girls' in 1965 and the French Girls' in 1969. She was a girl international in 1964, 1965 and 1966, played in the Curtis Cup in 1968, 1970, 1972 and 1976, the Vagliano in 1967, 1969 and 1971, the Espirito in 1970 and the Commonwealth in 1967 and 1971. She played in the European in 1971 and 1977 and in the home internationals in 1967, 1968, 1969, 1970, 1975, 1976, 1977 and 1978 (b.1948).

The seventh twice-running winner of the Open Amateur was Michelle Walker, who also made the transition to professional status. She was lady champion in 1971 and 1972, and won the English in 1973, the Portuguese in 1972, the Trans-Mississippi in 1972 (the first major event won in the US by a British lady since 1936), the Spanish in 1973 and was Kent champion in 1971. She won the French Girls' in 1971 and was a girl international in 1969, 1970 and 1971. She played in the Curtis Cup in 1972, the Commonwealth in 1971, the Espirito in 1972, the Vagliano in 1971, the European in 1971 and 1973, and in the home internationals in 1970 and 1972. She was awarded the Golf Writers' Trophy in 1972 and designated Daks Woman Golfer of the Year in 1972. She turned professional in 1973, signed with Mark McCormack and played in Brazil and America, qualified for her USLPGA card in 1974 and retained it until 1981. She was elected chairman of the WPGA in May 1981 (b.1952).

Comprehensive qualifications

Another lady who successfully made the transition to professional status was Vivien Saunders, who won the Open in 1977 and was runner-up in the Open Amateur in 1966. She was a girl international in 1964, 1965, 1966 and 1967, played in the Curtis Cup in 1968, the Vagliano in 1967, the Commonwealth in 1967, the European in 1967 and in the home internationals in 1967 and 1968. In 1969 she turned professional and qualified for the USLPGA circuit that same year, the first European to do so. In 1971 she was the first non-American to qualify at the LPGA teaching exams, and took the PGA course at Lilleshall in the early nineteen-seventies. A few years later she was the first lady professional to sign up with Golf Management and played successfully in Australia, the Far East and the USA. In 1973 she played in the Kenyan Open, Nairobi, and was thus the first woman to play in a national open tournament. She won the Schweppes Tarax Open and the Chrysler Open in Australia in 1973, and won the WPGA British Car Auctions in 1980. She was founder of the WPGA and chairman of it from 1978 to 1979. She has been attached to Horsley, Selsdon Park, Moore Place, Fairmile, Royal Manhattan and Tyrrells Wood and writes regular instructional articles. She has a particular flair for coaching and encouraging young champions.

Miss Saunders started playing at the age of eight, and was off 12 at the age of twelve. By the age of twenty she held six course records. She obtained an honours degree in psychology at Bedford College, University of London, in

Mickey Walker, lady champion in 1971 and 1972, turned professional in 1973 and has had a flourishing career ever since

Vivien Saunders gets it right again!

1969, and qualified as a solicitor in 1981 – leaving a major golf tournament at 4.30 one afternoon and sitting her finals at 9.00 a.m. the next day. She took her MBIA around the same time. Her legal training has been of immense benefit to the WPGA, particularly during its troubles and wrangles towards the end of 1982.

She is the author of *The Complete Woman Golfer*, *The Young Golfer*, *Tee to Green* (video) and *Successful Golf*. She has been prominent in the coaching and encouragement of young players and her ambition (when asked in March 1981) is to coach a Curtis Cup squad. It is doubtful that any other lady golfer in the UK has ever been as well qualified to do so (b.1946).

Two members of the same family who attained distinction during the 1950s and are still competing at championship level in the 1980s are Angela, née Ward, Bonallack and her sister-in-law Sally, née Bonallack, Barber. Angela Ward Bonallack won the English in 1958 and 1963, the Swedish and the German in 1955, the Scandinavian in 1956 and the Portuguese in 1957.

She won the Astor Salver in 1957, 1958, 1960, 1961 and 1966, the Astor Prince's in 1968 and the Roehampton Gold in 1980. She was leading amateur in the Colgate European Ladies' Open in 1975 and 1976, Essex champion in 1968, 1969, 1973, 1974, 1976, 1977, 1978 and 1982, South-Eastern champion in 1957 and 1965, and Kent champion in 1955, 1956 and 1958. She played in the Curtis Cup in 1956, 1958, 1960, 1962, 1964 and 1966, the Vagliano in 1959, 1961 and 1963 and in the home internationals in 1956, 1957, 1958, 1959, 1960, 1961, 1962, 1963, 1964, 1966 and 1972.

She began playing golf at the age of thirteen at North Foreland 'mostly in self-defence': both parents had started playing and talked about nothing else which, she said 'was enough to drive a girl to distraction'. Wanda Morgan, after beating her in a Kent Championship, suggested to her father that she had enough talent to make taking a year off to play golf worthwhile. He agreed. After winning the Girls', in 1955, she was disappointed at not being including in the junior team which was about to tour Australia, so borrowed £50 from her father, played golf successfully in four countries, and came home with £11 after paying all her travelling expenses (b.1937).

Sally, née Bonallack, Barber won the English in 1968, the German in 1958, the Astor Salver in 1972, and was Essex champion in 1958, 1959, 1960, 1961, 1962, 1963, 1966, 1967, 1970 and 1971. She played in the Curtis Cup in 1962, the Vagliano in 1961 and 1969, the European in 1969 and 1971, and in the

Angela Bonallack bunkering out

home internationals in 1960, 1961, 1962, 1963, 1968, 1970 and 1972 and as captain in 1977; she was non-playing captain in 1978. She joined the WPGA in March 1979 but later regained amateur status (b.1938).

Ann Irvin was lady champion in 1973, having previously won the inaugural Open Amateur Stroke Play in 1969. She also won the English in 1967 and 1974, and the Roehampton Gold in 1967, 1968, 1969, 1972, 1973 and 1976. She was Lancashire champion in 1965, 1967, 1969, 1971, 1972 and 1974, and won the French Girls' in 1963, being a girl international in 1960 and 1961. She played in the Curtis Cup in 1962, 1968, 1970 and 1976, and was deputy captain in 1982. She played in the Vagliano in 1961, 1963, 1965, 1967, 1969, 1971, 1973 and 1975, the Commonwealth in 1967 and 1975, in the European in 1965, 1967, 1969, 1971, 1973 and 1975, and in the home internationals in 1962, 1963, 1965, 1967, 1968, 1969, 1970, 1971, 1972, 1973 and 1975. She was designated Daks Woman Golfer of the Year in 1968, captained the LGU touring team to Australia in 1973 and the Espirito in 1981. She was thirty years of age when she won the Open Amateur, and, at a height of only 5 feet 3 inches, wasted no distance in wild play; she was never in the rough and never off line. Precision and accuracy have always been features of her game (b.1943).

The Open Amateur title went overseas three times in the 1970s, and British attention was drawn to the Open Amateur Stroke Play title. This was won by Mary, née Everard, Laupheimer in 1970. She also won the English in 1972, the Astor Salver in 1967, 1968 and 1978 and the Roehampton Gold in 1970. She was North of England champion in 1972, Yorkshire champion in 1964, 1967, 1972, 1973 and 1977. She played in the Curtis Cup in 1970, 1972, 1974 and 1978, in the European in 1967, 1971, 1973 and 1977 and in the Home Internationals in 1964, 1967, 1970, 1972, 1973, 1977 and 1978. She played in the Vagliano in 1967, 1969, 1971 and 1973, the Commonwealth in 1971 and the Espirito in 1968 and 1978, being captain in 1972. She toured Australia in 1973 and captained England in Kenya in 1973.

Married to an American and therefore resident in the USA, on one of her return trips to the UK she commented on the difference in standards of the two countries, pointing out that it could be based on the difference in handicap systems. 'As a rule [in America]', she said, 'one hands in a card every time one goes out. The result is that handicaps reflect average play as opposed to how someone plays when at her best. It's all very different from back in Britain when, on a day when an extra day score isn't going well, you simply tear up your card. Which, of course, is only natural, in that it doesn't really matter to anyone what you do with it' (b.1942).

The oldest lady champion

In 1971, Belle Robertson took the Open Amateur Stroke Play title, as she did in 1972, and thus consolidated her championship wins which had begun in 1957. Ten years later, in 1981, she became lady champion by winning the Open Amateur, having been runner-up three times. She won at the age of forty-five, thus becoming the oldest winner, eclipsing Jessie Anderson Valentine's record of being the oldest when she won in 1958 at the age of

forty-three. Isabella, née McCorkindale, Robertson, MBE, won the Scottish in 1965, 1966, 1971, 1972, 1978 and 1980, the Helen Holm Trophy in 1973 and 1979 and the Roehampton Gold in 1978, 1979, 1981 and 1982. She was West of Scotland champion in 1957, 1964, 1966 and 1969, and Dunbartonshire champion in 1958, 1959, 1960, 1961, 1962, 1963, 1965, 1966, 1968, 1969 and 1978. She won the New Zealand in 1971.

She played in the Curtis Cup in 1960, 1966, 1968, 1970, 1972 and 1982, being non-playing captain in 1974 and 1976. She played in the Vagliano in 1959, 1963, 1965, 1969, 1971 and 1981, in the Espirito in 1964, 1966 and 1968 (captain), 1972, 1980 and 1982. She played in the Commonwealth in 1971 and was non-playing captain in 1975. She played in the European in 1965, 1967 (captain), 1969, 1971, 1973 and 1981, and in the home internationals in 1958, 1959, 1960, 1961, 1962, 1963, 1964, 1965, 1966, 1969, 1972, 1973, 1978, 1980, 1981 and 1982. She was awarded the Frank Moran Trophy in 1971 and was designated Daks Woman Golfer of the Year in 1971 and 1981.

When she opened the Women Golfers' Museum in February 1982, she made the point that she was a suitable person to perform the opening, as 'When I play in international matches these days, I am not chosen by the selectors but by the National Trust.' Her rigorous practice system has stood her in good stead for many years. The routine consists of one and a half hours, twice a day, one session with the short clubs and one with the long irons, plus a quarter hour after each session on the putting green, as well as a number of bunker shots. She also runs a mile each evening in order to keep her fitness in line with her opponents, many of whom are nearly three decades younger.

Julia Greenhalgh also won the Open Amateur Stroke Play in the 1970s, twice running, in 1974 and 1975. She also won the English in 1966 and 1979 and the Welsh Stroke Play in 1977. She won the Astor Salver in 1969 and 1979, the Hampshire Rose in 1977, was Lancashire champion in 1961, 1962, 1966, 1968, 1973, 1975, 1976, 1977 and 1978, and Northern champion in 1961 and 1962. In 1963 she won the New Zealand. She was a girl international in 1957, 1958 and 1959, and won the Scottish Girls' Open in 1960. She played in the Curtis Cup in 1964, 1970, 1974, 1976 and 1978, the Vagliano in 1961, 1965, 1975 and 1977, and in the Commonwealth in 1963 and 1975. She played in the Espirito in 1970 and 1974, both as captain, and in 1978. She played in the European in 1971, 1975, 1977 and 1979, and in the home internationals in 1960, 1961, 1963, 1966, 1969, 1970, 1971, 1976, 1977 and 1978. She was designated Daks Woman Golfer of the Year in 1974 (b.1941).

In 1976, Cathy Panton and Jenny Lee Smith shared the championship honours and both made successful careers as professionals after that. Catherine Panton won the Open Amateur in 1976, the Scottish Girls' in 1969 and was East of Scotland champion in 1976. She was a girl international in 1969, 1970, 1971, 1972 and 1973. She played in the Espirito in 1976, the Vagliano in 1977 and in the home internationals in 1972, 1973, 1976, 1977 and 1978, and in the European in 1973 and 1977. She toured Canada with the LGU team in 1973 and was designated Scottish Sportswoman of the Year in 1976. She turned professional in January 1979 and headed the WPGA lists in

ABOVE: *Cathy Panton shows her suppleness and power*

ABOVE RIGHT: *Jennie Lee Smith gives that ball all she's got*

that year. In 1981 she was overall Carlsberg European Women's champion, and in the same year she broke the course record at Moortown with a 71 in the first round of the Carlsberg European. She broke that record in the second round with 70, and then Jenny Lee Smith came in with a 69. Miss Panton also had bad luck in the Open in 1981, when she was disqualified for removing a stone from a bunker, permitted under professional regulations but not LGU rules. A graduate, she learned her golf from her father, a professional, who still coaches her (b.1955).

Jenny Lee Smith won the Open Amateur Stroke Play and the inaugural Open in 1976. She was Northumberland champion in 1972, 1973 and 1974, played in the Curtis Cup in 1974 and 1976, in the European in 1975 and in the home internationals in 1973, 1974, 1975 and 1976. She played in the Femenino in 1975, the Espirito in 1976 and the Commonwealth in 1975. She was designated Daks Woman Golfer of the Year in 1976, turned professional in June 1977 and gained her USLPGA card in July 1977. She topped the WPGA lists in 1981 and 1982.

Formerly a hairdresser, and coached by John Jacobs, Jenny Lee Smith is among the longest British hitters, but not among the luckiest. She had to undergo surgery after dropping a heavy wardrobe on her foot, spent part of the 1981–2 winter in hospital after becoming allergic to drugs taken for a stomach ailment and later on developed ankle tendon trouble. One of her techniques for coping with the stress and strain of final rounds is to practise deep breathing exercises (b.1948).

Angela, née Carrick, Uzielli was lady champion in 1977. She also won the Astor Salver in 1971, 1973, 1977 and 1981 and the Roehampton Gold in 1977. She was Berkshire champion in 1976, 1977, 1978, 1979, 1980 and 1981. She played in the Curtis Cup in 1978, the Vagliano in 1977, in the European in 1977 and in the home internationals in 1976, 1977 and 1978. She was designated Daks Woman Golfer of the Year in 1977. In 1982 she won the Avia, with Wilma Aitken, at her fifteenth attempt, and also the Mother and Daughter Foursomes for the twelfth time; her mother, Peggy, née Bullard, Carrick was Norfolk champion in 1938, 1939, 1947, 1949, 1952, 1954, 1956, 1958, 1961, 1965 and 1977. When Mrs Uzielli won the Open Amateur, she had two young children, and her practice was confined to those hours when the children were at school. During the 1977 championship, as she progressed from round to round, pleading phone calls to her husband and friends ensured that the baby-sitting rotas were continued. She was thirty-seven when she won the championship, and thus boosted the morale of many lady golfers who were in the same age group (b.1940).

In 1978 the Open Amateur Stroke Play and the Open were played concurrently and Janet Melville held both titles. She was a girl international in 1976, played in the Vagliano in 1979, the European in 1979 and in the home internationals in 1978, 1979 and 1981 (b.1958).

Next lady champion was Maureen Madill in 1979. She shared championship honours with Mary McKenna, who won the Open Amateur Stroke Play in 1979, but retained them in 1980 when she too won the Open Amateur

BELOW LEFT: *Angela Uzielli battles through a snow storm to urge on a vital putt*

BELOW: *Maureen Madill plays a high pitch during the 1980 Curtis Cup*

ABOVE: *Kitrina Douglas was lady champion at her first attempt in 1982. In 1984 she turned professional*

ABOVE RIGHT: *Jane Connachan, dropped by the selectors for the 1984 Curtis Cup at Muirfield, immediately turned professional. She hails from Musselburgh, where the first ladies' golf competition was played in the early nineteenth century*

Stroke Play. Maureen Madill was also Ulster champion in 1980 and 1983, a girl international in 1972, 1973, 1974, 1975 and 1976, played in the Curtis Cup in 1980, the Espirito in 1980, the Vagliano in 1979 and 1981, the Commonwealth in 1979, the European in 1979 and 1981, and in the home internationals in 1978, 1979, 1980, 1981, 1982 and 1983 (b.1958). With Miss McKenna, she led an upsurge in the popularity of ladies' golf in Ireland, unprecedented since early this century. Miss McKenna spent some time in America and that experience helped her conquests in Britain and Ireland. A tall, powerful woman, who frequently booms drives 50 yards past her rivals, she works as a bank clerk in the Dublin branch of the Royal Bank of Ireland. Her first major success outside Ireland was the Open Stroke Play in 1979 at the age of 30. She won the Irish in 1969, 1972, 1974, 1977, 1979, 1981 and 1982. She played in the Curtis Cup in 1970, 1972, 1974, 1976, 1978, 1980 and 1982, the Vagliano in 1969, 1971, 1973, 1975, 1977, 1979 and 1981 and in the Espirito in 1970, 1974 and 1976. She played in the European in 1969, 1971, 1973, 1975, 1977, 1979 and 1981 and in the home internationals in 1968, 1969, 1970, 1971, 1972, 1973, 1974, 1975, 1976, 1977, 1978, 1979, 1980 and 1982. She captained the LGU team to South Africa in 1974, was leading amateur in the Colgate European LPGA in 1977 and 1979 and was voted Daks Woman Golfer of the Year in 1979. One of Miss McKenna's comments after her American stay was: 'we suffer because our practice greens are not of the same pace and texture as those on the course' (b.1949).

The youngsters take over

In 1981, Janet Soulsby distinguished herself by winning three titles in the space of three weeks. She won the English Girls' Under 23, the English Girls', and the Open Amateur Stroke Play. By winning the latter, she became the youngest person of either sex to win a major championship, at the age of sixteen. At the age of fourteen, she was Aer Lingus Schools' champion and also De Beers' Junior champion, and was English Schoolgirl champion for three successive years. Coached by Vivien Saunders, she is a well-built player with great power. Henry Cotton has said: 'Janet knows what it is to hit the ball, rather than merely swing at it.' She played in the home internationals in 1981 and 1982 and in the Curtis Cup in 1982 (b.1964).

Runner-up to Janet Soulsby in the Open Amateur Stroke Play in 1981 was Jane Connachan, who won in 1982. She also won the Scottish in 1982, was East Lothian champion in 1978 and 1979 and won the Girls' in 1980 and 1981, being the only player to retain the title since Pauline Doran won it three times in succession (1930–32). She also won the Scottish Girls' in 1978, 1979 and 1980 and the Scottish Girls' Open in 1978 and 1980.

She was a girl international in 1976, 1977, 1978, 1979 and 1980, played in the Curtis Cup in 1980 and 1982, the Espirito in 1980 and 1982, the Femenino in 1981 and 1983, the Vagliano in 1981 and the home internationals in 1979, 1980, 1981 and 1982. Miss Connachan spent a year at Indiana University and undoubtedly reaped the benefit in golfing experience. After her return from Denver and the unsuccessful team attempt on the 1982 Curtis Cup, she described the differences in standards on the two sides of the Atlantic thus: 'We are taught to compete. Americans are taught to *win*. When we play golf, we hit the ball around the golf course. When Americans play golf, *they play golf.*' Miss Connachan was a scratch player at the age of thirteen and was designated 1982 Lady Golfer of the Year by Avia Watches who took over the award from Daks (b.1964).

Lady champion in 1982 was Kitrina Douglas, who had been playing golf for only four years at that time. She won the Scottish Girls' in 1981, was Gloucester champion in 1980, 1981, 1982 and 1983 and played in the Curtis Cup in 1982 and in the home internationals in 1982. Tall and well-built, she is an accurate rather than a long hitter. When she won the Open Amateur, the LGU had increased the number of qualifiers from 32 to 64, otherwise she would not have survived the preliminaries. Coached by Vivien Saunders, her training schedule consists of a four-mile training run in the mornings, followed by practice during all the daylight hours, including at least two hours on the putting green. In 1978 her handicap came down from 30 to 19; in 1979 from 19 to 3, in 1980 from 3 to 1; in 1981 from 1 to scratch, and in 1982 from scratch to plus one. She played in the 1983 Vagliano. Later, not selected for the Curtis Cup, she turned professional and won the first major tournament for which she entered (b.1961).

Glories of Combat

There are very occasional gaps in these records where war, strikes or simple lack of information have intervened. The contestants' names are recorded as they appear in the competition results so, for example, a woman may one year register as Mrs Smith and in another as Mrs E. Smith.

THE CHAMPIONSHIPS

LADIES' BRITISH OPEN AMATEUR CHAMPIONSHIP

In November 1890 a letter appeared in *Golf* magazine which suggested that a ladies' championship would be popular. The letter was signed 'Toots', Glenalmond, Perth:

> If once started, it would not only help to encourage ladies to indulge in this healthy pastime, but as years roll by the general interest in such an event would increase, and in time it would become one of the most attractive gatherings of the year. I feel sure, if a championship was held in such places as St Andrews, North Berwick and Eastbourne, they would attract many a fair golfer.

In 1893 two championships were mooted, the ladies of St Anne's and Wimbledon having the same idea. They joined forces and the first was played from 13 to 18 June over the then 9-hole St Anne's, organized by the newly formed LGU. The original cup cost £50. It was called the Ladies' Championship for many years and is generally referred to as the British Ladies' Championship. Its correct name is the Ladies' British Open Amateur Championship.

Today it is open to all ladies of recognized amateur status, with a handicap of 4 or the overseas equivalent. It is decided by match play.

One round of 18 holes is played on each of the first two days, according to the draw. The thirty-two (or more if special conditions demand) players returning the lowest scores over the 36 holes qualify for match play. Apart from the Championship Cup, the winner of which is titled Ladies' British Open champion, other trophies competed for in this championship are the Pam Barton Memorial Salver (champion), the Diana Fishwick Cup (runner-up), the Springbok and Lion Trophies (semi-finalists), the SLGA Cup (team with lowest aggregate score in qualifying rounds), the Doris Chambers Trophy (lowest score for the 36 holes) and the Angus Trophy (lowest score for 18 holes).

After the first championship was played, a strong objection was lodged in *Golf* from 'I am, sir, etc., Scotchman' who wrote:

> Scotland possesses several lady golfers who are stronger players than the present champion . . . it is ridiculous to call the present Lady Champion by any other title than Champion of *England*. It should be clearly understood that the Union which promotes these championships only includes a very few of the existing Golf Clubs of the country.

There promptly followed a reply from 'A Scot' who wrote:

> Will anyone dispute the following facts: 1) that golf has taken firm root in England; 2) that it is much the larger nursery of the two; 3) that England has now, and is laying out, ladies' links which would astonish most St Andrew's Ladies. Your best friends, Scotia, say: 'Wake up! It is high time, or you may have to woo instead of being wooed'.

Many letters followed, for and against the above views.

During the championship's history, the handicap limit has changed, up and down, but the format has remained largely the same. Cecil Leitch and Janet Jackson, six-times Irish champion, suggested changes in 1925. The championship had remained the same for twenty-one years, except that ten years previously the final had been changed from 18 holes to 36. Miss Leitch and Miss Jackson suggested that there should be three rounds of stroke play on three successive days, each of 18 holes, the first four to qualify for two semi-finals and a final, each match to consist of 36 holes. The LGU Executive counterproposed two rounds of stroke play, with thirty-two to qualify for match play, each match to be of 18 holes except the final, which should be 36.

There was a storm of protest against changing the original conditions of play thought out by Laidlaw Purves, and it was considered that one human being versus another 'brings out the very essence of progress and brilliant achievement which is totally opposed to general tactics of successful card and pencil'. After much discussion, including thought being given to the fact that balls and equipment had changed, although players and conditions had not, Joyce Wethered proposed that conditions should remain the same 'except that LGU handicaps should be 12 or less, non-union players 8 or less, and open to foreign proposals'. This was carried by 320 votes to 81.

Since 1893, the championship cup has – although not always physically – gone to an overseas winner seventeen times, out of a total of eighty times played – to seven French, eight Americans, one Canadian and one Australian. Only two people have won it four times, Cecil Leitch and Joyce Wethered, five people have won it three times, Lady Margaret Scott, May Hezlet, Enid Wilson, Brigitte Varangot and Jessie Anderson Valentine. Twice-running winners have been Marley Spearman, Elizabeth Chadwick and Michelle Walker. The largest margin by which it has been won was 9 and 7, when Joyce Wethered defeated Cecil Leitch at Prince's in 1922.

Year	Winner	Runner-up	Venue	By
1893	Lady Margaret Scott	I. Pearson	St Anne's	7 & 5
1894	Lady Margaret Scott	I. Pearson	Littlestone	3 & 2
1895	Lady Margaret Scott	E. Lythgoe	R. Portrush	5 & 4
1896	A.B. Pascoe	L. Thomson	R. Liverpool	3 & 2
1897	E. Orr	Miss Orr	Gullane	4 & 2
1898	L. Thomson	E. Nevile	Yarmouth	7 & 5
1899	M. Hezlet	J. Magill	Newcastle, Co. Down	2 & 1
1900	R. Adair	E. Nevile	Westward Ho!	6 & 5
1901	M. Graham	R. Adair	Aberdovey	3 & 1
1902	M. Hezlet	E. Nevile	R. Cinque Ports	19th
1903	R. Adair	F. Walker-Leigh	R. Portrush	4 & 3
1904	L. Dod	M. Hezlet	Troon	1 hole
1905	B. Thompson	M.E. Stuart	R. Cromer	3 & 2
1906	Mrs Kennion	B. Thompson	Burnham	4 & 3
1907	M. Hezlet	F. Hezlet	Newcastle, Co. Down	2 & 1

Year	Winner	Runner-up	Venue	By
1908	M. Titterton	D. Campbell	St Andrews	19th
1909	D. Campbell	F. Hezlet	R. Birkdale	4 & 3
1910	E. Grant-Suttie	L. Moore	Westward Ho!	6 & 4
1911	D. Campbell	V. Hezlet	R. Portrush	3 & 2
1912	G. Ravenscroft	S. Temple	Turnberry	3 & 2
1913	M. Dodd	E. Chubb	St Anne's	8 & 6
1914	C. Leitch	G. Ravenscroft	Hunstanton	2 & 1
1920	C. Leitch	M. Griffiths	Newcastle, Co. Down	7 & 6
1921	C. Leitch	J. Wethered	Turnberry	4 & 3
1922	J. Wethered	C. Leitch	Prince's	9 & 7
1923	D. Chambers	Mrs A. MacBeth	Burnham	2 holes
1924	J. Wethered	Mrs Cautley	R. Portrush	7 & 6
1925	J. Wethered	C. Leitch	Troon	37th
1926	C. Leitch	Mrs P. Garon	R. St David's	8 & 7
1927	S. de la Chaume (France)	D. Pearson	Newcastle, Co. Down	5 & 4
1928	N. le Blan (France)	S. Marshall	Hunstanton	3 & 2
1929	J. Wethered	G. Collett	St Andrews	3 & 1
1930	D. Fishwick	G. Collett	Formby	4 & 3
1931	E. Wilson	W. Morgan	Portmarnock	7 & 6
1932	E. Wilson	C.P.R. Montgomery	Saunton	7 & 6
1933	E. Wilson	D. Plumpton	Gleneagles	5 & 4
1934	H. Holm	P. Barton	R. Porthcawl	6 & 5
1935	W. Morgan	P. Barton	Newcastle, Co. Down	3 & 2
1936	P. Barton	B. Newell	Southport	5 & 3
1937	J. Anderson	D. Park	Turnberry	6 & 4
1938	H. Holm	E. Corlett	Burnham	4 & 3
1939	P. Barton	Mrs T. Marks	R. Portrush	2 & 1
1946	J. Hetherington	P. Garvey	Hunstanton	1 hole
1947	M. Zaharias (USA)	J. Gordon	Gullane	5 & 4
1948	L. Suggs (USA)	J. Donald	R. Lytham	1 hole
1949	F. Stephens	V. Reddan	R. St David's	5 & 4
1950	L. de St Sauveur (France)	J. Valentine	Newcastle, Co. Down	3 & 2
1951	Mrs P.G. MacCann	F. Stephens	Broadstone	4 & 3
1952	M. Paterson	F. Stephens	Troon	39th
1953	M. Stewart (Canada)	P. Garvey	R. Porthcawl	7 & 6
1954	F. Stephens	E. Price	Ganton	4 & 3
1955	J. Valentine	B. Romack	R. Portrush	7 & 6
1956	M. Smith (USA)	M. Janssen	Sunningdale	8 & 7
1957	P. Garvey	J. Valentine	Gleneagles	4 & 3
1958	J. Valentine	E. Price	Hunstanton	1 hole
1959	E. Price	B. McCorkindale	Ascot	37th
1960	B. McIntire (USA)	P. Garvey	R. St David's	4 & 2
1961	M. Spearman	D. Robb	Carnoustie	7 & 6
1962	M. Spearman	A. Bonallack	R. Birkdale	1 hole
1963	B. Varangot (France)	P. Garvey	Newcastle, Co. Down	3 & 1
1964	C. Sorenson (USA)	B. Jackson	Prince's	37th

Year	Winner	Runner-up	Venue	By
1965	B. Varangot (France)	B. Robertson	St Andrews	4 & 3
1966	E. Chadwick	V. Saunders	Ganton	3 & 2
1967	E. Chadwick	M. Everard	R. St David's	1 hole
1968	B. Varangot (France)	C. Rubin	Walton Heath	20th
1969	C. Lacoste (France)	A. Irvin	R. Portrush	1 hole
1970	D. Oxley	B. Robertson	Gullane	1 hole
1971	M. Walker	B. Huke	Alwoodley	3 & 1
1972	M. Walker	C. Rubin	Hunstanton	2 holes
1973	A. Irvin	M. Walker	Carnoustie	3 & 2
1974	C. Semple (USA)	A. Bonallack	R. Porthcawl	2 & 1
1975	N. Syms (USA)	S. Cadden	St Andrews	3 & 2
1976	C. Panton	A. Sheard	Silloth	1 hole
1977	A. Uzielli	V. Marvin	Hillside	6 & 5
1978	E. Kennedy (Australia)	J. Greenhalgh	Nottinghamshire	1 hole
1979	M. Madill	J. Lock	Nairn	2 & 1
1980	A. Sander (USA)	L. Wollin	Woodhall	3 & 1
1981	B. Robertson	W. Aitken	Caernarvonshire	20th
1982	K. Douglas	G. Stewart	Walton Heath	4 & 2
1983	J. Thornhill	R. Lautens	Silloth	4 & 2

LADIES' BRITISH OPEN CHAMPIONSHIP

This was instituted in 1976 and open to professionals and amateurs with a handicap of not more than 4, the winner receiving the Hickson Trophy plus cheque if professional, plus voucher if amateur. The lowest scoring amateur receives the Smyth Salver, presented in 1979. Before its institution, overseas and home professionals and amateurs had been pressing for such a championship for some time. Two girls, who were discussing with the LGU the possibility of such a championship, asked how much it would cost to run. They were told £500. One girl reached into her handbag for her cheque book, but was told it was not necessary to write the cheque until the championship was set up. When the time drew near, she enquired about paying but learned that had been taken care of by an anonymous donor. During its seven years, the only UK professional to have won it has been Vivien Saunders. Overseas players have won three times – one South African and one American (twice). Amateurs have won three times. Pretty Polly sponsored the event from 1978 to 1982 inclusive. Hitachi took over for 1984. The championship consists of 72 holes stroke play. [* = professional]

Year	Winner	Runner-up	Venue
1976	J.L. Smith	M. McKenna	Fulford
1977	V. Saunders *	M. Everard	Lindrick
1978	J. Melville	W. Aitken	Foxhills
1979	A. Sheard * (SA)	M. Walker *	Southport
1980	D. Massey * (USA)	B. Robertson	Wentworth
1981	D. Massey * (USA)	B. Robertson	Northumberland
1982	M. Figueras-Dotti	J.L. Smith * and R. Jones	R. Birkdale
1983	cancelled		

LADIES' BRITISH OPEN AMATEUR STROKE PLAY CHAMPIONSHIP

Competitors must have an LGU handicap of not more than 4 for this championship, which consists of 72 holes stroke play and was instituted in 1969. The winner receives the Nicholls Trophy and the runner-up the Holden Trophy. The player who returns the lowest score for 18 holes receives the Taunton Trophy, and the player under the age of twenty-three who returns the lowest score for the 72 holes receives the Duncan Salver. The player under eighteen who returns the lowest score for the 72 holes receives the Dinwiddy Trophy; there is also the Team Award Trophy for the lowest aggregate score for the 36 holes of the qualifying rounds.

Year	Winner	Runner-up	Venue	Year	Winner	Runner-up	Venue
1969	A. Irvin	D. Oxley	Northumberland	1977	M. Everard	D. Henson	Lindrick
1970	M. Everard	F. Smith	R. Birkdale	1978	J. Melville	W. Aitken	Foxhills
1971	B. Robertson	M. Everard	Ayr Belleisle	1979	M. McKenna	V. Rawlings	Moseley
1972	B. Robertson	M. Walker	Silloth	1980	M. Madill	P. Wright	Brancepeth Castle
1973	A. Stant	M. Everard	Ipswich	1981	J. Soulsby	J. Connachan	R. Norwich
1974	J. Greenhalgh	T. Perkins	Seaton Carew	1982	J. Connachan	B. Bunkowsky and C. Waite	Downfield
1975	J. Greenhalgh	S. Cadden	Northumberland				
1976	J.L. Smith	M. McKenna	Fulford	1983	A. Nicholas	J. Connachan	Moortown

ENGLISH LADIES' CLOSE AMATEUR GOLF CHAMPIONSHIP

Instituted in 1912 at Prince's, Sandwich, the first two championships were run by the National Golf Alliance and held by the National County Golf Club. The Alliance was a group of several English counties which formed a body independent of the LGU in 1910. The first championship took place during the week commencing 15 April, and the entrance fee was 5 shillings (25p). Qualifications for the first two championships were a little hazy, and indeed the second championship was won by a Scot. Today, entrants must have a handicap of 7 or under, and national qualifications of birth, or English parentage or five years' residence in England.

Year	Winner	Year	Winner	Year	Winner	Year	Winner
1912	M. Gardiner	1931	W. Morgan	1954	F. Stephens	1969	B. Dixon
1913	F.W. Brown	1932	D. Fishwick	1955	F. Stephens Smith	1970	D. Oxley
1914	C. Leitch	1933	D. Pearson	1956	B. Jackson	1971	D. Oxley
1919	C. Leitch	1934	P. Wade	1957	J. Bisgood	1972	M. Everard
1920	J. Wethered	1935	Mrs M. Garon	1958	A. Bonallack	1973	M. Walker
1921	J. Wethered	1936	W. Morgan	1959	R. Porter	1974	A. Irvin
1922	J. Wethered	1937	W. Morgan	1960	M. Nichol	1975	B. Huke
1923	J. Wethered	1938	E. Corlett	1961	R. Porter	1976	L. Harrold
1924	J. Wethered	1947	L. Wallis	1962	J. Roberts	1977	V. Marvin
1925	D. Fowler	1948	F. Stephens	1963	A. Bonallack	1978	V. Marvin
1926	M. Gourlay	1949	A.C. Critchley	1964	M. Spearman	1979	J. Greenhalgh
1927	E. Guedalla	1950	Hon. Mrs A. Gee	1965	R. Porter	1980	B. New
1928	E. Wilson	1951	J. Bisgood	1966	J. Greenhalgh	1981	D. Christison
1929	M. Gourlay	1952	P. Davies	1967	A. Irvin	1982	J. Walter
1930	E. Wilson	1953	J. Bisgood	1968	S. Barber	1983	L. Bayman

GIRLS' BRITISH OPEN AMATEUR CHAMPIONSHIP

In 1914, J.S. Wood of the *Gentlewoman* and Mabel Stringer evolved the idea of a girls' championship, and organized the first one for that year. However, World War I intervened and the championship was not played until 1919, with the age limit adjusted so that the original entrants were not disappointed. It is a match play championship open to girls under eighteen years of age on the last day of the championship, and the handicap limit is 15. The winner receives the Challenge Cup and the runner-up the Leven Trophy. Until 1938 the championship was always held at Stoke Poges, but after that at different venues.

Year	Winner	Year	Winner	Year	Winner	Year	Winner
1919	A. Croft	1933	J. Anderson	1957	B. Varangot	1971	J. Mark
1920	C. Clark	1934	N. Jupp	1958	T. Ross Steen	1972	M. Walker
1921	W. Sarson	1935	P. Faulkner	1959	S. Vaughan	1973	A-M. Palli
1922	M. Wickenden	1936	P. Edwards	1960	S. Clarke	1974	R. Barry
1923	M. Mackay	1937	L. Vagliano	1961	D. Robb	1975	S. Cadden
1924	S. de la Chaume	1938	S. Stroyan	1962	S. McLaren-Smith	1976	G. Stewart
1925	E. Wilson	1949	P. Davies	1963	D. Oxley	1977	W. Aitken
1926	D. Esmond	1950	J. Robertson	1964	P. Tredinnick	1978	M. de Lorenzi
1927	D. Fishwick	1951	J. Redgate	1965	A. Willard	1979	S. Lapaire
1928	D. Fishwick	1952	A. Phillips	1966	J. Hutton	1980	J. Connachan
1929	N. Baird	1953	S. Hill	1967	P. Burrows	1981	J. Connachan
1930	P. Doran	1954	R. Jackson	1968	C. Wallace	1982	C. Waite
1931	P. Doran	1955	A. Ward	1969	J. de Witt Puyt	1983	E. Orley
1932	P. Doran	1956	R. Porter	1970	C. le Feuvre		

UNDER-23 ENGLISH CLOSE AMATEUR CHAMPIONSHIP

At its institution in 1978, the National Westminster Bank helped the launch and presented the trophy. Until then, there was no other championship of such a nature for this age group. It is a 54-hole stroke play competition, and national qualifications of birth, or parentage or five years' residence in England apply. The handicap limit is 9. The runner-up receives the Lorna Peters Trophy, and the Frances Smith Trophy goes to the player under 21 with the lowest aggregate score for the championship. There is also a Counties Trophy.

Year	Winner	Year	Winner	Year	Winner
1978	S. Bamford	1980	B. Cooper	1982	M. Gallagher
1979	B. Cooper	1981	J. Soulsby	1983	P. Grice

ENGLISH LADIES' INTERMEDIATE CHAMPIONSHIP

Inaugurated in 1982, this is a match play event for the eighteen to twenty-three year olds, and is played concurrently with the Girls' British Open Amateur Championship. It is for those who have left school and are at college, university, or job hunting. The event is supported by the National Westminster Bank who presented the trophy, designed by international master silversmith Stuart Devlin. The event is held over three days, with two preliminary medal rounds determining places in three separate flights of sixteen players each. Foursomes pairings takes care of losing players in Flights 2 and 3. The format is designed to give as much competitive match play to as many players as possible in three days. It is intended to supplement the Under-23 English Close Amateur Championship held the week before.

Year Winner
1982 J. Rhodes
1983 L. Davies

ENGLISH GIRLS' CHAMPIONSHIP

When this was instituted in 1964, there was no handicap limit, but for the 1982 event handicaps were eliminated down to 11 as the championship is limited to eighty players. The first championship was held at Wollaton Park. The winner receives the *Golf Illustrated* Challenge Cup. This cup was first played for in 1912, and won by May Leitch; then Cecil Leitch won it on three consecutive occasions, making it her property for ever.

The *Golf Illustrated* was competed for until just after World War II; it was presented to the ELGA for the new girls' championship in 1964. Prior to that date, there was only the Girls' British Open Amateur Championship in which English girls could play, and ELGA realized that by then there were quite enough girls to make a national championship worthwhile.

Year	Winner	Year	Winner	Year	Winner	Year	Winner
1964	S. Ward	1969	C. le Feuvre	1974	C. Langford	1979	L. Moore
1965	D. Oxley	1970	C. le Feuvre	1975	M. Burton	1980	P. Smillie
1966	B. Whitehead	1971	C. Eckersley	1976	H. Latham	1981	J. Soulsby
1967	A. Willard	1972	C. Barker	1977	S. Bamford	1982	C. Waite
1968	K. Phillips	1973	S. Parker	1978	P. Smillie	1983	P. Grice

IRISH GIRLS' CLOSE CHAMPIONSHIP

The championship is open to Irish girls under eighteen on the last day of the Girls' British Open Amateur Championship. Competitors must hold an ILGU handicap, maximum 36. The player with the best gross score receives the Muwick Cup; the player with the best nett score, the Dorothy Glendinning Trophy; the Violet Haslett Cup goes to the player under sixteen with the best gross score.

Year	Winner	Year	Winner	Year	Winner	Year	Winner
1951	J. Davies	1963	P. Atkinson	1970	E.A. McGregor	1977	A. Ferguson
1952	J. Redgate	1964	R. Hegarty	1971	J. Mark	1978	C. Wickham
1953	J. Redgate	1965	V. Singleton	1972	P. Smyth	1979	L. Bolton
1954	no competition	1966	M. McConnell	1973	M. Governey	1980	B. Gleeson
1960		1967	M. McConnell	1974	R. Hegarty	1981	B. Gleeson
1961	M. Coburn	1968	C. Wallace	1975	M. Irvine	1982	D. Langan
1962	P. Boyd	1969	E.A. McGregor	1976	P. Wickham	1983	E. McDaid

IRISH LADIES' CLOSE AMATEUR CHAMPIONSHIP

Instituted in 1894, this championship is the second oldest one. There is no handicap restriction for entrants, but the competition is limited to the sixty-four players with the lowest handicaps. National qualifications consist of birth, or parentage, or five years' residence. The winners' cup is held for one year by the club from which she entered, and the winner also receives a medal and replica cup; the runner-up and the semi-finalists receive brooches.

Year	Winner	Year	Winner	Year	Winner	Year	Winner
1894	Miss Mulligan	1914	J. Jackson	1938	Mrs J. Beck	1964	Mrs Z. Fallon
1895	Miss Cox	1919	J. Jackson	1939	C. MacGeagh	1965	E. Purcell
1896	M. Graham	1920	J. Jackson	1946	P. Garvey	1966	E. Bradshaw
1897	M. Graham	1921	Miss Stuart-French	1947	P. Garvey	1967	G. Brandom
1898	J. Magill	1922	Mrs C. Gotto	1948	P. Garvey	1968	E. Bradshaw
1899	M. Hezlet	1923	J. Jackson	1949	C. Smye	1969	M. McKenna
1900	R. Adair	1924	C.G. Thornton	1950	P. Garvey	1970	P. Garvey
1901	R. Adair	1925	J. Jackson	1951	P. Garvey	1971	E. Bradshaw
1902	R. Adair	1926	P. Jameson	1952	D. Forster	1972	M. McKenna
1903	R. Adair	1927	Miss M'Loughlin	1953	P. Garvey	1973	M. Mooney
1904	M. Hezlet	1928	Mrs Dwyer	1954	P. Garvey	1974	M. McKenna
1905	M. Hezlet	1929	Mrs M.A. Hall	1955	P. Garvey	1975	M. Gorry
1906	M. Hezlet	1930	Mrs J.B. Walker	1956	P. O'Sullivan	1976	C. Nesbitt
1907	F. Walker-Leigh	1931	E. Pentony	1957	P. Garvey	1977	M. McKenna
1908	M. Hezlet	1932	B. Latchford	1958	P. Garvey	1978	M. Gorry
1909	Miss Ormsby	1933	E. Pentony	1959	P. Garvey	1979	M. McKenna
1910	M. Harrison	1934	P. Sherlock Fletcher	1960	P. Garvey	1980	C. Nesbitt
1911	M. Harrison	1935	D. Ferguson	1961	Mrs K. McCann	1981	M. McKenna
1912	M. Harrison	1936	C. Tiernan	1962	P. Garvey	1982	M. McKenna
1913	J. Jackson	1937	Mrs H.V. Glendinning	1963	P. Garvey	1983	C. Hourihane

IRISH LADIES' CLOSE 54-HOLES STROKE PLAY FOURSOMES

The cup for this championship, called the Bicentennial Perpetual Challenge Cup, was presented to the ILGU in 1976 by the US ambassador to Ireland to commemorate the Bicentenary of the USA. National qualifications, as for the Irish Ladies' Close Amateur Championship, apply and entrants must have a handicap of 12 or under.

Year	Winners	Year	Winners
1976	C. Nesbitt and L. Malone	1980	M. Madill and M. Gorry
1977	M. McKenna and M. Gorry	1981	C. Hourihane and P. Wickham
1978	S. O'Brien Kenny and T. Moran	1982	C. Hourihane and P. Wickham
1979	S. O'Brien Kenny and T. Moran	1983	B. Gleeson and A. O'Sullivan

SCOTTISH LADIES' CLOSE AMATEUR CHAMPIONSHIP

Instituted in 1903, seven cups are now played for at this championship. The winner holds the championship cup, the runner-up the Beddows Trophy, and the semi-finalists hold the Coupar Quaichs. The winner in the second sixteen qualifiers match play holds the Clark Rosebowl, and the player under twenty-one years of age returning the lowest scratch aggregate in the qualifying rounds holds the St Rule Salver. The player returning the lowest nett score in the second qualifying round holds the Lyon Salver, and the Eglinton Quaich and Grainger Cup is competed for by teams playing one stroke play round in conjunction with the first qualifying round of the championship. In addition, eight other trophies are played for in connection with the championship. National qualifications of birtl. or parentage or five years' residence in Scotland and British nationality apply. Entrants with handicaps over 18 may be rejected. The championship consists of two qualifying rounds of stroke play followed by match play.

Year	Winner	Year	Winner	Year	Winner	Year	Winner
1903	A. Glover	1926	M.J. Wood	1951	J. Valentine	1969	Mrs J.H. Anderson
1904	M.A. Graham	1927	B. Inglis	1952	J. Donald	1970	A. Laing
1905	D. Campbell	1928	J. McCulloch	1953	J. Valentine	1971	B. Robertson
1906	D. Campbell	1929	C. Watson	1954	M. Peel	1972	B. Robertson
1907	F. Teacher	1930	H. Holm	1955	J. Valentine	1973	Mrs J. Wright
1908	D. Campbell	1931	J. McCulloch	1956	J. Valentine	1974	Dr A.J. Wilson
1909	E. Kyle	1932	H. Holm	1957	M. Speir	1975	L. Hope
1910	E. Kyle	1933	M. Couper	1958	D. Sommerville	1976	S. Needham
1911	E. Grant-Suttie	1934	N. Baird	1959	J.S. Robertson	1977	C. Lugton
1912	D.M. Jenkins	1935	M. Robertson-Durham	1960	J.S. Robertson	1978	B. Robertson
1913	J. McCulloch	1936	D. Park	1961	Mrs I. Wright	1979	G. Stewart
1914	E. Anderson	1937	H. Holm	1962	J.B. Lawrence	1980	B. Robertson
1920	C. Watson	1938	J. Anderson	1963	J.B. Lawrence	1981	A. Gemmill
1921	C. Watson	1939	J. Anderson	1964	J.B. Lawrence	1982	J. Connachan
1922	C. Watson	1947	J. Donald	1965	B. Robertson	1983	G. Stewart
1923	Mrs W.H. Nicolson	1948	H. Holm	1966	B. Robertson		
1924	C.P.R. Montgomery	1949	J. Donald	1967	J. Hastings		
1925	J. Percy	1950	H. Holm	1968	J. Smith		

SCOTTISH GIRLS' CLOSE AMATEUR CHAMPIONSHIP

SLGA committee member Mary Menzies realized that more competitive opportunities should be given to Scottish girls and eventually persuaded the committee to grant permission to start this championship, inaugurated in 1958 at West Kilbride. National qualifications of birth or parentage, or three years' residence in Scotland, or British nationality, apply and competitors must be under eighteen years of age on 1 September of the appropriate year.

Year	Winner	Year	Winner	Year	Winner	Year	Winner
1958	J. Burnett	1965	J.W. Smith	1972	G. Cadden	1979	J. Connachan
1959	A. Lurie	1966	J. Hutton	1973	M. Walker	1980	J. Connachan
1960	J. Hastings	1967	J. Hutton	1974	S. Cadden	1981	D. Thomson
1961	I. Wylie	1968	M. Dewar	1975	W. Aitken	1982	S. Lawson
1962	I. Wylie	1969	C. Panton	1976	S. Cadden	1983	K. Imrie
1963	M. Norval	1970	M. Walker	1977	W. Aitken		
1964	J.W. Smith	1971	M. Walker	1978	J. Connachan		

SCOTTISH GIRLS' OPEN STROKE PLAY CHAMPIONSHIP

This championship was instituted in 1955, on a suggestion of Mr Sam Bunton, who organized the Youth Championship for boys at Erskine. He asked Mary Menzies to organize a similar one for girls and donated the championship cup. The event was first called the Youth Championship, then the Open Stroke Play and then the Scottish Girls' Open Stroke Play. Competitors must be under twenty-one on the last day of the championship, and the handicap limit is 30. Play consists of three medal rounds. The championship cup goes to the winner, and the Menzies Cup to the player under eighteen who returns the best aggregate for the three rounds.

Year	Winner	Year	Winner	Year	Winner	Year	Winner
1955	M. Fowler	1963	A. Irvin	1971	B. Huke	1979	A. Gemmill
1956	B. McCorkindale	1964	M. Nuttall	1972	L. Hope	1980	J. Connachan
1957	M. Fowler	1965	I. Wylie	1973	G. Cadden	1981	K. Douglas
1958	R. Porter	1966	J. Smith	1974	S. Lambie	1982	J. Rhodes
1959	D. Robb	1967	J. Bourassa	1975	G. Cadden	1983	S. Lawson
1960	J. Greenhalgh	1968	K. Phillips	1976	S. Cadden		
1961	D. Robb	1969	K. Phillips	1977	S. Cadden		
1962	S. Armitage	1970	B. Huke	1978	J. Connachan		

WELSH LADIES' OPEN AMATEUR 54-HOLE STROKE PLAY CHAMPIONSHIP

Instituted in 1976, the championship offers the Dragon Salver, the Mary Nicholls Runner-up Trophy and finally the Under-21 Trophy for competition.

Year	Winner	Year	Winner	Year	Winner	Year	Winner
1976	P. Light	1978	S. Hedges	1980	T. Thomas	1982	V. Thomas
1977	J. Greenhalgh	1979	S. Crowcroft	1981	V. Thomas	1983	J. Thornhill

WELSH GIRLS' CLOSE AMATEUR CHAMPIONSHIP

Instituted in 1954 at Llandrindod Wells, twelve trophies are played for: Blethyn Rees Championship Cup, Nicholls Runner-up Cup, Dennis Smalldon Trophy, Golf Foundation Trophy, Ingham Trophy, K. Norman Jones Cup, Jones Lewis Salver, Melissa Trophy, North versus South Girls' Team Cup, Pressdee Cup, Jane Roberts Cup and the Tenby Trophy. Competitors must be under eighteen years of age on the last day of the Girls' British Open Championship, have Welsh parentage, or be born in Wales or have two years' consecutive residence in Wales.

Year	Winner	Year	Winner	Year	Winner	Year	Winner
1954	D. Lewis	1962	J. Morris	1970	T. Perkins	1978	S. Rowlands
1955	A. Gwyther	1963	A. Hughes	1971	P. Light	1979	M. Rawlings
1956	A. Gwyther	1964	A. Hughes	1972	P. Whitley	1980	K. Davies
1957	A. Coulman	1965	A. Hughes	1973	V. Rawlings	1981	M. Rawlings
1958	S. Wynne-Jones	1966	S. Hales	1974	L. Isherwood	1982	K. Davies
1959	C. Mason	1967	E. Wilkie	1975	L. Isherwood	1983	N. Wesley
1960	A. Hughes	1968	L. Morris	1976	K. Rawlings		
1961	J. Morris	1969	L. Morris	1977	S. Rowlands		

WELSH LADIES' CLOSE AMATEUR CHAMPIONSHIP

Instituted in 1905, today this is open to all Welsh amateur lady golfers who were born in Wales, have Welsh parentage or ten years' residence in Wales or have represented Wales in a junior international. There are no overt handicap restrictions. Trophies include the Lord Tredegar Championship Cup, Lady Cory Runner-up Cup, Caernarvonshire Cup, Lady Windsor Cup, Porthcawl Cup, Radyr Cup, Swansea Bay Cup, Glamorganshire Cup, Marriner Brigg Trophy, Newport Cup, Prince of Wales Investiture Cup and the Rhyl Cup.

Year	Winner	Year	Winner	Year	Winner	Year	Winner
1905	E. Young	1927	Mrs Duncan	1951	Mrs E. Bromley-Davenport	1967	Mrs M. Wright
1906	Miss Duncan	1928	Mrs Duncan			1968	S. Hales
1907	Miss Duncan	1929	Mrs Rieben	1952	E. Lever	1969	P. Roberts
1908	Miss Duncan	1930	M.J. Jeffreys	1953	N. Cook	1970	Mrs A. Briggs
1909	Miss Duncan	1931	M.J. Jeffreys	1954	N. Cook	1971	Mrs A. Briggs
1910	Miss Lloyd Roberts	1932	I. Rieben	1955	N. Cook	1972	A. Hughes
1911	Miss Clay	1933	M.J. Jeffreys	1956	P. Roberts	1973	Mrs A. Briggs
1912	Miss Duncan	1934	I. Rieben	1957	M. Barron	1974	Mrs A. Briggs
1913	Miss Brooke	1935	abandoned	1958	Mrs M. Wright	1975	Mrs A. Johnson
1914	V. Phelps	1936	Mrs Rieben	1959	P. Roberts	1976	T. Perkins
1920	Mrs R. Phillips	1937	Mrs G.S. Emery	1960	M. Barron	1977	T. Perkins
1921	M. Marley	1938	B. Pyman	1961	Mrs M. Oliver	1978	P. Light
1922	J. Duncan	1939	Mrs B. Burrell	1962	Mrs M. Oliver	1979	V. Rawlings
1923	M.R. Cox	1947	M. Barron	1963	P. Roberts	1980	M. Rawlings
1924	M.R. Cox	1948	Mrs N. Seely	1964	Mrs M. Oliver	1981	M. Rawlings
1925	M.R. Cox	1949	S. Bryan-Smith	1965	Mrs M. Wright	1982	V. Thomas
1926	M.C. Justice	1950	Dr Garfield Evans	1966	A. Hughes	1983	V. Thomas

THE INTERNATIONALS

GREAT BRITAIN VERSUS FRANCE

1931 Great Britain 8½	France ½	**1937** Great Britain 6½	France 2½
1932 Great Britain 7	France 1	**1938** Great Britain 7	France 2
1933 Great Britain 7	France 2	**1939** Great Britain 6½	France 2½
1934 Great Britain 4	France 4	**1947** Great Britain 6½	France 2½
1935 Great Britain 5	France 4	**1948** Great Britain 6½	France 2½
1936 Great Britain 6	France 3	**1949** Great Britain 7½	France 1½

1951 Great Britain 8	France 1
1953 Great Britain 5½	France 3½
1955 Great Britain 7	France 2
1957 Great Britain 5½	France 3½

GREAT BRITAIN VERSUS BELGIUM

1949 Great Britain 8	Belgium 1	**1952** Great Britain 9	Belgium 0	**1957** Great Britain 7	Belgium 1
1951 Great Britain 8	Belgium 1	**1955** Great Britain 7½	Belgium 1½		

VAGLIANO TROPHY – GREAT BRITAIN VERSUS EUROPE

1959 Great Britain 12	Europe 3	**1973** Great Britain 20	Europe 10
1961 Great Britain 8	Europe 7	**1975** Great Britain 13½	Europe 10½
1963 Great Britain 20	Europe 10	**1977** Great Britain 15½	Europe 8½
1965 Europe 17	Great Britain 13	**1979** Great Britain 12	Europe 12
1967 Europe 15½	Great Britain 14½	**1981** Europe 14	Great Britain 10
1969 Europe 16	Great Britain 14	**1983** Great Britain 14	Europe 10
1971 Great Britain 17½	Europe 12½		

CURTIS CUP

Year			Venue	Year			Venue
1932 USA 5½	GB and I 3½		Wentworth	**1964** USA 10½	GB and I 7½		R. Porthcawl
1934 USA 6½	GB and I 2½		Chevy Chase	**1966** USA 13	GB and I 5		Hot Springs
1936 USA 4½	GB and I 4½		Gleneagles	**1968** USA 10½	GB and I 7½		Newcastle,
1938 USA 5½	GB and I 3½		Essex County Club				Co. Down
1948 USA 6½	GB and I 2½		R. Birkdale	**1970** USA 11½	GB and I 6½		Brae Burn
1950 USA 7½	GB and I 1½		Buffalo	**1972** USA 10	GB and I 8		Western Gailes
1952 GB and I 5	USA 4		Muirfield	**1974** USA 13	GB and I 5		San Francisco
1954 USA 6	GB and I 3½		Merion	**1976** USA 11½	GB and I 6½		R. Lytham and
1956 GB and I 5	USA 4		Prince's				St Anne's
1958 GB and I 4½	USA 4½		Brae Burn	**1978** USA 12	GB and I 6		Apawamis
1960 USA 6½	GB and I 2½		Lindrick	**1980** USA 13	GB and I 5		St Pierre
1962 USA 8	GB and I 1		Colorado Springs	**1982** USA 14½	GB and I 3½		Denver

ESPIRITO SANTO – WOMEN'S WORLD AMATEUR TEAM CHAMPIONSHIP

Year	Winners	Runners-up	Venue
1964	France	USA (GB and I 3rd)	St Germain
1966	USA	Canada (GB and I 5th)	Mexico
1968	USA	Australia (GB and I 6th)	Melbourne
1970	USA	France (GB and I 6th)	Madrid
1972	USA	France (GB and I joint 5th)	Buenos Aires
1974	USA	GB and I, S. Africa	Dominican Republic
1976	USA	France (GB and I 13th)	Portugal
1978	Australia	Canada (GB and I joint 4th)	Fiji
1980	USA	Australia (GB and I 5th)	Pinehurst
1982	USA	New Zealand (GB and I 3rd)	Geneva

FEMENINO DE GOLF

Year	Winner	GB and I placing	Year	Winner	GB and I placing	Year	Winner	GB and I placing
1975	China	6th	1979	China	7th	1983	USA	6th equal
1977	Brazil	4th	1981	Sweden	4th			

COMMONWEALTH TOURNAMENT

Year	Winner	Venue	Year	Winner	Venue	Year	Winner	Venue
1959	GB and I	St Andrews	1971	GB and I	Hamilton, N. Zealand	1979	Canada	Perth
1963	GB and I	Melbourne				1983	Australia	Edmonton, Canada
1967	GB and I	Ontario, Canada	1975	GB and I	Ganton			

EUROPEAN LADIES' AMATEUR TEAM CHAMPIONSHIP

Year	Winner	Venue	Year	Winner	Venue	Year	Winner	Venue	Year	Winner	Venue
1965	England	Holland	1971	England	England	1977	England	Spain	1983	Ireland	Belgium
1967	England	Portugal	1973	England	Belgium	1979	Ireland	Eire			
1969	France	Sweden	1975	France	France	1981	Sweden	Portugal			

EUROPEAN LADY JUNIORS' TEAM CHAMPIONSHIP

Year	Winner	Venue	Year	Winner	Venue	Year	Winner	Venue	Year	Winner	Venue
1968	Belgium	Holland	1972	Italy	Germany	1976	Italy	Denmark	1980	Scotland	Austria
1969	Holland	Switzerland	1973	France	Spain	1977	Spain	Luxembourg	1981	Sweden	England
1970	France	France	1974	France	Sweden	1978	Sweden	Italy	1982	England	Sweden
1971	France	Italy	1975	Spain	Belgium	1979	France	France	1983	England	Holland

HOME INTERNATIONALS

The matches consist of six singles and three foursomes, each of 18 holes, and scoring is by team results, each team scoring one point for a team win and half for a halved match. Each country may nominate eight players, eligibility being the same as for the countries' own close championships.

1909

Scotland beat England	7 to 2
Scotland beat Ireland	7 to 2
Scotland beat Wales	9 to 0
England beat Ireland	6 to 3
England beat Wales	7 to 2
Ireland beat Wales	7 to 2

1910

Scotland beat Wales	9 to 2
Scotland beat England	6 to 2
Scotland beat Ireland	8 to 1
England beat Ireland	7 to 2
England beat Wales	6 to 3
Ireland beat Wales	7 to 2

1911

Scotland beat Ireland	5 to 2
England beat Ireland	8 to 1
England beat Scotland	5 to 4
(Wales did not compete)	

1912

England beat Ireland	5 to 4
England beat Wales	6 to 3
England beat Scotland	6 to 3
Ireland beat Scotland	6 to 3
Ireland beat Wales	7 to 2
Scotland beat Wales	6 to 3

1913

England beat Wales	8 to 1
England beat Scotland	5 to 4
England beat Ireland	7 to 2
Scotland beat Ireland	6 to 3
Scotland beat Wales	6 to 3
Ireland beat Wales	5 to 4

1914

England beat Scotland	6 to 3

England beat Wales	9 to 1
England beat Ireland	7 to 2
Scotland beat Wales	8 to 1
Scotland beat Ireland	5 to 4
Ireland beat Wales	6 to 3

1920

England beat Scotland	9 to 0
(Wales and Ireland did not compete)	

1921

England beat Scotland	8 to 1
England beat Wales	7 to 2
England beat Ireland	8 to 1
Scotland beat Wales	7 to 2
Scotland beat Ireland	6 to 3
Ireland beat Wales	7 to 2

1922

England beat Wales	8 to 1
England beat Ireland	8 to 1
England beat Scotland	8 to 1
Scotland beat Ireland	7 to 2
Scotland beat Wales	9 to 0
Wales beat Ireland	5 to 4

1923

England beat Wales	9 to 0
England beat Scotland	6 to 3
England beat Ireland	8 to 1
Scotland beat Ireland	9 to 0
Scotland beat Wales	7 to 2
Ireland beat Wales	6 to 3

1924

England beat Scotland	7 to 0
England beat Ireland	7 to 2
England beat Wales	8 to 1
Ireland beat Wales	8 to 1

Ireland beat Scotland	8 to 1
Ireland beat Wales	8 to 1

1925

England beat Scotland	8 to 1
England beat Scotland	9 to 0
England beat Wales	9 to 0
Scotland beat Wales	7 to 2
Scotland beat Ireland	5 to 4
Ireland beat Wales	7 to 2

1926

Not played because of general strike

1927

Scotland beat Wales	7 to 2
Scotland beat Ireland	7 to 2
Scotland beat England	5 to 4
England beat Ireland	9 to 0
England beat Wales	8 to 1
Ireland beat Wales	6 to 3

1928

England beat Scotland	5 to 4
England beat Ireland	7 to 2
Scotland beat Ireland	6 to 3
England beat Wales	9 to 0
Scotland beat Wales	7 to 2
Wales beat Ireland	5 to 4

1929

England beat Scotland	6 to 3
England beat Wales	8 to 1
England beat Ireland	7 to 2
Scotland beat Ireland	8 to 1
Scotland beat Wales	7 to 2
Ireland beat Wales	5 to 3

1930

England beat Ireland	7 to 2
England beat Scotland	8 to 1
England beat Wales	9 to 0
Scotland beat Wales	7 to 2
Scotland beat Wales	5 to 2
Ireland beat Wales	5 to 4

1931

Scotland beat England	5 to 4
Scotland beat Wales	7 to 4
Scotland beat Ireland	6 to 3
England beat Wales	8 to 1
England beat Ireland	7 to 2
Ireland beat Wales	5 to 4

1932

England beat Ireland	9 to 0
England beat Wales	9 to 0
England beat Scotland	8 to 1
Ireland beat Scotland	5 to 4
Ireland beat Wales	6 to 4
Scotland beat Wales	7 to 2

1933

England beat Wales	8 to 1
England beat Scotland	5 to 4
England beat Ireland	8 to 1
Scotland beat Ireland	7 to 2
Scotland beat Wales	8 to 1
Wales beat Ireland	5 to 4

1934

England beat Ireland	7 to 2
England beat Wales	8 to 1
Scotland beat England	5 to 4
Scotland beat Ireland	7 to 2
Wales beat Ireland	6 to 3
Wales beat Scotland	5 to 4

1935

Scotland beat England	6 to 3
Scotland beat Ireland	6 to 3
Scotland beat Wales	6 to 3
Ireland beat Wales	6 to 3
Ireland beat England	5 to 4
England beat Wales	5 to 4

1936

England beat Scotland	8 to 1
England beat Ireland	8 to 1
England beat Wales	8 to 1
Scotland beat Wales	7 to 2
Wales beat Ireland	6 to 3
Ireland beat Scotland	6 to 3

1937

England beat Scotland	6 to 3
England beat Ireland	7 to 2
Scotland beat Wales	9 to 0

(Contest abandoned because of the death of Bridget Newell)

1938

Scotland beat Wales	6 to 3
Scotland beat Ireland	6 to 3
Scotland beat England	6 to 3
England beat Ireland	6 to 3
England beat Wales	8 to 1
Ireland beat Wales	8 to 1

1939

Scotland beat Ireland	5 to 4
Scotland beat England	7 to 2
Scotland beat Wales	8 to 1
Ireland beat England	5 to 4
England beat Wales	7 to 2

1947

Scotland beat Wales	9 to 0
Scotland beat Ireland	6 to 3
Scotland beat England	7 to 2
England beat Ireland	8 to 1
England beat Wales	9 to 0
Ireland beat Wales	6 to 3

1948

England beat Scotland	5 to 4
England beat Ireland	7 to 2
England beat Wales	8 to 1
Scotland beat Ireland	7 to 2
Scotland beat Wales	7 to 2
Ireland beat Wales	6 to 3

1949

England beat Scotland	5 to 4
England beat Ireland	7 to 2
England beat Wales	8 to 1
Scotland beat Ireland	8 to 1
Scotland beat Wales	8 to 1
Ireland beat Wales	8 to 1

1950

Scotland beat England	6 to 3
Scotland beat Ireland	6 to 3
Scotland beat Wales	8 to 1
England beat Ireland	6 to 1
England beat Wales	8 to 1
Ireland beat Wales	6 to 3

1951

Scotland beat England	9 to 0
Scotland beat Ireland	5 to 4
Scotland beat Wales	6 to 3
England beat Ireland	6 to 3
England beat Wales	9 to 0
Ireland beat Wales	6 to 3

1952

Scotland beat England	6 to 3
Scotland beat Ireland	5 to 4
Scotland beat Wales	6 to 3
England beat Wales	9 to 0
Ireland beat England	6 to 3
Ireland beat Wales	7 to 2

1953

England beat Ireland	6 to 3
England beat Scotland	5 to 4
England beat Wales	7 to 2
Scotland beat Ireland	6 to 3
Scotland beat Wales	8 to 1
Ireland beat Wales	7 to 1

1954

England beat Ireland	5 to 4
England beat Scotland	7½ to 1½
England beat Wales	9 to 0
Scotland beat Ireland	5 to 4
Scotland beat Wales	9 to 0
Ireland beat Wales	7 to 2

1955

Scotland halved with England	4½ and 4½
Scotland beat Wales	9 to 0
Scotland beat Ireland	6 to 3
England beat Wales	6½ to 2½
England beat Ireland	6½ to 2½
Ireland beat Wales	6½ to 2½

1956

Scotland beat England	5 to 4
Scotland beat Ireland	8 to 1
Scotland beat Wales	7½ to 1½
England beat Wales	8½ to ½
England halved with Ireland	4½ and 4½
Ireland beat Wales	7 to 2

1957

Scotland beat England	3 to 2 (two matches halved)
Scotland beat Ireland	5 to 2
Scotland beat Wales	7 to 0
England beat Ireland	5 to 0
England beat Wales	5 to 2
Ireland beat Wales	5 to 2

1958

England beat Wales	6 to 1
Ireland beat Scotland	4 to 3
Ireland beat Wales	5 to 2
England beat Scotland	6 to 1
England beat Ireland	4 to 3
Scotland beat Wales	6 to 1

1959

Scotland beat Wales	9 to 0
England beat Ireland	6 to 3
England beat Scotland	6 to 3
Ireland beat Wales	8 to 1
England beat Wales	9 to 0
Scotland beat Ireland	5½ to 3½

1960

England beat Scotland	7 to 2
England beat Ireland	8½ to ½
England beat Wales	7 to 2
Scotland beat Wales	7 to 2
Scotland beat Ireland	7 to 2
Ireland beat Wales	4 to 3

1961

Scotland beat Wales	8 to 0
Scotland beat Ireland	8 to 1
Scotland beat England	4 to 2
England beat Ireland	5 to 4
England beat Wales	9 to 0
Ireland beat Wales	7 to 1

1962

Scotland beat England	4 to 3
Scotland beat Ireland	6 to 3
Scotland beat Wales	6 to 1
England beat Ireland	8 to 0
England beat Wales	9 to 0
Ireland beat Wales	7 to 2

1963

England beat Scotland	5 to 3
England beat Ireland	6 to 2
England beat Wales	8 to 1
Scotland beat Ireland	5 to 2
Scotland beat Wales	9 to 0
Ireland beat Wales	6 to 2

1964

England beat Scotland	7 to 1
England beat Wales	7 to 1
England beat Ireland	7 to 2
Scotland beat Ireland	6 to 1
Scotland beat Wales	6 to 3
Ireland halved with Wales	4 and 4

1965

England beat Ireland	7 to 0
England beat Scotland	5 to 3
England beat Wales	7 to 2
Scotland beat Ireland	5 to 4
Scotland beat Wales	9 to 0
Ireland beat Wales	7 to 2

1966

England beat Ireland	6 to 2

1966 (cont.)

England beat Scotland	5 to 3
England beat Wales	9 to 0
Scotland beat Wales	7 to 1
Scotland beat Ireland	7 to 1
Ireland halved with Wales	4 and 4

1967

England halved with Scotland	4 and 4
England beat Wales	8 to 1
England beat Ireland	6 to 2
Scotland beat Ireland	6 to 2
Scotland beat Wales	7 to 0
Ireland halved with Wales	4 and 4

1968

England halved with Scotland	4 and 4
England beat Ireland	4 to 3
England beat Wales	7 to 2
Scotland beat Ireland	5 to 4
Scotland beat Wales	6 to 3
Ireland beat Wales	5 to 3

1969

Scotland beat Wales	8 to 0
Scotland beat Ireland	7 to 2
England beat Scotland	4 to 2
England beat Wales	8 to 0
Ireland beat England	5 to 4
Ireland halved with Wales	4 and 4

1970

England beat Ireland	7 to 1
England beat Scotland	8 to 0
England beat Wales	6 to 2
Ireland beat Scotland	5 to 3
Ireland beat Wales	8 to 1
Scotland beat Wales	7 to 1

1971

England beat Scotland	6 to 3
England beat Ireland	6½ to 2½
England beat Wales	8 to 1
Scotland beat Ireland	8 to 1
Scotland beat Wales	7 to 2
Ireland beat Wales	5½ to 3½

1972

England beat Scotland	5½ to 3½
England beat Ireland	9 to 0
England beat Wales	8 to 1
Scotland halved with Ireland	4½ and 4½
Scotland beat Wales	8 to 1
Ireland beat Wales	5 to 4

1973

England beat Scotland	5½ to 3½
England beat Wales	7 to 2
England beat Ireland	8 to 1
Scotland halved with Wales	4½ and 4½
Scotland beat Ireland	5 to 4
Wales beat Ireland	5 to 4

1974

Scotland beat Ireland	7 to 2
Scotland beat Wales	7½ to 1½
England beat Scotland	5½ to 3½
England beat Wales	5½ to 3½
Ireland beat England	5 to 4
Ireland beat Wales	5 to 4

1975

England beat Wales	5½ to 3½

England beat Ireland	6 to 3
England beat Scotland	6 to 3
Wales beat Ireland	7 to 2
Ireland beat Scotland	6 to 3
Scotland beat Wales	5 to 4

1976

England halved with Wales	4½ and 4½
England beat Ireland	7½ to 1½
England beat Scotland	5 to 4
Wales halved with Ireland	4½ and 4½
Wales halved with Scotland	4½ and 4½
Ireland beat Scotland	5 to 4

1977

England beat Ireland	5½ to 3½
England beat Scotland	6 to 3
England beat Wales	7½ to 1½
Ireland beat Scotland	7½ to 1½
Scotland beat Wales	8 to 1

1978

England beat Ireland	5½ to 3½
England beat Scotland	5 to 4
England beat Wales	½ to 3½
Ireland beat Scotland	5½ to ½
Ireland beat Wales	6½ to 2½
Scotland beat Wales	6½ to 2½

1979

Scotland beat Wales	5 to 4
Scotland beat England	7 to 2
Ireland beat Scotland	5½ to 3½

Ireland beat England	5 to 4
Wales beat Ireland	5½ to 3½
England beat Wales	6 to 3

1980

Ireland beat Scotland	6½ to 2½
Ireland beat England	5 to 4
Ireland beat Wales	8½ to ½
Scotland beat England	5½ to 3½
Scotland beat Wales	5 to 4
England halved with Wales	4½ and 4½

1981

Scotland beat England	5½ to 3½
Ireland beat Wales	7 to 2
Scotland beat Ireland	6 to 3
Wales halved with England	4½ and 4½
Scotland beat Wales	8½ to ½
England beat Ireland	5½ to 3½

1982

England beat Scotland	5 to 4
England halved with Ireland	4½ and 4½
England beat Wales	7 to 2
Scotland beat Ireland	5½ to 3½
Scotland beat Wales	6½ to 2½
Ireland beat Wales	7 to 2

1983

abandoned

GIRLS' INTERNATIONALS

At first these were played only between England and Scotland; then in 1967 and 1968 Ireland tackled Wales and beat her. Since 1969 all four countries have done battle. Out of twenty-four matches played between the wee Scots and the little Sassenachs, from 1935 to 1968, there were three draws, five wins for Scotland, and sixteen wins for England. Today the winning team collects the Stroyan Cup, held by the captain, and the runner-up the Swansea Spoon. Players must be under eighteen on the last day of the Girls' British Open Championship of the appropriate year and have the same qualifications as those for the girls' national close championships.

1969

England beat Scotland	5½ to 1½
England beat Ireland	5 to 2
England beat Wales	7 to 0
Scotland beat Ireland	5 to 2
Scotland beat Wales	5 to 2
Ireland beat Wales	6 to 1

1970

England beat Scotland	4 to 3
England beat Ireland	5 to 2
England beat Wales	6 to 1
Scotland beat Ireland	4½ to 2½
Scotland beat Wales	6 to 1
Ireland beat Wales	6½ to ½

1971

England beat Scotland	4½ to 2½
England beat Ireland	5 to 2
England beat Wales	5 to 2
Scotland beat Ireland	4½ to 2½
Scotland beat Wales	5½ to 1½
Ireland beat Wales	4 to 3

1972

Scotland beat England	5 to 2
Scotland beat Wales	5½ to 1½
Scotland beat Ireland	6½ to ½
England beat Wales	5 to 2
England beat Ireland	6½ to ½
Wales beat Ireland	4 to 3

1973

Scotland beat England	5 to 2
Scotland beat Ireland	6 to 1
Scotland beat Wales	5 to 2
England beat Ireland	4½ to 2½
England beat Wales	4 to 3
Ireland beat Wales	6½ to ½

1974

England beat Scotland	5 to 2
England beat Ireland	5½ to 1½
England beat Wales	4 to 3
Scotland beat Ireland	6½ to ½
Scotland beat Wales	5 to 2
Ireland beat Wales	5 to 2

1975

England halved with Scotland	3½ and 3½
England beat Ireland	6½ to ½
England beat Wales	6 to 1
Scotland beat Ireland	5 to 2
Scotland beat Wales	5 to 2
Ireland beat Wales	5 to 2

1976

Scotland beat England	4½ to 2½
Scotland beat Wales	5 to 2
Scotland beat Ireland	4 to 3
England beat Wales	6 to 1
England beat Ireland	6½ to ½
Wales beat Ireland	4 to 3

1977

England halved with Scotland	3½ and 3½
England beat Wales	7 to 0
England beat Ireland	6 to 1
Scotland beat Wales	5 to 2
Scotland beat Ireland	7 to 0
Wales beat Ireland	5 to 2

1978

England beat Scotland	5 to 2
England beat Wales	6 to 1
England beat Ireland	7 to 0
Scotland beat Wales	6 to 1
Scotland beat Ireland	4½ to 2½
Wales beat Ireland	5 to 2

1979

England halved with Wales	3½ and 3½
England beat Ireland	7 to 0
England beat Scotland	5½ to 1½
Wales beat Ireland	4½ to 2½
Wales beat Scotland	4½ to 2½
Ireland beat Scotland	4 to 3

1980

England beat Scotland	5½ to 1½
England halved with Ireland	3½ and 3½
England beat Wales	5½ to 1½
Scotland beat Ireland	4 to 3
Scotland beat Wales	6 to 1
Ireland beat Wales	4½ to 2½

1981

England beat Wales	6½ to ½
England beat Scotland	4½ to 2½
England beat Ireland	5½ to 1½
Scotland halved with Ireland	3½ and 3½
Scotland beat Wales	5 to 2

1982

England beat Ireland	7 to 0
England beat Scotland	5 to 2
England beat Wales	6 to 1
Ireland beat Scotland	4 to 3
Ireland beat Wales	4½ to 2½
Scotland beat Wales	6 to 1

1983

England beat Ireland	4½ to 2½
England beat Scotland	4 to 3
England beat Wales	7 to 0
Ireland beat Scotland	4 to 3
Ireland beat Wales	6 to 1
Scotland beat Wales	5½ to 1½

OTHER MAJOR EVENTS

ANGUS LADIES' CHAMPIONSHIP

The name of the county golf association was changed from Forfarshire Ladies' County Golf Club to Angus Ladies' County Golf Club in 1920. On 1 October 1932, and 7 October 1933, proposals and dates for a championship were discussed and 'should the entry be sufficient it was agreed to give a cup to be called the Dickson Trophy'. On 26 January 1934 'The question of the Championship was discussed and it was decided that owing to the very small entry . . . the conditions be changed.' It was decided that a medal round should be played at Carnoustie on 22 September, those with the eight best scores to play another round at Carnoustie on the following Saturday, 29 September. The championship became a 'knock-out' event preceded by a qualifying round in 1958.

Year Winner	Year Winner	Year Winner	Year Winner
1934 Miss Harris	1953 Mrs E.F. Duncan	1964 J. Smith	1975 J.W. Smith
1935 Miss Milliken	1954 Mrs E.F. Duncan	1965 N. Duncan	1976 B. Huke
1936 Mrs Tocher	1955 Mrs E.F. Duncan	1966 K. Lackie	1977 J.W. Smith
1937 Mrs Tocher	1956 Mrs E.F. Duncan	1967 J. Smith	1978 J.W. Smith
1938 Miss Milliken	1957 Mrs E.F. Duncan	1968 S. Chalmers	1979 J.W. Smith
1939 Miss Milliken	1958 M. Walker	1969 I. Taylor	1980 N. Duncan
1948 Mrs Henderson	1959 Mrs A.G. Duncan	1970 J. Smith	1981 K. Sutherland
1949 Mrs Wright	1960 S. Cushnie	1971 K. Lackie	1982 K. Imrie
1950 Mrs E.F. Duncan	1961 E. Allan	1972 K. Lackie	1983 K. Imrie
1951 Mrs C. Johnstone	1962 Mrs A. Beattie	1973 K. Lackie	
1952 Mrs Harris	1963 E. Allan	1974 N. Duncan	

ASTOR SALVER

Instituted in 1951, this stroke play championship has been tied twice, won five times by Angela, née Ward, Bonallack, and abandoned once, in 1982, because of floods.

Year Winner	Year Winner	Year Winner	Year Winner
1951 J. Bisgood	1959 E. Price	1968 D.M. Everard	1976 H.D. Clifford
1952 J. Bisgood	1960 A. Bonallack	1969 J. Greenhalgh	1977 A. Uzielli
1953 J. Bisgood	1961 A. Bonallack	1970 B. Whitehead	1978 D.M. Everard
1954 J. Donald	1962 R. Porter	1971 A. Uzielli	1979 J. Greenhalgh
1955 E. Price	1963 R. Porter	1972 Mrs J.R. Thornhill	1980 J. Lock
1956 Mrs J. Barton and E. Price	1964 M. Spearman	1973 L. Denison-Pender and A. Uzielli	1981 A. Uzielli
1957 A. Ward	1965 M. Spearman	1974 C. Barclay	1982 abandoned – floods
1958 A. Bonallack	1966 A. Bonallack	1975 J.R. Thornhill	1983 L. Bayman
	1967 D.M. Everard		

AVIA WATCHES FOURSOMES CHAMPIONSHIP

Organized by Mrs Joan Rothschild, Douglas Caird and a team of twenty, and played at the Berkshire since 1966, this foursomes event is in two divisions according to handicap (plus to 16, 17 to 24) and is played towards the beginning of the season. It attracts the largest number of potential competitors of any ladies' championship, and there is always a waiting list for places. For four years it was also open to professionals. From 1958 to 1963 it was sponsored by Kayser-Bondor, and in 1964 it became the Casa Pupo Women's Foursomes.

Winners – Division I

1966 Vicomtesse de St Sauveur and
B. Varangot

1967 B.A.B. Jackson and
V. Saunders

1968 A. Irvin and
R. Porter

1969 L. Denison-Pender and
C. Reybroeck

1970 G. Cheetham and
J. Thornhill

1971 L. Denison-Pender and
C. Reybroeck

1972 D. Frearson and
B. Robertson

1973 L. Denison-Pender and M. Walker,
A-M. Palli and B. Varangot

1974 C. le Feuvre and
C. Redford

1975 abandoned – snow

1976 S. Barber and
A. Bonallack

1977 M. McKenna and
T. Perkins

1978 M. Everard and
V. Saunders

1979 L. Bayman and
A. Sander

1980 L. Bayman and
M. Madill

1981 B. Robertson and
I. Wooldridge

1982 W. Aitken and
A. Uzielli

1983 J. Nicholson and
J. Thornhill

Winners – Division II

1966 Mrs A. Joll and
Mrs M. Satchell

1967 Mrs D. Campbell and
Mrs R. Lavelle

1968 Mrs S. Lloyd and
H. Stileman

1969 Mrs I. Cowper and
Mrs M. Garrett

1970 Mrs E. Phillips and
Mrs J. Young

1971 Mrs I. Cowper and
Mrs M. Garrett

1972 Mrs P. Cardy and
Mrs B. McIntosh

1973 C. Denneny and Mrs P. Freeman,
Mrs J. Cowper and Mrs M. Garrett,
R. Arnell and R. Fleming

1974 Mrs H. Dykes and
Mrs R.G. Mickel

1975 abandoned – snow

1976 Mrs E. Morgan and
Mrs S. Newman

1977 Mrs P. Benka and
Mrs S. Sutton

1978 Mme P. Chrétien and
Mrs D. Jacobs

1979 J. Bisgood and
Mrs M. Garrett

1980 Mme P. Chrétien and
Mrs E. Jacobs

1981 Mrs H.N. Hubbard and
Mrs D.J. Youngman

1982 Mrs E. Evans and
P. Stedman

1983 H.N. Hubbard and
D.J. Youngman

AYRSHIRE LADIES' CHAMPIONSHIP

This was inaugurated in 1923 by Miss Ethel Robertson, of Sandyhills, Prestwick, who was secretary of the county that year. The first championship was held at St Nicholas, Prestwick. Jean McCulloch, West Kilbride, won the first championship in 1923, and in 1982 was honorary president of the Ayrshire Ladies' County Golf Association. Winner by the largest margin was Helen Holm, by 8 and 7 in 1950.

Year	Winner	Year	Winner	Year	Winner	Year	Winner
1923	J. McCulloch	1937	J.B. Walker	1958	Mrs B. Singleton	1972	I. Wylie
1924	J. McCulloch	1938	J.B. Walker	1959	Mrs B. Singleton	1973	I. Wylie
1925	C. Martin	1939	B. Henderson	1960	J. Hastings	1974	Mrs J.M. Sharp
1926	J. Gow	1947	H. Holm	1961	J. Hastings	1975	S. Lambie
1927	J. McCulloch	1948	H. Holm	1962	Mrs B. Singleton	1976	S. Lambie
1928	J. McCulloch	1949	Mrs Q. McCall	1963	J. Hastings	1977	S. Lambie
1929	Mrs G. Coats	1950	H. Holm	1964	J. Hastings	1978	T. Walker
1930	Mrs W. Greenless	1951	H. Holm	1965	Mrs I.D. Hamilton	1979	S. Lambie
1931	Mrs W. Greenless	1952	Mrs M. Park	1966	J. Hastings	1980	A. Gemmill
1932	J. McCulloch	1953	Mrs B. Singleton	1967	J. Hastings	1981	A. Gemmill
1933	J. McCulloch	1954	Mrs P.H. Wylie	1968	Mrs I.D. Hamilton	1982	A. Gemmill
1934	J.B. Walker	1955	Mrs A. McCall	1969	I. Wylie	1983	A. Gemmill
1935	H. Holm	1956	Mrs B. Singleton	1970	I. Wylie		
1936	H. Holm	1957	Mrs B. Singleton	1971	I. Wylie		

BEDFORDSHIRE LADIES' CHAMPIONSHIP

Instituted in 1923, the championship cup is known as the Lady Ludlow Cup.

Year	Winner	Year	Winner	Year	Winner	Year	Winner
1923	Mrs Antliff	1936	B. Gorrell	1956	Mrs Greer	1971	Mrs S. Kempster
1924	Mrs J.P. White	1937	N. Sanderson	1957	Mrs Greer	1972	Mrs P. Deman
1925	Miss Dalton	1938	Mrs Crew	1958	F.W. Wood	1973	Mrs J. Hawkins
1926	Mrs Payne	1939	Mrs Crew	1959	Mrs L. Cook	1974	Mrs S. Kempster
1927	Mrs Antliff	1947	Mrs Oakins	1960	Mrs Turner	1975	Mrs P. Deman
1928	Miss Dalton	1948	Miss Walsh	1963	Mrs Murray	1976	Mrs S. Kempster
1929	Miss Dalton	1949	Miss Walsh	1964	Mrs Greer	1977	Mrs P. Deman
1930	Mrs Antliff	1950	Mrs Seale	1965	G. Brandom	1978	Mrs P. Deman
1931	Miss Dalton	1951	Mrs Crew	1966	G. Brandom	1979	Mrs J. Latch
1932	Miss Dalton	1952	Mrs Crew	1967	G. Brandom	1980	S. Kiddle
1933	R. Payne	1953	Mrs Crew	1968	Mrs S. Kempster	1981	S. Kiddle
1934	Miss Dalton	1954	Mrs B. Allen	1969	Mrs S. Kempster	1982	S. Kiddle
1935	Mrs Hedges	1955	Mrs Arnold	1970	Mrs B. Hawkins	1983	S. Kiddle

BERKSHIRE LADIES' CHAMPIONSHIP

Since the event was inaugurated in 1925, Angela Uzielli holds the record for the most victories – seven – preceded by J. Cave – four times. Largest winning margin was in 1938 by Miss N. Gibbons and Miss Stokes in 1939; both won by 11 and 10.

Year	Winner	Year	Winner	Year	Winner	Year	Winner
1925	Mrs Oldman	1937	N. Gibbons	1961	D. Buchanan	1973	Mrs P. Cardy
1926	Mrs Morris	1938	N. Gibbons	1962	E. Clifton	1974	Mrs Leatham
1927	Mrs Morris	1939	Miss Stokes	1963	Mrs A.C. Marks	1975	S. Jolly
1928	J. Cave	1950	Mrs Tegner	1964	Mrs A.C. Marks	1976	A. Uzielli
1929	Mrs Morris	1951	Miss Bryant	1965	Mrs Garnett	1977	A. Uzielli
1930	J. Cave	1952	Mrs Simmons	1966	Mrs D. O'Brien	1978	A. Uzielli
1931	J. Cave	1954	Miss Bryant	1967	Mrs W. Henney	1979	A. Uzielli
1932	J. Cave	1955	Mrs Van Oss	1968	Mrs M.K. Garnett	1980	A. Uzielli
1933	Miss Timberg	1956	Miss Bryant	1969	Mrs D. Hanbury	1981	A. Uzielli
1934	Miss Slade	1958	I. Clifton	1970	Mrs M. Garnett	1982	C. Caldwell
1935	Miss Timberg	1959	Mrs E. Simmons	1971	Mrs D. Hanbury	1983	A. Uzielli
1936	Miss Timberg	1960	M.K. Garnett	1972	Mrs D. Hanbury		

BORDER LADIES' CHAMPIONSHIP

This event was introduced in 1974. S. Gallagher has won it four times so far.

Year	Winner	Year	Winner	Year	Winner	Year	Winner
1974	M.A.T. Sanderson	1977	S. Gallagher	1980	S. Gallagher	1983	E. White
1975	S. Simpson	1978	S. Gallagher	1981	A. Hunter		
1976	S. Simpson	1979	S. Gallagher	1982	S. Simpson		

BUCKINGHAMSHIRE LADIES' CHAMPIONSHIP

Since institution in 1924, the largest winning margin was by Mrs Adams in 1930, 8 and 7. Mrs Gold won it nine times.

Year	Winner	Year	Winner	Year	Winner	Year	Winner
1924	Miss Kelway	1938	Mrs A. Scott	1959	A. Mobbs	1973	Mrs G. Gordon
1925	P. Cotgrave	1939	Mrs Barnes	1960	A. Mobbs	1974	L. Harrold
1926	Mrs Kelway	1947	Mrs Gold	1961	Mrs E. Braithwaite	1975	L. Harrold
1927	Mrs Kelway	1948	Mrs Whitworth Jones	1962	Mrs A.W.H. Baucher	1976	L. Harrold
1928	Mrs Gold	1949	Mrs Whitworth Jones	1963	Mrs A.W.H. Baucher	1977	L. Harrold
1929	no competition	1950	Mrs Gold	1964	A. Mobbs	1978	Mrs M. Purdy
1930	Mrs Adams	1951	Mrs Gold	1965	Mrs B. Dutton	1979	J. Lee
1931	Mrs Gold	1952	Mrs Braddon	1966	A. Mobbs	1980	K. Copley
1932	Mrs Gold	1953	D.M. Speir	1967	A. Mobbs	1981	J. Warren
1933	Mrs Greenly	1954	Mrs W.M. Paul	1968	Mrs R.B. Parton	1982	J. Warren
1934	Mrs Gold	1955	Mrs C.W. Stothert	1969	Mrs P. Newman	1983	G. Bonallack
1935	Mrs O. Jones	1956	Mrs A.W.H. Baucher	1970	Mrs A. Baucher		
1936	Mrs Gold	1957	Mrs A.W.H. Baucher	1971	Mrs M. Baxter		
1937	Mrs Gold	1958	Mrs M. Baxter	1972	Mrs J. Marshall		

CAERNARVONSHIRE AND ANGLESEY LADIES' CHAMPIONSHIP

This championship was instituted in 1924, although the county association was in being well before that date.

Year	Winner	Year	Winner	Year	Winner	Year	Winner
1924	Mrs N. Jones	1938	A. Mellor	1959	Mrs D.V. Ingham	1973	Mrs J.H. Brown
1925	Mrs N. Jones	1939	S. Deeping	1960	Mrs B.J. Jenkin	1974	V.J. Brammer
1926	Mrs N. Jones	1947	A. Stockton	1961	Mrs M. Wright	1975	Mrs R. Ferguson
1927	Mrs Windsor Smith	1948	N. Cook	1962	Mrs D.V. Ingham	1976	Mrs M. Wright
1928	Mrs B.A. Jones	1949	E.H.A. Lever	1963	N. Seddon	1977	A. Thomas
1929	Mrs N. Jones	1950	E.H.A. Lever	1964	A. Hughes	1978	Mrs A. Johnson
1930	Miss Cooper-Davies	1951	E.H.A. Lever	1965	Mrs M. Wright	1979	A. Thomas
1931	S. Deeping	1952	E.H.A. Lever	1966	Mrs J.H. Brown	1980	A. Thomas
1932	E. Cummins	1953	N. Cook	1967	Mrs J.H. Brown	1981	S. Jump
1933	E. Cummins	1954	Mrs J.H. Brown	1968	A. Hughes	1982	F. Connor
1934	Mrs N. Jones	1955	E.H.A. Lever	1969	A. Hughes	1983	S.L. Roberts
1935	A. Mellor	1956	E.H.A. Lever	1970	Mrs M. Wright		
1936	N. Cook	1957	N. Seddon	1971	Mrs J.H. Brown		
1937	N. Cook	1958	N. Seddon	1972	A. Hughes		

CAERNARVON AND DISTRICT LADIES' CHAMPIONSHIP

This championship has been played for since 1927 by the ladies' section of the Caernarvonshire and District Golfing Union.

Year	Winner	Year	Winner	Year	Winner	Year	Winner
1927	Mrs W. Lloyd Jones	1940	Mrs F.F. Crosley	1959	Mrs D.V. Ingham	1972	Mrs M. Wright
1928	Mrs E. Hall	1946	N. Cook	1960	Mrs M. Wright	1973	Mrs J. Moon
1929	Mrs M. Hill	1947	N. Cook	1961	Mrs F.H.B. Jenkin	1974	Mrs J. Moon
1930	Mrs W. Lloyd Jones	1948	Mrs Ravenscroft	1962	Mrs M.G. Robinson	1975	Mrs F.W. Ferguson
1931	J. Bottomley	1950	N. Cook	1963	Mrs J.H. Brown	1976	Mrs F.W. Ferguson
1932	J. Bottomley	1951	N. Cook	1964	Mrs M. Wright	1977	Mrs F.W. Ferguson
1933	Mrs H.F. Dyer	1952	N. Cook	1965	Mrs M. Wright	1978	Mrs F.W. Ferguson
1934	A. Mellor	1953	Mrs E.D. Brown	1966	Mrs M. Wright	1979	Mrs F.W. Ferguson
1935	R. Appleby	1954	A. Mellor	1967	Mrs M. Wright	1980	Mrs C.A. Burnell
1936	A. Mellor	1955	E. Lever	1968	Mrs M. Wright	1981	Mrs C.A. Burnell
1937	N. Cook	1956	Mrs M. Wright	1969	Mrs J.H. Brown	1982	S.L. Roberts
1938	Mrs Hulbert	1957	Mrs D.M. Parry	1970	Mrs M. Wright	1983	Mrs R. Ferguson
1939	A. Mellor	1958	Mrs M. Wright	1971	Mrs J.H. Brown		

CAMBRIDGESHIRE AND HUNTS LADIES' CHAMPIONSHIP

Mrs Baker won this four times in succession, out of a total of seven wins, and Julie Walter also won it four times in succession, out of a total of eight wins.

Year	Winner	Year	Winner	Year	Winner	Year	Winner
1932	Mrs A.B. Coote	1951	Mrs Baker	1963	N. Richmond	1975	M. Maddocks
1933	Mrs W.B. Carter	1952	Mrs Holland	1964	J. Peck	1976	J. Walter
1934	Mrs Hamblyn-Smith	1953	Mrs Holland	1965	Mrs J. Sedgwick	1977	J. Walter
1935	Mrs Hamblyn-Smith	1954	Mrs Hill	1966	Mrs V.J. Mackenzie	1978	J. Walter
1936	Mrs W.B. Carter	1955	Mrs Croxton	1967	Mrs V.J. Mackenzie	1979	J. Walter
1937	Miss Goodlipp	1956	Mrs Baker	1968	Mrs V.J. Mackenzie	1980	J. Richards
1938	D. Drew	1957	Mrs Baker	1969	Mrs J. Honey	1981	J. Walter
1939	D. Drew	1958	Mrs Baker	1970	Mrs M. Gray	1982	J. Walter
1947	Mrs Holland	1959	Mrs Baker	1971	Mrs S. Stephenson	1983	J. Walter
1948	Mrs Baker	1960	Mrs Thomas	1972	Mrs M. Gray		
1949	Mrs A. Newport	1961	Mrs Croxton	1973	Mrs D. Baker		
1950	Mrs Holland	1962	Mrs Baker	1974	J. Walter		

CHANNEL ISLANDS LADIES' CHAMPIONSHIP

Mrs A. Lindsay holds the record for this championship, having won it ten times in succession. In 1970 her victory was by 15 and 13.

Year	Winner	Year	Winner	Year	Winner	Year	Winner
1937	Mrs J.P. Ross	1956	Mrs J.A. McDade	1966	Mrs A. Lindsay	1976	M. Darbyshire
1938	Mrs H.M. de la Rue	1957	Mrs J.A. McDade	1967	Mrs A. Lindsay	1977	M. Darbyshire
1939	Mrs J.P. Ross	1958	Mrs J.A. McDade	1968	Mrs A. Lindsay	1978	Mrs E. Roberts
1949	Mrs N.B. Grant	1959	Hon. Mrs Siddeley	1969	Mrs A. Lindsay	1979	Mrs J. Bunbury
1950	Mrs J.A. McDade	1960	P. Stacey	1970	Mrs A. Lindsay	1980	Mrs E. Roberts
1951	Mrs W.F. Mauger	1961	Mrs D. Porter	1971	Mrs A. Lindsay	1981	L. Cummins
1952	Mrs D.W.M. Randell	1962	P. Stacey	1972	Mrs A. Lindsay	1982	V. Bougourd
1953	Mrs J.A. McDade	1963	Mrs J.A. McDade	1973	Mrs A. Lindsay	1983	D. Heaton
1954	Mrs D.W.M. Randell	1964	Mrs A. Lindsay	1974	Mrs P. Haley		
1955	Mrs D. Porter	1965	Mrs A. Lindsay	1975	M. Darbyshire		

CHESHIRE LADIES' CHAMPIONSHIP

The AGM of the Cheshire County Ladies' Golf Association in December 1911 saw the decision to hold this championship taken, and the first course on which it was played was Wallasey, on 4–5 June 1912.

Year	Winner	Year	Winner	Year	Winner	Year	Winner
1912	G. Ravenscroft	1932	Mrs A. MacBeth	1954	A. Christian-Jones	1970	Mrs C. Comboy
1913	G. Ravenscroft	1933	E. Wilson	1955	B. Lloyd	1971	Mrs A. Briggs
1914	G. Ravenscroft	1934	Mrs Clement	1956	M. Wolff	1972	Dr H. Lyall
1920	Mrs Temple-Dobell	1935	Mrs A. MacBeth	1958	S. McNicoll	1973	Mrs A. Briggs
1921	Mrs Temple-Dobell	1936	Mrs Hartley	1959	C. Grott	1974	Mrs S. Graveley
1922	Mrs A. MacBeth	1937	Mrs A. MacBeth	1960	Mrs T. Briggs	1975	Mrs E. Wilson
1923	Mrs A. MacBeth	1938	Mrs Whitfield	1961	Mrs C. Comboy	1976	Mrs A. Briggs
1924	D. Chambers	1939	Mrs J.B. Hartley	1962	Mrs C. Comboy	1977	H. Latham
1925	Miss Bridgford	1947	J. Pemberton	1963	E. Chadwick	1978	Mrs J. Hughes
1926	Mrs Temple-Dobell	1948	J. Pemberton	1964	E. Chadwick	1979	H. Latham
1927	Mrs A. MacBeth	1949	Mrs Cowper	1965	E. Chadwick	1980	Mrs A. Briggs
1928	Mrs Temple-Dobell	1950	Mrs Horabin	1966	E. Chadwick	1981	Mrs A. Briggs
1929	Mrs Clement	1951	Miss Lloyd	1967	E. Chadwick	1982	H. Latham
1930	Mrs Cooper	1952	Mrs Horabin	1968	Mrs C. Comboy	1983	H. Latham
1931	Mrs Clement	1953	Mrs M. Appleby	1969	Mrs C. Comboy		

CLACKMANNANSHIRE COUNTY LADIES' GOLF CHAMPIONSHIP

This championship was instituted in 1922. In 1969 the county was amalgamated with Stirling (see Stirling and Clackmannan County Ladies' Championship).

Year	Winner	Year	Winner	Year	Winner	Year	Winner
1922	D. Black	1933	N. Foggo	1949	Mrs McQueen	1960	M. Buick
1923	Miss Stevenson	1934	N. Foggo	1950	Mrs McQueen	1961	J. Baikie
1924	I. Stirling	1935	N. Foggo	1951	Mrs McQueen	1962	Mrs J.M. Patton
1925	Miss Gibb	1936	N. Foggo	1952	N. Foggo	1963	J.M. Peattie
1926	N. Foggo	1937	N. Foggo	1953	Mrs McQueen	1964	Mrs M.E. Given
1927	Miss Anderson	1938	N. Foggo	1954	N. Foggo	1965	Mrs M.E. Given
1928	J. Black	1939	Mrs McQueen	1955	A.Y. Sorlie	1966	Mrs M.E. Given
1929	N. Foggo	1940	C. Dudgeon	1956	A.Y. Sorlie	1967	Mrs M.E. Given
1930	Mrs Barclay	1941	N. Foggo	1957	A.Y. Sorlie	1968	Mrs D. Russell
1931	N. Foggo	1947	Mrs McQueen	1958	N. Foggo		
1932	N. Foggo	1948	Mrs McQueen	1959	R.A. Millar		

CORNWALL LADIES' CHAMPIONSHIP

One of the oldest championships in the country, it was won by Muriel Roskrow a record eighteen times. It was instituted in 1896.

Year	Winner	Year	Winner	Year	Winner	Year	Winner
1896	Miss Every	1921	Mrs Le Messurier	1947	M. Roskrow	1966	M. Roskrow
1897	Miss Parker-Smith	1922	Mrs Wise	1948	M. Roskrow	1967	E. Luxon
1898	Miss Parker-Smith	1923	Mrs Le Messurier	1949	Mrs Wills	1968	Mrs M.C. Rowe
1899	N.M. Carter	1924	Mrs Wallace	1950	M. Roskrow	1969	S. Mitchell
1900	Miss Parker-Smith	1925	Mrs Prideaux	1951	H. Trant	1970	Mrs D. Luxon
1901	O. Miles	1926	Mrs V.B. Hilton	1952	M. Roskrow	1971	Mrs D. Luxon
1902	O. Miles	1927	Miss Notman	1953	M. Roskrow	1972	S. Mitchell
1903	Mrs Michael	1928	Mrs H.S. Prideaux	1954	B. Soper	1973	Mrs J. Clowes
1904	O. Miles	1929	E. Ratcliffe	1955	M. Roskrow	1974	J. Dodd
1905	K.S. Horn	1930	Miss Cornwall	1956	M. Roskrow	1975	E. Luxon
1906	O. Miles	1931	E. Ratcliffe	1957	M. Roskrow	1976	J. Ryder
1907	G. Cary	1932	Mrs Cornelius	1958	M. Roskrow	1977	J. Ryder
1908	K.S. Horn	1933	Miss Cornwall	1959	M. Roskrow	1978	S. Cann
1909	H.S. Rogers	1934	Mrs Cornelius	1960	Mrs J. Rodgers	1979	L. Moore
1910	H.S. Rogers	1935	E. Ratcliffe	1961	M. Roskrow	1980	L. Moore
1911	Miss Hardwick	1936	E. Ratcliffe	1962	M. Roskrow	1981	L. Moore
1912	H.S. Rogers	1937	M. Roskrow	1963	M. Roskrow	1982	S. Cann
1913	O.M. Rogers	1938	M. Roskrow	1964	Mrs W.A. Tomlinson	1983	J. Ryder
1920	Mrs Wise	1939	M. Roskrow	1965	M. Roskrow		

CUMBRIA LADIES' CHAMPIONSHIP

The Cumberland County Ladies' Golf Club was formed in December 1924, with the Hon. Mrs Donald Howard being elected president, and the Countess of Carlisle, Mrs Edwardes and Mrs Stead vice-presidents; Mrs Saul was captain. In October 1928 Westmoreland joined, and the name was changed to the Cumberland and Westmoreland Ladies' County Golf Association. In November 1980, this became the Cumbria Ladies' County Golf Association. The first championship was played at Silloth in April 1925.

Year	Winner	Year	Winner	Year	Winner	Year	Winner
1928	M. Howe	1948	H. Scott	1961	L.B. Clark	1974	H. Long
1929	E. Hartley	1949	J.I. Johnstone	1962	L.B. Clark	1975	J. Allison
1930	M. Howe	1950	L.B. Clark	1963	Mrs J. Stafford	1976	J. Allison
1931	M. Howe	1951	L.B. Clark	1964	M.A. Peile	1977	H. Long
1932	Mrs R.D. Burgess	1952	L.B. Clark	1965	Mrs M.J. Ward	1978	N. Pieri
1933	D.J. Jordan	1953	L.B. Clark	1966	P. Brough	1979	D. Thomson
1934	M. Howe	1954	Mrs P.E. Gillman	1967	P. Brough	1980	D. Thomson
1935	M. Howe	1955	L.B. Clark	1968	P. Brough	1981	D. Thomson
1936	L.B. Clark	1956	L.B. Clark	1969	N. Peile	1982	D. Thomson
1937	L.B. Clark	1957	Mrs J.H. French	1970	P. Brough	1983	P. Brumwell
1938	L.B. Clark	1958	L.B. Clark	1971	P. Brough		
1939	L.B. Clark	1959	L.B. Clark	1972	M. Stavert		
1947	H. Scott	1960	Mrs J. Stafford	1973	M. Stavert		

DENBIGHSHIRE LADIES' CHAMPIONSHIP

The first annual general meeting of the Denbighshire Women's County Golf Association was held on 26 January 1925, and began with an account of the formation of the Denbigh County Association. Lady Naylor Leyland was president, and the captain, honorary secretary and treasurer were all from Rhos-on-Sea. Forty-nine members joined at a subscription of 2s 6d (12½p). When the 1982 honorary secretary joined in 1960, the subscription was still the same.

Year	Winner	Year	Winner	Year	Winner	Year	Winner
1924	Mrs O. Bland	1937	Miss Appleby	1958	Mrs J.W. Johnson	1971	Mrs O.W. Jones
1925	Mrs Byford	1938	Mrs C.R. Taylor	1959	Mrs J.W. Johnson	1972	P. Whitley
1926	Miss Baldwin	1939	Mrs C.R. Taylor	1960	Mrs M. Hartley	1973	P. Whitley
1927	Miss Baldwin	1947	Mrs M. Hartley	1961	Mrs M. Hartley	1974	P. Whitley
1928	Miss Ashe	1949	Mrs R. Haberreiter	1962	Mrs H.M. Bellis	1975	M. Hayes
1929	Miss Baldwin	1950	Mrs M. Hartley	1963	Mrs M. Hartley	1976	E. Davies
1930	Mrs MacAlpine	1951	Mrs M. Hartley	1964	Mrs O.W. Jones	1977	P. Whitley
1931	Mrs C.R. Taylor	1952	Mrs M. Hartley	1965	Mrs O.W. Jones	1978	P. Whitley
1932	Mrs C.R. Taylor	1953	Mrs M. Hartley	1966	Mrs O.W. Jones	1979	P. Whitley
1933	Mrs C.R. Taylor	1954	Mrs J.W. Johnson	1967	Mrs H.M. Bellis	1980	K. Davies
1934	Mrs D. Evans	1955	Mrs M. Hartley	1968	M. Lea	1981	E. Higgs
1935	M. Brearley	1956	Mrs M. Hartley	1969	M. Lea	1982	K. Davies
1936	Miss Turner	1957	Mrs J.W. Johnson	1970	Mrs O.W. Jones	1983	E. Davies

DERBYSHIRE LADIES' CHAMPIONSHIP

In January 1921 it was proposed by Chevin and seconded by Derbyshire that a championship should be held. In January 1922 the minutes note: 'The Committee have much pleasure in reporting that their President, Her Grace the Duchess of Devonshire, kindly gave a Championship Cup which was played for the first time at the Spring Meeting, held at the Chevin Golf Club and won by Miss W. Abell of Duffield.' Miss Abell beat Miss Evershed, the 1982 President of the Derbyshire Ladies' County Golf Association.

Year	Winner	Year	Winner	Year	Winner	Year	Winner
1921	W. Abell	1935	B. Newell	1956	Hon. Mrs J. Gee	1970	D. Rose
1922	Mrs Fryer	1936	P. Shard	1957	Mrs E.S.C. Pedley	1971	Mrs E.M.J. Wenyon
1923	Mrs Farrington	1937	J. Hives	1958	Hon. Mrs J. Gee	1972	M. Mason
1924	Miss Bennett	1938	J. Hives	1959	Mrs R. Gascoyne	1973	E. Clark
1925	E. Wilson	1939	J. Hives	1960	Mrs J.H. Gibbs	1974	E. Colledge
1926	E. Wilson	1947	Mrs A. Gee	1961	Hon. Mrs J. Gee	1975	Mrs A. Bemrose
1927	Miss Reah	1948	Mrs A. Gee	1962	Mrs J. Burns	1976	Mrs M. Close
1928	Mrs Ellis	1949	Mrs A. Gee	1963	Hon. Mrs J. Gee	1977	Mrs M. Close
1929	Miss Hartropp	1950	Mrs A. Gee	1964	Hon. Mrs J. Gee	1978	Mrs M. Close
1930	Mrs Ellis	1951	Mrs A. Gee	1965	M. Grey	1979	Mrs M. Close
1931	Miss Hartropp	1952	Mrs A. Gee	1966	Hon. Mrs J. Gee	1980	A. Howe
1932	Miss Hartropp	1953	Hon. Mrs J. Gee	1967	M. Wenyon	1981	A. Howe
1933	Miss Spalding	1954	Mrs E.M. Jones	1968	Hon. Mrs J. Gee	1982	V. MacWilliams
1934	Miss Hartropp	1955	Mrs K. Dickie, Jr	1969	M. Wenyon	1983	J. Williams

DEVON LADIES' CHAMPIONSHIP

Instituted in 1922, the first championship was held at the East Devon Golf Club, and the championship cup was presented by the Rt Hon. Lord Clinton.

Year	Winner	Year	Winner	Year	Winner	Year	Winner
1922	Mrs Dering	1936	P. Williams	1957	A. Nicholson	1971	Mrs J. Dymond
1923	Mrs Dering	1937	Miss Dent	1958	Mrs B. Ord	1972	Mrs B. Salz
1924	Miss Hewitt	1938	Miss Dent	1959	Mrs K. Sharp	1973	Mrs R. Coleman
1925	Miss Hewitt	1939	M. Foster	1960	Mrs Anstey	1974	Mrs J. Lawson
1926	M. Kingston	1947	Mrs Ord	1961	Mrs Greenwood	1975	Mrs J. Mason
1927	Mrs S.H. Murphy	1948	Miss Pynan	1962	Mrs R. Emerson	1976	M. Wardrop
1928	P. Williams	1949	M. Taylor	1963	Mrs T.W. Slater	1977	Mrs J. Mason
1929	Mrs Dering	1950	Mrs Anstey	1964	J. Buswell	1978	Mrs D. Baxter
1930	Miss Radford	1951	M. Taylor	1965	Mrs Anstey	1979	S. Tyler
1931	L. Foster	1952	Mrs Anstey	1966	Mrs P. Anstey	1980	Mrs J. Mason
1932	B. Radford	1953	Mrs Anstey	1967	Mrs Fox	1981	S. Tyler
1933	P. Williams	1954	Mrs Anstey	1968	Mrs J. Mason	1982	J. Hurley
1934	B. Radford	1955	P. Morris	1969	Mrs J. Mason	1983	J. Hurley
1935	P. Williams	1956	P. Morris	1970	Mrs J. Mason		

DORSET LADIES' CHAMPIONSHIP

Instituted at Broadstone on 22 October 1923, the championship has been won most often by Mrs P.M. Crow, ten times in all.

Year	Winner	Year	Winner	Year	Winner	Year	Winner
1923	Miss Arkell	1937	Mrs Jones	1959	Mrs J. Cooper	1973	Mrs P. Crow
1924	Miss Arkell	1938	Mrs C. Beard	1960	Mrs J. Cooper	1974	Mrs W. Russell
1925	Mrs Peppercorn	1947	Miss Bannister	1961	Mrs P.M. Crow	1975	Mrs J. Sugden
1926	Mrs Morant	1948	Mrs Stuart Smith	1962	Mrs P.M. Crow	1976	Mrs J. Sugden
1927	Mrs Morant	1949	Mrs McPherson	1963	Mrs P.M. Crow	1977	Mrs W. Russell
1928	M. Beard	1950	Mrs McPherson	1964	Mrs J. Sugden	1978	Mrs W. Russell
1929	K. Beard	1951	Mrs Stuart Smith	1965	Mrs S. Smith	1979	S. Reeks
1930	K. Beard	1952	Mrs P.M. Crow	1966	B. Dixon	1980	Mrs C. Stirling
1931	Mrs Latham-Hall	1953	D.E. Kyle	1967	Mrs P. Crow	1981	Mrs R. Page
1932	Mrs Morant	1954	Mrs P.M. Crow	1968	B. Dixon	1982	Mrs B. Langley
1933	Mrs Latham-Hall	1955	Mrs P.M. Crow	1969	Mrs A. Humphreys	1983	J. Sugden
1934	Miss Arkell	1956	Mrs P.M. Crow	1970	B. Dixon		
1935	Mrs Jones	1957	J. Alexander	1971	Mrs P. Crow		
1936	Mrs Morant	1958	Mrs S. Smith	1972	D. Chalkley		

DUMFRIESSHIRE LADIES' CHAMPIONSHIP

The South Division of Scottish Golf was inaugurated in 1973 after the South had been for many years 'in the wilderness'. There had been North, West and East Divisions of Scottish Golf, but the South had never been accepted as it was only possible for it to form three 'counties', all the other divisions having four. After a lot of hard work and persuasion, the South was accepted, the three counties being Borders, Galloway and Dumfriesshire. The Dumfriesshire Ladies' Championship was instituted in 1973.

Year	Winner	Year	Winner	Year	Winner	Year	Winner
1973	A. Barclay	1976	A. Barclay	1979	D.M. Hill	1982	E. Hill
1974	M. McCalley	1977	A. Barclay	1980	Mrs G. Barclay	1983	E. Hill
1975	A. Barclay	1978	E. Hill	1981	E. Hill		

DUNBARTONSHIRE AND ARGYLL LADIES' CHAMPIONSHIP

The Dunbartonshire Ladies' County Golf Association was formed on 28 January 1909 at Dunbarton. On 6 December 1927, it was decided to hold a championship in the spring of 1928, to be played over two days. The intention was to replace the four medal days which had proved to be badly attended. In 1956 Dunbartonshire amalgamated with Argyll. In 1982 the association had three honorary members, M. Bell, B. Hendry and Belle Robertson.

Year	Winner	Year	Winner	Year	Winner	Year	Winner
1928	H.M. Johnstone	1948	Mrs Scott-Cochrane	1961	B. Robertson	1974	V. McAlister
1929	H.M. Johnstone	1949	M. Paterson	1962	B. Robertson	1975	V. McAlister
1930	H.M. Johnstone	1950	Mrs T.S. Currie	1963	B. Robertson	1976	S. Cadden
1931	Mrs E. White	1951	Mrs S. Cochran	1964	I. Keywood	1977	S. Cadden
1932	B. Hendry	1952	M. Bell	1965	B. Robertson	1978	B. Robertson
1933	B. Hendry	1953	I. Keywood	1966	B. Robertson	1979	Mrs S. McMahon
1934	M. Bell	1954	I. Keywood	1967	E. Low	1980	Mrs M.P. Grant
1935	Mrs D. Herbert	1955	Mrs T.S. Currie	1968	B. Robertson	1981	V. McAlister
1936	R. Adam	1956	B. Geekie	1969	B. Robertson	1982	V. McAlister
1937	Mrs A. Turnbell	1957	I. Keywood	1970	V. McAlister	1983	V. McAlister
1938	K.D. Adam	1958	B. McCorkindale	1971	F. Jamieson		
1939	Mrs A. Turnbell	1959	B. McCorkindale	1972	V. McAlister		
1947	Mrs Scott-Cochrane	1960	B. McCorkindale	1973	V. McAlister		

DURHAM LADIES' CHAMPIONSHIP

The championship bowl was presented in 1922 by the then president, the Marchioness of Londonderry, DBE, and the engraving indicates that the first winner was Mrs C.W.M. Potts of Wearside.

Year	Winner	Year	Winner	Year	Winner	Year	Winner
1922	Mrs C.W.M. Potts	1936	Miss Waugh	1959	Mrs Riddell	1973	C. Barker
1923	Miss Walker	1937	Mrs Richardson	1960	Mrs J. Kinsella	1974	Mrs C. Bowerbank
1924	S. Newlands	1938	Miss Curry	1961	Mrs Riddell	1975	Mrs A. Biggs
1925	Mrs C.W.M. Potts	1939	Miss Bell	1962	E. Reed	1976	R. Kelly
1926	Miss Walker	1949	Mrs J.H. Carter	1963	Mrs J. Riddell	1977	C. Barker
1927	Miss Westall	1950	Mrs Birbeck	1964	Mrs J. Riddell	1978	C. Barker
1928	Mrs Morton	1951	Mrs J.H. Carter	1965	Mrs Bennett	1979	P. Hunt
1929	Miss Rowland	1952	Mrs Butler	1966	P. Dinning	1980	Mrs L. Still
1930	Miss Walker	1953	Mrs J.H. Carter	1967	Mrs M. Whitehead	1981	C. Barker
1931	Miss Walker	1954	Mrs C. Wright	1968	Mrs P. Twinn	1982	P. Hunt
1932	Miss Sardler	1955	Mrs Birbeck	1969	Mrs D. Harrison	1983	P. Hunt
1933	Miss Waugh	1956	Miss Paton	1970	L. Hope		
1934	Miss Waugh	1957	Mrs Riddell	1971	Mrs M. Thompson		
1935	Miss Waugh	1958	Mrs Riddell	1972	R. Kelly		

EAST LOTHIAN LADIES' CHAMPIONSHIP

In its present form, the championship was instituted in 1934, the minute recording it stating that 'it should be a knockout competition instead of the present two rounds of scoring.' Sir Patrick Handyside was president when the East Lothian County Golf Club was formed in April 1922, and presented the Handyside Trophy as a scratch prize. The trophy is a sheet of 9ct gold and a gold brooch, both in a fitted case, and is now presented to the winner, the names being engraved on the sheet. Sir Patrick resigned as president in 1929 and was succeeded by Sir Harold Stiles who presented the championship bowl, which is now played for, in 1934. Marjorie Fowler won the championship eight times running.

Year	Winner	Year	Winner	Year	Winner	Year	Winner
1924	M.T. Smith	1936	M.M. Robertson-Durham	1957	M. Fowler	1971	C. Lugton
1925	M.T. Smith			1958	M. Fowler	1972	C. Lugton
1926	M.T. Smith	1937	Mrs I.H. Bowhill	1959	M. Fowler	1973	C. Lugton
1927	M.J. Cowper	1938	M.J. Couper	1960	M. Fowler	1974	Mrs A.J.R. Ferguson
1929	R. Durham and M.R. Durham	1939	Mrs E.C. Mackean	1961	M. Fowler	1975	Mrs D. McIntosh
		1948	J. Donald	1962	M. Fowler	1976	C. Lugton
1930	M.M. Robertson-Durham	1949	J. Donald	1963	M. Fowler	1977	C. Lugton
		1950	Mrs R.T. Peel	1964	M. Fowler	1978	J. Connachan
1931	Mrs Hilton	1951	J. Donald	1965	C. Lugton	1979	J. Connachan
1932	M.J. Cowper	1952	J. Donald	1966	M. Fowler	1980	C. Lugton
1933	M.M. Robertson-Durham	1953	J. Donald	1967	M. Fowler	1981	M. Ferguson
		1954	Mrs E. Woodcock	1968	C. Lugton	1982	F. McNab
1934	M.J. Couper	1955	Mrs E. Woodcock	1969	Mrs A.J.R. Ferguson	1983	M. Thomson
1935	M.J. Couper	1956	Mrs Paton	1970	C. Lugton		

EAST OF SCOTLAND LADIES' CHAMPIONSHIP

Played for only by members of the County Associations of Fife, East Lothian, Midlothian and Stirling and Clackmannanshire, the championship was instituted in 1931.

Year	Winner	Year	Winner	Year	Winner	Year	Winner
1931	Mrs J.B. Watson	1949	J. Donald	1961	Mrs C. Draper	1974	C. Lugton
1932	Mrs J.B. Watson	1950	J. Valentine	1962	M. Fowler	1975	Mrs A.J.R. Ferguson
1933	D. Park	1951	Mrs R.T. Peel	1964	B. Crichton	1976	C. Panton
1934	H. Nimmo	1952	Mrs R.T. Peel	1965	J. Bald	1977	L. Hope
1935	Mrs R.H. Wallace-Williamson	1953	J. Donald	1966	A. Laing	1978	L. Hope
		1954	Mrs R.T. Peel	1967	Mrs A. McIntosh	1979	M. Stavert
1936	J. Anderson	1955	Mrs R.T. Peel	1968	N. Duncan	1980	Mrs J. Marshall
1937	C.P.R. Montgomery	1956	Mrs R.T. Peel	1969	J. Hutton	1981	E. Miskimmin
1938	J. Anderson	1957	Mrs R.T. Peel	1970	J. Hutton	1982	J. Bald
1939	J. Anderson	1958	Mrs J. Aitken	1971	J. Lawrence	1983	J. Marshall
1947	J. Donald	1959	M. Fowler	1972	J. Lawrence		
1948	J. Donald	1960	M. Fowler	1973	J. Bald		

ESSEX LADIES' CHAMPIONSHIP

Instituted in 1923, the championship cup was donated by Miss M. Parkinson, who won it in its inaugural year.

Year	Winner	Year	Winner	Year	Winner	Year	Winner
1923	M. Parkinson	1937	K. Garnham	1958	S. Bonallack	1973	A. Bonallack
1924	Mrs P. Garon	1938	K. Garnham	1959	S. Bonallack	1974	A. Bonallack
1925	Mrs P. Garon	1939	K. Garnham	1960	S. Bonallack	1975	cancelled
1926	Mrs Simpson	1947	Mrs K. Hawes	1961	S. Bonallack	1976	A. Bonallack
1927	Mrs P. Garon	1948	Mrs Munro	1962	S. Bonallack	1977	A. Bonallack
1928	Mrs P. Garon	1949	M.A. McKenny	1963	S. Barber	1978	A. Bonallack
1929	Mrs P. Garon	1950	Mrs S. Munro	1964	E. Collis	1979	B. Cooper
1930	Mrs P. Garon	1951	A. Barrett	1966	S. Barber	1980	Mrs E. Boatman
1931	D. Wilkins	1952	Mrs M.R. Garon	1967	S. Barber	1981	P. Jackson
1932	K. Garnham	1954	Mrs Hanson-	1968	A. Bonallack	1982	A. Bonallack
1933	K. Garnham		Abbott	1969	A. Bonallack	1983	Mrs E. Boatman
1934	Mrs P. Garon	1955	Mrs J. Willis	1970	S. Barber		
1935	D. Wilkins	1956	J. Hetherington	1971	S. Barber		
1936	D. Wilkins	1957	J. Hetherington	1972	B. Lewis		

FIFE COUNTY LADIES' CHAMPIONSHIP

The Fife County Ladies' Golf Association was formed in 1909, but the first championship was not played until 1930. Before that, the ladies seemed more interested in their finances, holding golf ball raffles, and a ladder competition between 1 January 1928 and 30 June 1928, presumably to buy a cup for the commencement of the championship. Joan Lawrence won it nine times running.

Year	Winner	Year	Winner	Year	Winner	Year	Winner
1930	Dr M.C. Alexander	1950	Mrs Lockhardt-	1961	J.B. Lawrence	1973	J. Bald
1931	M. Cook		Cowan	1962	J.B. Lawrence	1974	J. McNeill
1932	M.G. Fortune	1951	Mrs T.M. Burton	1963	J.B. Lawrence	1975	M. Speir
1933	M. Everard	1952	Mrs T.M. Burton	1964	J.B. Lawrence	1976	Mrs J. Louden
1934	A. Hopwood	1953	J.B. Lawrence	1965	J.B. Lawrence	1977	Mrs J. Louden
1935	A. Hopwood	1954	Mrs T.M. Burton	1966	J. Bald	1978	D. Mitchell
1936	M. Everard	1955	L. Doman	1967	J.B. Lawrence	1979	J. Bald
1937	N. Orr	1956	A.D. Thomson	1968	J.B. Lawrence	1980	Mrs J. Louden
1938	N. Orr	1957	J.B. Lawrence	1969	J.B. Lawrence	1981	J. Bald
1939	N. Orr	1958	J.B. Lawrence	1970	J. Bald	1982	J. Bald
1949	Mrs Lockhardt-	1959	J.B. Lawrence	1971	J. Bald	1983	R. Scott
	Cowan	1960	J.B. Lawrence	1972	J. McNeill		

FLINTSHIRE LADIES' CHAMPIONSHIP

Winner by the largest margin since 1924 is Mrs P. Davies, who beat Miss P. Strange by 8 and 6 in 1975.

Year	Winner	Year	Winner	Year	Winner	Year	Winner
1924	Miss Selkerk	1936	G. Satchwell	1963	Mrs P. Rogers	1975	Mrs P. Davies
1925	Miss Selkerk	1939	Mrs Edwards	1964	Mrs P. Rogers	1976	S. Rowlands
1926	Miss Selkerk	1953	Mrs H.C. Johnson	1965	Mrs P. Griffiths	1977	Mrs P. Davies
1927	Mrs Nicholson	1954	Mrs R. Johnson	1966	Mrs J. Hughes	1978	Mrs P. Davies
1928	Miss Martin	1955	Mrs R. Johnson	1967	Mrs M. Lloyd-Jones	1979	P. Strange
1929	M. Lloyd-Price	1956	Mrs H. Griffiths	1968	Mrs J. Hughes	1980	Mrs P. Davies
1930	Mrs Morrell	1957	Mrs Johnson	1969	Mrs P. Davies	1981	Mrs E.N. Davies
1931	G. Satchwell	1958	Mrs R. Johnson	1970	Mrs J. Hughes	1982	Mrs P. Davies
1932	G. Satchwell	1959	Mrs R. Johnson	1971	Mrs J. Hughes	1983	S. Thomas
1933	Mrs Crabbe-Davies	1960	Mrs M. Davies	1972	L. Hughes		
1934	G. Satchwell	1961	Mrs R. Johnson	1973	L. Hughes		
1935	Miss Morrell	1962	P. Griffiths	1974	F. Ellard		

GALLOWAY LADIES' CHAMPIONSHIP

The championship was instituted, along with Galloway's entry to county golf, in 1973.

Year	Winner	Year	Winner	Year	Winner	Year	Winner
1973	M.P. Rennie	1976	M. Clement	1979	F.M. Rennie	1982	M. Clement
1974	M.P. Rennie	1977	M. Clement	1980	F.M. Rennie	1983	S. McDonald
1975	M. Clement	1978	F.M. Rennie	1981	M. Clement		

GLAMORGAN COUNTY LADIES' CHAMPIONSHIP

Instituted in 1927 at Royal Porthcawl, the minutes of the early meetings record the numbers of entries but they do not record the names of the winners.

Year	Winner	Year	Winner	Year	Winner	Year	Winner
1932	B. Pyman	1951	Mrs R.B. Roberts	1963	Mrs J. Treharne	1974	T. Perkins
1933	J. Jeffreys	1952	Mrs H. Jenkins	1964	Mrs J. Treharne	1975	T. Perkins
1934	J. Jeffreys	1953	Mrs H. Jenkins	1965	Mrs J. Treharne	1976	L. Isherwood
1935	J. Jeffreys	1954	Mrs R.B. Roberts	1966	J. Morris	1977	T. Perkins
1936	Mrs G.S. Emery	1955	Mrs R.B. Roberts	1967	C. Phipps	1978	T. Perkins
1937	Mrs G.S. Emery	1956	H. Wakelin	1968	J. Morris	1979	V. Rawlings
1938	Mrs G.S. Emery	1958	Mrs C. Robinson	1969	C. Phipps	1980	T. Thomas
1939	M. Thompson	1959	E. Owen	1970	V. Rawlings	1981	T. Thomas
1948	Mrs R.B. Roberts	1960	Mrs J. Treharne	1971	V. Rawlings	1982	M. Rawlings
1949	Mrs R.B. Roberts	1961	Mrs M. Fisher	1972	T. Perkins	1983	T. Thomas
1950	E. Owen	1962	E. Owen	1973	C. Phipps		

GLOUCESTERSHIRE LADIES' CHAMPIONSHIP

Instituted in 1913, this championship was played for by stroke play until 1929, and thereafter by match play.

Year Winner	Year Winner	Year Winner	Year Winner
1913 Miss Barry	1933 V. Bramwell	1956 Mrs J. Reece	1971 Mrs P. Reece
1914 Miss Bryan	1934 V. Bramwell	1957 R. Porter	1972 B. Huke
1920 Miss Bryan	1935 Mrs Whitley	1958 Mrs B. Popplestone	1973 R. Porter
1921 Mrs Whitley	1936 Miss Bramwell	1959 R. Porter	1974 R. Porter
1922 Miss Prince	1937 Miss Bramwell	1960 Mrs P. Reece	1975 R. Porter
1923 Mrs Whitley	1938 Mrs Whitley	1961 R. Porter	1976 R. Porter
1924 V. Bramwell	1939 Mrs Collier	1962 R. Porter	1977 R. Porter
1925 V. Bramwell	1947 Mrs Dickinson	1963 R. Porter	1978 D. Park
1926 V. Bramwell	1948 Mrs Whitley	1964 R. Porter	1979 Mrs P. Reece
1927 Mrs Whitley	1950 Mrs Whitley	1965 Mrs P. Reece	1980 K. Douglas
1928 V. Bramwell	1951 Mrs S.L. Dickinson	1966 R. Porter	1981 K. Douglas
1929 Mrs Whitley	1952 Mrs J. Reece	1967 R. Porter	1982 K. Douglas
1930 V. Bramwell	1953 Mrs J. Reece	1968 Mrs P. Reece	1983 K. Douglas
1931 V. Bramwell	1954 Mrs J. Reece	1969 R. Porter	
1932 W. Williams	1955 Mrs J. Reece	1970 Mrs P. Reece	

HAMPSHIRE LADIES' CHAMPIONSHIP

Instituted in 1924, the record for the most number of wins is held by Mrs B. Bavin, with eight.

Year Winner	Year Winner	Year Winner	Year Winner
1924 Miss Pearce	1938 P. Wade	1959 Mrs B. Green	1973 C. le Feuvre
1925 Mrs Lamplough	1939 R.S Morgan	1960 Mrs B. Green	1974 C. le Feuvre
1926 A. Kyle	1947 M. Wallis	1961 Mrs B. Green	1975 S. Thurston
1927 S. Lamplough	1948 Mrs Bavin	1962 J. Morrison	1976 Mrs C. Gibbs
1928 Miss Aitchison	1949 Mrs Bavin	1963 Mrs B. Green	1977 C. Mackintosh
1929 Mrs W.H. Hunt	1950 Mrs J.S.F. Morrison	1964 Mrs Bavin	1978 C. Mackintosh
1930 Miss Uthoff	1951 Mrs J.S.F. Morrison	1965 Mrs B. Bavin	1979 C. Mackintosh
1931 Mrs Clark	1952 F. Allan	1966 Mrs B. Bavin	1980 C. Mackintosh
1932 W.H. Hunt	1953 B. Lowe	1967 H. Clifford	1981 S. Pickles
1933 P. Wade	1954 Mrs Bavin	1968 P. Shepherd	1982 A. Wells
1934 Mrs Clark	1955 Mrs Bavin	1969 H. Clifford	1983 C. Hayllar
1935 P. Wade	1956 B. Lowe	1970 C. le Feuvre	
1936 N. Diamond	1957 Mrs B. Green	1971 C. le Feuvre	
1937 P. Wade	1958 Mrs Bavin	1972 C. le Feuvre	

HAMPSHIRE ROSE

This was instituted in 1973 by Heather Clifford Glynn-Jones, who tied for the winner's place in 1976 and 1978. It is a stroke play championship.

Year	Winner	Year	Winner	Year	Winner	Year	Winner
1973	C. Redford	1976	H. Clifford and W. Pithers	1978	V. Marvin and Mrs H. Glynn-Jones	1980	B. New
1974	Mrs P. Riddiford			1979	Mrs C. Larkin	1981	J. Nicholson
1975	V. Marvin	1977	J. Greenhalgh			1982	Mrs J. Thornhill
						1983	J. Pool

HELEN HOLM TROPHY

Instituted in 1973, this is a stroke play event won by Wilma Aitken three times so far.

Year	Winner	Year	Winner	Year	Winner	Year	Winner
1973	B. Robertson	1976	M.N. Thomson	1979	B. Robertson	1982	W. Aitken
1974	S.C. Needham	1977	B. Huke	1980	W. Aitken	1983	J. Connachan
1975	M.N. Thomson	1978	W. Aitken	1981	G. Stewart		

HERTFORDSHIRE LADIES' CHAMPIONSHIP

The cup for this championship was presented in 1923 by Mrs Albert Pam and first played for in 1924.

Year	Winner	Year	Winner	Year	Winner	Year	Winner
1924	Mrs R. Fleming	1937	Mrs Gilbertson	1960	P. Lane	1973	S. Parker
1925	Mrs Farquharson	1938	Miss Goddard	1961	Mrs R. Oliver	1974	Mrs R. Turnbull
1926	Mrs Martin-Smith	1939	Mrs Gilbertson	1962	Mrs R. Oliver	1975	Mrs M. Rumble
1927	Mrs Brindle	1947	Mrs Mawson	1963	Mrs R. Oliver	1976	Mrs R. Turnbull
1928	Mrs Brindle	1950	Mrs Davis	1964	Mrs R. Oliver	1977	J. Smith
1929	Mrs V. Miles	1951	Mrs Oliver	1965	Mrs M. Cuneen	1978	J. Smith
1930	Miss Harley	1952	Mrs Davies	1966	M. Paton	1979	S. Latham
1931	P. Horpfield	1954	Mrs H.J. Davies	1967	Mrs P. Rumble	1980	Mrs H. Kaye
1932	Miss Flint	1955	Mrs R. Oliver	1968	Mrs R. Oliver	1981	Mrs U. Pearson
1933	Miss Flint	1956	Mrs E. Beck	1969	Mrs R. Oliver	1982	N. McCormack
1934	Mrs Gilbertson	1957	A. Gardiner	1970	Mrs B. Smith	1983	E. Provan
1935	Z. Davies	1958	Mrs R. Oliver	1971	Mrs J. Kaye		
1936	V. Miles	1959	P. Lane	1972	Mrs R. Turnbull		

ISLE OF WIGHT CHAMPIONSHIP

The members of the Isle of Wight Ladies' Golf Club (Bembridge), together with the Ladies' Branch of the Needles and Freshwater Club, were instrumental in starting this championship, subscribing to and purchasing the trophy. The championship trophy was first played for on the Isle of Wight Ladies' Golf Club links at Bembridge on 26 April 1897.

Year	Winner	Year	Winner	Year	Winner	Year	Winner
1897	C. Henry	1912	M.H. Tankard	1937	L. Storr	1967	Mrs A.B. Oliveira
1898	Mrs C.P. Winfield Stratford	1913	J. Lee-White	1938	Mrs White	1968	H. Day
		1914	Mrs Laidlay	1939	L. Storr	1969	S. Baker
1899	Mrs C.P. Winfield Stratford	1923	E.L. Buck	1953	Mrs W.M. Driver	1970	Mrs A.B. Oliveira
		1924	Mrs W.H. Trinder	1954	Mrs W.J. Bennett	1971	Mrs P. Oliveira
1900	Mrs C.P. Winfield Stratford	1925	Mrs Newnham	1955	Mrs W.J. Bennett	1972	Mrs P. Mathews
		1926	Mrs W.H. Trinder	1956	H. Day	1973	Mrs P. Mathews
1901	J. Gordon	1927	Mrs M. White	1957	Mrs D. Boyd	1974	G. Wright
1902	E. Hull	1928	H.M. Fishwick	1958	H. Day	1975	Mrs P. Mathews
1903	Mrs M.L. Wilkinson	1929	Mrs P. Snelling	1959	Mrs K. Webb	1976	G. Wright
1904	B. Alexander	1930	Mrs P. Snelling	1960	H. Day	1977	Mrs P. Oliveira
1905	Mrs J. Lee-White	1931	Mrs Buchanan	1961	Mrs K. Webb	1978	Mrs P. Mathews
1906	Miss Dauntese	1932	L. Storr	1962	H. Day	1979	Mrs M. Butler
1907	C. Bloxsome	1933	L. Storr	1963	Mrs K. Webb	1980	G. Wright
1908	Mrs Laidlay	1934	L. Storr	1964	H. Day	1981	G. Wright
1909	Mrs J. Lee-White	1935	L. Storr	1965	H. Day	1982	G. Wright
1910	Mrs Laidlay	1936	L. Storr	1966	Mrs C.G. Dinham	1983	G. Wright

KENT LADIES' CHAMPIONSHIP

This was officially instituted in 1920, although in existence before World War I, when Mrs Cautley won it in 1911 and 1913.

Year	Winner	Year	Winner	Year	Winner	Year	Winner
1920	Mrs Cautley	1934	D. Fishwick	1956	A. Ward	1970	C. Redford
1921	H. Prest	1935	W. Morgan	1957	S.B. Smith	1971	M. Walker
1922	N. Wickenden	1936	W. Morgan	1958	A. Bonallack	1972	L. Denison-Pender
1923	Mrs K. Morrice	1937	W. Morgan	1959	Mrs C. Falconer	1973	L. Denison-Pender
1924	Mrs Cautley	1938	B. Mackenzie	1960	E. Hearn	1974	A. Langford
1925	Mrs J.R. Mason	1939	Miss Jackson	1961	Mrs R. Brown	1975	C. Redford
1926	Mrs J.H. Mason	1948	Mrs Z. Bolton	1962	Mrs R. Brown	1976	Mrs S. Hedges
1927	L. Doxford	1949	Mrs M. Richards	1963	Mrs M. Richards	1977	Mrs C. Caldwell
1928	Miss Oswald	1950	B. Jackson	1964	Mrs S. Ward	1978	Mrs L. Bayman
1929	D. Pearson	1951	B. Jackson	1965	Mrs D. Neech	1979	Mrs S. Hedges
1930	W. Morgan	1952	B. Jackson	1966	Mrs D. Neech	1980	Mrs A. Robinson
1931	W. Morgan	1953	W. Morgan	1967	S. Ward	1981	J. Guntrip
1932	I. Doxford	1954	Mrs C. Falconer	1968	L. Denison-Pender	1982	Mrs S. Hedges
1933	W. Morgan	1955	A. Ward	1969	S. German	1983	J. Guntrip

LANARKSHIRE LADIES' CHAMPIONSHIP

Miss M. Maitland, who was an original member and office bearer of the Lanarkshire County Association, donated the championship cup in December 1927.

Year	Winner	Year	Winner	Year	Winner	Year	Winner
1928	H. Gray	1948	J. Hill	1961	H. Murdoch	1974	Mrs W. Norris
1929	H. Holm	1949	S. Conacher	1962	H. Murdoch	1975	Mrs W. Norris
1930	M. Fogo	1950	G. Galbraith	1963	B. McCormack	1976	Mrs A. Burden
1931	Mrs T.M. Burton	1951	H. Murdoch	1964	J. Smith	1977	S. Needham
1932	H. Holm	1952	H. Murdoch	1965	M. Park	1978	B. McCormack
1933	Mrs W. Reid	1953	J. Cadzow	1966	Mrs M. Norris	1979	Mrs W. Norris
1934	W. Morrison	1954	J. Robertson	1967	B. McCormack	1980	Mrs J.C. Scott
1935	N. Forrest	1955	J. Robertson	1968	Mrs W. Norris	1981	E. Dunn
1936	W. Morrison	1956	J. Robertson	1969	S. Needham	1982	J. Norris
1937	Mrs Ballantine	1957	J. Robertson	1970	Mrs W. Norris	1983	S. Roy
1938	W. Morrison	1958	J. Robertson	1971	Mrs W. Norris		
1939	Mrs Ballantine	1959	J. Robertson	1972	S. Needham		
1947	J. Hill	1960	H. Murdoch	1973	S. Needham		

LANCASHIRE LADIES' CHAMPIONSHIP

The first championship was played at Formby in 1907 for the present trophy, which was presented by Lady Derby. Initially the handicap limit was 6, with one round only played and eight players qualifying for the match play stages. The present method of playing the championship was first used in 1921 when sixteen players qualifying from the 36-hole medal test entered the match play stages, the handicap limit being raised to 12.

Year	Winner	Year	Winner	Year	Winner	Year	Winner
1907	Mrs E.M. Gittins	1929	E. Corlett	1953	F. Stephens	1970	P. Burrows
1908	Mrs E. Garner	1930	Mrs D.E.B. Soulby	1954	F. Stephens	1971	A. Irvin
1909	F.E. Crummack	1931	B. Brown	1955	Mrs F. Smith	1972	A. Irvin
1910	F.E. Crummack	1932	J.D. Firth	1956	S. Stewart	1973	J. Greenhalgh
1911	E. Marsden	1933	J.D. Firth	1957	Mrs D. Howard	1974	A. Irvin
1912	Miss Maudsley	1934	W.M. Berry	1958	S. Vaughan	1975	J. Greenhalgh
1913	Miss Marden	1935	W.M. Berry	1959	Mrs F. Smith	1976	J. Greenhalgh
1914	Mrs Catlow	1936	W.M. Berry	1960	Mrs F. Smith	1977	J. Greenhalgh
1920	Mrs A.C.P. Medrington	1937	J.D. Firth	1961	J. Greenhalgh	1978	J. Greenhalgh
1921	B.M. Brown	1938	Miss Robinson	1962	J. Greenhalgh	1979	A. Norman
1922	Mrs A.C.P. Medrington	1939	B. Edwards	1963	S. Vaughan	1980	A. Brown
1923	Mrs E.S. Carlow	1947	B. Edwards	1964	S. Vaughan	1981	A. Brown
1924	B. Brown	1948	F. Stephens	1965	A. Irvin	1982	Dr G. Costello
1925	B. Brown	1949	F. Stephens	1966	J. Greenhalgh	1983	J. Melville
1926	B. Brown	1950	F. Stephens	1967	A. Irvin		
1927	Miss Corlett	1951	F. Stephens	1968	J. Greenhalgh		
1928	B. Brown	1952	F. Stephens	1969	A. Irvin		

LEICESTERSHIRE AND RUTLAND LADIES' CHAMPIONSHIP

Mr P.L. Baker donated the cup for this competition in 1922. He had a great interest in women's golf as his wife was a good player and keen competitor who won the championship four times. The first event was played at Birstall Golf Club on 27 September 1922 and was decided by stroke play until 1931, when match play was introduced for that year only; it reverted to stroke until 1950 and match play thereafter.

Year	Winner	Year	Winner	Year	Winner	Year	Winner
1922	P. Harrison	1936	Mrs Duncan	1958	F. Brunton	1972	J. Stevens
1923	P. Harrison	1937	E. Martin	1959	Mrs W. Howard	1973	J. Stevens
1924	P. Harrison	1938	Mrs A. Kerslake	1960	Mrs A. Kerslake	1974	Mrs O. Sturton
1925	Mrs Morton	1947	Mrs A. Kerslake	1961	Mrs J.F. Walton	1975	Mrs J. Chapman
1926	Mrs P.L. Baker	1948	Mrs L. Baxter	1962	Mrs J.F. Walton	1976	Mrs J. Chapman
1927	Mrs P.L. Baker	1949	Mrs L. Baxter	1963	Mrs A. Marrion	1977	Mrs J. Chapman
1928	Mrs Sturgess-Wells	1950	Mrs A. Kerslake	1964	Mrs G.A. Wheatley	1978	Mrs R. Reed
1929	Mrs Sturgess-Wells	1951	F. Brunton	1965	Mrs G.A. Wheatley	1979	Mrs A. Mansfield
1930	Mrs Sturgess-Wells	1952	Mrs A. Kerslake	1966	M. Howard	1980	J. Roberts
1931	Mrs Sturgess-Wells	1953	Mrs A. Kerslake	1967	Mrs R. Reed	1981	Mrs R. Reed
1932	Mrs P.L. Baker	1954	Mrs A. Kerslake	1968	Mrs A.M. Reed	1982	Mrs P. Gray
1933	Mrs Lashmor	1955	F. Brunton	1969	Mrs H. McKay	1983	Mrs R. Reed
1934	Mrs P.L. Baker	1956	F. Brunton	1970	Mrs P. Martin		
1935	V. King	1957	F. Brunton	1971	J. Stevens		

LEINSTER LADIES' CHAMPIONSHIP

This championship was inaugurated as a result of a resolution passed at the annual general meeting of the Eastern District of the ILGU in January 1931.

Year	Winner	Year	Winner	Year	Winner	Year	Winner
1931	Mrs N. Todd	1943	M. O'Neill	1957	Mrs V. Reddan	1971	J. Mark
1932	Mrs N. Todd	1944	Mrs V. Reddan	1958	Mrs P.G. MacCann	1972	J. Mark
1933	F. Blake	1945	P. Garvey	1959	E. Brooks	1973	M. Earner
1934	Mrs N. Todd	1946	P. Garvey	1960	M. Earner	1974	S. Gorman
1935	F. Blake	1947	P. Garvey	1961	M. Earner	1975	Dr G. Costello
1936	Mrs N. Todd	1948	K. Smye	1962	E. Brooks	1976	S. Gorman
1937	Miss Gildea	1949	P. Garvey	1963	I. Burke	1977	M. Gerry
1938	Miss Gildea	1950	P. Garvey	1964	I. Burke	1978	S. O'Brien
1939	no competition due to uncertainty caused by war	1951	D.M. Forster	1965	B. Hyland	1979	M. Gerry
		1952	P. O'Sullivan	1966	B. Hyland	1980	C. Hourihane
		1953	P. Garvey	1967	I. Butler	1981	M. McKenna
1940	C. Carroll	1954	E. Brooks	1968	E. Bradshaw	1982	M. McKenna
1941	S. Moore	1955	P. O'Sullivan	1969	E. Bradshaw	1983	P. Wickham
1942	S. Moore	1956	Mrs P. Fletcher	1970	V. Singleton		

LINCOLNSHIRE LADIES' CHAMPIONSHIP

Miss R. Gale and Mrs B. Watson have each won this three times in succession, the latter winning it a further three times.

Year	Winner	Year	Winner	Year	Winner	Year	Winner
1936	Mrs Sparrow	1954	Mrs C. Jones	1965	Mrs R. Winn	1976	Mrs P. West
1937	Mrs D. Taylor	1955	J. Johnson	1966	Mrs D. Frearson	1977	Mrs B. Hix
1938	C. King	1956	Mrs P. Powell	1967	Mrs D. Frearson	1978	Mrs P. West
1939	Mrs Sparrow	1957	Mrs C. Jones	1968	Mrs B. Watson	1979	Mrs B. Hix
1947	D. Taylor	1958	Mrs L. Jones	1969	Mrs B. Dawson	1980	Mrs E. Annison
1948	J. Johnson	1959	R. Gale	1970	Mrs B. Watson	1981	R. Broughton
1949	F.E. Kearney	1960	R. Gale	1971	Mrs E. Annison	1982	Mrs B. Hix
1950	Mrs C. Jones	1961	R. Gale	1972	Mrs P. Chatterton	1983	Mrs B. Hix
1951	Mrs C. Jones	1962	Mrs B. Watson	1973	Mrs P. Harvey		
1952	Mrs P. Powell	1963	Mrs B. Watson	1974	Mrs B. Watson		
1953	J. Johnson	1964	Mrs B. Watson	1975	Mrs P. Harvey		

MIDLAND LADIES' CHAMPIONSHIP

The championship was first held in 1897 at Kings Norton, Worcestershire. Each club was permitted to send one, two or three representatives to compete for medals. Only three counties were and Staffordshire. The championship has been played for by match play since 1932.

Year	Winner	Year	Winner	Year	Winner	Year	Winner
1898	E. Nevile	1922	Mrs E.B. Bayliss	1948	M. Hampson	1967	Mrs R. Tomlinson
1899	L. Smith	1923	D. Harthill	1949	Mrs Sheppard	1968	Mrs J. Roles
1900	M. Wolseley	1924	Miss Robinson	1950	Mrs Gaskell	1969	B. Jackson
1901	E. Nevile	1925	D. Harthill	1951	Mrs Denham	1970	J. Blaymire
1902	Mrs Phillips	1926	E. Wilson	1952	P. Davies	1971	J. Stant
1903	E. Nevile	1927	B. Law	1953	Hon. Mrs J. Gee	1972	J. Blaymire
1904	E. Nevile	1928	E. Wilson	1954	B. Jackson	1973	Mrs A. Stant
1905	Miss Bryan	1929	E. Wilson	1955	Mrs Beeson	1974	Mrs B. Bargh
1906	Miss Foster	1930	E. Wilson	1956	B. Jackson	1975	Mrs A. Stant
1907	L. Moore	1931	Mrs Peppercorn	1957	B. Jackson	1976	Mrs J. Chapman
1908	L. Moore	1932	M. Fieldhouse	1958	B. Jackson	1977	Mrs S. Westall
1909	Miss Foster	1933	G. Craddock-Hartopp	1959	B. Jackson	1978	Mrs S. Westall
1910	Miss Hemingway	1934	G. Craddock-Hartopp	1960	B. Jackson	1979	Mrs M. Carr
1911	L. Moore	1935	K. Bentley	1961	S. Armitage	1980	J. Walter
1912	L. Moore	1936	B. Newell	1962	A. Higgott	1981	J. Walter
1913	Miss Barry	1937	E. Pears	1963	A. Higgott	1982	S. Kiddle
1914	Mrs Bell-Scott	1938	E. Pears	1964	A. Coxhill	1983	T. Hammond
1920	Mrs E.B. Bayliss	1939	Mrs Jackson	1965	S. Armitage		
1921	Mrs E.B. Bayliss	1947	Mrs Sheppard	1966	Mrs D. Frearson		

MIDDLESEX LADIES' CHAMPIONSHIP

This championship was instituted in 1914, with the Challenge Bowl being presented by Mrs Symmons.

Year	Winner	Year	Winner	Year	Winner	Year	Winner
1914	Edith Leitch	1934	A.C. Regnart	1955	M. Spearman	1970	Mrs M. Barton
1920	Mrs Lewis-Smith	1935	R. Harris	1956	M. Spearman	1971	S. Hills
1921	Mrs S.H. Fletcher	1936	B. Taylor	1957	M. Spearman	1972	C. Macintosh
1922	Mrs McNair	1937	Mrs J.B. Beck	1958	M. Spearman	1973	Mrs R.E. Garrett
1923	E. Leitch	1938	Mrs C. Eberstein	1959	M. Spearman	1974	A. Daniel
1924	C. Leitch	1939	M. Ruttle	1960	Mrs M. Barton	1975	A. Daniel
1925	Mrs W.A. Gavin	1947	J. Gordon	1961	M. Spearman	1976	J. Boulter
1926	A. Croft	1948	J. Gordon	1962	Mrs M. Barton	1977	A. Daniel
1927	A. Croft	1949	Mrs C.R. Eberstein	1963	P. Moore	1978	Mrs A. Gems
1928	Miss Ramsden	1950	J. Gordon	1964	M. Spearman	1979	Mrs C. Turnbull
1929	Miss Clayton	1951	Mrs Bromley-	1965	M. Spearman	1980	Mrs C. Turnbull
1930	E. Guedalla		Davenport	1966	Mrs A. Denny	1981	M. Allen
1931	R. Rabbidge	1952	J. Gordon	1967	B. Hayhurst	1982	Mrs A. Gems
1932	Mrs J. Fleming	1953	Mrs R.E. Garrett	1968	Mrs B. Jones	1983	C. McGillivray
1933	Miss Daniell	1954	J. Gordon	1969	S. Hills		

MIDLOTHIAN LADIES' CHAMPIONSHIP

At the county annual general meeting in 1922, it was proposed that the association should hold a spring and an autumn meeting, in addition to a hole-and-hole competition and five-a-side matches, but this proposal was not implemented until 1924.

Year	Winner	Year	Winner	Year	Winner	Year	Winner
1924	M.J. Wood	1938	C.M. Park	1959	E. Phillip	1973	C. Hardwick
1925	M.J. Wood	1939	Mrs S.H. Morton	1960	P. Dunn	1974	Dr M. Norval
1926	M.J. Wood	1947	C.M. Park	1961	E. Phillip	1975	J. More
1927	Q. Smith	1948	C.M. Park	1962	Mrs J. Milton	1976	M. Stavert
1928	D. Park	1949	Mrs J. Scott	1963	Mrs M. Duthie	1977	M. Stavert
1929	D. Park	1950	E. M'Larty	1964	Mrs D. Antonio	1978	M. Stavert
1930	D. Park	1951	Mrs W.C. Ritchie	1965	F. Miller	1979	M. Stavert
1931	D. Park	1952	J.L. Dunbar	1966	E. Phillip	1980	Mrs B.M. Marshall
1932	Mrs J.N. Duncan	1953	Mrs W.C. Ritchie	1967	M. Norval	1981	P. Broughton
1933	C.M. Park	1954	Mrs J.J.G. Thomson	1968	Mrs E. Jack	1982	Mrs S. Little
1934	C.M. Park	1955	Mrs J.B. Cormack	1969	M. Norval	1983	J. Marshall
1935	C.M. Park	1956	Mrs W.C. Ritchie	1970	S. MacDonald		
1936	C.M. Park	1957	Mrs J.B. Cormack	1971	Mrs J. Marshall		
1937	M. Nicoll	1958	Mrs C.H. Ritchie	1972	C. Hardwick		

MONMOUTHSHIRE LADIES' CHAMPIONSHIP

The Monmouthshire Ladies' County Golf Association was formed on 2 May 1925, with the object of playing county matches. At that meeting, Mrs F.D. Llewlyn was elected treasurer; she is president today. The championship was decided by stroke play till 1934, then by match play.

Year	Winner	Year	Winner	Year	Winner	Year	Winner
1920	E. Clay	1935	Dr P. Whitaker	1957	P. Roberts	1972	P. Roberts
1921	D. Oswald-Thomas	1936	M. Williams	1958	Mrs P. Inglis	1973	E. Davies
1922	E. Clay	1937	Mrs J.G. Meredith	1959	P. Roberts	1974	E. Davies
1923	Mrs Phillips	1938	Mrs G. Evans	1960	Mrs R. Hartley	1975	Mrs B. Chambers
1924	Mrs Phillips	1939	H. Reynolds	1961	Mrs R. Hartley	1976	E. Davies
1925	L. Newman	1947	M.P. Roberts	1962	P. Roberts	1977	C. Parry
1926	C. Freeguard	1948	Mrs Garfield Evans	1963	P. Roberts	1978	E. Davies
1927	Mrs R.W. Meacock	1949	M.P. Roberts	1964	P. Roberts	1979	E. Davies
1928	Mrs W. Phillips	1950	M.P. Roberts	1965	P. Roberts	1980	M. Davis
1929	L. Newman	1951	Mrs Garfield Evans	1966	P. Roberts	1981	M. Davis
1930	G. Evans	1952	P. Roberts	1967	Mrs G. Gallies	1982	M. Davis
1931	Mrs B.T. Rees	1953	P. Roberts	1968	P. Roberts	1983	K. Beckett
1932	L. Newman	1954	P. Roberts	1969	Mrs B. Chambers		
1933	Mrs R.W. Meacock	1955	P. Roberts	1970	P. Roberts		
1934	Mrs R.W. Meacock	1956	P. Roberts	1971	Dr M. Smith		

NORFOLK LADIES' CHAMPIONSHIP

Mrs Sumpter, vice-president, presented the challenge cup for this championship, which was instituted on 31 July 1912, and first played for at Sheringham on 24 and 25 September that same year. The challenge cup, which bears Mrs Sumpter's name, is an exact copy, but smaller, of the Ladies' British Open Amateur Challenge Cup.

Year	Winner	Year	Winner	Year	Winner	Year	Winner
1912	Mrs Steinmetz	1932	M. Kerr	1954	Mrs B.T.F. Carrick	1970	Mrs N. Rains
1913	Miss Cooper	1933	G. Watts	1955	J.M. Harrison	1971	V.E. Cooper
1914	Miss Stocker	1934	G. Watts	1956	Mrs B.T.F. Carrick	1972	Mrs N. Rains
1920	S. Marshall	1935	Mrs V.M. Cross	1958	Mrs B.T.F. Carrick	1973	Mrs N. Rains
1921	S. Marshall	1936	G. Watts	1959	H. Smith	1974	Mrs M. Davies
1922	Miss Watts	1937	Mrs Jackson	1960	H. Smith	1975	Mrs M. Davies
1923	J. Kerr	1938	P. Bullard	1961	Mrs B.T.F. Carrick	1976	Mrs N. Rains
1924	J. Kerr	1939	Mrs Carrick	1962	A.M. Rust	1977	Mrs P. Carrick
1925	V. Kerr	1947	Mrs Carrick	1963	V.E. Cooper	1978	Mrs M. Davies
1926	E.G. Gower	1948	Mrs Richardson	1964	A.M. Rust	1979	Mrs D. Sutton
1927	Mrs Barnard	1949	Mrs Carrick	1965	Mrs B. Carrick	1980	V.E. Cooper
1928	V.S. Reeve	1950	Mrs J.H. Martin	1966	Mrs M. Leeder	1981	J. Dicks
1929	Mrs Cross	1951	J. Cowell	1967	Mrs M. Leeder	1982	V. Cooper
1930	M. Kerr	1952	Mrs Carrick	1968	Mrs M. Leeder	1983	Mrs M. Davies
1931	M. Kerr	1953	J.H. Harrison	1969	Mrs N. Rains		

NORTHAMPTONSHIRE LADIES' CHAMPIONSHIP

The championship was instituted in 1930, when Lady Annaly presented the trophy, but appears to have been first played for in 1932.

Year	Winner	Year	Winner	Year	Winner	Year	Winner
1932	Mrs R.T. Phipps	1950	Mrs W. Taylor	1959	Mrs L. Everard	1972	Mrs A. Duck
1933	D.R. Wooding	1951	Mrs R. Larratt	1960	Mrs L. Everard	1973	Mrs J. Sugden
1934	Mrs C. Everard	1952	Mrs K. Lock	1962	Mrs G. Hollingsworth	1974	J. Dicks
1935	Mrs R.T. Phipps	1953	Marchioness of	1963	Mrs L. Everard	1975	J. Lee
1936	Mrs G.E. Dazeley		Northampton	1964	Mrs L. Everard	1976	J. Lee
1937	Mrs W.T. Swannell	1954	Marchioness of	1965	Mrs N. Paton	1977	J. Lee
1938	Mrs R.T. Phipps		Northampton	1966	Mrs S. Stephenson	1978	J. Dicks
1939	Mrs W.T. Swannell	1955	Miss Spencer	1967	Mrs S. Stephenson	1979	V.J. Dicks
1946	Mrs W.T. Swannell	1956	Marchioness of	1968	Mrs J. Sugden	1980	Mrs M. Hutcheson
1947	A.M. Troup		Northampton	1969	Mrs M. Stephenson	1981	K. Beckett
1948	Mrs W.T. Swannell	1957	Mrs L. Everard	1970	Mrs K. Lock	1982	Mrs P. Coles
1949	A.M. Troup	1958	Mrs W.T. Swannell	1971	Mrs J. Blezard	1983	J. Dicks

NORTHERN COUNTIES LADIES' CHAMPIONSHIP

The Moray County Ladies' Association, formed during the 1920s, was joined in the 1930s by Nairn, and after the war by Banffshire. Later on, in 1967, it was decided that Inverness-shire and all counties north of there should combine with these three and be known as the Northern Counties Ladies' Golf Association. This came about because the counties are so thinly populated. In 1982 the association had 325 members belonging to twenty-five clubs.

Year	Winner	Year	Winner	Year	Winner	Year	Winner
1930	H. Cameron	1951	Dr M.G. Thomson	1963	M. McIntosh	1975	Mrs I. McIntosh
1931	H. Cameron	1952	Mrs M. Main	1964	M. McIntosh	1976	G. Stewart
1932	H. Cameron	1953	C. McGeagh	1965	Mrs I. McIntosh	1977	S. Ross
1933	H. Tomes	1954	C. McGeagh	1966	Mrs I. McIntosh	1978	G. Stewart
1934	Mrs B. Miller-Stirling	1955	Mrs M. Main	1967	Mrs B. Drakard	1979	Mrs I. McIntosh
1935	J. Alexander	1956	B. Chetham	1968	J. Cumming	1980	Mrs I. McIntosh
1936	I. Thomson	1957	Dr M.G. Thomson	1969	Mrs I. McIntosh	1981	S. Ross
1937	Mrs Graser	1958	Mrs M. Main	1970	Mrs I. McIntosh	1982	G. Stewart
1938	Mrs Smith	1959	Mrs M. Main	1971	M. Kirk	1983	L. Anderson
1939	Mrs J.G. Shiach	1960	M. McIntosh	1972	J. Cumming		
1949	Mrs M. Main	1961	B. Chetham	1973	Mrs I. McIntosh		
1950	Lady Inglis	1962	I. Storm	1974	Mrs I. McIntosh		

NORTH OF SCOTLAND LADIES' CHAMPIONSHIP

Instituted in 1970, the trophy for the winner was presented by Mrs Sophia J.C. Gifford, that for the runner-up by Mrs E.C. Thomson, and in the following year Mrs Lackie of Angus presented the Angus Trophy for the handicap winner. The first championship was played at Edzell, Angus, and the venue is rotated round the four counties of the Northern Section in alphabetical order.

Year	Winner	Year	Winner	Year	Winner	Year	Winner
1970	Mrs I. Wright	1974	M. Thomson	1978	G. Stewart	1982	G. Stewart
1971	Mrs I. McIntosh	1975	G. Stewart	1979	Mrs J. Self	1983	G. Stewart
1972	A. Laing	1976	A. Laing	1980	G. Stewart		
1973	M. Thomson	1977	F. Anderson	1981	F. McNab		

NORTHUMBERLAND LADIES' CHAMPIONSHIP

Since the institution of the event in 1921, the most number of wins, fifteen, has been achieved by Maureen, née Nichol, Pickard.

Year	Winner	Year	Winner	Year	Winner	Year	Winner
1921	Mrs Fraser	1935	Mrs H. Percy	1957	M. Nichol	1971	Mrs M. Pickard
1922	Miss Middlemass	1936	M. Hodgson	1958	M. Nichol	1972	J.L. Smith
1923	M. Conning	1937	Mrs H. Percy	1959	Mrs G. Kennedy	1973	J.L. Smith
1924	Miss Middlemass	1938	Mrs H. Percy	1960	Mrs G. Kennedy	1974	J.L. Smith
1925	Mrs H. Percy	1939	H. Hodgson	1961	M. Nichol	1975	Mrs E. Elliott
1926	Mrs H. Percy	1947	Mrs A. Dodds	1962	M. Nichol	1976	Mrs M. Pickard
1927	M. Moorhouse	1948	Mrs G. Moore	1963	Mrs G. Kennedy	1977	Mrs M. Pickard
1928	Mrs H. Percy	1949	Mrs A.M.H. Wardlaw	1964	M. Nichol	1978	Mrs E. Elliott
1929	Mrs H. Percy	1950	Mrs Storey	1965	M. Nichol	1979	H. Wilson
1930	M. Tate	1951	Mrs Storey	1966	M. Nichol	1980	D. Glenn
1931	Mrs Bird	1952	Mrs A.M.H. Wardlaw	1967	Mrs M. Pickard	1981	Mrs E. Elliott
1932	Mrs H. Percy	1953	Mrs A.M.H. Wardlaw	1968	A. Mortimer	1982	Mrs M. Pickard
1933	Mrs H. Percy	1955	Mrs Thatcher	1969	Mrs M. Pickard	1983	J. Soulsby
1934	Mrs H. Percy	1956	M. Nichol	1970	Mrs M. Pickard		

NOTTINGHAMSHIRE LADIES' CHAMPIONSHIP

The Nottinghamshire Ladies' Association was formed in December 1908. At the 1925 annual general meeting, it was decided to hold a championship in 1926. The trophy is in the form of a cleek, mounted on green velvet and surrounded by a silver band on which the names of the winners were engraved; the band has been filled and the names are now engraved on a silver plate inserted in the box containing the cleek. Mrs J.D. Player presented it.

Year	Winner	Year	Winner	Year	Winner	Year	Winner
1926	K. Watson	1939	Mrs A.S. Bright	1959	Mrs B. Baker	1972	R.M. Clay
1927	Miss Tate	1947	Mrs A.H. Taylor	1960	Mrs J. Redgate	1973	Mrs B. Brewer
1928	Mrs Bloomer	1948	Miss Lowe	1961	Mrs J. Redgate	1974	K. Horberry
1929	D. Snook	1949	J. Hetherington	1962	Mrs B. Brewer	1975	K. Horberry
1930	Mrs Bingley	1950	J. Hetherington	1963	Mrs B. Brewer	1976	K. Horberry
1931	D. Snook	1951	J. Hetherington	1964	Mrs B. Brewer	1977	K. Horberry
1932	Mrs Bristowe	195?	Mrs C.H.V. Elliott	1965	A. Payne	1978	Mrs J. Brewer
1933	Mrs Bristowe	1953	J. Redgate	1966	Mrs B. Brewer	1979	M. Elswood
1934	N. Watson	1954	J. McIntyre	1967	Mrs B. Brewer	1980	M. Elswood
1935	Mrs A.S. Bright	1955	Mrs B. Baker	1968	Mrs G. Marshall	1981	M. Davies
1936	Mrs Elliott	1956	Mrs J. McIntyre	1969	K. Horberry	1982	K. Horberry
1937	Mrs Elliott	1957	Mrs G.R. Needham	1970	Mrs J. Brewer	1983	M. Elswood
1938	A.H. Bloomer	1958	Mrs B. Baker	1971	V. O'Sullivan		

OXFORDSHIRE LADIES' CHAMPIONSHIP

Lady Rathcreedan, the county captain, proposed in October 1925 that a championship should be held annually, the championship to take the form of a knock-out scratch tournament, and to be held in the spring on a different course each year, provided that a county member was a member of the course chosen. The 1926 championship did not take place because of the General Strike and there appear to be no records for 1927 and 1928, but at the 1929 annual general meeting members were asked to contribute towards the trophy and did so.

Year	Winner	Year	Winner	Year	Winner	Year	Winner
1929	Mrs Barrington-Ward	1950	Mrs Bamberger	1962	Mrs L. Abrahams	1974	Mrs L. Davies
1930	Mrs Woodward	1951	Mrs Richards	1963	Mrs J. Grandison	1975	Mrs L. Davies
1931	Mrs Evers	1952	Mrs Abrahams	1964	Mrs L. Abrahams	1976	Mrs L. Davies
1932	Mrs Woodward	1953	Mrs L. Abrahams	1965	G. Hanks	1977	Mrs L. Davies
1933	Mrs Woodward	1954	Mrs L. Abrahams	1966	T. Ross Stein	1978	Mrs L. Davies
1934	Mrs Evers	1955	Mrs L. Abrahams	1967	Mrs J. Glennie	1979	Mrs L. Davies
1935	Mrs Evers	1956	Mrs Nightingale	1968	Mrs A. Delany	1980	Mrs L. Davies
1936	Mrs Coggins	1957	Mrs L. Abrahams	1969	Mrs L. Davies	1981	K. Horberry
1937	Mrs Evers	1958	Mrs L. Abrahams	1970	Mrs A. Delany	1982	Mrs M. Glennie
1938	Mrs Woodward	1959	Mrs L. Abrahams	1971	Mrs L. Davies	1983	Mrs M. Glennie
1948	Mrs Trepte	1960	V. Morris	1972	Mrs L. Davies		
1949	Mrs Halban	1961	Mrs L. Abrahams	1973	N. Sparks		

PERTH AND KINROSS LADIES' CHAMPIONSHIP

The A.K. Bell Rose Bowl was presented to the county association in 1921 by Mr Bell of Bell's Whisky as a handicap trophy. When the time came to play for it again after World War II, a long search had to be made, and it was finally found in the safe of Cairncross Jewellers. The county captain, Mrs Nan Gibb, and committee that year decided that it should be a scratch trophy and so it has been ever since.

Year	Winner	Year	Winner	Year	Winner	Year	Winner
1921	M. Brown	1934	J. Anderson	1957	E. Aitken	1971	Mrs Aitken
1922	M. Graham	1935	P. Russell-Montgomery	1958	J. Hay	1972	Mrs Aitken
1923	M. Vallings			1959	E. Aitken	1973	Mrs W. Hay
1924	M. Brown	1936	J. Anderson	1960	E. Aitken	1974	Mrs W. Hay
1925	M. Brown	1937	P. Russell-Montgomery	1961	Mrs Norwell	1975	F. Anderson
1926	S.C. Scott			1962	E. Aitken	1976	Mrs J. Hay
1927	S.C. Scott	1938	S.C. Scott	1963	Mrs Hay	1977	F. Anderson
1928	M. Meikle	1950	E. Crawford	1964	Mrs Norwell	1978	F. Anderson
1929	M. Brown	1951	E. Young	1965	Mrs Hay	1979	F. Anderson
1930	P. Russell-Montgomery	1952	E. Young	1966	Mrs Gibb	1980	Mrs J. Aitken
		1953	E. Young	1967	Mrs Norwell	1981	E. Aitken
1931	M. Brown	1954	E. Crawford	1968	Mrs Norwell	1982	E. Aitken
1932	J. Anderson	1955	N. Gibb	1969	Mrs Norwell	1983	F. Anderson
1933	J. Anderson	1956	N. Gibb	1970	Mrs Norwell		

RENFREWSHIRE COUNTY LADIES' CHAMPIONSHIP

The cup for this championship was presented by Lady Blythswood in 1927, the county association having been inaugurated in 1909. Wilma Aitken has so far won it five times in succession, eclipsing the record set by Dorothea Sommerville and Heather Anderson.

Year	Winner	Year	Winner	Year	Winner	Year	Winner
1927	D. Herbert	1939	Mrs Fleming	1960	Mrs J.H. Anderson	1972	Mrs J.H. Anderson
1928	Mrs Houston-Rowan	1949	Mrs Drummond	1961	D. Sommerville	1973	Mrs J.H. Anderson
1929	Mrs Fleming	1950	Mrs Drummond	1962	J. Letham	1974	Dr A.J. Wilson
1930	V. Lamb	1951	Mrs Drummond	1963	D. Sommerville	1975	L. Bennett
1931	Mrs Fleming	1952	Mrs A.R. Gray	1964	Mrs J.H. Anderson	1976	Dr A.J. Wilson
1932	Mrs Fleming	1953	M. Pearcy	1965	E. Gibb	1977	L. Bennett
1933	V. Lamb	1954	Mrs J. Drummond	1966	Mrs J.H. Anderson	1978	W. Aitken
1934	Mrs Fleming	1955	N. Menzies	1967	Mrs J.H. Anderson	1979	W. Aitken
1935	J. McLintock	1956	D. Sommerville	1968	Mrs J.H. Anderson	1980	W. Aitken
1936	M. Pearcy	1957	D. Sommerville	1969	E. Gibb	1981	W. Aitken
1937	Mrs C.M. Falconer	1958	D. Sommerville	1970	Mrs J.H. Anderson	1982	W. Aitken
1938	J. McLintock	1959	D. Sommerville	1971	Mrs J.H. Anderson	1983	J.L. Hastings

ROEHAMPTON GOLD CUP

Instituted in 1926, the Gold was competed for over 18 holes' stroke play until 1964, when it was increased to 36. Winners with the lowest scores during its 18-hole stage were Maureen Ruttle Garrett in 1950 and Jeanne Bisgood in 1952, both with 72. Winner with the lowest score since extension to 36 holes was Angela Ward Bonallack, with 147 in 1980. Lowest score ever was Ann Irvin's 71 in the second round in 1973.

Year	Winner	Year	Winner	Year	Winner	Year	Winner
1926	Mrs W. McNair	1948	M. Ruttle	1961	Mrs L. Abrahams	1974	L. Harrold
1927	M. Gourlay	1949	F. Stephens	1962	Mrs L. Abrahams	1975	W. Pithers and
1928	C. Leitch	1950	Mrs M. Garrett	1963	R. Porter		C. Redford
1929	L. Doxford	1951	J. Bisgood	1964	C. Archer	1976	A. Irvin and
1930	E. Wilson	1952	J. Bisgood	1965	M. Spearman		V. Marvin
1931	V. Lamb	1953	J. Bisgood	1966	G. Brandom	1977	A. Uzielli
1932	Mrs A. Gold	1954	Mrs J. Bromley-	1967	A. Irvin	1978	C. Caldwell and
1933	Mrs A. Ramsden		Davenport	1968	A. Irvin		B. Robertson
1934	J. Hamilton	1955	Mrs L. Abrahams	1969	A. Irvin	1979	B. Robertson
1935	P. Barton	1956	Mrs S. Allon	1970	M. Everard	1980	A. Bonallack
1936	B. Newell	1957	Mrs M. Roberts	1971	B. Huke	1981	B. Robertson
1937	P. Barton	1958	P. Moore	1972	A. Irvin and	1982	B. Robertson
1938	P. Barton	1959	M. Glidewell		C. Redford	1983	B. New and
1939	P. Barton	1960	E. Price	1973	A. Irvin		V. Thomas

SHROPSHIRE LADIES' CHAMPIONSHIP

This championship began in 1923, the youngest winner being Gillian Foster in 1972 at the age of sixteen. The county association had its fiftieth anniversary in 1980.

Year	Winner	Year	Winner	Year	Winner	Year	Winner
1923	Mrs Beard	1937	M. Black	1959	Mrs G.M. Argles	1969	Mrs G. Geddes
1924	H. Corser	1938	M. Black	1960	Mrs M. Wynne-Thomas	1970	Mrs J. Shrimpton
1925	Mrs Beard	1939	Mrs A.R. Blockley			1971	Mrs G. Geddes
1926	M. Deedes	1948	Mrs V. Jones	1961	Mrs J. Shrimpton	1972	G. Foster
1927	M. Deedes	1949	Mrs Argles	1962	Mrs M. Scott	1973	Mrs D. Watkin
1928	M. Barnes	1950	M. Loy	1963	Mrs M. Wynne-Thomas	1974	Mrs G. Geddes
1929	M. Barnes	1951	Mrs Argles			1975	Mrs G. Geddes
1930	M. Barnes	1952	Mrs Argles	1964	Mrs M. Wynne-Thomas	1976	S. McLachlin
1931	M. Barnes	1953	Mrs Beetham			1977	Mrs J. Shrimpton
1932	Mrs A.R. Blockley	1954	Mrs Beetham	1965	Mrs M. Wynne-Thomas	1978	J. Dingley
1933	M. Barnes	1955	Mrs Argles			1979	Mrs S. Pidgeon
1934	M. Black	1956	M. Loy	1966	Mrs M. Wynne-Thomas	1980	Mrs S. Pidgeon
1935	M. Black	1957	Mrs A.M. Argles			1981	Mrs S. Pidgeon
1936	Mrs Wycherly	1958	M. Loy	1967	Mrs G. Geddes	1982	Mrs S. Pidgeon
				1968	Mrs G. Geddes	1983	C. Gauge

SOMERSET LADIES' CHAMPIONSHIP

For 12 December 1912, the minutes state that a challenge bowl or cup was necessary and subscriptions towards the purchase were invited. The first championship was played at Burnham and Berrow links on 5–6 March 1913, when there were seventeen entries, each paying 2s (10p). Enough money had been collected to purchase the cup. The largest winning margin was in 1964 when J. Jurgens beat Mrs O. Hawkes 15 and 13.

Year	Winner	Year	Winner	Year	Winner	Year	Winner
1913	Mrs Hart	1935	D.R. Fowler	1954	Lady Katharine Cairns	1969	Mrs C. Walpole
1914	B. May	1936	D.R. Fowler			1970	Mrs M. Perriam
1920	Mrs R.E. Tomkinson	1937	M. Wall	1955	Mrs S. Jones	1971	Mrs S. Chambers
1921	D.R. Fowler	1938	Lady Catharine Cairns	1956	Mrs G. Lovell	1972	Mrs S. Chambers
1922	D.R. Fowler			1957	Mrs G. Lovell	1973	Mrs S. Chambers
1923	D.R. Fowler	1939	Lady Katharine Cairns	1958	Mrs P. Watford	1974	Mrs S. Chambers
1924	D.R. Fowler			1959	Mrs F.R. Brown	1975	C. Hammond
1925	D.R. Fowler	1947	Mrs B. Popplestone	1960	Mrs F.R. Brown	1976	Mrs M. Perriam
1927	Miss Penruddock	1948	Mrs B. Popplestone	1961	Mrs R. Watford	1977	C. Trew
1928	Miss Brownlow	1949	Mrs B. Popplestone	1962	Mrs F.R. Brown	1978	C. Trew
1929	Miss Penruddock	1950	Lady Katharine Cairns	1963	Mrs R. Watford	1979	B. New
1930	P. Reed			1964	J. Jurgens	1980	B. New
1931	P. Reed	1951	Mrs G. Lovell	1965	Mrs C. Walpole	1981	B. New
1932	Mrs Skrimshire	1952	Mrs G. Lovell	1966	Mrs A. Alford	1982	B. New
1933	Mrs Skrimshire	1953	Lady Katharine Cairns	1967	Mrs P. Watford	1983	B. New
1934	Mrs Skrimshire			1968	Mrs K. Counsell		

SOUTH-EASTERN LADIES' CHAMPIONSHIP

From 1950 to 1967 this was competed for by stroke play, and changed to match play until 1972. It then reverted to stroke play.

Year	Winner	Year	Winner	Year	Winner	Year	Winner
1950	J. Bisgood	1958	M. Spearman	1967	Mrs J. Baucher	1976	L. Harrold
1951	Lady Katharine Cairns	1959	E. Price	1968	E. Collis	1977	S. Bamford
1952	J. Bisgood	1960	E. Price	1969	Mrs E. Fisher	1978	C. Caldwell
1953	B. Lowe	1961	M. Spearman	1970	A. Warren	1979	B. Cooper
1954	B. Jackson	1962	Mrs B. Green	1971	H. Clifford	1980	J. Rumsey
1955	E. Price	1963	J. Thornhill	1972	H. Clifford	1981	C. Caldwell
1956	M. Spearman	1964	J. Thornhill	1973	C. Redford	1982	J. Nicholson
1957	A. Ward	1965	A. Bonallack	1974	C. le Feuvre	1983	L. Davies
		1966	H. Clifford	1975	W. Pithers		

SOUTH-WESTERN LADIES' CHAMPIONSHIP

The resolution to hold the championship was proposed by Dorset and seconded by Wiltshire on 14 November 1929, the first championship being held at Ferndown in 1931. Miss Huleatt, chairman at the meeting, presented the trophy which is still used today. The original format was a 36-hole qualifying round on the first day, sixteen to qualify, and an 18-hole final. In 1934 the number of qualifiers was increased to thirty-two and in 1936 the final became 36 holes. This continued until 1965 when the qualifying round and the final were both reduced to 18 holes, with thirty-two to qualify. In 1982 the competitors urged the organizers to change either the qualifying round or the final to 36-holes and so in that year there was a 36-hole qualifying round played over two days with 18 holes on each day and only sixteen players qualifying for the final. In one of the quarter finals, Mrs Peggy Reece, aged over sixty and playing off scratch, lost to Miss Pat Johnson, aged sixteen and playing off plus one, at the twenty-first hole.

Year	Winner	Year	Winner	Year	Winner	Year	Winner
1931	M. Beard	1950	P. Roberts	1961	R. Porter	1973	T. Perkins
1932	Mrs G. Jones	1951	P. Roberts	1962	R. Porter	1974	T. Perkins
1933	Mrs V. Bramwell	1952	Mrs P.J.E. Reece	1963	Mrs P. Reece	1975	P. Light
1934	B. Pyman	1953	Lady Katharine Cairns	1964	R. Porter	1976	T. Perkins
1935	M.J. Jeffreys			1965	R. Porter	1977	R. Porter
1936	Mrs G. Emery	1954	P.M. Crow	1966	R. Porter	1978	P. Light
1937	Mrs G. Emery	1955	P.M. Crow	1967	R. Porter	1979	Mrs R. Slark
1938	Mrs C. Beard	1956	R. Porter	1968	Mrs P. Reece	1980	L. Isherwood
1939	Mrs V. Bramwell	1957	R. Porter	1969	R. Porter	1981	L. Moore
1947	M. Roskrow	1958	T. Ross Steen	1970	Mrs S. Chambers	1982	L. Moore
1948	Mrs B. Wills	1959	Mrs P.J.E. Reece	1971	Mrs P. Reece	1983	P. Johnson
1949	M. Roskrow	1960	R. Porter	1972	R. Porter		

STAFFORDSHIRE LADIES' CHAMPIONSHIP

The formation of this county's golf association came in 1907 and 1921 saw the presentation of the championship cup by the then president, Lady Lewisham. The cup first went to the player with the best gross score over 36 holes, and the championship became match play in 1934. With the exception of 1947 and 1948 it has been match play ever since.

Year	Winner	Year	Winner	Year	Winner	Year	Winner
1921	Mrs E.B. Bayliss	1935	A. Dobson	1956	B. Jackson	1970	Mrs A. Booth
1922	Mrs E.B. Bayliss	1936	A. Dobson	1957	B. Jackson	1971	Mrs A. Booth
1923	Mrs Lloyd-Smith	1937	M. Evershed	1958	B. Jackson	1972	Mrs A. Booth
1924	A. Dobson	1938	A. Dobson	1959	B. Jackson	1973	M. Hood
1925	Mrs E.B. Bayliss	1939	Mrs A.E. Parks	1960	A. Higgott	1974	Mrs B. Bargh
1926	Mrs E.B. Bayliss	1947	M. Evershed	1961	D. Robb	1975	Mrs A. Stant
1927	A. Dobson	1948	M. Evershed	1962	A. Higgott	1976	B. Jackson
1928	A. Dobson	1949	Mrs G. Parrott	1963	B. Jackson	1977	Mrs A. Booth
1929	A. Dobson	1950	Mrs H. Pritchards	1964	B. Jackson	1978	Mrs A. Stant
1930	A. Dobson	1951	Mrs F. King	1965	A. Coxhill	1979	Mrs A. Smith
1931	A. Dobson	1952	Mrs A. Denham	1966	B. Jackson	1980	Mrs A. Booth
1932	Mrs A.E. Parks	1953	M. Evershed	1967	B. Jackson	1981	J. Brown
1933	A. Dobson	1954	B. Jackson	1968	B. Jackson	1982	J. Brown
1934	Miss Birkett	1955	Mrs A. Denham	1969	B. Jackson	1983	D. Christison

STIRLING COUNTY LADIES' GOLF ASSOCIATION CHAMPIONSHIP

From May 1950 this was played over Glenbervie golf course but the Stirling County Ladies and Clackmannanshire County Ladies amalgamated in 1969 to form the Stirling and Clackmannan County Ladies' Golf Association. The championship took this name, and used the Stirling County Ladies' Cup.

Year	Winner	Year	Winner	Year	Winner	Year	Winner
1950	H. Nimmo	1955	H. Glennie	1960	H. Glennie	1965	M.F. Myles
1951	M.F. Myles	1956	M.F. Myles	1961	H. Glennie	1966	M.F. Myles
1952	M.F. Myles	1957	H. Glennie	1962	Mrs D.H. Smith	1967	M.F. Myles
1953	Mrs G.E. Mitchell	1958	M.F. Myles	1963	Mrs G.E. Mitchell	1968	Mrs D.H. Smith
1954	M.F. Myles	1959	M.F. Myles	1964	M.F. Myles		

STIRLING AND CLACKMANNAN COUNTY LADIES' CHAMPIONSHIP

Year	Winner	Year	Winner	Year	Winner	Year	Winner
1969	Mrs D. Smith	1973	Mrs D. Smith	1977	Mrs D. Smith	1981	E. Miskimmin
1970	Mrs G.E. Mitchell	1974	Mrs G.E. Mitchell	1978	Mrs J. MacCallum	1982	declared void
1971	Mrs D. Smith	1975	E. Miskimmin	1979	Mrs J. MacCallum	1983	J. Harrison
1972	Mrs G.E. Mitchell	1976	Mrs R. Frame	1980	E. Miskimmin		

SUFFOLK LADIES' CHAMPIONSHIP

The Suffolk Ladies' County Golf Club was instituted on 12 January 1926, the meeting being attended by representatives from six county clubs – Aldeburgh, Bungay, Felixstowe, Ipswich, Royal Worlington and Woodbridge. The championship event was also instituted in that year. Miss Joy Winn was elected county captain and in 1982 was still a member of the association. The championship has always been match play. In 1982 a stroke play championship was inaugurated, Dr Jeanne Gibson winning the event, which was played at Aldeburgh.

Year	Winner	Year	Winner	Year	Winner	Year	Winner
1926	Mrs Long	1939	Lady Eddis	1961	Mrs M. Openshaw	1974	S. Dawson
1927	J. Winn	1947	Lady Eddis	1962	S. Dawson	1975	S. Dawson
1928	J. Winn	1948	P. Marsh	1963	Mrs M. Openshaw	1976	Mrs V. Cullen
1929	Mrs Garrett	1949	Mrs Evans	1964	Mrs A.M. Eddie	1977	S. Dawson
1930	Miss Griffiths	1950	Mrs Gaskell	1965	S. Dawson	1978	S. Field
1931	J. Winn	1951	Mrs Gaskell	1966	Mrs A.M. Eddis	1979	S. Dawson
1932	Miss Griffiths	1952	Mrs Wilkins	1967	A. Willard	1980	S. Field
1933	Lady Eddis	1953	Lady Eddis	1968	Mrs R.D.R. Biggar	1981	D. Marriott
1934	Lady Eddis	1954	Mrs A. Smith	1969	A. Willard	1982	D. Marriott
1935	J. Winn	1956	J. Winn	1970	A. Willard	1983	D. Marriott
1936	J. Winn	1958	Mrs Wilkins	1971	A. Willard		
1937	Lady Eddis	1959	Mrs M. Openshaw	1972	Mrs A. Eddis		
1938	Mrs A. Eddis	1960	Mrs Gaskell	1973	Mrs J. Biggar		

SUNNINGDALE LADIES' FOURSOMES COMPETITION

Instituted in 1950, the competition was adminis-
tered on behalf of the Sunningdale Ladies' Golf
Club by *Fairway and Hazard* magazine, until 1965.
Since 1966 it has been run by the club.

Year	Winners	Year	Winners	Year	Winners
1950	B. Cheney and J. Percy	1962	Mrs G.A. Joll and Mrs H.G. Satchell	1974	Mrs J. Roberts and Mrs I.G. Thorburn
1951	G. Watts and J. Winn	1963	Mrs J.M. Kaye and Mrs J.R. Thornhill	1975	Mrs M. Archer and Mrs J. Morrogh
1952	Mrs J.B. Beck and J. Donald	1964	Mrs C. Abrahams and H. Abrahams	1976	Mrs E.E. Morgan and Mrs B.C. Newman
1953	E.H. Lever and N. Seddon	1965	L. Denison-Pender and Mrs D.H. Martin	1977	Mrs J. Roberts and Mrs I.G. Thorburn
1954	B.A. Jackson and E. Price	1966	P. Greaves and Mrs K.S. Schapel	1978	Mrs E.E. Morgan and Mrs B.C. Newman
1955	L. Denison-Pender and Mrs D.H. Martin	1967	Mrs R.A.C. Cobley and H.M. Stileman	1979	J. Blaymire and S. Gordon
1956	W. Morgan and M. Roskrow	1968	Mrs G. Lumsden and Mrs A.D. McIlwraith	1980	Mrs D. Dixon and Mrs J. Martyn
1957	Mrs W.D. Beck and A. Gardner	1969	Mrs E.G. Benn and Mrs T.A. Hussey	1981	Mrs H. Hubbard and Mrs J. Penna
1958	R. Porter and Mrs T. Popplestone	1970	Mrs G. Chase-Gardener and Lady Rosemary Muir	1982	J. Blaymire and S. Gordon
1959	Mrs G.A. Joll and Mrs H.G. Satchell	1971	Mrs S.G. Sillem and F.J. Taylor	1983	E.E. Morgan and D.W. Wates
1960	E. Price and M. Spearman	1972	Mrs J. Shaw and Mrs S. Standaloft		
1961	Mrs J. Barton and Mme des Courtis	1973	Mrs J.B. Bickley and Mlle B. le Garrères		

SURREY LADIES' CHAMPIONSHIP

Year	Winner	Year	Winner	Year	Winner	Year	Winner
1921	J. Wethered	1935	P. Barton	1959	E. Price	1972	Mrs S. Birley
1922	J. Wethered	1936	D. Fishwick	1960	E. Price	1973	J. Thornhill
1923	M. Gourlay	1937	J. Hamilton	1961	Mrs C.A. Barclay	1974	J. Thornhill
1924	J. Wethered	1938	M. Gourlay	1962	J. Thornhill	1975	D. Strickland
1925	Mrs Latham-Hall	1939	J. Kerr	1963	A. Rampton	1976	Mrs D. Henson
1926	M. Gourlay	1946	D. Critchley	1964	J. Thornhill	1977	J. Thornhill
1927	M. Gourlay	1951	J. Bisgood	1965	J. Thornhill	1978	J. Thornhill
1928	Mrs Potter	1952	Mrs C.A. Barclay	1966	C. Denneny	1979	S. Peters
1929	J. Wethered	1953	J. Bisgood	1967	D. Oxley	1980	D. Dowling
1930	Mrs Atherton	1954	E. Price	1968	Mrs R. Sutherland Pilch	1981	J. Thornhill
1931	M. Gourlay	1955	E. Price	1969	J. Bisgood	1982	J. Thornhill
1932	J. Wethered	1956	E. Price	1970	D. Oxley	1983	J. Thornhill
1933	M. Gourlay	1957	E. Price	1971	D. Oxley		
1934	M. Gourlay	1958	E. Price				

SUSSEX LADIES' CHAMPIONSHIP

From its institution in 1923, Mrs P. Riddiford has won ten times. Mrs Riddiford also won the LGU's Seniors' (over 50) Championship in 1982.

Miss J. Yuille was the winner by the largest margin – 12 and 10 in 1956. After 1936, the final has been played over 36 holes.

Year	Winner	Year	Winner	Year	Winner	Year	Winner
1923	Miss Archer	1937	B. Norris	1958	B. Strange	1972	Mrs P. Riddiford
1924	Miss Sarson	1938	B. Norris	1959	Mrs J. Hayter	1973	Mrs P. Riddiford
1925	Mrs Davies	1939	R. Powell	1960	B. Strange	1974	Mrs P. Riddiford
1926	Mrs de Winton	1947	Mrs Dennler	1961	Mrs P. Riddiford	1975	Mrs P. Tredinnick
1927	Mrs Davies	1948	Mrs Cleary	1962	Mrs P. Riddiford	1976	Mrs C. Larkin
1928	S. Marshall	1949	Mrs Jerdein	1963	P. Tredinnick	1977	S. Bamford
1929	Mrs Hambro	1950	Mrs Jerdein	1964	Mrs P. Riddiford	1978	Mrs J. Tate
1930	S. Archer	1951	Mrs Dennler	1965	Mrs P. Tredinnick	1979	Mrs S. Sutton
1931	Mrs de Winton	1952	Mrs Dennler	1966	Mrs P. Riddiford	1980	C. Pierce
1932	V.G. Davies	1953	Mrs P. Riddiford	1967	Mrs P. Riddiford	1981	C. Larkin
1933	Mrs R. Harker	1954	Mrs M. Groom	1968	Mrs P. Riddiford	1982	C. Larkin
1934	Mrs Gallatley	1955	Mrs Grant-White	1969	A. Brown	1983	C. Larkin
1935	V.G. Davies	1956	J. Yuille	1970	Mrs P. Tredinnick		
1936	Mrs G. White	1957	B. Strange	1971	E. Mountain		

ULSTER LADIES' CHAMPIONSHIP

The cup for this championship was presented by the proprietors of the *Belfast Newsletter* to the Northern Executive of the ILGU in 1923.

Year	Winner	Year	Winner	Year	Winner	Year	Winner
1923	Mrs Corbett	1937	B. Ellis	1958	M. Smyth	1972	Mrs D. Morton
1924	J. Rice	1938	Mrs J. Marks	1959	M. Smyth	1973	Mrs P. Rooney
1925	J. Rice	1939	Mrs J. Marks	1960	Mrs S. Bolton	1974	Mrs A. McLean
1926	Mrs Cuttell	1947	Mrs S. Bolton	1961	no championship	1975	L. Malone
1927	J. Rice	1948	Mrs S. Bolton	1962	A. Sweeney	1976	C. Nesbitt
1928	B. Gardiner	1949	Mrs S. Bolton	1963	A. Sweeney	1977	Mrs D. Morton
1929	J. Rice	1950	Mrs S. Bolton	1964	H. Colhoun	1978	C. Nesbit
1930	Mrs J. Marks	1951	M. Smyth	1965	S. Owen	1979	M. Gorry
1931	D. Ferguson	1952	D. Foster	1966	J. Beckett	1980	M. Madill
1932	J. Marks	1953	D. Foster	1967	E. Barnett	1981	Mrs L. Starrett
1933	D. Ferguson	1954	Mrs J. Marks	1968	E. Barnett	1982	Mrs C. Robinson
1934	J. Mitchell	1955	Mrs S. Bolton	1969	Mrs M. Madeley	1983	M. Madill
1935	Mrs B. Lee	1956	Mrs S. Bolton	1970	C. McAuley		
1936	Mrs J. Marks	1957	Mrs D. Humphries	1971	M. McConnell		

WARWICKSHIRE LADIES' CHAMPIONSHIP

Since its institution in 1923, Enid, née Pears, Sheppard has won this championship ten times.

Year	Winner	Year	Winner	Year	Winner	Year	Winner
1923	D. Harthill	1937	E. Pears	1958	V. Anstey	1972	Mrs V. Beharrell
1924	D. Harthill	1938	Mrs Peppercorn	1959	S. Armstrong	1973	Mrs S. Westall
1925	D. Harthill	1939	M. Frysche	1960	V. Anstey	1974	Mrs S. Westall
1926	D. Harthill	1947	Mrs E.M. Sheppard	1961	Mrs J. Roles	1975	Mrs V. Beharrell
1927	D. Harthill	1948	Mrs E.M. Sheppard	1962	J. Roberts	1976	Mrs M.F. Roles
1928	Mrs Peppercorn	1949	Mrs E.M. Sheppard	1963	J. Roberts	1977	A. Middleton
1929	D. Harthill	1950	Mrs E.M. Sheppard	1964	J. Roberts	1978	Mrs S. Westall
1930	Mrs Peppercorn	1951	Mrs E.M. Sheppard	1965	J. Roberts	1979	Mrs S. Nicholson
1931	Mrs Peppercorn	1952	P. Davies	1966	Mrs J. Roles	1980	T. Hammond
1932	Miss Fyshe	1953	M. Peppercorn	1967	Mrs J. Tomlinson	1981	J. Evans
1933	Mrs Peppercorn	1954	Mrs E.M. Sheppard	1968	Mrs J. Tomlinson	1982	T. Hammond
1934	E. Pears	1955	V. Anstey	1969	J. Roberts	1983	T. Hammond
1935	E. Pears	1956	V. Anstey	1970	Mrs J. Roles		
1936	E. Pears	1957	V. Anstey	1971	Mrs V. Beharrell		

WEST OF SCOTLAND LADIES' CLOSE CHAMPIONSHIP

Instituted on 23 January 1928, the participating counties being Argyllshire, Ayrshire, Dunbartonshire, Lanarkshire, Renfrewshire and Stirlingshire, the first championship was held on 3 September and following days in 1928 at Western Gailles on a match play format. Stirlingshire withdrew in 1929 and in 1958 Argyllshire and Dunbartonshire amalgamated as one county. Since then, four counties have participated: Ayrshire, Argyllshire and Dunbartonshire, Lanarkshire and Renfrewshire. In 1969 a qualifying 18-hole stroke round was needed, the sixteen best scores going into automatic draw for match play. In 1947 the ladies clubbed together and a cheque for £240 was presented to the Red Cross Society towards the purchase of an ambulance, which was named 'Fairways'.

Year	Winner	Year	Winner	Year	Winner	Year	Winner
1928	Mrs Coats	1948	H. Holm	1960	B. Singleton	1972	S. Needham
1929	J. McCulloch	1949	H. Holm	1961	D. Sommerville	1973	S. Needham
1930	J. McCulloch	1950	H. Holm	1962	S. McKinven	1974	G. Cadden
1931	N. Baird	1951	Mrs B. Singleton	1963	Mrs B. Singleton	1975	S. Needham
1932	Mrs Greenlees	1952	Mrs K. McNeil	1964	B. Robertson	1976	S. Lambie
1933	H. Holm	1953	Mrs B. Singleton	1965	Mrs I.D. Hamilton	1977	S. Lambie
1934	H. Holm	1954	Mrs J. Drummond	1966	B. Robertson	1978	W. Aitken
1935	H. Holm	1955	B. Geakie	1967	S. Needham	1979	S. Lambie
1936	H. Holm	1956	J. Robertson	1968	Mrs W. Norris	1980	W. Aitken
1937	H. Holm	1957	B. McCorkindale	1969	B. Robertson	1981	W. Aitken
1938	B. Henderson	1958	J. Robertson	1970	F. Jamieson	1982	S. Lawson
1947	J. McCulloch	1959	J. Robertson	1971	S. Needham	1983	S. Lawson

WILTSHIRE LADIES' CHAMPIONSHIP

At a meeting on 25 February 1910, at the Golf Pavilion, Warminster, it was decided to form the Wiltshire Ladies' County Golf Club, and to adopt the Hampshire Ladies' Rules. Since 1933 the club has been called the Wiltshire Ladies' County Golf Association. At West Wilts (Warminster) Golf Club on 14 November 1923, Mrs Leys proposed, seconded by Miss Pinkney, that Wiltshire should have a county championship, the cup to be subscribed for by individual subscription from each member. The first championship commenced on 1 May 1924, with a qualifying round of 18 holes, the first eight scratch scores to qualify for play-off in match play. The entry fee was 2s 6d (12½p). £14 15s 0d (£14.75) had been collected for the cup which, with its plinth, cost £6 15s 0d (£6.75). The balance of £8 was used for miniature replicas and wood for the Championship Cup Board, which was to be a light oak with red and black lettering. In 1937 a silver salver was purchased for the championship, 'the cost to be not more than £20', the old original cup being used for bronze division players and called the Wiltshire County Plate. Claire Waite, when aged fifteen, was the youngest winner, in 1980.

Year	Winner	Year	Winner	Year	Winner	Year	Winner
1924	P. Kempe	1938	Miss Pywell	1959	Mrs Taunton	1973	Mrs P. Bucher
1925	P. Kempe	1939	Miss Pywell	1960	Mrs J. Taunton	1974	Mrs V. Morgan
1926	Miss Erskine	1947	Mrs Evans	1961	Mrs J. Taunton	1975	Mrs J. Lawrence
1927	Mrs Cole	1948	Mrs Potts	1962	Mrs M. Strong	1976	Mrs V. Morgan
1928	Mrs Hart	1949	Mrs Kennard	1963	Mrs M. Morris	1977	Mrs J. Lawrence
1929	Miss Kempe	1950	Mrs Greenland	1964	Mrs C. Jones	1978	Mrs P. Millar
1930	Mrs Lonnon	1951	Mrs Greenland	1965	Mrs Taunton	1979	Mrs P. Board
1931	Mrs Hoare	1952	Mrs Glendinning	1966	Mrs R.J.A. Morris	1980	C. Waite
1932	Mrs Collins	1953	Mrs Glendinning	1967	N.A. Mackenzie	1981	C. Waite
1933	Mrs B. White	1954	Mrs Greenland	1968	Mrs A. Bucher	1982	F. Dawson
1934	Mrs Hart	1955	Mrs Curnick	1969	P. Lord	1983	C. Waite
1935	Mrs Deacon	1956	Mrs Curnick	1970	P. Lord		
1936	Mrs Hart	1957	Mrs Taunton	1971	Mrs V. Morgan		
1937	Mrs Potts	1958	Mrs Taunton	1972	Mrs P. Board		

WORCESTERSHIRE LADIES' CHAMPIONSHIP

Miss M. Hampson has won the championship eleven times and Miss J. Blaymire twelve times.

Year	Winner	Year	Winner	Year	Winner	Year	Winner
1924	Miss Robinson	1938	Mrs Challen	1959	A. Cawsey	1973	J. Blaymire
1925	K. Nicholls	1939	M. Hampson	1960	M. Hampson	1974	Mrs V. Cotterill
1926	K. Nicholls	1947	M. Hampson	1961	M. Hampson	1975	J. Blaymire
1927	K. Nicholls	1948	M. Hampson	1962	Mrs G. Strang	1976	J. Blaymire
1928	K. Nicholls	1949	Miss M. Hampson	1963	J. Odell	1977	J. Blaymire
1929	Mrs Fieldhouse	1950	M. Hampson	1964	Mrs R.L. Brinton	1978	S. Crowcroft
1930	B. Law	1951	Mrs Challen	1965	Mrs C. Banner	1979	J. Blaymire
1931	Mrs Challen	1952	M. Fyshe	1966	Mrs C. Banner	1980	Mrs R. West
1932	Mrs Challen	1953	M. Hampson	1967	J. Blaymire	1981	J. Blaymire
1933	M. Fieldhouse	1954	M. Fyshe	1968	Mrs M. Hayes	1982	J. Blaymire
1934	B. Law	1955	M. Hampson	1969	J. Blaymire	1983	S. Nicklin
1935	Mrs E. Fiddian	1956	M. Hampson	1970	J. Blaymire		
1936	Mrs Brinton	1957	M. Hampson	1971	J. Blaymire		
1937	Mrs E. Fiddian	1958	Mrs M. Downing	1972	J. Blaymire		

WORPLESDON MIXED FOURSOMES

When this was instituted in 1921, it was considered a very brave thing to do, for, in the words of Eleanor Helme, 'mixed foursomes were on a par with the Post Office pen, the station sandwich, mothers-in-law and other staples of a comedian's cheap humour.' Miss Helme won the inaugural event, with Tony Torrance, beating Joyce Wethered and her brother Roger, but Joyce Wethered holds the record for the most number of wins, eight, with several different partners.

Year	Winners	Year	Winners	Year	Winners
1921	Miss E. Helme and T.A. Torrance	1931	Miss J. Wethered and the Hon. Michael Scott	1947	Miss J. Gordon and A.A. Duncan
1922	Miss J. Wethered and R. Wethered	1932	Miss J. Wethered and R.H. Oppenheimer	1948	Miss W. Morgan and E.F. Storey
1923	Miss J. Wethered and C.J.H. Trolley	1933	Miss J. Wethered and B. Darwin	1949	Miss F. Stephens and L.G. Crawley
1924	Miss S.R. Fowler and E. Noel Layton	1934	Miss M. Gourlay and T.A. Torrance	1950	Miss F. Stephens and L.G. Crawley
1925	Miss C. Leitch and E. Esmond	1935	Miss G. Craddock-Hartopp and J. Craddock-Hartopp	1951	Mrs A.C. Barclay and G. Evans
1926	Mlle S. de la Chaume and R. Wethered	1936	Miss J. Wethered and the Hon. T. Coke	1952	Mrs R.T. Peel and G.W. Mackie
1927	Miss J. Wethered and C.J.H. Trolley	1937	Mrs Heppel and L.G. Crawley	1953	Miss J. Gordon and G. Knipe
1928	Miss J. Wethered and J.S.F. Morrison	1938	Mrs M. Garon and E.F. Storey	1954	Miss F. Stephens and W.A. Slark
1929	Miss M. Gourlay and Major C.O. Hezlet	1946	Miss J. Gordon and A.A. Duncan	1955	Miss P. Garvey and P.F. Scrutton
1930	Miss M. Gourlay and Major C.O. Hezlet				

Year	Winners	Year	Winners	Year	Winners
1956	Mrs L. Abrahams and Major D. Henderson	1966	Mrs C. Barclay and D.J. Miller	1976	Mrs B. Lewis and J. Caplan
1957	Mrs B. Singleton and W.D. Smith	1967	Miss C. Lacoste and J.F. Gancedo	1977	Mrs D. Henson and J. Caplan
1958	Mrs M. Bonallack and M. Bonallack	1968	Miss D. Oxley and J.D. van Heel	1978	Miss T. Perkins and R. Thomas
1959	Miss J. Robertson and I. Wright	1969	Mrs R. Ferguson and A. Wilson	1979	Miss J. Melville and A. Melville
1960	Miss B. Jackson and M.J. Burgess	1970	Miss R. Roberts and R.L. Glading	1980	Mrs L. Bayman and I. Boyd
1961	Mrs R. Smith and B. Critchley	1971	Mrs D. Frearson and A. Smith	1981	Mrs J. Nicholson and N. Stern
1962	Vicomtess de St Sauveur and D.W. Frame	1972	Mlle B. le Garrères and C.A. Strang	1982	Miss B. New and K. Dobson
1963	Mrs G. Valentine and J.E. Behrend	1973	Miss T. Perkins and R.J. Evans	1983	Miss B. New and K. Dobson
1964	Mrs G. Valentine and J.E. Behrend	1974	Mrs S. Birley and R.L. Glading		
1965	Mrs G. Valentine and J.E. Behrend	1975	Mrs J. Thornhill and J. Thornhill		

YORKSHIRE LADIES' CHAMPIONSHIP

The Yorkshire Gentlemen's Union started the ladies' championship in 1896 and it was handed over to the ladies ten years later. The men also handed over the sum of £20 for the running of the event.

Year	Winner	Year	Winner	Year	Winner	Year	Winner
1896	N. Haigh	1919	Mrs Harrop	1938	K. Merry	1965	Mrs T.J. Briggs
1897	K.G. Moeller	1920	Miss Heaton	1947	J. McIntyre	1966	C. Bell
1898	K.G. Moeller	1921	M. Wragg	1948	Mrs Kyle	1967	M. Everard
1899	H.M. Firth	1922	Mrs White	1949	Mrs Kyle	1968	K. Phillips
1900	K.G. Moeller	1923	Mrs White	1950	Mrs Hartley	1969	K. Phillips
1901	Mrs H.J. Lister	1924	M. Wragg	1951	G. Rudgard	1970	Mrs J. Hunter
1902	B. Thompson	1925	E. Griffiths	1952	A. Scargill	1971	G. Ringstead
1903	E. Steel	1926	Mrs Shalders	1953	Mrs E. Hartley	1972	M. Everard
1904	E. Steel	1927	M. Wragg	1954	J. Mitton	1973	M. Everard
1905	E. Steel	1928	M. Wragg	1955	Mrs E. Hartley	1974	Mrs B. Allison
1906	Miss Swayne	1929	M. Wragg	1956	Mrs E. Hartley	1975	V. Marvin
1907	K.G. Moeller	1930	M. Wragg	1957	P. Bagley	1976	P. Wrightson
1908	E. Steel	1931	M. Wragg	1958	Mrs E. Hartley	1977	M. Everard
1909	B. Thompson	1932	M. Johnson	1959	Mrs E. Hartley	1978	V. Marvin
1910	E. Steel	1933	Miss Swincoe	1960	Mrs E. Hartley	1979	J. Rhodes
1911	Mrs Melrose	1934	M. Johnson	1961	Mrs P. Foster	1980	L. Batty
1912	Miss Branson	1935	Miss Platts	1962	G. Coldwell	1981	P. Grice
1913	Mrs Gwynne	1936	Mrs Rhodes	1963	G. Hickson	1982	P. Grice
1914	Miss Heaton	1937	Mrs Rhodes	1964	H. Everard	1983	P. Grice

Appendix

1 Early Ladies' Golf Clubs

(Within single years, clubs are given in alphabetical order).

1867 St Andrews

1868 Westward Ho!
and North Devon

1872 Musselburgh
Wimbledon

1873 Carnoustie

1882 Troon

1883 Bath

1884 Hayling
Elie and Earlsferry

1885 Cupar
Exmouth
Gladwyns
Great Yarmouth

1886 Lytham and St Anne's

1887 Stirling
Warwickshire

1888 Royal Belfast
North Berwick
Royal Eastbourne

1889 Ashdown Forest
Elie and Earlsferry
Minchinhampton
North Warwickshire
Royal Blackheath
West Cornwall

1890 Barham Downs
Grantown
Kenilworth
Lundin
Macrihanish
Montrose
Nairn
Royal Leamington Spa
Rhyl
Torquay

1891 Barnes
Cotswold
East Sheen
Lancashire
Leven
Littlestone
North West
Old Manchester
Rochester
Royal Portrush
Scarborough
Sutton Coldfield
Thames Ditton and Esher
Wakefield
West Lancashire
Windermere
Woodhall Spa

1892 Aberdeen
Aberdovey
Brighton and Hove
Burnham
Chester
Coventry
Didsbury
Folkestone
Hawick
Leicestershire
Mid-Surrey
St Neots
Sheffield and District

2 Handicap Differences in 1902

Short-links handicap	Long-links handicap	Long-links handicap	Short-links handicap
1	2	2	1
2	3	3	2
3	5	5	3
4	6	6	4
5	8	7	5
6	9	8	5
7	11	9	6
8	12	10	7
9	14	11	7
10	15	12	8
11	17	13	9
12	18	14	9
13	20	15	10
14	21	16	11
15	23	17	11
16	24	18	12
17 and over	25	19	13
		20	13
		21	14
		22	15
		23	15
		24	16
		25	17

3 Variations in Pars of the Green

Course	1890s	1980s	Course	1890s	1980s
Ashdown	80	69	Royal Belfast	100	70
Bath	76	70	Royal Lytham and St Anne's	88	73
Beckenham	78	67	Royal Portrush	76	73 and 69
Dulwich and Sydenham Hill	80	69	Scarborough	88	70 and 68
Eltham	66	68	Seaford	64	72 and 71
Formby	82	73 (ladies 71)	Southport	104	71
Freshwater	60	67	Wakefield	88	72
Great Yarmouth	90	70	West Lancashire	78	73
Hastings	86	70	Wimbledon	72	67 and 66
Hoylake	66	70	Windermere	86	65
Ilkley	90	70	Wirral	70	68
Kenilworth	84	70	Woking	96	70
Littlestone	76	71	Worcester	84	69
Minchinhampton	76	72 and 70			
Rochester	76	70	*Maximum variation*	44	8

Bibliography

Armour, Tommy, *How to play your best golf all the time*, Hodder and Stoughton, 1954

Barton, Pamela, *A Stroke a Hole*, Blackies, 1937

Batchelor, Gerald, *Golf Stories*, A. & C. Black, 1914

Bauchope, C.R., *The Golfing Annual*, 1888

Beldam, George W., *Great Golfers: Their Methods at a Glance*, Macmillan, 1904

Braid, James, *The Ladies' Field Golf Book*, Newnes, 1908

Brown, Thomas, *Golfiana*, private, 1869

Browning, Robert H.K., *Moments with Golfing Masters*, Methuen, 1932

Carnegie, George Fullarton, *Golfiana*, 1833

Chambers, Robert, *Golfing*, 1887

Clark, Robert, *Golf: A Royal and Ancient Game*, private, 1875

Cotton, Henry, *This Game of Golf*, Country Life, 1948

Cundell, John, untitled, 1826

Darwin, Bernard and Duncan, George, *Present-Day Golf*, Hodder and Stoughton, 1925

Darwin, Bernard, *Pack Clouds Away*, Collins, 1941

Darwin, Bernard, *Golf between Two Wars*, Chatto and Windus, 1944

Darwin, Bernard, *Golfing By-Paths*, Country Life, 1946

Darwin, Bernard, *History of Golf in Britain*, 1947

Darwin, Bernard, *Golf*, Burke, 1954

Dunlop-Hill, Noël, *History of the Scottish Ladies' Golfing Association*, 1929

Everard, H.S.C., *History of the Royal and Ancient Club*, 1907

Farnie, Henry B., *The Golfer's Manual*, 1857

Halma's Dictionary, 1708

Helme, Eleanor, *The Lady Golfer's Tip Book*, Mills and Boon, 1923

Helme, Eleanor, *After the Ball*, Hurst and Blackett, 1931

Hezlet, May, *Ladies' Golf*, Hutchinson, 1904

Hughes, J., *Historical Gossip about Golf and Golfers*, Robb, 1863

Hughes, W.E., *Chronicles of Blackheath Golfers*, 1897

Hutchinson, Horace G., *Golf*, Badminton Library, 1890

Hutchinson, Horace G., *Hints on the Game of Golf*, Blackwood, 1893

Hutchinson, Horace G., *The Book of Golf and Golfers*, Longmans, 1899

Hutchinson, Horace G. (ed.), *The New Book of Golf*, Longmans, 1912

Hutchinson, Horace G., *Fifty Years of Golf*, Country Life/Newnes, 1919

Kennard, Mary G., *Sorrows of a Golfer's Wife*, 1896

Kerr, Rev. John, *Golf Book of East Lothian*, 1869

Kincaid, Thomas, *Instructions in the Form of a Poem*, 1687

Lang, Andrew, *A Batch of Golfing Papers*, 1892

Leitch, Cecil, *Golf*, Butterworth, 1922

Leitch, Cecil, *Golf Simplified*, Butterworth, 1924

Linskill, W.T., *Golf*, 1889

Lonsdale Library of Sports, Games and Pastimes, Seeley, 1931

McAndrew, J., *Golfing Step by Step*, Mitchell, 1935

Macdonald, Charles Blair, *Scotland's Gift – Golf*, 1928

Matheson, T., *The Goff*, 1743

Murdoch, Joseph S.F., *The Library of Golf*, Gale, 1968

Pearson, Issette, *Our Lady of the Green*, 1899

Player, Gary, *Gary Player's Golf Secrets*, Pelham, 1964

Ray, Edward, *Some Hints for Lady Beginners*, 1912

Ray, Ted, *Golf: My Slice of Life*, W.H. Allen, 1972

Reminiscences of Golf on St Andrews Links, 1887

Salmond, J.B., *The Story of the R and A*, Macmillan, 1956

Seton-Kerr, Sir Henry, *Golf*, 1907

Scott, Tom, *A Century of Golf*, 1960

Shadwell, Thomas, *Westminster Drollery*, 1671

Simpson, Sir Walter G., *The Art of Golf*, Douglas, 1887

Smith, Garden G., *Golf*, 1897

Souvenir Book of the Ladies' Championship 1893–1932, private, 1933

Stirling, Mrs, *Sedgeley Court*, 1860

Stringer, Mabel, *Golfing Reminiscences*, Mills and Boon, 1924

Stringer, Mabel, *History of the LGU*, unpublished

Stuart, Ian, *Golf in Hertfordshire*, Carling, 1973

Stuart, Patrick, *Golf Grave and Gay*, 1906

Summers, Montague (ed.), *Complete Works of Thomas Shadwell*, 1927

Taylor, J.H., *Taylor on Golf*, Hutchinson, 1902

Vardon, Harry, *The Complete Golfer*, Methuen, 1905

Ward-Thomas, Pat, *The Long Green Fairway*, Hodder and Stoughton, 1966

Ward-Thomas, Pat, *The Royal and Ancient*, Academic Press, 1980

Wethered, Roger and Joyce, *Golf from Two Sides*, Longmans, 1922

Wilson, Enid, *Golf for Women*, Barker, 1964

Annuals

Golfer's Annual 1869–70; *Nisbets Golf Year Book 1906*; *Golfer's Handbook* (1902–82); *Lady Golfer's Handbook* (1894–1982 under various titles)

Periodicals and Newspapers 1870–1982

Blackwoods, Boudoir, Bystander, Cornhill, Country Life, The Daily Telegraph, Eve, Fairway and Hazard, Gentlewoman, Golf, Golfing, Golf Illustrated, Golf International, Golf Monthly, Golf World, Illustrated London News, Ladies' Field, Ladies' Golf, Lady's Pictorial, Pall Mall, Punch, Tatler, The Times.

General Index

Index of Persons

Many of the records to which this index in part refers do not distinguish between unmarried names with or without initials; for example, the author has sometimes not been able to establish so many decades later whether Miss Smith was in fact Miss E. Smith. There has also been the insurmountable difficulty that, for example, such Miss Smiths may later appear under married names. On occasions it has been necessary, except in the case of relatively major names, to index such ladies strictly according to the information supplied by official organizations. Therefore one person may have two or more separate entries. Figures in *italic* refer to the captions of the illustrations.

THE END